BLOOD OF MOLDARA

BLOOD OF MOLDARA

BOOK 2 IN THE MOLDARA SERIES

BRIANNE EARHART

J. NORWOOD

CONTENTS

Dedication	ix
Prologue	1
Chapter 1	17
Chapter 2	25
Chapter 3	29
Chapter 4	37
Chapter 5	46
Chapter 6	52
Chapter 7	59
Chapter 8	70
Chapter 9	80
Chapter 10	85
Chapter 11	94
Chapter 12	100
Chapter 13	107
Chapter 14	111
Chapter 15	118
Chapter 16	124
Chapter 17	134
Chapter 18	141
Chapter 19	151
Chapter 20	157
Chapter 21	166
Chapter 22	176
Chapter 23	185
Chapter 24	194
Chapter 25	203
Chapter 26	208
Chapter 27	214
Chapter 28	221
Chapter 29	226
Chapter 30	234

Chapter 31	241
Chapter 32	250
Chapter 33	258
Chapter 34	266
Chapter 35	277
Chapter 36	285
Chapter 37	290
Chapter 38	295
Chapter 39	306
Chapter 40	310
Epilogue	322
Acknowledgments	331
And my deepest thanks to you,	333
About the Author	337
About the Co-Author	339
Back Cover	343

BLOOD OF MOLDARA

COPYRIGHT © 2017 BRIANNE EARHART & J. NORWOOD

ALL RIGHTS RESERVED. PUBLISHED IN THE UNITED STATES OF AMERICA. NO PART OF THIS BOOK MAY BE USED OR REPRODUCED IN ANY MANNER WHATSOEVER WITHOUT WRITTEN PERMISSION EXCEPT IN THE CASE OF BRIEF QUOTATIONS EMBODIED IN CRITICAL ARTICLES AND REVIEWS. FOR INFORMATION, ADDRESS MYTH MACHINE AT INFO@MYTHMACHINE.COM

THIS IS A WORK OF FICTION. NAMES, CHARACTERS, BUSINESSES, PLACES, EVENTS AND INCIDENTS ARE EITHER THE PRODUCTS OF THE AUTHOR'S IMAGINATION OR USED IN A FICTITIOUS MANNER. ANY RESEMBLANCE TO ACTUAL PERSONS, LIVING OR DEAD, OR ACTUAL EVENTS IS PURELY COINCIDENTAL.

Cover Illustration Copyright © 2017 by Myth Machine, LLC

Cover design by © Alfie

Book design and production by Myth Machine, LLC

Development Editor J. Norwood

Editing by Leslie Lutz of Eliot Bay Editing

Author Brianne Earhart photograph by Robin Johnson

Author J. Norwood photograph by Evan Lurker

DEDICATION

For Grandma Ruth~
Your love of creating stories, art,
and all things beautiful has
taught me the sky's the limit.
Thanks you for believing in me.
I love you!

PROLOGUE

"We have more Exiles at our city gates every season. If we have to distribute more than our allotment of grain, my people will face starvation this winter. Terrshon has threatened to tax even more of our trade routes. My hands are tied."

The heavyset man stopped his wild gestures long enough to glance out the tent flaps, which had been stirred by another procession. The delegation from Niniever was making its way with its finest meats to the feast tents.

"I hear your concerns," Ayla reassured DaVu as soon as she was sure they couldn't be overheard. "But as the ambassador of Galistan, you have the opportunity to intercede on behalf of those who are more vulnerable to Terrshon's bullying. Why let him divide the kingdoms further and weaken a valuable ally when your coffers enjoy a surplus of dried fish from two expeditions—"

"Three. There will be another before the winds change."

"Three?! DaVu, our ancestors watch over you."

He leaned back in his chair with a heavy sigh. Ayla pretended not to notice DaVu as he rubbed his stubbly chin and glared at her across the crude table. In the growing silence, she sipped her tea and adjusted her gloves, in no hurry. Her compliment was as much a courtesy as it was a damning call to action, and they both knew it.

A crowd cheered in the distance and the drums sounded. The dancing between the pavilions had nothing on the revelry spilling out of dozens of tents like this one. It was Ayla's eighth negotiation, and there was still one more day to the three-day festival.

"Ayla, you are still of Galistan," DaVu whispered. "Your mother may refuse to return or claim any of her birthrights, but yours still awaits you. Our people would welcome a woman of your foresight and diplomacy. Age breeds fear, and I'm not long for this post."

"You are very kind, DaVu, but you know I serve all the kingdoms of this world until peace is restored, not just the province of my birth. Any official position would be a direct challenge to Terrshon, which would endanger the people I represent," Ayla said, reciting her mother's words as if they were her own. Each negotiation made them more her personal mantra, reminding her of the work they'd pledged their lives to. But it was little comfort to people caught between the impossible hope for a long-dead princess and a fear of Terrshon's increasingly divisive maneuvers.

"Surely enough time has passed that your mother—"

"Ambassador," Ayla cut him off before he could speak the words that, if they got back to Terrshon, could end both their lives and start a war. No shadows lingered at the edge of their tent, but she knew better than to act like they were completely alone. "Following the untimely death of Queen Mira and King Norwyck, it was my family's honor to answer the call of the people of Moldara. That we were unable to discover and punish the murderers of my beloved aunt and uncle remains our family's greatest shame. As a result, my father also fell by their hands. We are disgraced, a queen and a princess in memory only, as we must remain. We owe our lives to the people of Moldara, who forgave us and compelled a pardon from Terrshon."

"Yes, yes, we all know the official story. Forgive me for asking you to speak of such dark times. I meant no insult." He looked around the tent nervously. "I would never speak ill of a standing king, especially in his kingdom. I'll be sure to send the goods in three shipments, just like last winter."

"Thank you, for your generosity, DaVu. You have always been a truly courageous friend."

Ayla stood, patting him gently on his shoulder as she turned to leave. He stayed in his seat, his expression troubled. Before she had a chance to take a step, he grabbed her hand and pulled it down until it was over his heart. He held it with two shaking hands.

"DaVu, what is it?"

His dark skin suddenly looked a few shades lighter. Ayla scanned the edges of the tent. They were still alone. She went to one knee.

"The Sacred Waters. You are aware of the rationing?"

She nodded.

He continued, patting the hand he still held against his heart as if she were the one that needed soothing. "You are too young to remember a time when every sanctuary in every province had more than enough of the Sacred Waters to aid the people it served. The rationing we've endured all these years...it appears we are about to look back on even that time with longing."

"DaVu, what are you trying to tell me?"

"The Sages are now sending all who can make the journey to sanctuaries inside the borders of Moldara. At first, it was just an inconvenience, but now it's become dangerous. The lucky ones still have enough of the Waters to recover from the beatings of bandits, but others..."

"Who's missing?"

"A young couple from my own city. They were traveling with a dying friend."

"Are you sure?"

"The sources are reliable. Their own parents are afraid to search for them. My position limits my ability to intercede. Galistan needs the trade agreements and my king, your uncle, to stay neutral. But if this continues, and the Sages are blamed—"

"Yes, I see the problem."

"You're in a unique position—influential, respected in trusted circles, but politically overlooked. Your connections could help us avoid further bloodshed without threatening those in power." The ambassador let go of her hand and shifted in his seat, adjusting a tan waistcoat as if it held in the weight of the world.

This was neither new to her, nor was he the first ambassador to make this request. In fact, she was sure that if DaVu knew what she and her mother's spies had been reporting these last few months, he would find swallowing the last of his festival mead far more difficult.

"The people of Galistan should be honored to have your protection." Ayla stood, straitening DaVu's short, brimless cap and dusting off his high-collared coat. Brushing off the fear, her mother had called it. "Be assured, you are not alone in your concerns. I will look into what can be done and send word."

"The spirits be with you, child." DaVu bowed his head, lifting the end of his sash to kiss one of the many symbolic coins stitched into the heavy cloth.

"And with you, old friend," Ayla whispered, bestowing a kiss on his cheek before slipping between the tent flaps and disappearing into the crowd.

Ayla tucked the hem of her ruffled skirt into the wide belt that accented her corset before she stepped over horse manure and mud from the recent rain. The last thing she needed was to walk back into the main gathering smelling like she'd slept in the stables. The key was to move just fast enough to distance herself from her meeting with DaVu without drawing attention. The prominent guests, and their entourages of commoners who'd made this area their home for the last week, all had agendas beyond the annual harvest celebrations.

As she strode through the temporary village next to the imposing city walls of Moldara, children rushed around her, spattering mud on her boots. She chuckled. A highly anticipated wrestling match had just been announced. That night at the feast, the winner's province would be awarded the host city's surplus of honeycomb.

A straggler suddenly plowed straight into her.

"So sorry, my lady," the boy apologized. "A portion of my honey will be yours if you will pardon my clumsiness."

"Promise me you will share it with a friend from the losing side, and all is forgiven." The boy's eyes lit up and he nodded eagerly. Ayla returned his grin, tussling his blond hair as she sent him on his way. "Well, hurry. You'll not see this match again."

As much as she wanted to join the crowd and yell encouragements to the two men wrestling in the ring, she had unfinished business. Despite the disagreeable terrain and the growing crowd, she doubled her pace.

Usually, that year's host of the Harvest Feasts held the celebrations within the castle grounds, and the revelry spilled out into the surrounding city. This year Moldara's gates had closed at the arrival of the first delegation. Rumors of heightened security had every ambassador and their network of informants buzzing with predictions of war. Indeed, for Terrshon to treat century old allies as Exiles could be interpreted as an act of war. But without knowing why he'd broken with tradition in such an aggressive way, no one was willing to do more than protest.

So now the rolling hills between the nearby city of Oslo and the gates of Moldara had been filled with just that—an informal protest. The change had elevated a routine celebration and the usual updating of trade agreements to a full-blown allegiance reevaluation. It gave a normally carefree event an air of foreboding and made her moves against Terrshon all the more dangerous.

Ayla cut through one of the improvised main squares, passing merchants, and musicians setting up everywhere. She stopped at a table already filled with fruits and fresh baked goods. The sight of a bowl of berries with cream and a small butter pastry on a black plate made her mouth water. She slipped off her gloves and tucked them into her belt, took both the bowl and the plate, and claimed one of the few open benches in the crowd. What a relief to finally take a few seconds to enjoy herself and fill her growling belly. The food was the perfect distraction from her aching feet, and she savored the simplicity of the moment as she watched the crowd and waited for her signal to be seen.

Suddenly, a squirrel dressed in a little suit jumped up next to her. He straightened his bowtie, bowed, and stretched out his hand as if asking her to dance. Delighted, Ayla set the plate on her knee and offered her finger. The squirrel took it, swaying, twirling, and swishing his tail in a little dance until he was practically on her lap. In one deft move, the animal dropped her finger, snatched the last of her pastry from the plate, and shoved it into his mouth until his cheeks bulged. Then, tail in hand, he bowed and jumped from the bench, scurrying over to a young lady with an assortment of forest creatures following her like ducklings.

The woman leading the group smiled knowingly before turning her attention back to organizing the performing animals. Their whisperer, Ayla thought. Even though she had a different bond, Ayla had been taught that all creatures had a will of their own. The bond over them wasn't always strong enough to overpower the temptation of a butter pastry, no matter what mission they were on.

Ayla sighed as she looked at the sky. The sun was still warm and bright, even though they would soon sound the evening bell and light the bonfires. She stood and started walking, making sure she wasn't followed before she checked her pockets. Sure enough, there was a tiny note left by the squirrel.

The fire is in the hearth.

Ambassador Aht-see-lah, whose name literally meant "fire," was canceling her meeting with Ayla and returning home early. Ayla crumpled the paper and dropped it in a cook-fire as she passed, a dozen alternate plans forming in her head. She needed to reach the stubborn woman before she was too far away. She'd been counting on Aht-see-lah to guarantee the protection of the supplies DaVu had just promised. Aht-see-lah's departure, though separate from that of her delegation, did not bode well.

The air cooled just a little as Ayla approached a small stream that, in the absence of a city fountain, had been transformed for the festival. The normally dull footbridge had been painted with the colors of every nation, with more colorful rocks and baskets of offerings trailing off either side like marks on a compass, each pointing toward that people's home country. It was beautiful. An inspiring improvisation. The only thing that marred the overall effect was the dozen soldiers from Terrshon's personal guard standing watch.

The spring that fed the stream was believed to flow from the Waters of Creation. Tradition held that all water was once sacred. However, in this stream, only the crystal vial submerged near the footbridge held the true Sacred Waters. It was why Terrshon's men were there. When the event had concluded, they would return his one concession to the palace.

Reaching into her pouch, Ayla paused on the tiny bridge to look over the rail and take in the individual offerings—flowers, rocks of all shapes and colors, fruit, even some bright fish swimming in the clear water, although most were glass tokens. She'd chosen her glass token in Bronia, in honor of her late aunt.

She rubbed the smooth embossed glass, hesitating while she formed the message to the spirits in her mind. She reached out her hand toward the water, token between her fingers as she pictured all those who had been lost since that terrible night.

Ayla closed her eyes and began.

Spirits, it has been generations since one bonded to the healing waters has been discovered, and we are in need of such a person more every day—

A shove at her elbow pushed Ayla off balance. Her token slipped from her grasp and plopped into the water. Her eyes popped open. She was no longer alone on the bridge.

"I'm making mine first!"

"No, Father said I could!"

She glared at the two teens as each shoved and pulled on the other's clothes in hopes of being the first to throw their offerings into the water. Their opulent and heavily layered clothes told her their parents were people of influence, but their manners gave away their birth nation.

Moldara.

It was another disgusting reminder of how far the country, under Terrshon's rule, had strayed from its most basic tenets.

"What good is an offering stained by blood? Or are you both trying to curse your family for the rest of time?" Ayla demanded, glaring at the startled youths until they assumed a more respectful demeanor. They each mumbled something and dropped the offerings, silently shoving each other as they continued to the area designated for livestock. She caught one of the guards watching the exchange. When he noticed her gaze, he looked away quickly.

Ayla cursed herself for drawing attention and quickly disappeared back into the crowds.

Ayla found a seat inside the largest of the tents, a giant pavilion whose size rivaled many castle dining halls. She'd chosen a table near the back to give her a good view of the crowd without being noticed. She'd also picked a spot close to a door so she could slip out at a moment's notice. She longed to rid herself of the yards of fabric that advertised her station. The weight was already making her lower back ache.

Ayla placed her head in her hands, eyes closed, and took measured breaths. In a crowded tent, while music played, it was harder to hear the whisperings, but it could be done. Ayla's bond wasn't as powerful as some, but Soren's years of secret lessons came back quickly. Everybody picked up the vibrations of another whisperer in their own way; her awareness came through inner stillness.

Feeling a presence beside her, she lifted her head and watched a woman her mother's age pinching the wicks of the evening candles. The friction of her fingers created a spark, and the candle flamed to life. Ayla never ceased to be amazed by the mastery women like these had over their bonds, but it came at a steep price; a period of service— surrendering a decade of one's life to improve the lives of everyone else—was a burden not always offset by the honor.

Usually, those who trained with the Sages served right after being educated. But there were always a few instances where service wasn't suitable, due to pregnancy or a sudden death in the family. Those who buried a loved one could postpone the rest of their training and service for up to eight seasons. Those who conceived and chose to attempt delivery during training or service had their time deferred until their children were old enough to provide for themselves. The bonded could then go on with their lives or study to become a Sage. No person with a bond strong enough to be trained and to serve was allowed to rule a kingdom for any reason.

Ayla closed her eyes and took another slow breath, attempting to go deeper. Deeper into the stillness, deeper into the quiet, deeper into her bond. There—in the subtle ruffle of the tent flap—she felt it. It moved toward her through the tablecloth, stirred the flowers in the centerpieces and then the hem of her skirt, a connection she could trace back to its source and meant only for her.

Ayla.

The vibration filled her, blocking out all other distractions.

Men have emerged from the falls—

"You're tensing up."

She felt Taft's large body fill the space beside her, but she didn't open her eyes. The whisper wasn't complete.

"This is supposed to be a celebration, and you're working too hard. People are going to notice. Can I get you something to relax?" he asked. "They're sampling the wine from last year's crop. It's good, but if you ask me, the older vintage has a better kick."

Ayla glanced up at him through her fingers.

"The older vintage it is," he guessed knowingly. "Don't move or you might lose it."

When she tried to go back into her bond, she realized he was right. She had lost the connection.

"Sorry," Taft offered as he set a large stemmed glass filled with a deep purple liquid in front of her. "If I'd known what you were doing, I'd never have interrupted."

"It's not your fault I have to keep my bond a secret." Ayla took the glass, drinking deeply. Somedays she wished it was strong enough to train with the Sages, to erase her birthright, to lose herself in a service that had consistent, tangible results.

Taft finished his drink. "I saw Ambassador Yona outside. Have you met with her yet?"

"No."

"I could get her for you. Maybe the two of you will be overlooked in here."

A giant gong sounded from outside. The feast had begun.

"I'll find her in a minute. I have something she wants. It will be good for her to wait for me for a change."

Taft put down his glass and scooted closer to her.

"I keep hearing rumors of a royal union," he said, keeping his voice low.

Ayla snorted. "No doubt Terrshon has suddenly decided to take yet another helpless child-bride. We expected some stunt in an attempt to draw emissaries into more compromising treaties."

"These rumors are said to be coming from the dungeon guards."

"The dungeon? I thought all his wives were either the daughters of political adversaries or another 'little sister' his Sages were claiming as the long-lost princess."

"No one knows where this one came from," Taft continued. "The most repeated speculation is that she's royalty and that he kidnapped her to use as leverage against one of the northern kingdoms."

Ayla looked into the rich liquid she held, but she didn't see it. "Are you sure about your source?"

"He was very eager to share," Taft said, the corner of his mouth turning up slightly.

"Glad to hear someone is having fun. Did he happen to mention when this union might take place or will be officially announced, or were you too busy to ask?"

"All he said was it wasn't to be held in public," Taft replied, no longer hiding his proud grin. "But then why bother barring Moldara's gate to the festival at the last minute? Was this unplanned somehow?"

"Maybe. Another drink?" Ayla asked as she realized her glass was already empty. This was clearly going to be a longer night than first anticipated. Taft stood and bowed playfully, clearing their glasses and crossing the tent with his familiar swagger.

Ayla watched her most trusted bodyguard and close friend move through the growing throng of people toward the wine barrels. She marveled at the way he sweet-talked the young woman pouring the drinks, admiring his ability to so effortlessly mix work and play.

Maybe it was time she put herself in a more powerful position too. When there was no place else to turn, people looked to her for assistance. And this wasn't the first time she'd heard about the strange disappearances and attacks, or about Terrshon's men emerging from the falls.

Taft returned with another drink and sat beside her.

"I think it's time I accept a union of my own," she said.

"What did they put in this wine?!" He eyed the goblet suspiciously.

"I'm serious."

"Exactly why are you suddenly ready to fall on that sword?"

"Because it's time." Ayla took a deep breath. "Terrshon is slowly strangling our allies with all his plots, and I'm tired of how little I'm able to help them. Be it with this poor doomed union or the next, he is going to make his move soon, and I need to be strong enough to stop him. We need help, Taft."

"Ayla," he took her hand, rubbing it lightly. Her warm brown skin almost made his look black as midnight. "You don't have to do this. There are other ways."

She leaned into him, resting on that familiar place against his shoulder. His arm came up around her and he sighed heavily.

"You deserve so much more."

"We all deserve more. But this is what we have been given, so we must use it as best we can."

"Well, look at this." Prince Laurion of Niniever emerged from a passing group of people. He had a glass in one hand and a pitcher in the other. "Is this garishly oversized brute why you never return my letters?"

She felt Taft stiffen. He leaned in and whispered, "Say the word and no one will ever find his body." Then, he stood and offered a bow, "If you'll excuse me."

"Prince Laurion," she said, hoping her voice didn't sound strained when she'd spoken. "To what do I owe this loud and very public greeting?"

"You look stunning," he said, his eyes drinking her in as he filled Taft's seat.

"And you look drunk." She could smell the spirits on his breath.

"It is a celebration, Ayla. Not all of us have your patience for passing notes among impotent rulers," he said, his mouth set in a perpetual pout as he poured himself another drink. The alcohol had amplified his already arrogant demeanor.

"Any news from your little brother?" Ayla asked as she slid the pitcher out of his reach. "It's been years since I've enjoyed the pleasure of Zarian's company. He was always such a calming influence on you."

"He's an ungrateful brat who runs away from responsibility," he spat. The musicians changed songs, inviting others to join the new couples on the dance floor. The prince stood and offered his hand. "It's time you had a man who knows what to do with you."

Ayla thanked the years of diplomatic training that kept her from falling off her chair laughing. Instead, she swallowed her retort with a swig of his wine and a shake of her head. He took it as an invitation and pulled her onto the dance floor, nearly upsetting their table.

"As entitled as ever, I see," Ayla hissed.

He wrapped his arms around her waist, his eyes tracking the lines of her cascading silver necklaces before he pulled her close. His breath warming her neck, he pulled her still closer, until the brass buttons on his vest dug into her ribs. They swayed to the music, and Ayla tried to keep her stomach down.

"I'm serious, Ayla," he said into her ear. "Do you ever wonder what might have happened if I'd given us a real chance?"

She pulled away and gave him the coldest expression she could muster.

"I'm the firstborn of Niniever," he said. "I can choose who I want. I'm not bound by the oath of the second, like my brother. Denounce that crazy excuse for a mother, leave the shame of your family behind, and you can still be mine. We were good together once—"

"You never were good at change, or listening."

His fingers tightened around her hand and waist. "I'm serious. I've been with a lot of women. They clamor to me like bees to a flower. If I said the word, they would be mine."

"Then why don't you?"

"Because we have history, Ayla. You are my proper match. You have the bloodline of a queen, but you need a king like me to restore you. Together we can fight for whatever cause amuses you. But without me, you have no right pretending there is still a crown on your head. Face it, you need me. And most importantly"—his hand came up, fingers tracing the silver chains down her neck—"I want you."

He stopped in the middle of the floor, and suddenly his lips were crushing hers, his hand groping her as he searched for a way under her skirt. She knew from other encounters he wanted her to pull away, to fight him. He was most excited by a bit of danger, as long as the object of his affections was the one feeling the fear.

Latching onto him, Ayla returned the kiss, her arms disappearing into his coat like a snake coiling around its prey. Laurion struggled in shock, trying to pull away, to regain control. When Ayla finally loosened her grip, it was to place the dagger she'd pulled from his belt against his throat.

"If you ever insult me like that again, I will start by cutting off your lips and feeding them to your dogs," she murmured seductively. The menace behind her words registered in his eyes. He tried to sneer dismissively, but his expression was confused. "And I might not carry a title, but I have friends who do. They'll be more than happy to bury the tiny pieces of you that your dogs leave behind. Think on that the next time you wonder what remains between us."

Ayla shoved him. He stumbled back, hands going to his neck.

"Prince Laurion," she announced dramatically for anyone within earshot, "I must apologize for my poor dancing. My dinner doesn't seem to agree with me. I will have to leave you in the capable hands of our fellow countrymen."

Ayla used her curtsy to stash the newly acquired dagger in her boot. Laurion watched in silence as the trophy disappeared. A flock of youths descended on the now publicly recognized royalty with wreaths of fall leaves and bouquets of flowers for the next dance. Ayla slipped into the crowd and out the nearest exit. Taft was waiting for her by a merchant wagon, a smirk on his face.

"That was terrifying to watch." He held out his arm. "Who taught you to do that?"

"My mother. She'd always tell me, 'Your enemy's weakness lies in the weapon they think they wield over you. Whatever it is, find a way to turn it back on them, and you'll defeat them twice.' Since Terrshon's rise to power, it's possibly the most valuable thing she's ever taught me."

"I'm not sure I'd have handled an assault like that with such grace." Taft offered her a flagon. "Care to wash your mouth out before we both become ill?"

She rolled her eyes and took a swig. "Don't go soft on me now. I have two more negotiations to get through before this night is over."

"I can't help you with people, but you pit me against any wild animal, and I'm your man."

"Too much more of this and we won't be able to tell the difference." Ayla sighed, taking one more swig and handing the flagon back. They passed the merchant stands, their wares covered. When night's revels spilled around the bonfires, the merchants would return to set up shop again.

A young servant emerged from the thin crowd and approached her. "Excuse me, my lady," she said, looking around to be sure they were alone.

"What is it?" Ayla encouraged.

"Only for you." She looked at the man on Ayla's arm.

"What you have to say he can hear," she reassured the young lady.

"If you say. This came tonight from the castle." She looked over her shoulder and scanned the area to make sure they were still alone. "Your castle. Some still hope."

"You're too kind." Ayla sighed. "Who sent word?"

"They only sent this." The servant handed Ayla a small bundle wrapped in a dirty old rag. She then bowed and quickly excused herself.

Ayla met Taft's gaze before looking at the mysterious package in her hand. Carefully, Ayla unwrapped the bundle. Upon the cloth lay a leather cuff stained with blood. Embossed in the leather was a symbol: a circle with a line through it. Droplets of water cascaded down from that line.

The hairs on Ayla's neck stood up. The whisper came, weaving through her mind.

The blood call has been answered. You must steal back the Last Secret.

1

My whole body shook as I shrieked.

The girl Oydis lay lifeless on the stone floor. This couldn't be happening. It wasn't real. I had to be dreaming. The whole thing had to be one of my nightmares—a nightmare I knew I would never recover from if it continued for much longer. I had to wake up.

But the grip on my arm was too painful. The sickening in my stomach tasted too real. I screamed louder.

I struggled as Terrshon's men tied my wrists and then dragged me back to a dark cell. When rough hands finally released me, I swung my fists, connecting with nothing but air. A second later, a blow glanced off my face, and light exploded in my vision. I fell hard on my knees, my sobs calling after them as the door closed. I tasted blood on my lip again.

I frantically ripped at my bound hands and wrists, trying to force myself to find a grip on reality. They burned with every move. I didn't care. Cuts would eventually heal.

I couldn't get a good grasp. No matter how many times I tried, I couldn't find the end of the cord. I sobbed in panic. I was hyperventilating, and I knew it, or at least a part of my brain did. But I couldn't stop. The room spun. I lay on the straw-covered stone, trying to slow my breathing, but it was keeping pace with my mind.

Fear has taken more lives than evil men ever will.

My grandfather's words mercifully echoed in my mind, and my breathing slowed. I clung to the memory that bubbled to the surface.

The year before he'd disappeared, I'd started having new nightmares. I would wake up screaming in the middle of the night. The dreams weren't always the same, but certain symbols remained constant. I was in a nightgown, running from a burning building as giant talons descended from the sky and tried to tear me to ribbons. Sometimes I was crawling, and other times I could barely move. The claws always came, reaching for me. The dream filled my head with the most horrible noises.

When I finally told my grandfather about them, he fell silent for a long time. He looked so sad, but then he smiled at me.

"Lotty, I am going to tell you something that many people never learn, but you must learn it and live by it."

"What Grandpa?"

"Fear has taken more lives than evil men ever will."

"What does it mean?"

"It means there are many things in this world that are to be feared, but like your dreams, most of them are illusions. Until you can see the illusions, you will be controlled by your fear. When people are afraid, they hide. They hide until they're so small they might as well not be alive at all. Fear is its own monster, you see. But it has a weakness—an off switch. You must find that switch within yourself and become its master."

"But I don't know how. I'm just so scared. What if I can't?"

"You can, and you will," he answered, pulling me into a tight hug. "You'll find your courage and defeat that monster because you are stronger."

"How do you know?"

"In your dreams, you are already winning," he whispered, leaning close with a twinkle in his eye. "They never catch you, and they never will."

Blood of Moldara 19

The memory faded, and I realized I had calmed down a little.

But they did catch me this time, Grandpa! What do I do now?

No more answers came, so I imagined the fear inside me, like a demon made entirely of smoke. It was an exercise left over from when I was a child, but it was still effective. All one needed to get rid of smoke was a strong wind. I thought of the innocent girl they'd beaten and killed in my place until anger built up inside me like a tornado, clearing away the haze.

I fixated on one question. *How did I get here?*

It obviously had something to do with my grandpa because that murdering bastard, Terrshon, had said his name. But Elion had disappeared when I was ten. It had been eight years. If these people wanted me so bad, why wait all this time?

It was easy to say that none of this would have happened if my Aunt Karen and Uncle Bill hadn't moved us back to Virginia, to my grandparent's farm. But years of therapy had taught me to stop blaming one event for all my problems. Even being struck by lightning had omens that preceded it. I just had to establish what mine were.

In returning to my childhood home, I'd found the note left behind by Grandma Mable on that weird blue-flame lamp. It turned out to be a cipher for Grandpa's journals, and my desire for answers had been rekindled. In secret, I'd started searching his things and his writings, hoping to finally figure out what had happened all those years ago when he'd left us. But then, just when I'd really thought I was onto something, like a name for the man who might have attacked him, my cousin Tyler looked over what I'd found and decided Grandpa's journals were notes for a novel he'd been writing.

Nothing in Tyler's anthropology studies had suggested to him that any of Grandpa's writings could be rooted in reality. And I'd believed him, until Grandpa's fairytale characters and creatures started leaving signs that they were real.

I'd refused to talk to Tyler or my aunt and uncle about any of this until I had solid proof. Roah, an exchange student turned farmhand who had slowly stolen my heart, had ended up being the only one who could figure out how to translate the coded and hidden parts of my grandpa's journals. He was also the only witness to my kidnapping.

If he was still alive.

That thought alone threatened to send me spiraling back toward despair. I decided instead to focus on the mistakes I was sure I'd made.

Roah and I should never have gone back to my house after the break-in. That was obvious. The police had warned us. The vandals were violent. I replayed the attack in my room, when we'd gone back for my things and grandpa's journals. I'd thought I'd escaped. In my dark, mildewing cell, that idea now seemed laughable. It had always been a trap, one closing a little more every day. I just hadn't been able to see it.

What I couldn't stop seeing now was the look of horror and desperation on Roah's face as Conlen's men carried me off into the woods. He tried to follow us, but a man on foot was no match for mounted horsemen.

Now, this lunatic named Terrshon held me captive in a place called Moldara. He had tortured me, healed me, and tortured me again. But it hadn't been enough for him. I didn't have the stupid ring he was looking for, which meant that poor young woman had died for nothing. Now I was supposed to wait for him to drag me out and force me to marry him. This was not a fairytale. This was a horror movie.

And I had to find a way out of it.

I had no idea how long I sat in my cell, face swollen, body throbbing, thoughts looping. My only hope was beating back my fear with anger. A couple of times I tried to sleep, but the nightmares that came when I dozed off weren't worth it. Hours passed. Distant voices on the other side of my cell walls mingled with crying and more screaming. They never lasted long. But as my hunger and thirst grew, I began to worry it had been more than a few hours. I hoped and feared that I'd been forgotten.

When my cell door creaked opened and footsteps slid lightly across the damp stone floor, I made myself a promise. They weren't taking me anywhere without a fight.

I felt a hand on my head, and I kicked out blindly.

"Shh, child," a soft, and aged, feminine voice whispered. "I'm not going to hurt you. I'm here to help. We need to get you out of here before Terrshon comes back, but first, we have to untie you."

I was being rescued?! It seemed so impossible, but I didn't care; I just wanted to go home, and I was ready to take any door that led there. I offered my hands blindly. In an instant, someone was at my side. A pair of fingers worked to release the knot at my ankles. As the rope came off, I slowly peeled my puffy eyes open.

A small lantern flooded the room with a soft light, and I finally saw the prison I had known only through touch. A stone floor. Stone walls. A pile of straw that had become my bed. The room was small with no windows, and the only entrance was a narrow doorway guarded by a thick wooden slab.

In front of the door, an older lady with soft eyes looked me over. Her salt and pepper hair framed a wrinkled expression that was just visible under the deep hood of her long cloak. She gasped when I met her gaze and covered her mouth with her hand.

"Oh, Adelaide, it is you! I hardly dared to hope—"

It wasn't the older lady who spoke. It was the one who had untied me and now kneeled next to me. She wore a similar cloak, but even in the dim light I could clearly see her expression, which was full of remorse and pain. My rescuer was around my age, maybe a few years older. She was beautiful, with soft, full lips framing a small mouth, high cheekbones, and a slender nose. Her long black hair had been pulled back, allowing the full impact of her beauty to show. But it was her eyes that struck me the most. I couldn't quite see their true color in the dim light of the flame, but their intensity was unmistakable.

"Who are you? How did you—" I choked out in a low voice. Talking burned my dry throat.

"No time. We need to get you out of here. Do you understand?" she whispered, her eyes pleading.

"Yes." Anything was better than staying with the murderous psychopath.

"Quickly, Hattie, help me." She motioned for the old woman to stand behind me.

Hattie helped me sit up as the young woman worked at my wrists. The leather stung as it ripped from my skin, opening the scabs that had formed around the bands. The blood burned when it rushed into my numb fingers. I rubbed my hands, hoping to ease the heat pulsing through them. Every bruise and sore muscle throbbed. I had never dreamt up pain that excruciating. I bit the inside of my cheeks to keep from screaming.

Slowly, they helped me to my feet. The young woman spoke again.

"Adelaide, I need you to follow my every word. Once we are outside this room, except in a few archways, if we talk, we will be discovered, so I need you to understand your instructions before we exit this chamber. Our survival depends on it."

I nodded, even though my head swam with the effort of sitting. She read the concern on my face.

"I'll be by your side to help you. When we leave, stay as close to me as possible. We need to go as fast as you are able. If you need to lean on me for support, then so be it; I am strong enough for both of us tonight.

"The corridors to our exit are long and tedious. There will be no light to guide us. Just stay close. I know my way. As soon as we are outside the castle wall, we lessen our risk of being captured. My driver and guard will be waiting for us there with a carriage. Even so, we must hurry. We won't know when the guards will discover your absence. Tell me you understand."

My thoughts still felt sluggish due to lack of food and water, or sleep, or perhaps I'd been to too many Renaissance festivals. Either way, my brain couldn't process what she'd told me. Since when did a carriage replace a getaway car? I didn't want to be the one who got us caught, so I focused on the escape plan instead of trying to get things to make sense.

"I think I got it. Stay close. Go fast. Use you for help if I need it. It's going to be dark, but no worries, you know the way. Then it's into the…carriage?" I thought my brain might explode.

"Good. Put this on."

The older lady, Hattie, opened a long thick cloak identical to the ones my rescuers wore. I turned around as she gently lifted the heavy garment over my shoulders. With the cloak hanging on my body, I warmed up instantly. It hung to the ground and hid even the tops of my feet. She turned me to face her and fastened the four large metal buttons that held it shut. Then she reached up and lifted the hood, tucking in a few strands of hair that escaped.

"Only when you are safely out of the city walls can you remove this," Hattie said in a loving manner. "Until then, promise me you will remain hidden and follow every instruction Ayla gives you."

"I will," I promised.

"You are ready then?" the younger woman, Ayla I assumed, asked.

"I think so," I said, my voice cracking. There was something too real, almost heartbreaking about the way the old woman touched me, the look in her eyes.

Then Ayla turned for the door, motioning for Hattie to open it. As I moved toward the threshold, the older woman turned to give my hand a tight squeeze. Her fierce gaze penetrated me, burned into me. I tried to shake the feeling, but the depth of her conviction as she spoke was hard to ignore.

"Go in peace, my child. I now know the stories are true. You look just like her, you know," she paused, lowering her voice a whisper. "I loved your mother like my own daughter, and I loved you too. You have a great journey ahead of you. May the Spirits guide you and the Sages look over you, my dear, sweet Adelaide."

Smiling, she took my face in her hands. Her eyes spoke nothing but love to mine. With the gentleness of a grandmother's touch, she softly kissed my forehead.

Hattie turned to the younger woman and took her hands in the same loving fashion as she had mine. They looked into each other's eyes. No words were exchanged. They didn't need any. They kissed each other on the cheek, wet with their tears, and performed one last gesture.

Hattie held the glass trinket that hung from her neck and crushed it in her hand, flinching as the glass cut into her wrinkled skin. Smiling serenely, she held out her bloody palm. Ayla bowed her head, kissed her own fingers, and touched them to Hattie's fresh wound.

"Today my sorrow is ended," Hattie murmured.

"And with your vow, you end the sorrow of countless others," Ayla answered.

"You must hurry," Hattie ordered, even as she nodded her acknowledgment of the blessing. Hattie opened the heavy wooden door and poked her head out, checking to see if the way was clear. She motioned us forward with her other hand, stepping aside to let us pass.

I looked at her one last time. Strangely, I felt a deep love for this woman I didn't know. Somehow, she knew me and my mother, and had loved us both.

I had so many questions for her. Questions I was afraid I would never get to ask. She squeezed my hand one last time, holding the bloodied one up proudly as if it meant something to me, and then we were running.

2

We raced down the stone corridor. Torches shed a dim light along the walls, making it easy for me to get sidetracked by what I saw. Every ten feet stood statues of full armor holding swords or maces. My guide tugged my arm. I hadn't realized I slowed every time I passed one of those ancient guards. I quickened my pace, fighting my exhaustion. To keep me going, I focused on the rhythm of our feet hitting the hard stone.

We wound our way through the tight hall. With the last turn, the light faded behind us. I was totally dependent on my guide now. She held me close to her side and continued through the dark. We traveled down another black corridor, turning several times. How did she know which turn was the one that would lead us out?

We came to another pitch-black hall where the air grew cold. Chills rippled through my body. She slowed, pausing for just a second. Then, she whispered into my ear barely loud enough for me to hear.

"Steps."

She led the way, pulling me with her. The stairs felt narrower and higher than most, and as if I were taking stadium steps two at a time. My shoulder rubbed against the cold stone as we ascended the dark staircase. I struggled to keep up. Noticing I was growing weaker, my guide held me tightly to her, allowing me to use her as a crutch. When we got to the top of the stairs, the cold draft dropped a few degrees and grew stronger, brushing against my heated face.

We took one last turn. Then she stopped. I could hardly hear her breathing over my panting.

"Quickly," she whispered urgently. "Someone's coming."

She pulled my arm up to drape it over her shoulders, and with her hand on my waist, she half dragged me into the darkness. After several minutes, she stopped and I felt her body shift as she pushed against something. A faint light appeared, in a widening line. It was a door, small and heavy. She opened just enough for us to squeeze through into the cool night air. Once she'd dragged me to the other side, she pushed the door shut and slid a wooden beam in place to secure it. Whoever was trying to follow would have to find another exit.

Two fairly big men, one much larger and darker than the other, met us when we emerged on the other side. My hood was so deep it was almost like wearing a blindfold. Still, I tried to steal a glance at our surroundings, to get some sense of where I was. But a hand caught my tender wrist and pulled it down.

"They're coming. We need to hurry," Ayla said to them.

The big guy with dark brown skin and darker hair scooped me into his arms and half ran down a steep, crumbling staircase built into the wall. The others followed close behind. At the bottom, in the shadows, was a carriage with four horses harnessed to it. The door flew open, and he placed me lightly on a seat in the dim cabin. Then he was gone. My young guide ducked in, closed the door, and sat across from me.

After a loud snap, we jolted forward, fast. When we took a sharp corner, I slid down the smooth leather seat and slammed into a third person I hadn't even realized was there. I scrambled, finding something to hold onto as the carriage bumped and careened down the road.

A few more sharp turns had me sliding around in the cabin. Finally, the carriage slowed. We kept a swift pace, even after the road changed from stone to dirt. The ride was bumpy, but not unbearable. It reminded me of off-roading in an old pickup with bad shocks. I kept one hand on my hood and the other on a handrail that ran along the ceiling of the carriage, afraid to let go long enough to peek through the covered windows and be seen.

"Here, drink. You must be parched." Ayla handed me a small leather pouch heavy with water.

"Thank you." The words still burned when I spoke.

I put my dried lips to the spout. The cool water coated the fire in my mouth and throat. I drank the whole thing.

"Sorry, I didn't mean to finish it." The words still hurt when I spoke, but they didn't blaze anymore.

"Don't apologize, Lotty. That was for you. We have more if you'd like."

"Yes, please."

It didn't take long for me to empty the second water-skin. After I had my fill, my throat hurt only slightly. The water in my stomach sloshed with the bumps of the carriage, but it seemed as though the road was smoothing out.

"Try to get some sleep." She gestured to the bench, handing me something small and soft. "You need to rest."

"How long was I—" Kidnapped? That didn't seem like the right word. "Please don't think I'm ungrateful, but I don't know you. If you could just drop me off at a gas station, or bus stop, I can find my way to a police station from there. There are people looking for me, and I have to let them know I'm okay."

She looked at me with a puzzled expression. "I'm sorry. I don't understand what you're asking. I came for you as soon as my spies told me Terrshon had you. You're safe now. You should try to get some sleep."

I didn't want to sleep. I wanted answers. I wanted to go home! Hot fury blazed through me. Just as I was about to throw the most epic tantrum, the carriage dipped, and her cloak slipped open, revealing knee-high black lace-up boots that peeked out from under a heavy petticoat. Pinstriped ruffles and lace in descending shades of blue dripped from one gather to another. A white leather bodice with a matching white collar displayed the numerous silver chains that adorned her neck and disappeared between her breasts. I felt my eyes go wide as she hurried to cover herself under the cloak again.

Confused, and suddenly afraid I had not escaped all of the crazy people, I took the small pillow and laid my head on it. I wasn't going to sleep, but I closed my eyes anyway. My mind was the last place I could hide, and in my exhaustion, all I wanted to do was pretend I was somewhere else. Somewhere safe.

3

When I finally came out of my restless slumber, the bouncing of the carriage reminded me of the pain in my head and the sores on my wrists and ankles. As I lay with my eyes still closed, one thought occupied every square inch of my brain—I was still a prisoner.

The longer I was awake, the more I realized how much I had been hoping the last few days had been nothing but a bad dream. Now that I was better rested, and out of imminent danger, the fog of shock had cleared. My mind raced back through all that had happened; all the broken images I could remember:

The intense look of Hattie's face as she held up her bleeding hand. Oydis's cries of agony from the whipping. The cold stone of the cell floor against my cheek. The groping hands of my captors at the cavern entrance. Roah's bloodied fists and bruised face in the woods. Sinji's lifeless body in the grass. Trell's hushed conversation with Roah as he expressed concern for me. The break-in. My bedroom ransacked. Tyler's insistence that I stay at Roah's. Roah's hallucinations rising from the poison in his wounds. An eagle as big as a golden retriever, attacking from the sky.

I looked for details—new clues that might help me figure out who had taken me and what they wanted with me. And why on earth were they all in a mix of period clothing and using carriages? Impossibly, every conclusion led me back to excerpts from Grandpa's journals.

I told myself that I didn't know my supposed rescuers or their intentions for me. As soon as I could make a break for it, I would. I had to find a phone or a passing car—anything to return me to civilization. I clung to that one objective while my heart pounded in my ears.

The carriage slowed and then stopped. I stayed perfectly still, feigning sleep while people moved around me. A door closed, and a latch clicked into place. Hushed voices talked just out of range. Working up the courage, I counted to three and forced myself to open my eyes.

I was alone in the carriage, but the shadow of a figure stood in front of the only door. It was one of the guards, I realized. The big one. My heart sank and I bit my lip to keep from screaming. I had been right. I was still being held prisoner.

I chanced a look out one of the small windows of the carriage. The glass was wavy with tiny bubbles frozen in it, the kind found in the windows of old buildings, produced before there were machines that made it flawless.

Looking past the bubbles into the early morning light, I had to rub my eyes to be sure of what I saw. A village right out of a storybook, or old Europe, stretched at least a mile in either direction. The few buildings I could make out along the main road were short and appeared handcrafted. Hills with forests and meadows flowed beyond the village.

I watched a young man lead a horse, pulling a cart full of raw goods, down the dirt road. Another horse passed, pulling a small open carriage, driven by a man in a dark blue waistcoat. The woman next to him held a goose tightly on her lap. A few more people walked by carrying baskets under their arms or large satchels stretched across their shoulders. Their clothes were the most confusing part of the picture, as if someone had smashed a few centuries together into one time and place.

There were no jeans and no sneakers, but I saw as many women in variations of pants as the men. Simple leather corsets lay atop long shirts, and women wore close fitting pants as well as flowing skirts. For the men, blousy shirts with woven vests over longer pants and calf-high boots were the most common attire. I saw nearly every kind of hat and noticed that thick leather belts were as common as fingerless gloves and worn equally by both sexes.

But most alarming of all, I saw no cell phones and no personal tablets. Not even a single camera.

A new panic seized me as I rushed to the opposite side of the carriage and peeked through the curtain. We were parked in front of an old inn. The front was white stucco with dark wood beams that criss-crossed, making large triangular shapes. There were boxes of bright red and yellow flowers under the windows. An old worn sign hung over the door. It reminded me of the building Roah had taken me to at the Ren fest, the one with a small medical office inside.

I dropped the curtain and returned to my seat, my hope of escape slipping away. I had been kidnapped by crazies. Who bought into the festival life so much that they actually started a village like this? Who gave up real civilization for living in a commune full of Renaissance freakazoids?

I was doing everything in my power not to hyperventilate when the carriage door slowly opened. I froze. A beautiful face appeared, smiling brightly at me.

Last night the dim lantern light hadn't done her justice. She was even more breathtaking than I remembered. Her hair, still pulled back in a thick braid, was a midnight black. What I thought might be brown eyes were actually a dark emerald green with flecks of gold scattered throughout. The silken, mahogany tone of her skin made her eyes stand out. She sat next to me on the bench, closer than I wanted.

"Good morning, Lotty," she said, her tone more relaxed than it had been last night. "Let's have a look at your wounds in the light." She took my hand in hers and examined my wrist, poking at my sores.

"Ow! Please don't." I forced through gritted teeth, pulling my arm away.

"I'm sorry. I didn't mean any harm. We need to clean your lesions before they get any more infected, or I'll never forgive myself," she said, her expression apologetic and concerned.

I stared her down, my brow furrowed. I glanced at her guards, still hovering by the door, and scooted away from her like the caged animal I was.

"Look, you seem nice," I snapped, my voice hoarse from a day and a half of screaming...or had it been longer? "But I need answers because I am freaking out here!"

Her brow crumpled in distress as a hand went to her heart. "I'm so sorry. I just figured you knew." She slid next to me again as if to reassure me. "It has been a long time though, hasn't it? It's me, Ayla."

I just looked at her, perplexed. Why did everyone around here think I knew them?

"Ayla, is it? I have no idea what you're talking about, Ayla. I mean, I am grateful you saved me from that"—a shiver inched down my spine as my thoughts went back to the stone cell—"that creepy psycho and his fraternity of Halloween masks, but I think there's been a horrible mistake."

"No, there's no mistake. I'd know you anywhere." The compassion in her eyes shifted into certainty as she scooted closer and rested her hand on my leg. "Once I got word that Terrshon had found you, I didn't delay. I'm just relieved we were already so close to the castle, or things could have gotten complicated. You're safe now, and you have my word that as long as you're with me, nothing will harm you."

What in the hell was she talking about? I shook her arm off and moved to the other bench across from her.

"You know, this is all fine and dandy. I love role-playing as much as the next Ren geek, I really do, but I don't know you. This whole situation is starting to look like some elaborate good-cop-bad-cop routine. I'll tell you the same thing I told the last guy. Whatever you're looking for, I don't have it! Can we please drop all the crap and just talk straight? I'm tired of playing. I hurt, I'm hungry, and I just want to go home!"

Ayla stiffened; the kindness in her eyes cooling to disappointment.

"It's not that simple, Lotty."

"Sure it is! Just let me use your cell phone. Or better yet, point me to the nearest highway. I don't believe you want to hurt me. Just let me go, and I will tell people I got lost in the woods. It wouldn't be the first time."

Ayla watched me, measuring something. Her brow narrowed as if she were deciding how to answer.

"Lotty, there are a couple things you need to understand." She was trying to be gentle, but I sensed an air of command to her voice. She was angry. "The first is that I am in no way associated with Terrshon. I would kill him myself, with my bare hands, and smile doing it."

"The second is that you are not my prisoner, but neither are you in Virginia. You are in a different world altogether, one that is not safe for you. This little town, Vandervelde, is in a country fighting for its very existence, but we have more pressing things to worry about at the moment, like getting you out of the street."

"Wait. What?" How far were they going to take this charade? "Did you—or that other guy—take me across state lines?"

"You don't understand," she said to herself before she continued. "I'm sorry this is so confusing, but it's neither the time nor the place for this conversation. Our room is ready and time is short."

She stretched her hand out to me.

"Make the time! I'm not going anywhere else," I insisted, flinching away from her, "unless it's back to Lexington. Help me get home, and I will tell the cops you had nothing to do with this insanity, or just drop me off at the nearest police station. I don't care which, but if you keep me here, you are as bad as that guy."

"I am trying to help you, Lotty. I know you don't trust me." She emphasized each word as if I tried her patience. Clasping her hands, she leaned forward, her expression pleading. "But the longer you delay, the more dangerous it is for all of us. Can you not see that? The threat I rescued you from last night—that's real. Just look at your wrists; those weren't from me. I didn't tie you up. I'm not holding you prisoner. I'm trying to keep you alive because obviously, you have no inkling of what is happening. But I will tell you this: throughout this realm, I have never once heard of a station called 'police.'"

My head was about to explode. She believed every word of her speech. I had gone from one crazy person to another. The familiar sting of tears threatened to tear apart the last of my control as I pulled my knees up to my chest and fought to stay calm.

Ayla sighed. "Lotty, I knew you to be stubborn, but I never thought you would have forgotten so much. I'm sorry it has to come to this, but everything I've risked means nothing if you don't come with me."

Ayla took her fist and pounded twice on the door. It opened immediately, and the large man standing guard leaned in. Without any warning, he grabbed me by the waist and lifted me out of the carriage.

Before I could blink, he used the cloak I wore against me, wrapping it around my body as easily as if it were a rope. His large hands tightened, causing my bruises to flare in protest. Feeling my pain resurface, I gave in and let him carry me. I went totally limp in his arms, hoping my dead weight would make it harder for him.

In next to no time, we were inside the inn. Empty wooden tables were scattered across a tiled floor, the hearth at the end of the room was dark. A bucket and mop stood waiting by a pile of linens heaped in front of a side door. It was like the place had been abandoned. Still being carried, I was taken up a set of questionable wood stairs to a room on the second floor. Once inside, Ayla closed the door behind us. The aroma of food overwhelmed my senses. My stomach knotted in pain.

"Now, I'm going to let Taft release you, but only if you choose to contain yourself and follow my instructions. If you cooperate, it will make it much easier for all of us. If not, Taft can manage you for as long as need be."

His arms tightened slightly around my torso just to prove he could carry me like that for as long as he wanted.

The aroma was torturous. My mouth watered as I caught the scent of the fresh muffins, hot bread, and cold jams. I couldn't get my brain to think of any good reason to say no to food.

"Fine," I conceded. "I'll play nice. Just put me down already."

Taft set me on my feet and stepped back to stand against the wall. He continued to stare, just to let me know he would be watching.

Blood of Moldara 35

"Now that that's settled, please, freshen up," Ayla said, handing me a bowl of water, a small towel, and a bar of soap.

"Thank you," I said after I'd washed my hands.

"Let's eat," she offered with a smile.

I stared at the arrangement of food. I didn't know where to start. The table setting looked like something from a food magazine. Plates had been arranged in circles, the alternating slices of different colored cheeses and warm bread creating an artful pattern. A bowl of fresh fruit sat on one corner of the table, with a pitcher of some sort of drink at the other. In the middle was a large spiral cut ham, a crock steaming with soup, and a wooden platter of freshly baked muffins with jam. A bouquet of freshly cut flowers completed the arrangement.

If I weren't so hungry, I would've felt bad for destroying the creative layout. It didn't take long for my stomach to fill as I tried to stuff as much food in it as possible. After just two helpings, I was satisfied.

When I finished, Ayla pulled on a thin rope hanging in the corner.

"Let's get you cleaned up."

There was a low knock at the door.

"Come in, Enzi."

Taft slid the door open, revealing a woman who looked to be in her mid-forties. She wore a rust-colored sleeveless turtleneck under a brown and white striped jumper that had large metal buckles where the shoulder straps connected. Two gray pockets were stitched at waist height and matched the sturdy low-heeled boots that disappeared under the long tube dress.

Most surprising was her short, spiky white hair that went in every direction like animal fur. She had small laugh lines at the corners of her eyes, rosy cheeks, and a light crease in her brow. The several piercings in each ear didn't quite match the one necklace she wore right at the base of her throat, a single clear glass charm shaped like a drop of water on a white leather cord. It looked like the one Hattie had been wearing before she broke it in her hand.

Enzi carried a tray lined with different shaped bottles and a large towel. She walked across the room and stopped at a door I hadn't noticed before. She turned to me as if waiting for me to follow.

"This is Enzi. She'll see to your personal needs," Ayla said, helping me out of my seat. I hesitated, unsure of what she meant by personal needs. I began to question my resolve to play along.

Ayla sighed in surrender. "I will not become Terrshon and compel you at every turn. Perhaps if you had a reason to cooperate?"

Although she had misread my hesitation, I was curious to know what she thought she had to offer me.

"I can tell you about your parents," she offered quietly.

"Excuse me? How would you know my parents?" I demanded, trying to hide my astonishment at such a lie.

"I didn't say I knew them. I said I could tell you about them. To prove that I am not lying, I will show you the portrait I have of them in which your mother is wearing that same necklace you now wear."

My hand went to my pendant. She had my undivided attention, and I was sure I looked as astonished as I felt. My grandfather had described my parents to me a thousand times, but I had never seen a picture until Roah showed me one on my birthday.

"It's not here, of course," she continued. "It's at the end of our journey, in a safe place. If you cooperate, do everything I ask of you, I will tell you what I know. After that, if you still want to return to Virginia, we will make the necessary arrangements. Is that acceptable?"

I stood, nodding my surrender, and walked toward Enzi.

Ayla smiled sadly and gestured to Enzi, who curtsied. She had a bright, warm smile on her face. My smile felt much the opposite.

4

I wasn't used to bathing with anyone in the room with me, but Enzi was a master at averting her eyes and holding up curtains. My clothes were ruined. And while they felt like my only remaining connection to home, they'd also been touched by Terrshon. Peeling them off was my only way to scrub away any remaining residue. The resulting pile of rags looked more like something an animal had dug up, than the jeans and t-shirt they used to be.

I sank into the steaming water with a sigh of relief. The tub was just big enough for me to sit and collect myself. I picked up the bar of soap and started lathering.

An hour later, Enzi pulled the lace tight on the front of the leather half-bodice. I hardly recognized myself in the full-length mirror. Enzi hadn't missed one detail. I lifted my hand to my face, then to my neck, absently searching. I still wasn't used to the naked feeling at my throat. My mother's pendant had been modified with a new chain long enough to hide the stone between my breasts. Enzi had said Ayla was adamant that the necklace stay hidden, "for your own protection," whatever that meant.

The gown underneath the leather was beautiful—dark blue silk trimmed in gold. The cut of the skirt was unique, several layers of fabric gathered in different places in the front where it tucked into a thick leather belt hanging low on my hips. The skirt opened in the front allowing free movement of my legs, which were clothed in tight pants and knee-high boots that matched the leather of my bodice. The sleeves were just long enough to cover the bandages Enzi had placed around my wrists after tending my wounds. Sadly, there was nothing to cover the cut or the bruising on my cheek.

My mostly silent helper had pulled my long hair up off my neck in an intricate design held by pearl clips. A few loose dark blond ringlets lined my face and trailed down my back. The makeup she used took away the dark circles and the other signs of my ordeal, leaving me with bright eyes and dark red lips.

I couldn't believe how elegant, yet practical, the entire outfit was. The strange mix of leathers and metal buckles evoked a bold sense of daring I wasn't expecting. Despite how bewildered I felt by the last few days, I liked whatever style was going on in this freaky Ren-fest village.

I wished Roah could see me, and a flutter of fear went through me. I hoped he'd gotten away and was safely searching for me with the police.

A low knock sounded on the door, and Ayla entered. She had changed as well, into a dark red dress, almost the color of wine. Her bodice was made from the same light leather as mine, though the cut was different. It allowed for the plume of ruffles at her neckline to cascade down her front. Her skirt gathered in the same way mine did, at her waist, a square leather bag and a metal chain, with what looked like an old-fashioned compass at the end, hung from her belt. Her legs peeked through the silk of her skirt, her knee-high boots laced with a thick cream ribbon from toe to thigh.

She came over, taking both my hands in hers. She lifted them slightly, getting a closer look. Then, she met my gaze, and a warm smile brightened her eyes.

"Ah. Much better, Little Sister." She looked at me with an approving expression of a parent or older sibling. "Well done, Enzi. I think we are finished here. Could you please see to our things? It's almost time."

"Certainly, my lady. Little Sister." She nodded to us each in turn and then exited the room.

"I take it by what you've dressed me in, that you're taking me deeper into crazy country." Exactly how much more playing along was I expected to do before getting some real answers?

"Yes, it's deeper into crazy country," she quoted me with a wry smile.

She held out a sleeveless black cloak with gray stitching and a heavy metal clasp.

"What's this for?"

"Terrshon has spies everywhere. We need to keep you hidden, just until I know his spies aren't watching."

With our faces concealed in the deep hoods and her bodyguard leading the way, we walked down the stairs and out the back door of the inn. A new carriage awaited us in the street. This one lacked the fancy glass windows, polished trim, and padded seats.

Ayla assured me the arrangement was temporary. We were going to a sanctuary on the outskirts of town to wait for the horses and carriage that would take us the rest of the way. I resumed my silent position across from Ayla and Taft.

We turned off the main road onto a less worn path through the thick trees.

Trying to occupy my mind, I analyzed my surroundings. I could see why they had chosen that spot for their Renaissance commune. The jagged mountain range in the distance would isolate them from outside influences. I'd heard of hikers getting lost in treacherous terrain like that, but I was sure there wasn't anything like that in Virginia or even West Virginia. *Where am I?*

Cut off from the rest of civilization, the crazy Ren-fest people probably had trouble bringing in new blood to keep their population growing and healthy. Maybe those lost hikers had been abducted to keep the population from marrying their first cousins, and after they captured them, they brainwashed them into liking their prison. What if that's what happened to Grandpa?

The carriage jostled down the secluded dirt road for more than an hour before it made one last turn and climbed a slow rise. I risked a glance through the curtains just as a small modest building came into view. It was made of large chunks of stone and beautiful stained glass windows. Ivy grew up one side of the building. This had to be the sanctuary Ayla had mentioned earlier.

The carriage stopped, and the door opened to an older dark-skinned man with a trim white beard and athletic physique. He wore a high-collared, long-sleeved shirt that was forest green. His matching wide-legged pants were tied with a broad leather band that latched together on either side with ornate metal clasps. Over the shirt and pants was a white tunic, like a double-sided apron, which hung just below his knees. It bore a symbol that reminded me of some from Grandpa's journals.

"Welcome, my friends," he said cheerfully, helping us from the carriage, "and my dearest Ayla. To what do I owe this unscheduled visit?"

"Soren, you old bookworm, someone has to keep you on your toes and make sure you see the sun now and again," Ayla responded, warmly embracing him. When she pulled back, her expression sobered. "I was hoping you'd have some news from the dead. Why else would I come from the Harvest Feasts in a carriage not my own with a cloaked guest?"

As they greeted each other, I hung back, staying close to the carriage but within arm's reach of Taft. Guest? Hardly.

"What has happened?" He peered deeply into the shadow of my hood as all the levity drained out of his face.

"Soren, I'm sorry," Ayla answered. "We were all caught off guard by this. It's not fair to you, or your order, but we are in need of a place to hide, just until my people come for us."

"My lady, who would you risk all this for, and during the festival?"

"Only one person," she replied gravely. "Our little sister."

Soren finally stopped fidgeting and closed the distance between us in two strides, a fire lighting his eyes as he reached to lower my hood. I flinched, blinking against the sudden onslaught of sunlight. I looked to Ayla for a little help, but she seemed caught up in the moment, simply regarding me with somber pride.

I looked back to Soren and found a man who appeared caught between joy and a terrible grief.

"I assure you, you are looking at no spirit," Ayla whispered. "She is real."

"I can hardly believe what my old eyes are telling me. But she looks so much like her...her mother." His expression had gone pale as he continued to scrutinize me.

"Yes, she does. I would never have believed it myself, except that they have such a strong resemblance, and she bears the burn scars of the legend. She is also wearing this." Ayla motioned for me to reveal what was hidden at the end of the long chain around my neck. Self-consciously, I held up the only connection to a mother I didn't know. To everyone in this place, what I wore around my neck functioned like a pair of dog tags.

He reached out and held the stone, examining it closely. Then he glanced up, misty-eyed.

"Adelaide?" he whispered.

"Yes?" I answered, still not sure what to do. "How do you know me?"

He stared at me, completely spellbound. He scrutinized every detail of my face and even touched the exposed scar at my neck. When he got to my eyes, he gazed into them, searching for something. I felt my personal space alarm going off. It was starting to get weird.

His expression became concentrated. He took both my hands in his and closed his eyes. The lines on his face softened, one corner of his mouth turning up slightly. I stood perfectly still but couldn't help shooting a questioning glance at Ayla, hoping for a little assistance. She smiled and held a finger to her lips. I looked back at this man, who was now lost in thought. I wondered if he was ever going to let my hands free.

I had counted to fifty when his eyes opened again and found mine. His smile brightened, deepening the creases next to his eyes.

"You, child, have journeyed so much farther than most in your short and tragic life. I sense your mother's will in you and your father's insolence. Both qualities will serve you in ways your parents could not have imagined. They knew greatness, but it did not save them from loss. You are a result of their love and hope for a better future. Be a daughter that would make them proud by staying true to yourself, and you will find all the allies you need here."

I looked at the poor old man in front of me, sorrow pricking me deep in my chest. I was not who he thought I was, but how could I change his mind when he was so sure he knew me? He must have misinterpreted my placating nod because he started to speak again, bowing slightly as he explained himself.

"The pieces of a puzzle don't show the entire picture until all are in their place. Your questions all have answers, and you have landed among friends. Just be open to receive what will come." He released my hands and turned his attention to Ayla. "Now then, you were in need of something?"

"The use of your cemetery, my friend."

"Of course. Follow me."

Soren took us by foot some distance from the ruins. We walked through trees, following the bank of a large stream. It was warm, with the sun shining through a forest canopy full of gold, green, and red leaves. When the wind picked up, the air was crisp against my cheeks and smelled like pine. Even the bubbling water falling over stones reminded me of the woods by my house. The woods looked just like home, but every step felt like a deeper descent into a reality I didn't understand.

When we came to a small clearing in the woods, I was taken aback by the sight. The remains of three more sanctuaries filled the space, one larger than the other two; beautiful, even in their ruined state. The roofs were gone, and the interior was now made up of young trees, many reaching past the tall walls. The gray stone walls had disintegrated in some places and held together by vines in others. Arched openings lined a few of the walls, which must have been windows once.

I stumbled over some rocks as emotions washed over me. I felt the way these ruins looked. I choked back the feeling. All I wanted was to find my way home, to my family, to everything familiar, to everything normal. I wanted to find my way back to Roah. I missed him. I worried for him so much it hurt.

Pushing thoughts of him away again, I wandered slowly through the natural maze. A small cemetery appeared ahead, hidden behind some overgrown shrubs. It was well tended, which surprised me. Why would someone take the time to care for this small patch among the ruins? Intrigued and hoping for information about where I was, I stepped forward to get a closer look.

I wound through the headstones. Some had names and dates that didn't make sense. Some were blank. Most of them were modest slabs of smooth stone. Nothing indicated my location. But two memorials stood out from the rest and looked nothing like graves I expected to see in a little unknown cemetery. Large square granite rectangles, each a little larger than a coffin, rose from the manicured grass. I stood in front of the side-by-side tombs and examined the elaborate designs carved there. They were exquisite. At the head of each, jeweled gold compasses drew my gaze. When I got closer, I realized the designs were really the trick font from Grandpa's journals.

Here lies our Mighty King.

Here lies our Beloved Queen.

Lost in thought, I didn't notice Ayla standing next to me.

"Who are they?" I asked.

She stood there for a while, staring at the graves.

"They were my aunt and uncle," she whispered.

I didn't know what to say. No matter how misled she might be to believe in this silly charade, I knew what it was like to lose the people you love. No words ever fixed the ache left behind.

"I come here often," she said. "When they died, a lot changed for me. A lot changed here." She gestured around us, pointing to the buildings. "This used to be the place they came for reflection and spiritual connection. Our family's country manor isn't far from here. In the summers, we were welcomed guests at Soren's rituals and celebrations. Soren knows my family well. He performed the binding ceremony for my aunt and uncle.

"When the throne was threatened after the murder of the king and queen, Soren stepped in. He helped in the protection of their most sacred treasure.

"But some did not look favorably on this and burned his sanctuary. After the uprising here, not many would fight against the tyranny that threatened us, fearing they would be next. My family suffered for it. My uncle and aunt did have a royal burial and a proper resting place in the cemetery on the castle grounds. But after the uprising, we feared their graves would be desecrated. Soren, already having lost everything, took their bodies and gave them rest here.

"After their death, my father ascended the throne. He ruled for three years before the same end came to him. That very night, my mother and I fled as far north as we could, escaping death ourselves. I was seven at the time."

I had so many questions I wanted to ask, but there was only one burning in my throat.

"You think you're a princess?" I asked, dumbfounded.

She turned, looking me dead in the eyes. "No. Although royal blood runs through my veins, my mother and I are disgraced. We belong to no country now."

Before I could respond, we were interrupted by the sound of someone approaching. In that instant, the atmosphere of the group shifted. Ayla replaced my hood, grabbed my arm, and pulled me behind her. We reached the others, who formed a protective line in front of Ayla and me. The big guy placed himself directly in front of us, like a shield. The drumbeat of hooves grew louder. We stood rigid, waiting for what approached.

5

"Ayla. Ayla, it's only me, Kavish," someone shouted, straining to be heard above the sound of his horse.

The group exhaled in relief.

"Who is Kavish?" I asked Ayla softly.

"He's my...well, he does a lot of things. But today he is our eyes and ears."

A lanky boy of about seventeen, with blonde windblown hair and a red face, rode up on a speckled gelding. He dismounted when he reached us. I noticed he wore gear much like Taft's.

"What is it, Kavish?" Ayla stepped out from behind the now relaxed guards.

"They're coming. I don't know how many. Five or maybe six of Terrshon's guard. He is not with them. They are taking any little sisters that have sought refuge among the villagers. We can't risk it."

Kavish was breathless by the time he'd finished. At the sound of Terrshon's name, I had forgotten how to breathe.

"We must hide," Ayla said anxiously, turning to Soren. "Old friend, I—"

"Say no more. It's just a little farther," Soren said. "This way."

Soren led us back into the cemetery, and I followed in a haze of fear, stumbling on my suddenly weak knees. I clutched at my hood as we hurried to keep pace. The old man was surprisingly quick and light on his feet as we wound our way past the old forgotten headstones.

When he came to an abrupt halt in front of an ornate and oversized manhole cover, I nearly crashed into Ayla. I had noticed a few of these hatches scattered throughout the cemetery, but I couldn't imagine their purpose. Soren bent down, grabbed a small latch and turned it three times, as if working the combination to a safe. The hatch popped open. Soren lifted the thick cover and stepped aside.

"I know it's not ideal, but not one soul hidden here has been discovered on my watch," he reassured. "There will be plenty of space and enough air. I'm afraid I was not prepared for you, but there are enough blankets and water for one day. I can't vouch for how good the food is anymore."

"Thank you, Soren. I knew I could count on your cleverness." Ayla kissed him lightly on the cheek. He smiled. She turned to Kavish. "Stay alert and out of sight. I've sent whispers to our allies. Do not come back for us until they arrive in my carriage. Trust no one unless they prove beyond a doubt they're loyal. Do you understand?"

"Yes, my lady," Kavish replied.

"And Kavish," Ayla added in a commanding tone, "die before you give our location away, or you will wish you had."

"I swear it, my lady," he answered with a small bow as his hand clutched at something under his shirt. Ayla nodded her approval, and the youth took off like a shot, remounting his horse and disappearing into the surrounding woods.

"Harsh words for one so young," Soren observed, saying what I was already thinking. "How long until you expect the rest?"

"Late afternoon at the earliest, I'm afraid." Ayla sighed, scanning the horizon. "Can you hide us for that long?"

"All that is needed, I am prepared to do, child," he assured her, his face filled with compassion. He took her hands in his. "Now hurry; you don't have much time."

At a signal from Ayla, her driver, Brolin, was the first to climb down into the dark hole. He called up to Taft, who helped lower Enzi into the hole. Then, he looked at me.

"In you go, Adelaide." Taft took me under my arms and lowered me down into the darkness before I could take a step for myself or protest. The drop was brief. Brolin caught me on the other end and set me down, leading me to a musty corner where I sat next to Enzi.

"Just like old times," Soren said from above.

"Yes," Ayla replied. "Though let's pray for a different outcome this time."

I was surprised by how large the room was. The ceiling was low, the shaggy peeling bark from the beams that crossed it made it seem even lower. I imagined the builders must have used whole trees to take the weight of the dirt above them. The walls were rough-cut stone, but the floor and benches that lined the walls were hard packed dirt. The corner we had dropped into was opposite the water barrel and the pile of supplies Soren had mentioned. I could just make them out in the darkness.

The five of us didn't come close to filling the earthen bench on one side of the chamber. The cold seeped through my layers as if I were wearing nothing. The only light came from three small holes in the center of the hatch we'd come through that had not been visible from above. Still, it was so dark I could barely make out everyone's shape. I tried not to imagine the bodies in the graves around us or think about how easy it would be to decompose into the dirt that was our seat.

Shuddering at the thought, I pulled my legs to my chest, wrapped my thick cloak around them, and tried not to think about the people looking for us. A shiver, completely separate from the cold, ran down my spine, and I pulled my feet under the cloak. No one spoke, and slowly my body tugged at my consciousness, enticing it to give in to the pressing exhaustion. Curling up on one side, I closed my eyes and drifted off.

I wasn't sure how long I was out, but when I woke, the light from the three holes in the hatch above us seemed dimmer. I stretched and felt bruises where I had found rocks in my sleep. Sitting up, I took stock of the room. Everyone else seemed to have followed my lead and drifted off. But where Ayla and Enzi leaned on each other, and the other two men had slumped in their seats, it appeared I was the only one who had taken advantage of the space by lying down.

Before long, we heard a low rumbling sound, like an approaching car. All our heads popped up, and Ayla's guards shifted anxiously, hands hovering over weapons as the whole room filled with tension. When Ayla slid next to me and grabbed my hand, I nearly jumped out of my skin. I turned to glare at her and found an apologetic expression. She gave my hand a gentle reassuring squeeze. I wanted to believe her.

The noise stopped sooner than I'd expected. Low voices bled through the ceiling. The voices came closer, and my hand tightened around Ayla's. I felt the shared alarm in her grip as the lid slowly lifted, flooding the small space with light.

"Be still, friends," Soren called down to us. "Just one more to join your party. He is a trusted friend of our cause."

After so much darkness, the light from opening the manhole cover was nearly blinding. I blinked, focusing my eyes just enough to see a pair of dark boots fill the entrance, followed by their owner. He sat on the edge for only a second before making the final drop to the floor. Before he was upright again, the lid closed behind him, plunging the room back into near darkness.

I watched the changing shadows as he sat on the cold earthen bench across from our party. I couldn't see under his hood. He said nothing as he sat, elbows on his knees, clenching and unclenching his gloved fists. He looked like a caged animal. I shared his sentiment. No one spoke. But I knew I wasn't the only one watching his constant shifting, wary of the tension rolling off of him like he was about to explode.

Ten minutes later I heard it, a low rumble in the distance, like the sound an oncoming semi-truck made. As it grew in intensity, the ground started to vibrate. I clenched my teeth and pulled away from Ayla, holding my hands over my ears.

The sound became more varied as it got closer. Shouts filtered down from above and pounding hooves mixed with the rattle of metal. Dust and small clods of dirt fell from the ceiling, showering us. Particles swirled through the three beams of light. I curled into a tighter ball and fought back tears, terrified we would be discovered or buried alive.

Every second felt like an eternity as the noise above grew in volume.

As we waited, it was all I could do to keep calm. Just hearing my pursuers so close, searching in such great numbers, lent credibility to Ayla's story and only added to my fear of Terrshon. The cold dirt seat leached the warmth from my bones until I wasn't sure if I was shaking from the cold or my fear. I rubbed my arms, but no amount of friction could warm me. My mind was trapped by one question. What if he found me again?

Gradually, the noise above us faded, but I didn't relax.

I felt arms around me and shrugged them off angrily as the memory of Terrshon's hands flared in my mind unexpectedly. Suddenly, I felt violated again. I jumped to my feet in an explosion of anxiety, startling everyone else in the room. Without deciding to do it, I began to pace. I just kept putting one foot in front of the other, batting away any hand that rose to stop me.

"You need to calm down," Ayla hissed in a low voice. "We can't go anywhere until nightfall." Hearing her voice did nothing to calm my nerves, and my anxiety built with each step.

"Lotty!" Ayla snapped.

At the sound of my name, the stranger burst out of his seat, a familiar blade coming easily to hand as he pounced on Ayla. Before I could blink, Ayla's guards had daggers unsheathed and were on their feet ready to attack the cloaked man.

"That name is forbidden!" The stranger growled as if he were being strangled, his daggered hand shaking with anger as he held it to Ayla's throat. She had her own blade at his throat, but he barely seemed to notice it. "How dare you brandish it so casually? Tell me where you heard it, and I might spare your life!"

I watched in astonishment as Ayla slowly removed her hood, locking eyes with her assailant. As soon as her face was visible, the stranger recoiled, all blades falling away as his posture relaxed. I thought I heard a relieved sigh as he sheathed his weapon and urgently embraced her.

"You don't know how many nights I lay awake, fearing you were dead or lost to us in Oldworld," Ayla whispered, her voice full of emotion. "How on earth did you find us?"

"I've paid the worst price, and I fear I've failed in everything I set out to do!" he whispered back with equal emotion, the familiar voice cracking. "Ayla, he took her."

"I know," Ayla answered, squeezing him tighter before pulling away, her eyes shining. "Which is why I stole her back, Roah."

6

He turned, his hood coming down, finally revealing the face that went with the name.

I gasped.

When he reached over to push my hood away, I was too shocked to move. I watched in stunned awe as he touched my cheek, his eyes brimming with pain and longing so intense that the last of my control crumbled. When his protective embrace tightened around me, I lost it. Tears blurred my vision, and my body shook from the sobs.

"Roah," I wept, burying my face in his chest.

He held me there as I cried. He brushed my hair with his hand and repeated, "I'm here. I've got you."

I did my best to control my sobbing, to keep quiet in our mutual hiding place, but my nerves were already frayed to the breaking point. Seeing Roah, being in his arms—the change from terror to relief was so quick I didn't know how to process it. And then there was the shadow that loomed over that relief, the memory of the last man to touch me so insistently. I pulled away on instinct and regretted it at once.

"What did they do to you?" he asked. The muscles in his jaw tightened as he examined the wound on my cheek and the bandages on my wrists.

I tried to answer, but when the thought of Terrshon's devastatingly handsome face and his desire for me flashed across my memory, I shuddered, and my tears flowed again.

He pulled me close, his arms warm around me.

"You don't have to answer," he whispered in my ear. "It's enough knowing you're safe."

I was barely aware of Roah guiding me to the bench opposite the others. He retrieved a thick blanket from the stack of supplies and wrapped it around me as he sat both of us down. I let his embrace support me while the confused tears continued to streak down my cheeks.

Roah said nothing as he held me tightly, resting his cheek on my head.

When I finally gained some control of my breathing, I tried to talk.

"How...did...you...find me?" I choked out in a hoarse whisper.

"For you, I would have come so much farther than this. Ayla just beat me to it," he confessed, stroking my hair.

"For that I am grateful." I wiped my face with my sleeve. I was still in disbelief that he was there. Then I realized what his presence meant.

"We can go home now."

"It's not that simple," Roah started slowly, his voice guarded.

"Sure it is." I looked up at him. "We just get Tregr to bring the truck and drive home. Where are Daggon and Tregr anyway?"

"Lotty, didn't Ayla tell you?"

"Tell me what?"

"We're not in Virginia," Roah said the words slowly.

"I know, I got that part. We crossed state lines or something."

He and Ayla exchanged a weighted glance across the dirt room. She stood and walked over to sit on the bench next to him.

"She doesn't understand," Ayla explained to Roah. "I thought she'd have been more prepared than this, that she'd at least know who her parents were and how they died."

"By fire," I clarified. "I have the scars to prove it."

"Yes, but there is much more you should have been told. How is she not more prepared? What went wrong?" she asked Roah again.

"Nothing could have prepared me for being kidnapped by a psychopath," I blurted out. My own words terrified me, and I feared where my mind would take me next. I distracted myself by studying Roah's sleeve. The fabric was coarse and looked hand stitched. My heart started to pound as I involuntarily took in the rest of him.

He wore jeans, but the jeans were the only normal thing left on him. His shirt's short mandarin collar hung open under a padded leather vest. His black, military-style boots, which laced up to his knees, matched a plain leather belt. His long dark cloak was lined with fur at the shoulders and boasted brass buttons on both sides.

But more than his clothes, he had known Soren and Ayla, whose accents matched his perfectly.

I still heard everyone's voices, but they sounded far away, as if I were listening from a great distance, my brain barely processing what I was not willing to consider. It was preposterous. He was from Scandinavia, a foreigner with a strange and charming accent. Neither he nor my grandpa could have known any of these people!

"It was an oversight we have paid dearly for. I tried to make up for it by helping decipher Elion's journals for her. But growing up in Oldworld, without Elion's guidance, has shaped her. She has no understanding of our world," Roah said.

"None?" Ayla looked deeply troubled as she glanced from me to Roah.

"She thought he was writing a children's story," he explained flatly. "Though as inconvenient as it is, this may be the better way."

"How is this the better way?" I pressed, the statement pulling me out of my irrational thoughts. "I have no idea what the hell is going on!"

Roah looked at me, eyes serious. "You're not dead. If you had known more, truly believed what was written in those books, things may have ended very differently for you."

The bruise on my cheek flared with the thought.

Ayla turned to Roah. "What now?"

"We go home?" It came out more like a question.

"Lotty," she said, her voice thoughtful. "I know this doesn't make sense yet, but you must understand getting you back to Virginia is not easy. There are precautions we need to make and allies we need to find to help us achieve safe passage through Moldara to the Land of the Sages. All that takes time. Things work differently here than what you're used to. Communication can take longer. Travel takes longer. We have to account for all that."

I looked from Roah's face to Ayla's, not sure how to answer. All I wanted was to go home, to be where the world made sense. Even after my reunion with Roah, it seemed my liberation was still out of my grasp.

"Ayla has risked her life and the lives of those she commands to save you. We need time to prepare so that doesn't happen again," Roah explained.

"Can I at least help?"

"Lotty, it's complicated. What you don't know is just as dangerous as what you do," Ayla seemed optimistic, but it didn't mask the doubt in her voice. "No one outside our small circle knows of your true identity and that's how it must remain. It's why you're cloaked, and it's why we asked you to hide your mother's necklace. We need to take every precaution to keep you and your location secret."

"That, at least, I can agree with."

"Lotty, eventually you will need to understand what is going on and why you've been brought here," Ayla spoke kindly, but her words were sobering. "But for the sake of immediate plans, ignorance is best. Why don't we—"

The squeak of a door opening startled me, and a blinding lantern light filled the small space. I blinked several times, trying to get my eyes to adjust.

Soren leaned into the hole. "It's all clear."

The others stirred, dusting themselves off as they worked out sore muscles. Ayla, Roah, and I didn't move.

"Kavish just returned with your carriage and a dozen of your personal guard," Soren said. "I sent him back out to double check the road ahead for your journey."

Ayla motioned for her people to exit and then turned to Roah.

"You know what you must do now, right?"

He took a deep breath, wringing his hands as he exhaled loudly. "I'd been hoping to avoid that."

"I know." She placed her hand in his, squeezing his fingers. "But I've just come from the celebrations, and I've heard whispers. Things I shouldn't speak of. But they give me hope we will find all we need to help us there."

"Only your words could persuade me." He lifted her hand to his lips, kissing it gently.

"I will guard her," she said.

"As you have your entire life."

"But now I'm not the only one." She kissed him on the cheek and stood. "We will be at the manor." Then she turned and walked to the manhole.

Once she was out, Roah helped me pull myself through the hole. He followed. Soren closed the hatch and motioned for everyone to follow him. Just before we reached the carriage, Roah slowed and pulled me aside.

"I'm sorry. I should have prepared you properly. Been more forthcoming about everything. When I watched them carry you off like that, I thought it would be the last time I saw you alive. I've spent every second since then searching for you. And I..."

His eyes burned into mine, and the madness of my thoughts was silenced. He leaned his face toward mine. My heart accelerated as I felt his breath on my skin. Then, he hesitated slightly, searching my face for something.

I didn't know what was real anymore. I didn't know if he was one of these crazies or still the jousting boy who wanted to share summer sunsets on the barn roof. But I knew the feel of his hand, the way it grounded and soothed me. Emotionally raw and battered, I wanted that feeling again. I wanted it more than I wanted answers about how he got to this messed up place. My entire body ached for him, for his touch.

At that moment, giving into this fantasy world seemed a small price to pay for the security I felt in his arms.

My breath caught in my throat as he leaned in, closing the distance between us, and gently pressed his full lips to mine. The warmth shot through my body, assuaging every battered cell with its touch.

I was only aware of him in my arms and me in his, our lips silky against each other. The cloud that had followed me for days, the stain of Terrshon's invasion, melted away. At that moment, nothing else in the world existed. We were alone in the fading sunset with each other, and it was enough.

Still holding me, he slowly pulled away, his liquid crystal eyes blazing. My heart relaxed into a peace it hadn't known for days.

"Lotty, I..." Roah paused looking for the right words. "I have to go."

"What?!" Whatever I'd expected to hear, that wasn't it. "What do you mean you have to go? You just found me, and you want to leave me again? What about escaping so we can get back home?"

"Lotty, I have to."

"Why?"

"It's...complicated. Finding you in Ayla's capable hands is a miracle, but if I'm to get you home safely, there are things I must prepare, people I must face. I need Daggon and Tregr by my side for that. So, I must go now."

"Not you, too. I still have no answers—just more pieces of a puzzle that I can't make fit."

He pulled me tighter, leaning close to my ear. "Lotty, I don't want to, but I must. These allies—we need them. I would never leave you if I thought you would be safer with me, but you're not in danger now. You're well protected in your present company. Ayla would do anything to keep you safe. I know you don't trust these people. I can see that"—he paused, his body shifting slightly around mine—"but you trust me, don't you?"

"Yes." Mostly, I qualified in my head.

He exhaled faintly. "Then be certain of me today when I tell you I would entrust Ayla and her guards with my life, and in leaving you with them, that's exactly what I'm doing." He pulled me away, his eyes stern.

"Stay with Ayla and do exactly what she says." This wasn't a request. "No matter how crazy you think she is, besides me, she's your greatest friend right now. Trust her. Do you think you can do that? Can you trust her, for me?"

I took a deep breath before answering.

"I hate this. You're the only reason I'm not a blubbering puddle on the ground right now. How will I function in this place without you to keep me sane?"

"I hate this as much as you. I want nothing more than to get you home, but I need to assure our safety before I risk your life again. I'll return to you as quickly as possible."

"I will stay with Ayla, for you," I promised him. His lips gently brushed mine again.

"Thank you," he whispered.

Then, he was gone.

I watched him speak briefly to Ayla, and they exchanged something before he mounted his horse and rode off.

Ayla found me still staring in the direction Roah had disappeared into the dark woods. "Lotty, we are ready. The carriage is waiting."

Glossy eyed and dazed, I followed her to another carriage like the one we'd escaped in the night before. I would trust her, and her irrational ways.

Because I promised Roah I would.

7

The light shining through the room slowly woke me. I snuggled deeper under the covers, enjoying the comfort. If I let my mind wander, I could almost imagine I was in my bed at home, but I soon gave up my illusion and opened my eyes.

For a heartbeat, I thought I was still dreaming and last night's carriage ride, as well as the country manor where my trip had ended, had all been a hallucination. I rubbed my eyes and took in my elaborate accommodations. My room was lovelier than any hotel or cabin I'd ever seen. To my left, on either side of a stone fireplace, two tall windows looked out over a rippling pond. Trees edged the far side of the pond, swaying from a gentle breeze. The sky was a brilliant blue, free of any clouds. The scene reminded me of home.

There were two leather chairs in front of the fireplace; a large fur rug spread between them. A small wooden table sat next to the far chair, a tray of food perched on one end. On the other wall, facing the fireplace, were large double doors-their dark wood matching the heavy beams and rafters on the ceiling. An armoire topped with a few colored bottles stood beside them. The whole set up had a very soothing, old-world feel to it, homey in spite of its grand size.

I dragged my road-weary body out from under the warm comforter and met the chill of the day in a thin sleeping gown. Shivering, I pulled a knit blanket off the foot of the bed, wrapped up in it, and wandered over to one of the tall windows. I threw open the sash, and a stiff breeze of fresh, crisp air swept into the room. A chill ran through me as I looked at the pond but didn't really see it. My thoughts were on other things; things that I couldn't seem to escape.

The savory aroma coming from the tray across the room made my mouth water, and the gnawing in my stomach grew. I closed the window and sat at the table to eat, picking over the food, only eating what looked appetizing.

I wandered to the large chair next to the crackling fire, taking some of my food with me. The flame was low but very warm. Someone must have stoked it in the night. As I ate, my curiosity grew. I wanted to find Ayla. A good night's sleep had endowed me with a single conviction.

I wanted answers.

When I finished my brunch, I rummaged through the armoire, trying to find something suitable to wear. An outfit had been laid out for me, but I wanted options. I groaned as I dug through the confusing pieces. Most of it wasn't my style, as I rarely wore anything frilly.

Finally admitting defeat, I returned to what had been laid out for me. I donned the dark brown pants first, the soft cotton fitting closely, but well. Next, I pulled the ivory tank top over my head. It felt like silk and draped down to the top of my thigh like a short skirt. The green bodice that went over it fit like a corset and connected in the front with clasps instead of buckles.

A long-sleeved, short-collared emerald-green jacket went over the top of everything but didn't close all of the way in front. Instead of buttons, three small leather belts bearing beautiful silver buckles sewn into the fabric of the jacket fastened so that the embroidered vines on the lighter green bodice underneath showed through.

To finish the ensemble, I put on the knee-high black boots I'd been given the day before. I took a breath and stepped in front of the mirror.

The first thing I noticed was that my hair was a wreck. The second was that I looked a lot like a mad wood sprite.

Feeling a little ridiculous, I ran my fingers through my curls trying to smooth out the snarls. The braids and pins had given my hair waves I was not used to managing. Admitting defeat, I finger-combed the whole mess into a soft side braid, letting the strays go where they wanted. I lengthened the chain on my necklace so it hid under my silk tank, so that it wouldn't be the focal point where the coat opened, and checked my reflection again.

I leaned in to get a better look. Those few changes had pulled the whole outfit together. My neckline especially brought out the mature lines of the outfit. I turned, seeing the embroidered tree on the back of the jacket for the first time, my jaw dropping at the craftsmanship.

Secure in my determination, I headed for the door.

I walked slowly down the grand corridor. The rustic lodge feel of my room—the wood rafters and white-washed walls—continued through the manor. I stepped lightly on the stone floors, hoping I wouldn't draw attention. I wanted to look around without a tour guide.

I passed a couple of closed doors and left them alone, afraid of what I might find on the other side. The end of the hall opened to a large room filled with oil paintings. The artist in me just couldn't resist one tiny detour.

I meandered through the room, studying each piece. The paintings were a beautiful mix of landscapes and portraits. I longed to run my fingers over the swirls of dried paint, to feel the texture the artist's brush had left behind. One of a castle caught my attention and made the hair on my arms stand up.

With a start, I realized why it had caught my eye. It looked eerily close to the castle I had just painted in art class, although the perspective was different.

I pulled my gaze from the painting and continued through the room, telling myself I was imagining things. After several more paintings, I felt drawn to the far wall where the largest portrait hung. There were two people in the picture, a man and a woman. I had to refocus my eyes as I stared at their faces.

They were so lovely, so lifelike, that I half expected them to walk out of the painting to greet me. They carried themselves in a way that commanded respect, but not in an intimidating way. They wanted you to trust them. That came through very clearly in their eyes. And the way they held each other expressed the love in their relationship. It was inspiring. I wished that someday I could find someone who would stand by me the way they stood together.

But the longer I stared at the painting, the more I realized it wasn't their postures or the fact they were in love that struck me most. It was their faces. Well, her face to be exact. I studied the woman from every vantage point I could find. No matter how I looked at her, it was always the same. I couldn't comprehend it.

I ran through all the possibilities, but nothing made rational sense.

I stared into her eyes. *My* eyes. There were hardly any differences between the image in the painting and me, except for my hair color. I had the same dishwater blond hair as the man who stood beside her, not the chestnut brown of hers. I was baffled.

Footsteps approached, breaking my concentration. Ayla entered the room and walked toward me. I felt my eyes go wide.

She wore dark thigh-high boots with a cream-colored ribbon that laced up the front, cream pants covering the rest of her legs. A belt hung below a purple satin corset with polished metal work. She had no blouse under her bodice, but instead wore a high-collared sleeveless jacket that lightly brushed the floor when she walked. A dozen different necklaces, jeweled and simple gold, hung at her throat.

She was a vision in purple and cream, but the authority in her hard eyes could not hold back my questions.

"Explain that?" I demanded, pointing at the painting.

"I'm not sure you'll want me to," Ayla confessed. "At least not in a way you'll find comfortable. Maybe you should wait for Roah."

I exhaled with frustration. "What could possibly be so horrible?"

"I know I promised I would explain, but I need to start from a point you will understand." She walked over to a far corner of the room, waving for me to join her in front of a smaller painting.

"Do you remember when you were little? When you would go to the woods by El...I mean your Grandfather's?" she asked.

I nodded.

"You used to play there for hours."

"What does that have to do with anything?"

"Lotty, I have to start somewhere." She hesitated before she spoke again. "Do you remember who you used to play with?"

"Yeah, I had an imaginary friend. Just this pretend princess I made up who went on adventures with me," I admitted.

She gestured to a portrait of a young girl. "One who looked like this?"

"Perhaps." I looked at the portrait. She did look eerily similar to the girl I'd imagined all those years ago.

"What was her name? Do you remember?"

I closed my eyes. A scene with the two girls dancing through the dense woods became vivid. I watched the girls more intently, forcing myself to remember her name. In my vision, my younger self called to a playmate, a little girl with warm brown skin and ebony hair, her small frame clothed in the dress of a fairytale princess. My head snapped up with the memory.

"Aly?"

"You had trouble pronouncing Ayla, so yes, you called me Aly." A smile stretched across her face as she remembered with me.

"You're saying it was you? You were my imaginary friend?"

"Yes, I was. But I'm not imaginary." She pointed to the painting again.

"How?" I was puzzled. "Where did you come from?"

"I remember making many long trips through dark caverns to reach your world."

"*My* world?" I wasn't sure if I'd heard her correctly.

"The cave," she pulled out a small leather booklet the size of a stack of index cards and flipped through it. When she found what she was looking for, she looked up. "You'd call it... a magic door between our worlds."

"Of course, a magic doorway. Why didn't I think of that? Every good fairy tale has one of those. Does that make you my fairy godmother too?" I scoffed.

"I told you we should wait for Roah to explain," she said, pursing her lips in frustration. She closed the book and turned to leave.

"Wait." I reached out to her, grabbing her arm. "Sorry. I told you I'd listen, that I wanted answers. So, there's a magic doorway in a cave?"

"Yes," she answered slowly.

"Where am I then?"

"Elvae, a providence of Moldara."

"Where is that in relation to Virginia?"

She concentrated for a second or two before she consulted the little leather book again. "In Oldworld—in Virginia, I mean—they have stories of worlds that exist side by side with one another, seemingly existing in the same place but never touching, and—"

"Parallel universes aren't supposed to be real. They're science fiction, fantasy."

"You've heard stories then?" She lowered the book.

"Of course I've heard stories. Everyone's heard stories of other worlds."

"Well, they had to start somewhere," she stated matter-of-factly. "Why not here?"

Her question temporarily stumped me. It was as good an explanation as any for what I had seen and experienced so far. And even in the mountains of Virginia, this world was just too big to escape notice. People had circulated stories of parallel worlds for centuries. She was right; they would've had to start somewhere. Besides, who was I to claim to know every secret of the universe?

"I know you think your grandfather didn't prepare you for this, but I think he did, you just didn't realize it. Playing with me was one thing Elion did to bridge the gap between our worlds."

"That is another I suppose." I pointed to her mysterious little book.

"This?" Ayla lifted the journal, her finger holding her place. "No. This is Roah's. He gave me the book before leaving us at the sanctuary. He wanted me to be able to explain things in terms you'd understand."

I fought a rising sadness at the thought of Roah needing to keep notes to help him communicate with me. I didn't want to think of him as being from this place. But if he could be so pragmatic, then I could try to be as well.

"Why did you stop coming?"

Ayla looked away. "Terrshon's men murdered my father. After that, my mother took me out of Moldara, and Elion didn't protest the separation. I think he hoped our few years together would be enough."

"I'm sorry about your father."

"Thank you." Ayla's voice was soft. "We have both lost much in this. My father's passing helped shape who I am today, and I honor him for it. As you honor yours."

I was silent. I felt like I was just surviving, not living a life to honor anyone. "So does that little notebook of Roah's also explain where this world came from and why everyone here is stuck in a Ren-fest?"

Ayla flipped through the pages until she found what she was looking for and smiled. "You're speaking of the random festivals for merchants?"

"They're a little more than that," I mumbled.

"Oh, I meant no offense. We have similar gatherings. Some are formal, and others celebrate the change of seasons," Ayla said, flipping through more pages. "I'll explain those later. First, do you recall any stories of the people you know as... Vikings?"

I nodded, wondering who hadn't heard of Vikings and why it was such a strange word for her to say.

"As explorers and conquerors, they crossed your oceans and discovered new land. There they found tribes that spoke of a place ruled by the spirits, places they visited when they needed guidance. Here, those same Vikings found a place that they'd always believed existed in legend. A kind of Otherworld. It was their paradise."

"Sounds nice but"—I took in her dark complexion—"but there is no way you are only descended from ancient Vikings.

Ayla smiled checking her notes before she continued. "That was the first of three migrations. A great sickness swept through the people of your world...Native Americans, it says you called them. To escape certain death, as many as were able fled through the caverns, and one nation became two."

"Wait, you're saying that Vikings and Native Americans got along?"

"Not at first. There were some terribly dark times as they fought over the Waters of Creation. Only the Sages know all that happened. It's part of many stories we don't repeat because they no longer serve who we are trying to be as a people."

"The Waters of what? Never mind." I gestured for her to continue.

"From those times of great death, our ancestors chose to abandon all that divided them. Instead, they focused on inclusion and celebrating what they had in common from their respective cultures. So, when the third migration began—" Ayla flipped through several pages before she found the one she was looking for. "The country of America was being formed. Those people practiced something called slavery, stealing people from their homes and cultures to force them to work and build for their captors. Learning this, our Sages smuggled those who could escape into our world."

"Which you call Otherworld. And I've supposedly been living in…?"

"Oldworld."

"Right. But you're telling me that this place was one of the endpoints for the Underground Railroad?"

Ayla consulted Roah's book before nodding.

"There is so much more, centuries of history I've left out. I just thought if you had a sense of the foundations of this world, it would help make this more real to you." Ayla put the small book away. "But like I said, these histories are kept by the Sages who share them with our rulers only when it will help them make better choices. I'm trusting you to show equal restraint."

"But if this world is so far from Virginia, why do I recognize your clothes? I mean, you guys are really mixing it up. More importantly, why do you speak English?"

"The elite of the Sages, those that serve for life, have made frequent trips to Oldworld," Ayla began. "They bring back only what they feel is most aligned with our ways as a people. Remember I said we abandoned all that divided us? Well, that included language.

Blood of Moldara 67

Adopting a new language that belonged to no one proved to be a very healing solution."

"But what does this have to do with me?" I pleaded.

"Since the murder of your parents, Otherworld has been slowly drifting back toward those dark times. The only thing stopping Terrshon are royal tokens that were lost when he murdered your parents and took over Moldara. But now that you are back, and you carry one of those tokens, we have the leverage to unite the people against him."

I looked at her, one brow rising. "I carry a token?"

She put her hand on the small of my back and directed me back to the larger painting, the one of the couple. "You wear your mother's necklace," she pointed to the stone depicted in the painting and then to the one hidden at the end of my chain. "They are one and the same."

My hand automatically went to my necklace. As I studied the artist's rendition in front of me, I couldn't refute her claim.

"Do you know what your parents looked like?" Ayla asked.

"No, well, not for sure. Everything was lost in our house fire. I did have a drawing."

"But you knew your parents' names?"

"Of course. Norwyck and Mira."

Ayla reached toward the bottom of the frame and pulled at a cloth that had been draped across the bottom.

I looked at the portrait again. It was one thing to have a drawing in one of my grandpa's journals, but it was something else entirely to stand in a room like this and see a painting with my parent's names under it.

"It's a mistake." My breathing accelerated and my head swam. I knew if I didn't sit quickly, I would pass out. I sank to the stone floor and put my head between my knees. I tried to steady my breath, to ease the growing pressure in my head. This was too much.

Ayla followed me to the cold floor. Her voice was gentle when she spoke.

"Lotty, I know this is hard for you. But I would never lie to you about something like this."

"How would I know that?"

"I guess you can't. That's where you'll have to trust me. But Lotty, just look at her," she said, pointing to the portrait again.

I didn't need to look up to see that she looked almost exactly like me. It made it more difficult to argue with her.

"How can I be sure those are really my parents?" I knew my question sounded asinine before it left my mouth. Despite the names under the picture, anyone looking at the painting would have come to the same conclusion Ayla had. I just wanted to know how certain she was.

"Because I knew them well."

"How well?" I asked, lifting my head and looking her in the eyes, eagerly trying to paint her into a corner with her words.

Ayla eyed me from the side. "This was painted a long time ago. They had recently met and were so in love." She paused, taking her eyes off me and gazing at the figures. It was as if she yearned for them to tell her what to say next. She took a deep breath and let it out slowly, watching me as she spoke. Her words were soft, almost a whisper.

"Your parents were my aunt and uncle."

"You're my…cousin?" I blurted out. Her smile confirmed my question. "Does that mean…?"

I couldn't finish. It was too bizarre, too crazy to even consider. Then I gasped, covering my mouth with my hands.

"The cemetery," I forced through my fingers. "That was them?"

She nodded slowly.

My stomach churned, the blood draining from my face. My head started throbbing. I was going to be sick. I lay on the stone floor, pressing my clammy cheek against its coolness.

If I believed her, then I had been at my parents' graves. I felt more lost in the knowledge of who they were than having not known. The truth shattered the images I had conjured up of them as a little girl, and along with it, the foundation of who I was.

I was losing myself, my essence. Who was I really? And where did I belong? I didn't know anymore.

"Lotty, can I get you anything? You don't look well." Ayla's concerned voice brought me out of my downward spiral.

"I just need a minute, that's all." I kept my eyes closed as the cool stone continued to soothe my flushed skin. I saw flashes of light behind my dark eyelids. The stress of the whole situation was robbing me of all the good that sleep had done me. I was getting a headache, the beginnings of an awful, piercing migraine.

8

I paced the halls of the country manor, trying to find an escape from the noise in my head. Ayla had sensed my need to be alone. Thankfully, with only a minor protest and a promise that she would check on me later, she left me to myself. But Ayla's version of my history haunted me. The paintings on the walls, the books on the shelves, even the clothes I wore only confirmed what I desperately wanted to escape.

I tried to avoid being seen, but Ayla's guards stood around every corner, blocking every door. My stomach churned, and my head pounded even more with every step. I couldn't breathe. I couldn't focus. It was all too much.

A familiar scent wafted down a hallway—comforting, soothing. I craved its relief, so I followed it.

The smell led me into an expansive and rustic kitchen. I walked through the room, looking for the fresh bread that had lured me in, hoping to get some without being caught. Counters set on cabinets lined the far walls, and shelves hung over them. Next to a large water basin, cut into one of the counters, sat a cutting board full of chopped vegetables. A metal faucet dripped into the stone sink.

A huge stone fireplace, large enough for a person to stand upright inside, dominated the opposite wall. It had several spaces in the stone that I guessed were used as ovens. There were also large metal hooks mounted to its stone wall. One held a bubbling pot hanging over the hot flames. In the middle of the room sat a large wooden table and over it hung small bundles of dry herbs and flowers. It reminded me of Roah's kitchen, and the ache in my heart started to match the one in my head.

"Ahh!" I heard from behind a door. Rounding the corner was an older, portly woman carrying a basket of goods. She wore an outfit identical to what I remembered Enzi wearing. She looked very unhappy with me.

"Child, what in the name of the spirits are you trying to do, send an old woman to greet them?"

"I'm sorry. I just wandered in…" I started to explain but stopped when recognition lit her eyes and her jaw dropped.

"Forgive me, Your Highness. I did not recognize you," she begged, giving a slight curtsy.

"Please, don't call me that. I'm not a princess."

She stopped me before I could reach the door.

"As you wish, Little Sister. Nettie, at your service. Come child, you must be famished." She ushered me to a chair, seating me at the large table just like my Grandma Mable used to do.

"Thanks, I'm not that hungry," I started to explain, but she wouldn't hear it.

"Nonsense. No one can refuse my cooking, especially when it's fresh out of the fire," she boasted. "Besides, a little nurturing will do us both good."

She set her basket on the large wooden table and scurried around the room, gathering up a few things and bringing down jars from the shelves. As she passed in front of the fire, the light glinted off a glass tear-shaped charm on a white leather string at her neck. Why did almost everyone I'd seen wear one of those?

She grabbed a towel and used it to pick up one of the warm loaves of bread sitting on the far counter and set it on the table in front of me. She then found a knife, plate, and a small bowl of butter. Placing them next to the loaf, she proceeded to cut the bread into thick slices.

"I suspect Ayla has been trying to catch you up on a few thousand years of history?"

"Something like that. It's kind of a lot all at once."

"Weight of the world on that one. I don't envy Ayla the lot she's chosen for her life. Puts too much on herself, if you ask me," she rambled as she spread the soft butter on a slice of fresh bread.

"You really don't need to do this," I tried to tell her, but the smell of the bread was irresistible, and I was glad she ignored my protests.

"This isn't my first time in the kitchen; I know hunger when I see it, and Little Sister, it's plaguing you. Now, are you going to let me fulfill my duties, or are you going to be as stubborn as Elion?"

The sound of my grandfather's name had my instant attention.

"You knew Elion?" The ache in my head swelled. I started to rub my temples, hoping it would help.

"Yes, we all did. He and Ayla are the reason we keep this old manor alive." She set the plate of buttered bread in front of me. As she did, her sleeve caught on a nearby basket, exposing a bracelet on her wrist. Without thinking, I grabbed her hand and pushed back the sleeve.

"Where did you get that?" I demanded, pointing to the bracelet. It was a wide silver band wrapped in gold and inlaid with an intricate design. In the center of the bracelet was a symbol I'd seen in my grandpa's journals. It was identical to the design that he associated with Moldara—something I thought looked like a broken compass.

Nettie gently twisted her arm in my hand, being sure I got to see the full bracelet. "It's the insignia of Moldara, or what it was before Terrshon distorted it. All loyal to the house of Norwyck and Mira still wear it." Gradually, I released her arm, my thoughts swirling in my head. She pulled her sleeve back down and regarded me with motherly concern.

"Did Elion tell you stories?" she asked, changing the subject.

"Of course he told me stories. I wouldn't go to bed without them," I admitted, turning my attention to the buttered goodness in front of me.

"What was your favorite?"

Blood of Moldara 73

"What would that have to do with any of this?"

"In Moldara, we tell stories to pass on our histories. Rarely are stories told for pure entertainment. They hold a message or a greater meaning in them. I think the stories Elion told you would have done the same."

"You think my grandpa told me stories that were true?"

"Yes."

The beloved stories of my childhood rushed through my mind, taking on new life—a life I wasn't sure I was ready for.

"Start anywhere," she encouraged continuing to fuss in the kitchen.

I took a deep breath and began.

"There was a king and queen who had been great rulers over their kingdom. Their people loved them and rejoiced the day they had a child, a daughter who would one day inherit the throne.

"Not long after her birth, a man who didn't like how they were running the kingdom decided to kill them and take over. He tried to kill all of them, except the princess, who escaped with the help of a servant.

"She was taken into the woods by protectors who will guard her until she is ready to take back what was stolen from her." Even as I said the words out loud, I couldn't help making the connections I wasn't willing to consider before.

"That's a good start. Missing a few details though."

"That seems to be the theme of the day," I said, moaning as she placed a second piece of bread in front of me.

She grabbed a stool, sliding it closer to me, and sat.

"Norwyck took the throne after his father died. He was very young, but even so, the people adored him. We all did." A smile brightened her face, a smile born only by true memories.

"You knew him, my father?"

She took my hand in hers. "I knew them both. It was tragic all those years ago. Still is. They were so young, you just a babe. Terrshon was greedy and calculating. We didn't even know he was capable of such bloodshed. If we had known, if we had stopped that awful night from happening…" She looked at my hand in hers. "I am so sorry we couldn't do more to protect you, child."

"It's okay," I said, trying to reassure her. "I was too young to remember anything. Please, go on."

"Your father was young when he took his post, and very lonely. King Gannon, who ruled a kingdom to the north called Bronia, extended an offer of betrothal. His daughter, Mira, was their second child, their first having been a son. Bronia had been a great ally to his father's rule, so Norwyck traveled to Bronia. When he met Mira, he was instantly taken by her wit and beauty. They courted, and shortly thereafter they performed their bonding ceremony.

"When he introduced your mother to Moldara, the people fell instantly in love. She was beautiful, kind, and generous. The celebrations and offerings continued for weeks. A few years later, you were born.

"They didn't have many enemies, your parents. It took a greedy, grasping, silver-tongued young man in their inner circle to destroy what they had spent their lives building. It was seventeen years ago, at this very manor, and no one saw it coming. Terrshon had lain in wait with his men, men who betrayed their king as well."

"The same Terrshon who kidnapped me?" A shiver ran through me.

"Yes. He's been after you since we hid you away all those years ago. Your parents had traveled with a small party intending to spend the season here. They pulled up to the stables first. Norwyck was excited to show Mira her new gift, a beautiful mare. Terrshon ambushed them in the stables, killing them both. He set the building on fire to make it look like an accident. He also tried to kill all the witnesses, but a few eluded him."

"Are you one of them?"

"Yes, and my sister, Hattie. She was brave enough to rescue you from the fire and run into the woods. She hoped it looked like you had died in the fire with everyone else. Desperate, she ran all night, finally reaching the closest sanctuary."

"The ruins near the cemetery."

She nodded. More chills traveled down my spine as I ran my

fingers over my scars. The story had sounded too familiar, too much like the one my grandpa had left in his journals. Too much like the nightmares I'd endured as a child.

She nodded, "That's where Hattie found Elion."

"My grandfather?"

"Yes, though he's not really your grandfather, not by blood." She paused, taking in my reaction. "Sweetie, we can do this later."

"I'm okay," I lied, rubbing my temples to alleviate the growing pressure.

"Are you sure?"

"Yeah, yeah. I'm good." I forced a smile, hoping to fool her. Someone was finally willing to tell me what was going on and why I had been taken. "Who is Elion then, if he's not my grandfather? How does he fit into all this?"

"All right then," she continued slowly, as if trying not to scare me. "Elion was like a father to Norwyck. He had tutored him from his youth and counseled him since he had taken the throne. Some say their bond ran so deep that Norwyck had Elion meet Mira first, so Norwyck would not be taken in by a pretty face. Elion dedicated his life to the service of your family.

"Elion had heard rumors of someone moving against the royal family and had come to warn them. But he was too late. After searching the remains of the barn and the grounds, he vowed vengeance on Terrshon, the kind of blood oath made only in the presence of someone like Soren. He suddenly had his hands full—he needed the identity of your parents' assassin, as well as a suitable caretaker for you. You see, it was into his sanctuary that Hattie stumbled, delirious and out of her mind with terror and exhaustion, a wounded baby screaming in her arms. Only Elion was more distraught than you, nearly out of his mind with grief and guilt. That poor man.

"To this day, I don't know who came up with the plan as it was carried out. I imagine it was Hattie who thought up a way to save two lives that night. All of them knew that if Terrshon discovered that you had survived his betrayal, he wouldn't rest until he had finished the job.

"You were placed in Elion's care, and he hid you in the outlying towns, staying with families still loyal to your parents. But several years later, Terrshon killed the new king and plundered those not willing to support him as their king. Those were very dark times. After Terrshon slaughtered and burned the bodies of a family that had opened their home to Elion—thank the spirits that you had been hidden before the attack—Elion knew there was no safe place left in Moldara for you. So he spirited you away where no one could find you. Seems he fulfilled his oath well."

"That's not how my story goes," I said, my mind racing to catch up. "When Grandpa told me these stories he let me believe I was one of the protectors, the one who fights for her, keeps her safe."

"Of course, who better to protect your greatest secret than its source? You are heiress to Moldara. Anyone wearing a symbol like my bracelet or this one"—she reached up to the glass tear on the white leather cord at her throat—"would sacrifice everything to protect you. Many, including my sister, have already. But her loss is greatly eased as I serve you today."

I felt sick hearing another person had given up their life for mine.

"Little Sister, are you well?"

I was about to tell her I was fine, but the ache swelling in my head was almost unbearable. I couldn't pretend any longer.

"No, I'm not. I have a headache that keeps getting worse."

"I may have just the thing. It's what has cured all my ailments, and I'm positive it will alleviate yours."

She moved to one of the cupboards, gathered some dried herbs, and crushed them into a coarse powder. She then placed them in a small pot, adding water before hanging it over the fire.

"The tea only takes a few minutes to boil. Then it will be ready. It should do you good to drink it."

"Thank you."

"It's my pleasure to serve you, Little Sister."

"I'm sorry, but could you please stop calling me 'Little Sister'? Lotty, just call me Lotty."

"Elion would be infuriated if I didn't show you the amount of respect you deserve."

"Why? It doesn't really mean anything."

Nettie took my hands in hers. She had the same soft touch as Grandma Mable, and my heart ached at the similarity.

"Of course it does!" She smiled. "It may have morphed into a children's tale about taking in and caring for strangers, but the origin is rooted in truth. When you were in hiding from Terrshon, Elion would disguise you and take you to trusted people for shelter in their homes. He thought it was the best way to keep you hidden. Those caring for you would call you 'Little Sister,' never speaking your name in hopes of keeping the huntsmen confused. As years passed, strangers in need are lovingly called 'Little Sister,' or 'Little Brother,' because anyone of them could be a lost royal in disguise. Because of that, you are everyone's lost sister."

"I can't be made into something I'm not just by calling me 'Little Sister.'"

"No, you can't. But neither can you crush the hopes of generations by pretending to be someone you are not."

I let it go. There was a time when I would have given anything to hear stories of my parents and what kind of people they were, but the more I heard these stories, the harder it was for me to listen. I rubbed my temples, my head still pounding, wishing it would all go away.

"If the words of an old lady aren't convincing enough for you, maybe Elion's will be."

"What? How?!" I cried out, interrupting her. "You've seen Elion here? Recently?"

"No one has heard from Elion for almost three years now. Nevertheless, the last time he was here, he asked me to do something for him. I think this is the right time to fulfill that request since I vowed to keep it from Ayla. Wait here."

She walked around the table and headed down the cellar steps. When she entered the room again, her left hand carried a thick, sealed letter. She set the bursting parchment on the table and slid it to me.

"This is for you."

I lifted a shaking hand to retrieve the parcel. My grandfather had written a letter to be given to me when I arrived here. Was I strong enough to know the contents?

"Go on, it won't bite," Nettie encouraged.

I took a deep breath. As I exhaled, I wrapped my still shaking fingers around the smooth paper.

Unthinking, I lifted it up, gently stroking the rough edges. All those times and adventures in the woods with my grandfather came flooding back. All the letters and messages we would find and, in turn, hide for our imaginary friends in the forest all came back to me. But this time my imaginary friend knew nothing of it.

Curiosity consumed me, and I felt the paper would burst into flames any moment and burn my fingers.

I stood up from the table, the letter clutched to my chest.

"You'll want to read that in private," Nettie said. "I know just the place. Follow me."

She took me down a short hallway that led to a door I hadn't noticed earlier. It opened to a small garden. She paused in the doorway and turned to me.

"Don't, under any circumstances, leave this garden. I can't stress to you enough that you are safe only as long as you stay close to the manor. There is a small bench just beyond the berry patch that you may find suited to reading, and since you've hardly eaten anything, I'll bring you some food with the tea when it's ready." After a smile of encouragement, she bowed and walked back to the kitchen.

I found the bench. Still holding the letter close to my chest, I sat and looked around the garden. My fingers traced the lines of the folds. I was ready to break the seal when I saw someone out of the corner of my eye. They couldn't see me tucked behind the berry bushes, but I just didn't feel comfortable reading something so private with the threat of someone interrupting me.

I knew what Nettie had said about staying in the garden, but we were out in the middle of nowhere. Nothing threatened me out here, except the guards who kept me trapped. I didn't want to be trapped any longer.

I walked in the direction of an orchard. It wasn't too far from the large house, but it would give me the privacy I craved.

When I got to the grove of trees, the sweet smell of apples carried on the breeze. My mouth watered as I walked deeper into the grove. I searched for the right trunk to climb. After surveying the trees, I found it—on the outer corner of the orchard, the last one in the organized rows. It still held the majority of its summer foliage and would conceal me with all its leaves, yet I would still have a clear view of the manor. I grabbed the lowest branch and lifted myself into its lush boughs.

On a large branch, about midway up the center of the trunk, I let my legs dangle as I rested my back against the thick core. I took in the fresh air and exhaled forcefully. *What if I couldn't handle what the letter said?* I tried to push that aside as I shifted my weight on the bumpy branch. Whatever Grandpa had written was intended to help me, not hurt me.

My fingers traced the hard wax seal, an elaborate *L*, before breaking it. My hands trembled as the pages unfolded. I felt something heavy land in my lap. I looked down to see a small leather pouch tied shut. I picked up the pouch, clutching it in my fingers, and read the letter.

9

My Dearest Lotty,

I promise you, I fought long and hard to avoid this day, but if you are reading this, then I have not made it back to you. These meager pages are all that remains of me now. Forgive me, child. I should be there with you, to tell you of the great and terrible story that has been my burden.

I can only imagine the pain you have born because of our separation. Forgive me, but it was too dangerous to return to you and my beloved Mable. When they finally found me that day in the woods, my heart broke. At that moment, I knew I would never see her again. I couldn't allow myself to lead them back to you, and Mable's minimal knowledge of our true origins would not have protected her from Terrshon's sword. It was one of the most painful choices of my life.

You have every right to be angry with the people who, in trying to protect you, have conspired to control your future, who have taken your very identity and heritage from you and given you one that was false. And after what I am about to tell you, you may consider me one of them. I can only pray that somehow you will understand and forgive an old man his failures.

If you are reading these words, then you have traveled through the *passage to Otherworld and found your family's summer manor. If my plan was successful, then you should be around twelve or thirteen when you receive this letter. That leaves you plenty of time to acclimate and study with Soren. He will be instructed to teach you all I have written in the journals. Only a chosen few know your true location, and I need to keep it that way. Sweet child, I cannot let danger find you, not after all we have been through to keep you safe this long. Terrshon keeps a close eye on me, hoping I will lead him back to you. It is for that reason I cannot join you myself. I cannot risk your life this way. The burden of your parents' fate weighs heavily on me, and I will not add your death to what I already carry.*

I loved your parents and was honored to serve them. You may be faced with many doubts, but never doubt that I lost my closest friends— my family, too—the night your parents died. I might have been lost to my despair had I not learned of your escape. I knew then that they lived on in you, and that I must do all in my power to honor them by keeping you safe.

From the moment I saw your little face in Soren's sanctuary, terri- fied, tear-stained, and burned, I knew I had to do more than hide you. My allegiance to your parents wasn't merely a vow I made to honor their legacy; it became more—my purpose for living. That is why I took you through the caverns and into Oldworld, a place forbidden to all but the Sages. I thought it was the only way you'd be safe.

I had had no time to prepare and no way to know what I would find on the other side of those waterfalls. I went in blind, knowing only that Terrshon couldn't reach you there. The ancestors must have been looking out for us both because I never expected to find Trell and Brea —Sages in their own right and from Moldara as well. They opened their home and their hearts in the middle of the night to two rain- soaked strangers.

In that second life with you and Mable, I found renewed hope and love I never thought possible. Every day that I watched you grow, my confidence in your future was fortified, but I never forgot what hunted you. My greatest fear was that my escape route would be discovered, and they would come for you before you were prepared to fight back.

Lotty, the bedtime story I told you, the story I built all of my games and lessons around, is true. You were supposed to grow up as a princess. I prepared you as best I knew for one so young and left you journals of this land, of your family, and of myself. I set defenses to guard us and recruited help if I were to fail in my vow. Defenders loyal to your parents were each given a piece of your secret, to ensure that no one person could find you without alerting your protectors. Your aunt, Queen Kassil, is one such protector who will help you reclaim your rightful place. She, along with her daughter Ayla, have lost much to Terrshon's hand. If you find them on your journey, trust them at their word. They are your family.

Even this letter will have been preserved by one who would give her very life to preserve yours. She is one of many protectors, tied to your parents' legacy, all of whom are waiting to stand with you.

Still, I worry it may not be enough. If you need more help, follow the glass tears. They are worn by those who still grieve the loss of your parents and hope for your return.

Lotty, as you take in all that I've revealed, know this—you are the only daughter of the late King Norwyck and Queen Mira of Moldara. You are the rightful heiress to their throne. If your parents had lived, you, Princess Adelaide, would be the one ruling these good people. Terrshon, the assassin who robbed you of your parents and made exile necessary, has no claim to the power he stole. That authority is your birthright, and as long as you live, he lives in fear of losing it.

I know this is complicated and raises as many questions as it answers. Time has not been our ally. Remember what I have taught you. Have Soren help you study the journals I left for you. He can help decipher the Sage's script. The tools you require to find your answers are in those pages.

One last thing, dearest Lotty, has to do with the ring I've enclosed. It is not just a ring. It is the royal seal. It's what Terrshon was after when he killed your parents. It is the final piece that confirms one as the rightful ruler of Moldara. That, along with your mother's necklace, make it impossible to question your authority. Keep them with you always and guard them at all costs.

Along with the journals, there is one more item I've left for you in Virginia, a dagger with a name engraved on the blade. It was to be given to you on your return to Moldara. If Trell has not placed it in your hands before you've passed through the caverns, please seek it out. It will be important in finding allies across Otherworld.

The dagger also holds another purpose, if and when that time may come. It's the dagger that will bind you to the man you are to marry. If you will accept it, he has already been chosen for you, the match arranged by both your parents. It is tradition for a couple to make a blood oath that binds them body and soul to each other. It's with this particular dagger those oaths are made.

If you haven't met the prince yet, you must find him. His family rules the land of Niniever, and his name is Prince Zarian. I cannot say if he is still promised to you, for if you have been proclaimed dead, then his family could have sought out special allowance from the Sages to free him of his obligation. If he has married another, he may still be willing to pledge help to you for Moldara's sake. I am set to seek him out now to see if this is the case, for if he is still promised to you, then he will be your strongest ally.

My will is to ensure that his purpose is in line with mine in the matter of your safety and happiness, as well as the good of the people of Moldara. From my recollection, he has a good heart, and I believe he will be a just and loving ruler, as well as a good companion. The final choice is yours, of course, but I urge you to give him a chance.

Lotty, I would imagine an arranged marriage, at any age, is an overwhelming prospect. To add to that, the burden of a hostage kingdom and the wrath of its tyrant is a devastating path to lay at your feet, but you are strong. And you are not, nor have you ever been, alone in this.

I know how different Moldara is from the world you know. We, those who have fought to keep you alive, will not fault you if you choose to return to Virginia. We knew that in taking you through the caverns to Oldworld, this revelation alone might be too overwhelming to overcome. Remember that your inheritance was never meant to cost you your life. Not then and not now.

Above all, this is your journey, your path to walk. No matter how this ends, you must discover, as I have, that following your heart is always worth the price. Make your choices, not for your parents or an idea of obligation to a throne, but for yourself.

Lotty, I need you to know that I love you like you are my own blood. Nothing you do or don't do can ever change that. My own children, if I'd been blessed with them, could not have brought me as much love and joy as you have. I have, and always will, think of you as my granddaughter. I hope that if our paths cross again, you will still call me Grandfather, for bearing that name, protecting our family, has given me joy beyond measure.

-*E*lion Loxton

10

I wanted to reread what I'd just read, but I couldn't will my eyes to focus. The words still stung.

My own grandpa, in his own handwriting, had just confirmed what everyone else had been trying to tell me. My brain couldn't process it anymore. The words he had set down in his letter had seared my emotions, numbing me to all that was happening now, and to all that had played out in the last few days. The pounding in my head became constant—the only real thing I could feel as my world slowly crumbled around me.

I grabbed an apple hanging just above me and plucked it from the branch. Was it real? I knew what an apple was. I could smell it, squeeze it. It was tangible to me.

I used that fact as a base to cling to what I knew to be real. But when I used that same process for the ring that sat in my other hand, or the letter from my grandfather, I was lost again.

On the other side of the garden, the door to the kitchen opened, and Nettie emerged with a tray full of food. When she walked through the rows of flowers, concern flashed over her features.

"Little Sister," she called, scanning the garden and yard beyond. "I have your food." When I didn't answer, she dropped the tray on the bench and ran back into the building.

I felt bad for the panic I stirred in her, but not bad enough to alleviate it. I needed a little more time by myself to sort through everything.

Not a moment later, several men and women I recognized as Ayla's guard, exited the front and side doors. They moved quickly through the yard and corrals of animals, becoming more frenzied. Eventually, the gardeners and farmhands worked together with the guards to search for me.

Then something shifted, as if the wind had changed, warning of an impending storm. Everyone scurried away. Most of them ran for the outbuildings while others headed quickly into the manor—all except for Nettie, who stayed in the garden, searching in all directions. Suddenly, I heard it, what they were running from, and I knew from their reactions, this was bad.

When horses galloped into sight, I counted about ten men. They looked like the guards from the dungeon or the men who had abducted me. They all wore the same grotesque masks and each bore a large sword. A couple carried crossbows as well. Who knew what else they concealed under their clothing?

As they dismounted, my heart pounded against my rib cage.

Ayla, along with a couple of her large guards, greeted them just outside the door. I couldn't hear what was said, but it didn't look friendly. With a signal from their leader, they stormed the house.

Ayla stayed with a few of her guards as Taft followed the men inside. Even from this distance, the unrest happening within the manor drifted across the garden. I truly feared for the safety of those still inside. These guys weren't the neighborhood welcoming committee; they were more like the neighborhood bouncers.

With the men inside, Nettie moved unnoticed in the direction of the orchard. It didn't take her long to enter the trees on the opposite side of the grove from where I was sitting.

The men searched the immense house faster than I thought possible. When they emerged, I exhaled. They were done.

But all that changed with one phrase.

"Search the grounds!" a voice roared.

My breath caught in my throat. *They weren't going to stop until they found me!* I watched in horror as the men took their orders, splitting off into different directions. Some ran toward the barn and stables. Others searched through the gardens surrounding the house.

Then, my heart thundered in double time as two men ran in the direction of the orchard—in my direction! I forced my breathing to slow. They were almost to the edge of the trees. Luckily neither one carried a weapon, at least not one I could see.

I slowly lifted my legs onto the branch to screen myself in the leaves. I tucked the letter and pouch containing the ring into the top of my short bodice, not making a sound.

Stay still. Stay very still.

I didn't dare move to see where they were. I followed the sound of their footfalls instead. Boots disturbed the bed of dry leaves at the far end of the grove. The same side Nettie had.

"Why is it we always get assigned the sissy stuff? I mean, where's the fun in storming the orchard?" One of them complained, his voice drifting up into the boughs. I had no way of knowing which one had spoken without seeing them, and that wasn't possible.

"Just shut your trap and do your job," the other barked.

"So when we find her, we're just supposed to bring her to Waygar? That doesn't sound entertaining."

"This isn't for our entertainment, boy! Your Lord Regent wants another whore, so that's what we get him."

"I just don't see why this one is so special. Why we can't have a little fun first?"

"You are a lowly soldier who does what he's told, Trey. You so much as leer at her without his permission and he will cut out your eyes and feed them to you. Understand?"

"What, we have to treat her like royalty?"

"I didn't say that. Your master likes them softened up before they're brought in. That lets him play the hero."

"How soft?"

"Let's just say she won't be walking by the time we're done with her."

Both men shared a dark laugh, and I swallowed a gasp.

I lost my balance, and my left leg slipped. I stopped it before it fell, but not before it caught on a small branch. It snapped. The sound was so loud, it sent my stomach cringing. Their heads turned in my direction. As quickly as I'd slipped, I corrected my positioning, hoping they hadn't seen me.

"Did you hear that?" Trey asked.

"I sure did."

I watched as the two figures closed the distance between us. They were looking in my direction, their eyes scanning the branches on the trees. But before they got any closer, a figure came running toward them, arms flailing. I was astonished to see Nettie yelling at the top of her lungs.

"You boys should be ashamed, talking about a woman with such disrespect. You think no one heard you describing your unthinkable crimes." Nettie was in their faces now, almost spitting out her words. "That is no way to talk. The girl you're looking for has the blood of a queen in her! She is the kind of royalty that puts your master to shame."

"Stand down, old lady. You are now disputing the legitimacy of your Lord Regent and standing King. That's treason."

"I will no longer pretend to align myself with that assassin. He has taken the throne unlawfully. He is no king of mine," Nettie stated forcefully.

An older man on horseback burst into the orchard. He stopped right next to them. The same mountain symbol that had been tattooed on Conlen's forehead appeared on the horse's breast strap; three triangles overlapping with a line through them all and three dots.

"Silence," he commanded. "What is the meaning of this?" he demanded, looking from Nettie to his soldiers.

"This old lady was just saying how she doesn't stand with her king, sir," one of the men said, acid lacing his tone.

The confidence Nettie exuded was impossible. Not once did remorse show in her expression.

"Is that so?" the man on a horse demanded. "What else did she say?"

"That this girl we're tracking should be our queen," Trey added.

A look that sent a chill through me slowly filled the man's eyes.

"Well, well. I didn't think we would run into this today. But the witness of these two men confirms that what you've said cannot go unpunished. Seize her."

They grabbed Nettie by the shoulders, forcing her to her knees.

"See anything else out here?" the voice demanded.

"No, Captain Waygar, we haven't seen anything except this wind-bag," one of the men said.

"What about you?" he asked Trey.

"Right before she came ranting at us, I did hear something in the trees over there," Trey said, pointing in my general direction.

Panic spread through me like wildfire. I had to do something to kill their curiosity. I couldn't let them find me, too. But what?

Think, Lotty.

I had seconds to come up with a plan and found the only solution I could, hoping it was the right thing to do. Hoping it would be enough.

I took the apple that had been resting in my lap and dropped it. It fell through the lower branches, creating more snapping sounds. An angel of mercy smiled on me because a bird, one I hadn't noticed till then, had been resting on one of those lower branches. The commotion startled it. It shot out of the tree in their direction. Their heads all turned to follow the bird's flight.

Relief washed over Nettie's face, as if her silent prayers had been answered.

"Now that my men have found their bird, we are left with you," Waygar addressed Nettie. "You are an old woman. Swear, before me and my men that henceforth you renounce all other false claims to the throne and will serve King Terrshon, and I will let you go back to your knitting."

Do it, Nettie! I screamed inside. *Tell them what they want to hear so they don't hurt you!* My nails dug into the flesh of the tree as I waited for Nettie's response. She was quiet for a long moment, as if contemplating something. Then she reached up and pulled a cord from around her neck. The sunlight glinted off the small glass teardrop just before Nettie grasped it in one hand and squeezed. The familiar crunch of breaking glass drifted through the branches.

Waygar stared in shock as she opened up her bleeding palm in defiance.

"My tears stop this day. It's your false king's turn to weep for the reckoning that is coming!" Nettie vowed passionately.

I felt my jaw drop in horror.

The captain's horse danced nervously before he answered her.

"You are a foolish old woman who should have kept her mouth shut! I hereby find you guilty of treason and sentence you to death. Kill her."

Without hesitation, both men drew their swords and plunged them deep into Nettie's chest. As they withdrew bloodied blades, Nettie forced out her last garbled words.

"Long live the Blood of Moldara!" she gasped, then fell lifeless to the earth.

"She will be wearing a token. Find it and take the hand while you are at it. King Terrshon will need proof of exactly the kind of traitors we found here and how we dealt with them. Be quick about it. We have several more miles to search before nightfall if you expect to sleep tonight." He turned his horse back toward the rest of his men now gathered in front of the manor.

The two men roughly searched the body, finally revealing the insignia bracelet on her wrist. One of the men grabbed Nettie's arm just above the bracelet. Pulling a dagger from his belt, he vigorously worked the blade through the tissue. The bloody stump fell back into the dirt. He took the hand, still wearing the bracelet, glass embedded in the palm, and shoved it into a small burlap sack. Blood seeped through the cloth as they turned and followed Waygar back to their horses. Moments later, they all mounted and disappeared down the road.

The orchard was quiet again, unnaturally still.

My gaze locked on Nettie's lifeless form. A pool of crimson spread across her dress and darkened the earth. The stump, where her hand had been, lay in its own dark pool as all the color drained out of her once vibrant skin. Nettie's head had rolled to the side as they'd searched her and had been left facing me. I could see her half-closed eyes; the defiant look on her face had softened into a peaceful stare.

I didn't move. I could barely breathe. Raw terror coursed through my veins, cementing me to the tree.

The pain behind my eyes peaked, exploding lights into my vision until I was finally able to look away. I gasped for air as I searched for something else to focus on, anything other than the horror I couldn't escape. I covered my eyes with my hands, pushing back against the pounding in my head, trying to block it out.

My self-imposed darkness didn't hide the scene from me though. Instead, I watched the horror play out again and again in slow motion. Nettie running out to defend me. The commander passing sentence. The swords slicing through her as if she were nothing more than one of her loaves of bread.

"No," I heard myself gasp.

I forced my eyes open again, my grandfather's words from his letter playing in my head.

You are the only daughter of the late King Norwyck and Queen Mira of Moldara. You are the rightful heiress to the throne. If your parents had lived, you, Princess Adelaide, would be the one ruling these good people.

The words repeated, forcing me to listen, eroding my resistance.

The pain arcing through my skull eventually pushed away all memory or thought. I still couldn't catch my breath. I was drowning, my heart and mind on overload, and I was losing the will to fight it.

The sound of new footsteps approaching pushed me off the emotional edge. Wild with fear, tears streamed down my face as I turned to climb higher into the tree.

"I found Nettie!"

A man's voice. I continued to climb.

The rough bark cut into my trembling hands, but I kept pushing through the branches. A whimper was the only sound that escaped my tightly clenched jaw when the branch I had been reaching for broke.

I felt branch after branch catch on my clothes, like a thousand hands clawing at me in my descent. A couple of seconds of free fall later, the ground rushed up, and my head slammed into the rocky earth.

The impact sent lightning bolts of pain through me that stripped the last of my willpower. Giant sobs finally broke through the fear and spilled out of me. I let them come. I let them consume me.

"She's over here," someone shouted.

Several footsteps ran in my direction.

"Lotty," a kind deep voice tried to get my attention. "It's going to be okay. Are you hurt?"

It was Taft, but I couldn't answer him. Darkness ate away the edges of my consciousness. More footfalls brought more familiar people and more anxious questions. As I tried focusing on the people that surrounded me, the darkness retreated.

Without the darkness, a whole new round of sobs took over. The pain in my head was overwhelming, far beyond anything I had ever experienced. I just wanted it to stop. I would do anything to make it stop.

My perception of the world warped around me. I couldn't stay focused. Strong arms lifted me. The ground fell away. I wanted to tell them to leave me alone, but my mouth wouldn't form the words.

A voice said Roah's name, and my decline into full unconsciousness stopped. I tried to move my mouth, to plea for someone to bring Roah to me, but I was trapped in my body, the pain washing through my veins with every thud of my pulse. The agony twisted my stomach, threatening to turn inside out. I struggled against the arms that held me as bile filled my throat.

After the third retch, I blacked out.

11

Sounds registered first. The sound of a door opening, and then closing. Footsteps. A fire crackling. Muffled, distant, dreamlike.

My body felt foreign, heavy as my awareness moved from my fingers to my toes, checking if I was all there. I shifted, and my arms and shoulders burned with every readjustment, conjuring images of branches and tree bark. My back flared and flashes of metal and blood tore at the periphery of my mind. Muscles tightened around my eyes, pushing the images from memory. But the pain searing through my head trapped them.

My skull felt like it had shattered into thousands of pieces and was sloppily glued back together. I didn't lift it from the pillow. I was afraid if I did, it would come unglued again.

My mouth was like plaster, dry and sticky. I needed water.

I slowly opened my eyes. They were heavy and puffy. The room around me looked blurry. I was sure the silhouette in the window wasn't really there. I tried to bring the image into focus but was overcome with pain. I shut my eyes.

Soft fingers slowly caressed the skin of my cheek and brushed the hair from my damp brow. They traced softly down my neck and over my scars. I turned my head toward the sensations, wanting them to be more than just another part of my delusions. I tried opening my mouth to will my voice, but my lips stuck together.

An arm slid under my neck, gradually lifting me. A glass was set to my lips. The cool liquid rolled through my mouth, quenching the scorching pain. My head released back to the pillow, and again I drifted in the space between waking and dreaming.

A jolt forced me back to awareness. My head pounded. I blinked, trying to orient myself. Nothing seemed familiar, nothing was right; the sheets were too itchy, the comforter not heavy enough. I tried to sit up but couldn't. My body protested the movement and I moaned.

A heavy weight filled the space next to me. I turned toward it, sweet relief filling me as I saw him. This time I was sure I wasn't dreaming.

Roah reached for a pitcher, filling the glass. He lifted me, and I drank. As the cool liquid slid down my throat, it took with it a thin layer of the fog still rolling through my brain. I drank until I'd reached the bottom.

He replaced the glass on the side table and tucked the warm comforter around me.

I closed my eyes again. The throbbing in my body eased when the weight of his hand pressed on my shoulder. Another hand rested on my forehead. I relaxed under their touch, allowing him to help hold me together.

My thoughts were still an eddy of images. I pushed the unpleasant ones to the farthest reaches of my mind and concentrated on Roah's touch, his breath steady in my ear. The sound matched the rise and fall of my own chest. I didn't count the number of breaths we shared. Time was irrelevant. He was there. That was all that mattered.

When I found some strength, I brought a hand up, placing it over the one on my forehead. I exhaled as his touch soothed the ache deep within. I opened my eyes, and he was right there, gaze soft, expression concerned. I smiled, but I could tell he wasn't convinced.

He leaned in, warm fingertips gracing my temple and cheek. His expression was steady, kind, but he held something back. I squeezed his hand, both to reassure myself that he was really there, but also so he knew he could open up to me if he wanted to.

A soft knock interrupted the silence. With an apologetic glance, he pulled his hands from me and walked to the door. A low, murmuring conversation followed. I thought I could make out the words—awake...weak...needs some time—but I couldn't be sure.

He returned with a full plate and bowl, both steaming, and set them on the table. Ignoring my questioning eyes, he helped me sit up against a stack of pillows.

The stiffness in my muscles flared as I shifted. I wiggled my fingers and toes in hopes of alleviating it. I tried not to think about the events that had made them so tender, focusing instead on the food about to fill my stomach.

Roah sat on the edge of the bed next to me. He took the bowl in his hands, slowly blowing off the steam swirling just above it. Then he held it to my lips.

The warm liquid hit my mouth, sending a soothing, yet invigorating, sensation through me as it ran down my throat and warmed my stomach. My muscles gently released, and the comfort of the sensation swelled within me, unknotting the tight sensitive spots and waking the numb ones.

Roah dropped the bowl from my lips.

I sighed, the warmth of the soup growing in my center.

He lifted the bowl once more. After I had swallowed the last of its tangy sweetness, I noticed that the pain screaming through my body had hushed. My mental clarity, on the other hand, had only marginally improved. I felt stuck in the weird limbo between wakefulness and sleep. Either could claim me without much effort on my part.

He offered me a piece of bread from the plate, and with a weak but steady hand, I ate. The coarseness of the grains, the yeast with just a hint of garlic and thyme, all combined in my mouth until I could almost feel the rays of sunlight that had given it life. It was the same savory crumbles that Nettie had served me before—my throat suddenly tightened.

Roah swept back an errant strand of hair from my cheek as I sipped from the cup he handed me. I allowed his presence to revive me as much as the food had. Just being with him felt like a balm on my tattered soul.

Once satisfied, he took the cup and set it back on the table. I reached out; I needed to feel him, to know he was really there. When he filled my hand with his, the warmth from his touch was clear. His eyes searched my face; they looked tired. Or maybe he was just reflecting what he saw in mine.

Scared he might disappear again, I drew Roah to me. He scooted closer, tucking me under his arm. Feeling the weight of him around me, I relaxed into him further, finally being in the one place that felt right. He stroked my neck and my shoulder, playing with the unruly tendrils spilling down my back.

His fingers lingered, tracing their way to my cheekbone, lightly trailing the lines of my ears, and stopping at my temple. He fully opened his hand, placing his palm against my cheek. The warmth of his touch was like honey, sweet and irresistible, but it wasn't his touch that had me breathless. When I looked up at him, a tear glistened in the corner of his eye. Slowly, it trickled out.

He stood quickly and walked to the other side of the room. As he stood by the window, staring at something through the glass, his shoulders tensed as he balled fists against his side, trying to steady his breathing. Finally, he raked his hands through his long hair, rubbed his face, and turned to lock eyes with me.

They held me, their depth pulling me in, even from across the room. There was no wall, no pretending he was anything other than what I saw before me. They filled me with a longing, an openness, a desire I wasn't sure he meant me to see. Not after everything that had happened. The look was overwhelming, unbearable. I shut my eyes.

He was soon next to me again, arms around me. I kept my eyes closed but sank into his touch. Regardless of everything that had happened, I still wanted him—his touch, his strength, his ability to make me feel whole. He had shown me a side of himself he hadn't shared with anyone, and I had done the same. Even after being dragged to the ends of the earth, he'd still found me and tried to keep me safe. That wasn't something I could ignore.

Fingers brushed my cheek again. In that simple touch, I could feel that he desired the same reassurance I craved. And as much as I couldn't bear that I'd put him in harm's way, I couldn't deny him either.

I looked up.

He placed his hands on both my cheeks, eyes intent on mine. He searched my face, and I let him suck me into his world, his desires, his need for me, because I was sure he was only answering the call he saw in me.

Gradually, he closed the distance and kissed me. His lips fought to be gentle against mine, but the intensity won. The hand on my cheek gently coaxed my face forward. His other hand moved from my shoulders to my lower back, his muscled arms supporting my still fragile frame. I melted under their influence, and the contradicting sensations of pain and pleasure swirled through me, intensifying with every passing second.

Too soon he stopped, pulling away just enough to see my face. His grip on my cheek tightened as if he were afraid to let go. The look in his eyes matched the desperation of his touch.

"Lotty," he breathed.

My chest tightened, and I dug my fingers into his back. The raw pain in his voice had sapped any strength I'd managed to replenish.

"I had life figured out," Roah began. "I knew my path. I knew my duties. I knew nothing else. I see now I was going through the motions, discontented, searching for a purpose that would fill the void, but I didn't know what I was truly looking for. I didn't know life until you entered mine."

"I don't understand—"

"I thought I might lose you again. I was sick with myself, thinking you would be safe here, that he wouldn't have sent his legions here."

Roah's eyes were liquid fire. It took my breath away. "I am forever altered because of who you are. When they told me what had happened. I—"

He stopped, unable to finish the thought out loud. My heart drummed against my ribs.

"Lotty, I am lost without you."

As I leaned forward, my true feelings flowed unfiltered through my raw state. And I said the words, the only ones that made my jumbled reality finally make sense. A touchstone. An anchor.

"And I without you."

12

His eyes met mine again, pleading as he spoke. "Tell me what you want."

I hesitated, unsure of what he was truly asking. As I looked into his eyes, I wanted more than just his touch. I wanted something I wasn't sure he could give me.

I could believe that Moldara's existence was beyond my comprehension but still very real, excruciatingly so. I rubbed the sores on my wrists. Just like the apple in the orchard, I knew this pain was real. Ignoring this reality caused us both more pain. Mine I could live with, but I ached to ease his.

Suddenly, the memory of Nettie's death burst through the fog in my mind. Pulling away from Roah, I curled my knees in front of me under the comforter and hugged them tightly. It felt like such a childish way to try to keep the weight of Nettie's death from consuming me, but I couldn't help myself. My next words spilled out in a panic.

"Will you take me home? We can still get home, right?"

"You are home, Adelaide."

His words hung in the air between us and anxiety twisted my gut. I noticed that he'd used my full name, the name people who thought they knew me here used, the name they believed belonged to their lost princess. Roah's use of it reminded me of the weight that had been building on my shoulders since reading my grandfather's letter.

The letter drew my eye. It was sitting on the small wooden table beside the bed. The pouch containing the ring lay next to it. I couldn't take my eyes off of either of them as Elion's words rang through my mind.

"Talk to me, Lotty. You are not in this alone."

I sighed. There was just too much to put into words. "It's all in there," I said, nodding toward the parchment and small leather satchel.

Roah reached over, lightly fingering the edges of the paper.

"Elion confirmed everything Ayla and Nettie told me," I admitted as I rested my chin on top of my knees, hugging them closer. "How can I refute the words of my grandfather? How am I supposed to understand any of this when everything feels so surreal?"

"I can only imagine what you must be feeling. If you're sure that going back to Virginia is the right thing for you, then I will support you in that, but are you sure you're ready?"

"Of course I'm ready. I've been ready since I got here. Why wouldn't I be?"

"Maybe you still seek answers. If you leave too soon, how will you find them?"

"Roah, I'm more confused now than before I was kidnapped. I don't see how staying will change that."

Parallel universes were easy to swallow compared to the tale of my birth, my parents, and my duty to Moldara. Strangers were dying because of who they believed me to be. Whether or not any of it was true, I already felt the burden of that knowledge. "I'm not who everyone thinks I am."

"Never say that."

"It's true. Just look at me. Even if I was born here, I'm no princess. Tyler would tell you I'm barely a lady! I don't know how to be this person everyone expects me to be."

"It's not a secret formula. You, just be you. Everything else will take care of itself."

"Right. Like yesterday?"

"I will die before I let—"

"You can't promise that!" I interrupted, fear and frustration mingling in that single outburst. "Those guys are powerful. They were well armed and had no issues with killing a poor, innocent woman. Last I checked, you were just Roah. What gives you the idea you can protect yourself from them?"

Even as I said it, the very idea threatened to stop my heart completely. I couldn't bear the idea of him sharing Nettie and Oydis's fate. His expression darkened.

"As I said, there is still so much you don't know—"

"Like this prince my grandfather said I should find?"

"So, he did mention that then?" he asked coolly, watching my face.

"Yes, but truthfully, I have no interest in princes. Or royalty of any kind, for that matter. Even if everything in that letter is true, it's impossible now. I'm a simple girl who grew up in a different world, a world where fairy tales stay in books and don't kidnap their readers and then write them into the story! Plus, it was never the prince in those stories who won my heart. I loved the farm boys and the knights, the adventurers and sidekicks." Did he understand that I didn't want some spoiled, boring, faceless prince? I wanted him, but I couldn't find the words. "I just want to get out of here as fast as we can, before anyone else gets hurt because of me."

Roah didn't say anything, lost in his thoughts.

"Roah." I reached out, taking his hand again. "Can we please go home? I can't stay here."

His crystal eyes gazed into mine, their depth magnified by the firelight. "You were meant for great things, Lotty. This I know, but if you wish to go, to return to Virginia, then I will take you."

I flung my arms around his neck, kissing it. "Thank you."

"But it won't be easy."

"Sure it is. We just get on our horses and ride back through the magic doorway everyone keeps telling me about."

Roah laughed. It echoed through the rafters. "Well, when you put it that way, I'll just go fetch my magic wand and we'll be off in a jiffy."

"Be serious," I scolded.

"You want serious? Out there"—he pointed to the window, the mirth in his voice draining away with each word—"those people see you as their princess, and you know there are men who want you for their own terrible proposes. The stories you hear about your parents, about the tyranny that has taken over these lands, that is the reality here. It's as real to these people as your story of Virginia is to you. Navigating your situation will take a lot more than a few quips about magic wands."

"I didn't mean—" I couldn't finish. He was right. This world was complicated, and the consequences of my ignorance had already been catastrophic. "Okay, then teach me. What else do I need to know to go home? I'll do whatever it takes. Everyone will be safer without me here."

Roah's face fell, and he looked away.

"Hey, it's okay. Start with something small. Like—" I searched my memory and chose one of the hundred odd things that I'd noticed since I'd been freed. "Nettie and Hattie. They both did something odd. They had glass charms on white leather cords. Both broke them in their hands, cutting themselves. Why? What are they?"

"That's the first thing you want explained?" He still wouldn't meet my eyes.

"If I can't handle knowing the purpose of the jewelry here, then you should just leave me to the wolves. Wait, are there wolves here?"

"Yes, but—"

"Tell me."

"I guess you need to know." Roah sighed heavily, taking my hands and studying them as he spoke. "It's a tradition that dates back centuries. What you saw was a token known as a glass tear. It signifies a great personal loss. If it's worn on a white cord, it's a symbol of the loss of a member of a royal family. In most cases, the glass holds a special vial of salt water, representing tears. Mourners wear this charm until the void left behind is filled—a new spouse is found, a new baby is born, and so on—at which time it is cast into a fire. The fire boils the water inside, bursting the tear and allowing the water to mingle with the spirit world as steam. The glass then melts back into the earth.

The ashes of that fire are sacred and must be spread in the forest or at sea."

"That's really beautiful. But that's not what I saw."

"What you saw was an oath of vengeance. The glass cuts into the hand and the salt water mingles with the griever's blood, forever binding them to surrender their lives in the name of the one they lost. In a commoner, no healer may tend to such a wound, as it must be left to scar, a lifelong symbol of their fealty to a cause. In a royal, however, the wound is tended to immediately. They have only until the cuts fade to complete their vengeance, for their lives already belong to their people."

Terrshon's words came back to me. *Your life does not belong to you. It never did.* A shiver ran through me.

"Wait, so Hattie and Nettie knew what they were doing when they broke theirs, didn't they?" I was breathing too fast, but I couldn't slow down.

"Yes."

"And this Terrshon creep, his minions, they all knew what it meant?"

"Yes. Those rebellious, beloved old ladies were as good as dead the second that glass broke. No one dons a glass tear lightly. Even fewer will take a vow with one. Those who do will lay down their lives before they allow a single hair of your head to be harmed."

To wear one's grief as a talisman, a token of faith or a promise of vengeance, seemed as healing as it was foreign. A beautiful and terrible tradition. I found myself wishing I had a glass tear. But who would I mourn? My grandfather, my parents, or me? I wasn't sure.

"Lotty, your logical side must be on overload, but you've got to understand what it means to be here." His voice took on a quiet authority I'd never heard before. "As long as you are in Moldara, whether you want to believe it or not, you *are* a princess, the heiress to a kingdom that has been preparing for your return. Just because it's not the world you prefer does not diminish its validity or the consequences of being here. If you can't step into that role—or at least respect it—it would be best if I prepare for your return to Virginia without you."

The pain and determination in Roah's expression was almost as gut-wrenching as the terror building inside me.

"Roah, you have to understand—you can't leave me here alone again. You are the person I trust the most in all of this insanity. I know it's a different world out there. Believe me, I know. The princess thing, I can play along, because as soon as I'm home, it won't matter anyway. I promise to be more careful, but please, take me with you. I don't know if I can face another—" I choked on my words as those death scenes flashed in my head again, now in full context. My tears returned.

"Roah, I watched them die." I wept as my confession unleashed the full terror of Oydis and Nettie's deaths, the story finally spilling out in a torrent of tears and pain. I expelled every excruciating detail hoping if I spoke them aloud, the crushing grief inside me would finally have an outlet.

He listened, taking me in his arms and holding me until the tears passed. "Cry as much as you need to. Let it all out. I'm not going anywhere."

My sobs transformed into something cleansing, washing away the past few days and the agony of feeling so alone in all of it.

"Ayla saw to her body personally," Roah offered when I was finally still. "Though I don't think there will be a funeral until they recover her sister's body from the castle. It was their wish to be laid to rest together, I believe."

"They killed her sister, too?"

"Yes, but not for Nettie's actions yesterday. Hattie, as I understand it, was the one who took your place in Terrshon's cell to conceal your escape. Terrshon had her executed as soon as the deception was discovered."

My mind flashed back to Hattie's proud, gentle face as she held out her bloody hand toward me like an omen. Nettie had had that same look in her eyes. Guilt swelled inside me. Three lives had already ended to save mine.

"It's all my fault! I killed them—"

"No," Roah shook his head emphatically, taking my face in his hands. "Listen to me: you are not responsible for their choices. Though we all grieve for their loss, they were not the first to die for this cause, and they won't be the last."

"Why does anyone have to die?"

When he didn't pull me back into his chest but merely continued to hold my gaze, I knew he understood the layers within my question. I needed more than platitudes or stories; I needed to know what could make one person that important.

"Because great love often asks great things of us," he said, his eyes threatening to well up. "It is not for us to judge the worthiness of those tasks, only to be prepared to give everything we have in their service when it's our time."

13

As he gathered me back into his strong embrace, I realized there was still so much about him I didn't know. His wisdom seemed beyond his years, deeply rooted in experiences I did not yet understand. I molded my body to his chest as he held me, unwilling to let go. His deep breaths tickled my ear, sending pleasant chills across my skin.

"I would take all of this from you if I could," he whispered.

Slowly his fingers found my chin. He lifted it. My eyes searched for his. Then he leaned in, kissing me with the same force present in his eyes.

As our lips moved together, I felt something different about the way he held me, the way his fingers clung to my skin, as if he were trying to make our bodies one. He moved with more than desire, more than yearning. He moved with conviction, with certainty. It was something I'd never felt from him before, and I never wanted to be without it again.

"If you give me one ounce of trouble," he warned as he kissed my neck. "I'll return you to Ayla's keeping."

"No trouble. I promise," I replied breathlessly.

"Great. Now let's go find that prince of yours," he said as he trailed kisses from one side of my neck to the other.

"Wait, what?" I blurted, trying to pull my head away to see his face. He wouldn't let me move.

"If Elion said we needed to find him, then we should listen to his council. There must be a reason," he said calmly, as he continued moving his lips up and down my skin. *How did he talk and still do that?* The heat from his breath made my hair stand on end.

"But," I tried to protest. "Wouldn't he want that ring for himself, too?"

"You have the ring?" Roah stopped abruptly, pulling away.

I was somewhat confused by his anxiety, as my head was reluctant to come down from cloud nine. I took the small pouch from the table, opened it, and pulled out the insignia ring that had been my father's. On the thick and tarnished golden band, the engraved image of a broken compass shimmered in the light. The center gem glistened like a dim sun. I handed it to Roah.

He studied it with reverence.

"You do understand the significance of this now, right?"

"Yeah, I think I'm starting to."

"This emblem changes everything. This ring"—he held it to the light of the nearest candle—"proves without a shadow of a doubt that you are not just Adelaide of Moldara but heir to its throne. More men than I'd like to keep track of have died because of this ring. Who knows you have it?"

"No one, I think. Except for my grandpa. He's the one who gave it to me."

"How?" he pressed.

"With the letter."

"Who gave you that?"

"Nettie," I answered in a solemn voice.

"Of, course." Roah rolled his eyes as if searching for patience. "You must keep this hidden, and under no circumstances are you to tell anyone that you have this. Do you understand?"

"Yes, but why do we have to keep it?"

"Because if Terrshon ever got his hands on this, he will kill you, slowly and publicly."

I pictured yesterday, except it was me in Nettie's place, Terrshon standing over me, taking me to the brink of death and bringing me back just to do it again. Only now there would be a crowd cheering him on, screaming for my blood. Something cold and dark settled inside me.

"Keep it hidden, tell no one. Got it?"

I nodded, and Roah handed the ring back to me. I secured it in the small leather pouch, resolved never to take it out again as my mind worked on more places I could hide it.

"Roah, can I ask you something?"

"That which is in my power to give you is yours."

"Why are you doing all this? I mean, you've risked so much for me. I know that letter talks about those I can trust here, protectors who will help me. Ayla and her mother are named, and Soren. Even this prince I'm to find. But not you. Why?"

His brow furrowed as he answered. "I'm not sure."

"Who are you then if you're not a protector of the princess?" I tried to sound teasing, but he didn't seem to hear me.

"I never said I wasn't. I just didn't start as a protector. That part kind of found me."

"How?"

"Because," he paused as if trying to find the right words. "I'm the Captain of the Royal Guard of Niniever."

"You are from Niniever?"

"Yes."

"Then you know this prince."

"For many years."

"But my grandpa's letter is four years too late." I couldn't believe I was considering this. "What if he thinks I'm dead? What if he takes me prisoner? Is this still safe?"

He smiled that wry half-smile I loved.

"If the prince doesn't honor his oaths, I will kill him myself before I let him harm a hair on your head. No one is stopping me from getting you back to Virginia. Now, you get some rest. I'll tell Ayla that we'll be leaving first thing in the morning."

14

As we made preparations to leave the next day, the world looked different. I'd felt this way the morning after my grandfather—Elion, I reminded myself—had disappeared. Something about the world became starker. The details held more contrast, and everything felt a little closer. The effects also reminded me that my emotions were still raw and dangerously close to the surface.

Roah had brought with him six guardsmen from the royal army of Niniever, not counting the scout who went on ahead or the one who walked barefoot behind us covering our tracks. They surrounded us, protecting us on all sides. I was glad to see Tregr with them. In a small way, when he took his place next to me, opposite Roah, it felt like being home again.

As we left the country manor, thick fog muffled every sound. The quiet was almost deafening while we ventured farther into the shrouded wilderness. I pulled the woven cloak tighter around my neck in an effort to keep the chill away, but the heavy air settled on every-thing; there was no way to protect myself from its bite. Although I was as anxious as the others to get on the road, it felt like an ominous start; as if we were going toward more trouble instead of away from it.

After the first hour, I began to warm. The heat rising from my mount filled the cloak as efficiently as a space heater. For traveling, Enzi and Ayla had done my hair in an elaborate braid, a style that perfectly suited the outfit they had put together. Under my cloak, I wore a thick white cotton blouse with tight-fitting brown pants that tucked neatly into the tops of my now familiar knee-high boots.

In place of the usual full bodice, which I was too sore from my fall to wear, they had produced something similar to a tank top, made from an extra wide leather belt with shoulder straps. Worn over the white blouse, it functioned partly as a bra and partly to give my long draping shirt an empire waist. Enzi had fussed until Ayla had let her add a finely worked metal broach dripping with small woven chains that looped into the side buckles. I thought it was an unnecessary embell-ishment but had to admit that it was beautiful.

The sleeves of the blouse were long and secured with leather and metal cuffs—a feature I rejected until Ayla had removed the bandages around my wrists. To my astonishment, all signs of injury were gone, though they still ached. When I realized that the shattered feeling of my skull and the stabbing pain in my side had also been eased, I began questioning Ayla. Not meeting my eyes, she mumbled something about Sacred Waters and changed the subject.

No one spoke as we traveled. It made for a lot of time to think— time I didn't want. My mind wandered dangerously close to the memo-ries of the last few days. When it did, I looked at Roah and sought out happier thoughts. He still wore the same outfit I'd seen him in when we were at Soren's, although he'd added a wool cloak to his simple tunic, blue jeans, and black leather boots.

I found it a little odd that he hadn't changed into something less conspicuous, like his men, who all resembled seasoned woodsmen in an array of leathers and furs. At first it reassured me, as if his clothing choice was a sign of solidarity with my home in Virginia, but as the hours passed, I was less sure. The worn look of his clothes and the shadows under his eyes made me wonder when he'd last slept.

He stayed so close I could reach out and touch him, though I didn't dare break his concentration. He constantly searched the misty woods, looking for any warning signs left behind by the scout he'd sent ahead earlier. Roah's men shared in his burden of the watch, keeping a steady gaze in every direction, so I kept my thoughts to myself and tried to stay calm.

Unfortunately, there was a lot to consider and a lot of hours on the road. I had accepted I was in a different world. I told myself that I was having a very bad foreign exchange student experience, and as soon as I got home I could put it behind me. That worked great, for the most part, until I tried to imagine Roah back home with me. I couldn't watch him now without seeing how at home he was *here*. He didn't just blend in. He was in his element. And why shouldn't he be? He was captain of a king's guard, apparently.

His revelation about being captain of the guard explained so much —him coming to protect me in Virginia, the people he knew, the connections he had, and the resources. The horses and men he led seemed like natural extensions of himself.

As I watched him riding, shame washed over me, because I couldn't help but see him in a different light now. I tried not to think about how many lies he had told in Virginia to blend in. No wonder he had always dodged questions about where he'd grown up or his family. Obviously, he wasn't related to Trell or his cousins as he'd said. What else had he lied about in the name of protecting me? What else was there about him and his life here that was foreign to me?

He had promised to stay with me, but what about his responsibilities here? I had assumed he was like me, ordinary with a hint of oddball. Now I saw him as both the Roah I had come to love, and a man who might be bound to a kingdom and a world that were as familiar to me as the moon. He wasn't a free citizen; he was someone's subject. What if this prince Zarian tried to separate us? What if he ordered Roah away and locked me up until I agreed to the arranged marriage?

If only Roah were all I had to think about. It had been almost a week since my abduction into this Otherworld. What were my aunt and uncle going to think? Were they worried? Did they even know? What would Trell tell them? How would they react when I told them about this world, or would I? If Tyler heard the whole story, would he even look at me the same way again? Would I even get a chance to see them again, let alone explain any of this?

And then there was the pouch that hung heavily around my neck. Before we'd left, Ayla had brought me a thick, but elegant, silver chain; it had been Nettie's. All of Nettie's children had perished in the battles against Terrshon, or Ayla would have seen it passed on to them. She thought Nettie would have been honored to know I had accepted this gift from her. I couldn't say no, and I'd almost started crying again.

Its weight, and the concealed ring it hid down the front of my wide neck tunic, was my constant reminder of why I had to leave as soon as possible. Regardless of what anyone thought, I wasn't ready to handle that kind of responsibility. Even with the help of those who believed in a restoration of power, how could that happen without a fight? Being here didn't just endanger my life; it could get innocent people killed. I shuddered at the thought, concentrating instead on the rhythm of my horse as we made our way through the dense trees.

By midday, the sun had burned off most of the fog as it forced its rays through the branches overhead. With the path ahead clear, we picked up our pace. Roah was insistent we keep moving even though the horses showed signs of fatigue. More speed on the difficult terrain meant more concentration, which meant less time to think. I found the extra exertion to be a relief.

After yesterday, Roah wasn't sure where Terrshon might have sent his men and said it would be best if we kept moving. So when he asked how I was holding up, I lied and said I was fine. He didn't need to know I couldn't feel my butt anymore because it was so saddle sore. I wouldn't tell him that the pain throughout my body that I'd experienced earlier threatened to return with every step of the horse, or that I was afraid to be left alone with my thoughts again.

Most of all, I didn't want to be the one holding up the party; after all, I was the reason we were in a hurry in the first place. Consequently, after the horses drank from a small creek, we mounted and continued our journey.

We rounded a bend in the road, and the front rider stopped

Blood of Moldara 115

suddenly. He lifted his hand, signaling for us to halt. Then he dismounted and stood perfectly still in the middle of the road.

"What is he doing?" I asked Tregr as he scooted closer to me.

"He's listening."

"For what?"

He looked at me, measuring my expression before he continued. "It's his bond."

"His what?"

"His bond. Let's just say he can hear things, messages or feelings. I'm not positive how his works, but he's riding ahead to receive communication from our scout."

"Because he can send messages?" I asked skeptically.

"Yeah."

"Is that what the guy walking barefoot is doing too?"

"No," he spoke in a hushed tone. "His bond connects him to the earth. He is making our trail undetectable, shifting it so it's as if no one has come this way for weeks."

"He's moving the earth?"

"You can say that." He grinned as he took in my perplexed expression.

"Of course, because a whole new world isn't enough."

The front rider turned to face Roah. "It's from our man."

"What is it?" Roah asked.

"It seems that Icel has caught word of Terrshon searching all the villages for an escaped prisoner. They are gathering as many men as they can to protect their village from any threats of unlawful entry. It isn't clear if they know who they're looking for"—his eyes met mine briefly before turning back to Roah—"but I'm positive if we want to pass, we will be made to identify ourselves."

"Can we afford that?" Tregr asked.

"It's either that or bypass the village altogether," Roah said. "If we do though, we delay our arrival by almost a day and will be forced to make a river crossing that's taken many lives. With Terrshon searching these outer villages, his men won't be far. I don't think we have a choice."

Roah and Tregr both looked at me as they mulled over the new information. I stayed silent, trying to pull my stomach back out of my boots. If this concerned them, I knew I had good reason to be genuinely worried. Was today going to be a repeat of the orchard? Would more empty eyes haunt my dreams tonight? Instead of arousing the fear I had expected, quiet hot anger began to pulse slowly through me.

"Okay," Roah finally said. "When we get there, let me do the talking. Maintain a tight formation. Do not break rank for anyone and keep your heads. No one is to reveal our true identity, or I will see to it personally that you are disposed of when we reach the castle. Ignore insults and watch for distractions. This mission isn't about our pride. Am I understood?"

A round of "*Yes, Sir*" followed. It amazed me how these men respected him. He was younger than some of them, yet they would do anything he asked.

"Good. If all goes as planned, we shall be on the other side of Icel in no time. Let our man know," he said to the rider still standing in the road. He dismounted and tossed the reins to the rider in front of him. "Tie him to your steed. Make sure he's secure; I'd hate to lose him."

Next, he pulled parchment and a quill from his saddlebag. After scribbling something on the paper, he produced a stick of wax and something out of his pocket. When he flipped open the small Zippo lighter, I gawked at him, bewildered. *Where on earth had he gotten that?* He didn't answer my unspoken question. He just smiled that crooked smile that I loved as he lit the flame and melted the wax.

After sealing the letter, he closed the Zippo, tucking it safely out of sight again. I blushed guiltily realizing I liked seeing him with it. It made me feel I had a claim on him, as if he belonged in my world, too.

Roah took an arrow from one of his men and walked over to a tree by the road. Placing the note in a very visible place on the trunk of the tree, he plunged the arrow into the letter to hold it in place.

"If anyone was following our party, they will think we took the road heading toward the river."

Roah came over to my horse, grabbed the reins, and mounted,

landing heavily in the large saddle right behind me. With the reins in one hand, he encircled his other arm around my waist, pulling his body closer to mine.

"What are you doing?" I asked over my shoulder.

"My job," he whispered in my ear. "Why? Does this bother you?" he asked, his voice teasing. His lips tickled my lobe as he tightened his hold on my waist.

"No, I like this just fine," I breathed, wrapping my fingers around his arm, holding it to me like a lifeline.

"Good." I could hear the smile on his face. "You'll need to wear this." He lifted my hood over my head and tucked my hair inside. "I don't want anyone to see you. Just precaution, that's all."

His words melted away some of the pleasure as they reminded me that I was putting Roah in danger now, too.

When he was finally satisfied with our positioning, he gave the word to ride on. "Remember," he said as we started again, "once you see the village in sight, slow your pace. We don't want to give the impression we mean harm."

15

We rode for a good twenty minutes before seeing evidence of a village. When we did, I didn't know what to say or think. A sea of human suffering spread out before us.

Crude shelters made out of various materials had been built just off the road on either side. Some were makeshift tents pieced together from ratty pieces of canvas; others were small shacks constructed of random pieces of wood. The one thing they all had in common was that they were mobile. A small ocean of rickety carts and wagons bunched into circles around fires and lined paths marked with large rocks.

But it wasn't the structures that disturbed me; it was the number of people and the living conditions. I couldn't fathom how they were still alive. They huddled in small groups, dressed in layers of filthy rags, and tried to keep warm. Considering their impoverished conditions, I could hardly imagine what was boiling in the pots by the fires.

What broke my heart, what fueled the anger I was nursing, were the children. They were so cold, so skinny, and they shared the same forlorn, desperate expressions their parents wore.

"Who are they?" I asked in a hushed tone over my shoulder.

"They are the exiled, the cursed ones. Or as I was taught, the last

Blood of Moldara

remaining loyal subjects of the House of Norwyck and Mira," Roah whispered back, the seriousness in his tone matching mine.

"Where did they come from?"

"Other villages where their houses and lands have been seized by Terrshon in efforts to solicit submission," he explained without pretense. I sensed that their living conditions angered him as well.

"I don't understand. Why would he take their homes?"

"They were given a choice. If they renounced your family's right to rule and swore fealty to Terrshon, they could keep their wealth and remain in his service. So many refused that it would have crippled the kingdom to kill them all. His answer was what you see here. One by one he picked them off, going to their houses in the night, confiscating everything they owned, and distributing it among those who were loyal to him. Then he burned everything that remained to the ground.

"The ones who survived the purge are what you see here. They are forbidden from owning or tilling land. They are not allowed to even camp in one place for more than a month or near the same city for more than a season, or they risk flogging. They forage for food, do odd jobs, and sell small goods to survive. Any children born to them are considered the fruit of a poisonous tree and subject to the same judgment. When they die, no one may bury them. The bodies they don't burn are taken into the forest. They cover them with rocks as best they can, but it's hard to keep the animals away."

I felt my back straighten as my muscles tensed and flexed. "How long has this gone on? Why don't your people stop it?"

"It was years before anyone believed the reports. To this day, Terrshon refuses to meet an opposing army on the field of battle. Each time there is an uprising and another kingdom marches to help them, Terrshon massacres one of these encampments and scatters the bodies in the advancing army's path. His men don't leave so much as a blade of grass standing. It was decided that in order to spare lives, we would have to wait for the people of Moldara to rise up and lead a true rebellion."

Looking into the eyes of these poor people made my blood boil. No one deserved to live like this. These people had to endure every day what I had experienced only recently. They'd watched their loved ones die. My skin grew hot, and the air beneath the hood was stifling. I embraced my anger to keep tears of empathy at bay. I didn't want to look weak, not when they were suffering so much with no end in sight.

"Isn't there more the villages can do? How can they just leave these people out here?"

"No one dares take them in. No one may feed them, educate them, or give them charity without the risk of sharing the same fate. They aren't permitted forged weapons or to use their bond. If they are caught with as much as a dagger, their whole family is blinded. So they band together like this for protection. It's very common to see tent villages in the outlying cities of Moldara. They came here for help and protection, but the people of the village don't want to upset Terrshon, so they do very little for them."

"What about the other kingdoms, like Niniever? If Terrshon won't attack you directly, can't these people find asylum or something there?"

"Some of the kingdoms have opened their borders, but it's difficult to take many refugees without crippling trade treaties or declaring war. Niniever has taken in so many that our villages are now overrun with beggars and homeless. I have also heard that some have traveled to the mountains in the north. They have started their own nations there, giving shelter and protection to anyone who has been cast out, but most don't want to make the treacherous journey."

My mind was in overload, trying to find solutions. There had to be more that could be done for these people. Looking at their gaunt faces, I wondered how any ruler could be this cruel.

"Isn't there someone who can stop him from doing this?"

"There is."

"Who?"

But he didn't answer. Instead, he tightened his arms around me, pulling me closer.

Then I knew.

I knew who they were waiting for, who bore the responsibility to bring Terrshon down. I touched the ring hanging on the chain around my neck, and a hollow feeling met the growing fury in my chest.

The guards at the village gate waved for our attention, pulling me out of my thoughts. Roah shifted in the saddle behind me. I could feel the tension coursing through him, though his hands remained relaxed on the reins.

Gathered in front of the village gate was a group of about twenty men, weapons drawn. I unconsciously tightened my grip on Roah's arm.

"Halt!" A large burly man commanded. He stepped toward our party and raised his sword. The man behind him played with a lit torch.

Our group came to a stop, staying together in tight formation.

"Who goes there? State your business," he demanded.

"I am Rykan. This is my brother, Tovar," Roah gestured to Tregr, then to me, "and my sister, Dahlia. These are our cousins Callen, Hal, Brokk, Hoden, and Colton, sons of Jarik of Eston. They sent for us to stay with them after our parents died. We are just passing through on our way to Eston, which is our final destination."

"And you have no other dealings here?" he asked as he scrutinized our group. He looked at Roah the longest. Something about what he saw in Roah puzzled him greatly.

"No, sir. We are just passing through," Roah said with a bored expression, trying not to give more information than needed. I tried not to stare at the guy playing with fire. I was sure it was some kind of illusion or trick. Perhaps he'd covered his skin in a fire-retardant substance as he shaped and reshaped the flame with his bare hands as if it were clay.

"I'll need to see the girl before I decide," he insisted, smirking. "We can't have you sneaking off with one of our vagabond whores." The man turned hungry eyes to the huddled masses behind us before looking back at Roah. Then the fire images turned into crude shapes. Roah stiffened behind me as the guards chuckled.

"You will have to forgive my sister. She is not well and the light —" I heard Roah's lie, but my anger had reached its boiling point.

Roah's voice cut off as I reached up and lowered my hood, exposing my face to the hostile city guard.

I sat there, still as stone and stared at the men. The lead guard approached our horse, leering curiously. I met his gaze without flinching and saw the dark thoughts swimming behind his eyes, the pleasure he took in detaining us. He was a common bully, a troll without a bridge. I felt my chin jolt upward in defiance. I heard a wolf whistle and laughter from his men, and something in me snapped.

I met every eye in his blockade. I poured my pain, my fear, my anger and, most of all, my loathing into my gaze, willing them to shrink before us. How dare they perpetuate Terrshon's tyranny? How dare they be a party to such vulgarity and suffering? I hoped they saw the resemblance to Mira that I had been told was so obvious. I hoped it scared them enough to let us on our way.

Most of the men in the blockade didn't seem to recognize me; it was the villagers outside the wall watching the whole scene who had. People clutched at white leather straps hanging around their necks and gathered around us. A low murmur spread through the air as they leaned closer still, something about a spirit. I knew some of them had recognized my face, but it wasn't my name they had spoken. It was my mother's. I didn't care. It wasn't me they needed. It was her.

"Do I know you?" The troll inquired of me, starting to look concerned.

"You've had your look." Roah lifted my hood, concealing me once again. Our horse danced anxiously beneath us.

Hiding my face did nothing to ease the mutterings of the people. Instead, they continued to draw closer, a light igniting in their once lifeless eyes. Weapons in the form of crude clubs, hand tools, and kitchen knives had begun to appear from under grimy rags.

Roah's arm tightened around me as our horse continued to dance under the tension. His unease and impatience were palpable as the crowd closed in around us.

Roah reached into his cloak. The crowd froze, hesitating at his movements. He pulled out a good-sized leather pouch. It clinked as he lifted it, showing it to the burly man.

Blood of Moldara 123

"Let us pass," Roah roared in a voice that even I would never refuse.

"Yes, sir," he replied, greed replacing all his other thoughts. He lowered his weapon and turned to the men behind him, waving his hand while yelling, "Make way." When he turned back to Roah and motioned for us to move, Roah tossed the pouch at him.

"Pleasure doing business with you, stranger." The man licked his lips as he weighed his reward in his hand.

Roah kicked the horse with enough force that it reared. I lost my balance, but Roah's arm tightened around me, keeping me in the saddle. We galloped toward the gate. No one got in our way.

We moved through the village faster than I was comfortable. I kept one hand on Roah's arm, and one on my hood to keep it in place as the wind tried to wrestle it off my head, mentally kicking myself for being so reckless. Even though it was too late to keep some villagers from talking about what they saw, at least I could prevent it from happening again.

As we approached the gate at the other end of the village, Roah picked up speed. He had no intention of stopping this time. The guards all jumped out of the way before our horses could trample them. We heard their yells long after the village walls and tents were out of sight.

16

Even though we seemed to be out of danger, Roah never slowed. In fact, he pushed the horses harder than before, riding for more than an hour before stopping. I wanted to put as many miles between us and the town as Roah did, but his continued urgency kept me on edge.

When sunlight faded, we found a small grassy spot next to a clear stream, well off the main road.

Roah dismounted and addressed the group. "Water your horses and fill your canteens. If you're hungry, now would be a good time to eat. We won't be here long—only fifteen minutes, twenty at most." He turned to Tregr, "See to my horse and Lotty's, will you, please?"

"Sure thing," Tregr said, passing us with his mount, heading to the water's edge.

Roah reached up and grabbed my waist. I placed my hands weakly on his shoulders, expecting him to help me to the ground. Instead, he lowered me into his chest, wrapping his muscular arms around me. I melted into them, my body shaking like a leaf. As he pulled away, he stayed close, leaving a warm hand on the small of my back. Holding my gaze, he spoke in an urgent whisper.

"What were you thinking back there?"

I looked away, guilt replacing my anger. What *had* I been thinking? Had I lost my mind? Worst of all, I had put us in danger. It was just more proof I had no business being there.

"Roah, I am so sorry. I don't know what came over me. I was suddenly just so angry at seeing all those people, and then those men—the look in their eyes. I didn't mean to put us in danger. I didn't know. I—"

Lifting a finger to my lips, he cut me off. "It's okay, Lotty. We're safe now. I just needed to know if—" He paused as if searching for the right words. Then he lowered his voice even more. "It's just that...you had this look on your face. I thought you were about to proclaim yourself."

He seemed like he wanted to say more, but my reaction cut him off.

"No. I... No!" I shook my head frantically. I was shocked, horrified. How had he jumped to that conclusion?

He bowed his head and let out a deep breath—whether in relief or disappointment, I couldn't tell. Before I could ask, he pulled me back into his arms, changing the subject.

"Let's get you something to eat," he said, his voice soft in my ear.

Keeping one arm around my waist, he led me to a spot of grass lit by the golden light of early evening. He took off his cloak and spread it on the meadow. As he retrieved a sack from his saddlebag, I got as comfortable as I could on the hard, lumpy ground. It wasn't easy finding a position that didn't hurt; everything was sore from the rough ride.

"It's not a proper picnic, but it will have to do." He spread out the meager portions of food. "Sorry there isn't more. We didn't have extra room for much of anything." He ripped off a hunk of bread and handed it to me. Then he unfolded a piece of cloth, revealing a few pieces of cheese along with an apple. He offered the food to me first, before helping himself.

"No, this is fine," I said, taking a bite of bread. All the bouncing and nerves had kept my stomach churning. It hadn't fully recovered yet. "Roah," I started softly, picking at the bread in my hand. "I don't mean to pry, but what is a bond? How did that guy play with fire?"

He took another bite, chewing thoughtfully as he studied me. "A bond is a connection to the elements."

"What kind of connection?"

"Some can manipulate certain elements, like that guy with the fire."

"How is that even possible?"

"With training. He's taught how to concentrate on the heat around him and focus it between his hands. Or some can do that with earth or metal, shaping it by conducting heat. Like Wapi." He pointed to the guy who had just entered our encampment, barefoot and singing to himself. "His bond connects him to the earth."

"And others have supersonic hearing?"

"Hal has a bond that allows him to hear or sense vibrations on the wind or through the ground. I don't understand it completely. I just know it comes in handy when messages need to be sent long distances."

"How many bonds are there?"

"Five. Earth, air or spirit, fire, metal, and water. Though there haven't been any recorded with a water bond for several generations."

"How does someone get this power?"

"It's less of a power and more of an obligation. The bond is a strong connection that enables them to guide a natural force when they're in direct contact with that element. But getting the element to respond takes years of training."

"Okay. Do you have a bond?" I almost hated asking.

He shook his head. "No, thank the spirits. I have too much responsibility as it is."

"But Tregr does?"

"Yes. With metal. And Daggon too, with spirit. It lets him converse directly with animals."

I rubbed my forehead as memories came rushing back. That first day of working with them, seeing Daggon getting the hens to lay and Tregr straightening the nails. It hadn't been my imagination. I thought of Karen's horse, Brandy, and her sudden transformation into the perfect mount.

Blood of Moldara 127

"Next are you going to tell me that you have a pet dragon?"

He laughed. Loudly. "A dragon! I wish! Lotty, this is Otherworld, not a magical land with fairies, mermaids, or adventuring hobbits."

I grinned awkwardly. "Right. Of course. What was I thinking?"

The silence stretched out between us as we ate. Something else tugged at my awareness, something more pressing than people playing with the elements. I washed the dry bread down before beginning.

"At the gate, why didn't you tell them who you are? Wouldn't that have been easier? Surely they would've let the captain of a royal guard through without any trouble."

Roah looked at me, a smirk on his face. Either he didn't want to tell me the truth or he was still enjoying my comment about pet dragons. His reaction to my question reminded me of the distance I could once again feel between us, like a tiny stream that could swell its banks and sweep away everything familiar.

"Because," he explained, "we might have to go back that way."

I swallowed a mouthful of cheese and groaned audibly as a familiar knot reformed in my stomach. *Was there no end to this mess?*

"Your little stunt probably started some substantial rumors, but there may still be a way to use that to our advantage. With the look you were giving everyone, it's more likely they'll be claiming your mother has risen from the dead," he explained with a mixture of amusement and irritation.

"If I had announced myself, with you right there, and the size of the escort—" he stopped abruptly.

"What?" I asked, unsure as to why he suddenly looked like he'd said too much.

"It's complicated," he replied cryptically. "Regardless, you are too valuable to be found out like that. Word would've gotten back to Terrshon, and every road between you and Virginia would become impassable. You see, as long as your existence remains a myth, his power goes unchallenged, except by a weak few. Until you proclaim yourself, we must maintain that myth or risk an uprising to find you. Without leadership, they would be cut down before they were able to challenge Terrshon or aide us."

"Could that really happen?" I pressed. "You think there are still enough people who would do that? Would he really just kill them all?"

He nodded. "It's a possibility. No one knows for sure what support remains for your return to the throne. What I do know is that as long as you are never found or captured, people have hope and Terrshon has fear. That's why we were *supposed* to be keeping a low profile today."

"Sorry," I said faintly.

"Lotty," he spoke kindly, his gaze on the woods around us. "Even if they don't feel like yours, those were your parents' people you saw today. They have paid dearly for their loyalties and are a reminder of the destruction of your parents' legacy. Terrshon lets them live to remind others of the fate that awaits them if he is challenged. I would have been surprised if you did not react to seeing them. Never be sorry about that. Never."

"Thank you," I said, cringing a little at the formality in his tone. I wondered if he felt the same distance creeping between us that I did. "If it weren't for you, Roah, I don't know how I would ever get through this. Any of it."

"For you, Lotty, I would do it all again."

"Do you really mean that? Or am I just one of your orders?" The words escaped my lips before I could stop them. His hands clenched at my words, and his mouth went taught, as if he'd tasted something terrible.

"I'm sorry. That didn't come out right." I sensed I was bordering on rude but couldn't stop myself. "It's just that a few days ago you were just my neighbor. I mean you were more like my boyfriend. Then I find out that not only do you know this place, but you have a position in it, a job, a life. I'm worried about what else I don't know."

"You were never one of my *orders*, as you call it." His expression softened, but his voice remained grave. "And you have become so much more."

I felt the intensity of his words, but the distance between us only seemed to grow in the silence. His men laughed at a joke, and we both glanced toward the noise. When I looked back, his hands were twisting the empty cheesecloth over and over again, his expression clouded.

"It's like you said earlier, there is so much I don't know," I tried to amend, to put words to my fears. "I don't know the rules here. What if the prince sells me to Terrshon for more land or an end to the fighting? What if he sends you away, assigning someone else to guard me, and I never see you again? What if he decides to hold me prisoner until I agree to marry him? What if this is another trap, one I can't escape?"

I had mutilated the grass at the edge of his cloak as I spoke, but I couldn't make myself stop. My hands kept pulling at the helpless blades as I studied the lacing on my boots, waiting for a response. I felt warm hands close over mine, stilling them.

"I know I have lost a portion of your trust, but I will not rest until I get it back," he said calmly, but I could hear restraint in his voice, as if he were holding back some deeper frustration. "I will begin with quelling the fear I see haunting you. The first thing you need to understand is that Niniever has two princes." Roah's face took on a distant look as he explained. "The kingdoms, their borders, are set in stone. No marriage or alliance can change that. The eldest child, male or female, inherits the kingdom and is expected to marry for trade relations unless a second child is born. Then, the eldest is released to marry for love, and the duty to marry for the good of the kingdom is borne by their siblings. You are engaged to the second prince, not the first."

"Why does that matter?"

"For starters, a lot of choices were taken away from your prince the day he was born," Roah spoke as if he found the whole system distasteful. "If your parents had lived long enough to give you siblings, they would have been sold off to other countries, their only inheritance the power and status given them through marriage. This tradition keeps the royal family units strong. Instead of squabbling over their parents' kingdoms, the children protect each other."

"The younger kids don't grow up hating the firstborn?" I asked, skeptically.

"Why would they? As long as good matches are made for them, their inheritance is often as big as or bigger than the oldest child's. What is there to fight over?"

"What about the right to choose who they love or marry?" I asked in astonishment. "What about cases like mine? What if I was dead or lost forever? What would this Zarian do then?"

"There has never been a case like yours," Roah answered with a shrug, but he wouldn't meet my eyes as he continued. "The betrothal is binding unless you or he dies. If you had never been found or your death never proved, he would have been stuck, unable to marry another and without a legitimate claim to aid your people. Why else do you think he would risk so much to find you?"

"But that's my point. Once he has me, why would he let me go? How is he any less of a trap than Terrshon?"

"How do you know that he hasn't grown up feeling trapped by you? He has been asking these questions for much longer, Lotty," Roah answered with a small, sad smile. "This isn't a fairytale. I think you'd find him ordinary enough. He's a good commander and treats those closest to him with appreciation and respect. I think he'll be a good ruler, better than his father if he's ever awarded that honor, but this entire situation has made him question tradition, made him search for other options for both of you. I know we will find a sympathetic ally in Prince Zarian."

"Sir," Tregr called from behind, interrupting our conversation.

"Yes?" Roah responded, assuming a more formal posture. "Something from one of the scouts?"

"No, sir, but the horses are ready and light is growing dim. We should be on our way."

Roah nodded. "Before we go, Tregr could I ask a service of you?"

"Anything," Tregr offered.

"Lotty is wearing a silver chain. I need you to lock it."

Tregr stepped behind me. "May I?"

"Sure, I guess."

Tregr touched the nape of my neck, his fingers tickling as he gently moved the chain, locating the clasp. The sound of hands rubbing together rose behind me, and heat moved down the chain. I waited for the burn, but the metal never got hot. After a few moments, Tregr blew on the chain, causing the hairs on my neck to stand. Then he set the thick chain back in place.

Blood of Moldara 131

"Is that all?" Tregr asked Roah.

"Yes. Thank you."

Tregr made the slightest of bows and winked at me before wheeling around and jogging over to where the horses had been tethered.

"What was that for?" I looked for the clasp by sliding the necklace around my neck. It had disappeared. At one point in the chain, I noticed that the links glowed brighter than the rest.

"Just for precaution. Tregr made sure it won't open without help," he explained as I tucked the chain back under my tunic.

Once the leftover food was gathered, Roah stood and stretched his sore muscles, groaning again as he did. I stood, doing the same. It felt good to work out all the little aches. I hoped we didn't have much farther to go. I was suddenly nervous again as Roah shook out his cloak.

"So, when we get to the castle, will you introduce me to the prince right away?" I blurted out.

Roah scrutinized my face, replacing his cloak over his shoulders and guiding me toward the horses being saddled. "I thought you couldn't care less about the prince or any royalty for that matter."

"Do my questions bother you?" I asked, intrigued by his guarded tone. "It's not like I'm about to fall for this prince just because of some arrangements made a long time ago, but if getting to know him will help us get out of here faster, then I can be a team player."

"For the record, it's not your questions that worry me." He smiled, but I saw the pain in his eyes and tension still in his face. I sensed there was more he wanted to say but didn't.

"Good to know. So, when will I meet this prince?"

"I'm not sure," Roah said, his eyes flashing an emotion I didn't understand. "We won't know until we get there."

"Will I still get to see you?" I asked in a soft voice.

"Lotty, I will always do everything in my power to protect you," he vowed, but didn't meet my eyes. I felt the space between us return and widen as his voice took on the same formal tone he had used with Tregr. "Figuring out how to get you home safely is my greatest duty, but I have others as well - things that I must do while at the castle, so I won't always be with you. Within the castle, the prince's will is my will. Understand?"

"I'm trying to," I whispered, a familiar loneliness creeping back into my chest.

After helping me on my horse, Roah mounted his. As we rode, I felt bare without his arms around me. No matter what front I tried to put up for Roah, I wasn't ready to see this castle or meet a guy who felt he had a claim on my life.

Our guard spread out around us in the growing darkness.

The moon had just started to rise when we reached the village surrounding the castle. I was surprised to see hanging oil lamps blazing on either side of the road. Windows glowed with life, illuminating the scenes inside. We passed shops selling goods or food and houses with families engaged in their evening routines. The slight undertone of a harmony drifted from a side street as a group of musicians enjoyed the crisp night air together.

The architecture of the buildings, which were constructed of stone or wood, was hard to pinpoint. But the craftsmanship was undeniable. The design and execution showed an attention to detail I couldn't fully enjoy in the dim light.

Our road opened up to a large main square with trees, grass, and a fountain in the middle. Several roads found their origin in the square, like spokes of a wheel, making it a perfect marketplace or city center. Once we reached the fountain, Roah signaled for us to stop.

He rode over to Tregr and gave him instructions to stay by my side until I was safely inside the castle walls. Then without a word to me, he excused himself and continued ahead, taking half of the men with him. As he rode down one of the adjacent narrow streets without looking back, a knot formed in my stomach. Would I ever see him again?

By the time we arrived at the castle, I was so tired and sore all I wanted was sleep. After I nearly collapsed from exhaustion while dismounting, Tregr was kind enough to carry me the long way to my room. He left me in the care of two older women who, bless them, had a hot bath waiting.

When I finally slid into the silky sheets of my bed, I closed my eyes, wishing I had never left Virginia. I wished I had never seen the suffering or bloodshed that still haunted me. I wished I could go back in time to my last day on the farm and keep Roah from checking the barn. Between that thought and musing over my own ignorance, my eyes popped open.

The fear behind all of the rationalizations my mind had spun that day was blatantly clear and shouted for acknowledgment. There *was* no going back. No returning to who I had been before all of this. Whether I'd wanted it or not, a chapter of my life had closed.

My childhood had ended, and there was no going back. Ever.

As this realization sunk in, fresh tears burned in my eyes. It felt like a part of me had died, and I wept silent tears for the innocence that had been handled so roughly and ended so cruelly. I let the tears come, let my heart grieve for the death of that part of my life. There were no giant desperate sobs, just the ache of acceptance as I gave into the exhaustion and loneliness, and finally fell asleep.

17

The sunlight streaming into the room finally roused me from the exhaustion of the last few days. I brought my hand to my neck, feeling the two chains that hung there. One was thin and delicate, the other thick and simple, but each held priceless treasures. Too emotionally drained to face another day, I stayed hidden in the nest of fluffy white pillows and sheets. But I couldn't hide from what I knew. There was no returning to my life before.

Sure, I could leave this strange world and never return. But I could never erase what had happened, never free myself from the images seared into my memory or how they had changed me. I rolled over, burying myself deeper into the soft sheets, hiding from the piercing rays of light, hoping for sleep to rescue me. It didn't.

A soft knock sounded across the room. I startled, my heart leaping into my throat as I stifled a squeak. Was it him? Before I could answer, a timid feminine voice spoke through the door.

"Breakfast for you, my lady?"

I wanted to pretend to still be sleeping, but my stomach grumbled, and I gave in. I couldn't hide forever.

"Yes, thank you," I called from my hiding spot under the sheets.

I heard her enter and set down a tray. A few footsteps later, the door closed again. I sighed. *Time to face this world.* I threw the covers off all at once, my eyes blinking at the sudden brightness of the room. I stretched my sore muscles, and what I saw nearly took my breath away. The windows were astonishing pieces of art. Different sizes of clear cut glass had been arranged to create pictures of flowering vines winding through lattice of melted lead. The sunlight illuminated the intricate designs, somehow making the room seem larger and more spacious.

Worn wooden benches and colorful upholstered chairs lined with velvety pillows created a small sitting area in front of the largest stone fireplace I'd ever seen. It could have been its own room. The fire in it blazed behind the iron grates holding the large logs. I wondered how many men it took to rekindle its flame.

But no matter how lavish or ostentatious the room was, what captured my attention most were the paintings. There weren't that many—four to be exact—but they were some of the most detailed, most lifelike works of art I'd ever seen. That in itself would've been enough to impress me, but each canvas was taller than I was.

I kicked myself for hiding under the covers when I could've been studying masterpieces. I grabbed a handful of grapes and, in nothing more than my long nightgown, pulled up a chair by the nearest one and leaned in. The brushstrokes were poetry.

As soon as my grapes were gone, I returned for the whole tray. Abandoning the chair, I opted for sitting on the soft rug with my food and studying the detail of a castle in one of the canvases. I was captivated by the colors as they combined and divided, highlighting turrets and shading rough-cut stone. How had they gotten so much detail into every inch?

Suddenly, a thought hit me. I swallowed hard. Had the prince done this? Was putting me in this room his idea? I was sure Roah had sent reports back to him but had assumed they were only about my safety. Had Roah shared personal details about what I liked? I didn't want to believe he would have, but what if those were his orders?

I looked at the roses, my favorite flowers, the center point of every fresh cut arrangement in the room, and suddenly the whole set up wasn't so innocent. My gut told me this prince still intended to collect on our parents' contract. The more I looked around the room, the more it felt like a pretty jail cell.

What if I said, *Thanks for the offer but I'm already in love with your army captain?* Would Roah still make sure I got home, or would that be it? If the prince couldn't be talked out of this marriage nonsense, would Roah choose me over his world? Would it come to that? Could I ask that of him?

My head fell into my hands. What was I going to do?

Another gentle knock sounded at the door. There was only one person I wanted to see. "Yes," I answered, getting up off the floor. The two ladies from the previous night entered, and my hope went out the door as they closed it behind them.

They curtsied. "Sorry to interrupt you, my lady, but you are wanted in the Chamber Room."

"Oh," I said.

I had no idea what that meant, but it sounded important. I was obliging as they played dress up with me. Nevertheless, as they laced up the back of the bodice, I longed for my favorite jeans and t-shirt.

Over the flesh-colored shift, they had fitted yet another full corset. I had originally thought the look they were going for was simple. But my clothing was like nothing I'd ever seen.

The fabric was a nearly transparent ivory that matched my skin tone. Embroidered over the entire outer gown were the most exquisite red lines, like the iron patterns in a fancy gate. They crossed over each other to form windows and trellises on the dress that gave me a statuesque appearance. It naturally drew the eye without being too busy, and it was light on my skin. I would have expected that kind of full coverage to look matronly and feel heavy. Instead, it was cut to flatter all my curves; the transparency of the fabric between the red lines revealed my skin as if behind a smoky filter on a camera.

The skirt didn't come up in the front as the others had; rather the ruffles and overdress parted at midthigh when I took a step, briefly revealing a leg and the new knee-high black boots that laced up in the back. I examined the boot in the mirror, fascinated by the shiny metal heel and embroidered leather that made my legs look so long. If only I could take the clothes back home with me...

The two women continued fussing over me, pinning and twisting my hair into an intricate design of braids on top of my head until they were satisfied with every detail. They then decorated the up-do with pins topped with red stones. Just when I thought they were finished, they produced makeup and began to powder and paint. It took all of my self-control to hold still and let them do their job. When they had at last finished, they brought one of the full-length, gilded mirrors over to me. I hardly recognized the girl who gaped back at me through the glass.

After informing me that someone would arrive shortly to escort me through the castle, the women excused themselves. I stood in front of the mirror and examined my image. For the first time, I couldn't rationalize away the resemblance between my mother and myself. When I couldn't shake the heaviness settling on me as I considered who I might be, I abandoned the mirror altogether.

My anxiety grew as I paced the length of the long room, waiting.

I leaned against the windowpane and looked out, tracing the cool lead designs with my fingers. The castle was situated on a tall hill surrounded by acres of manicured gardens, orchards, and a small wilderness. Just outside the castle walls sat a village with narrow streets and thatched roofed buildings. As I watched the villagers going about their daily activities, I couldn't help but wonder what it would've been like to grow up in such a place—to grow up a princess, to know there was a prince waiting for me.

The knock on the door made me jump.

"Come in." I took a deep breath, trying not to fidget, but my dress suddenly felt too tight. What if I was about to meet the prince, or maybe even the king and queen? I started to hyperventilate a little bit while still trying to calm myself but was unable to squeeze a deep breath into my corset.

The door opened slowly and a man in uniform stepped inside. He had closed it behind him and turned to me before I recognized him.

Roah wore black breaches under boots polished to a high gloss. A white collared shirt was barely visible between the thick blue stripes of his vest and the matching silk kerchief at his neck. Open over the vest was a stiff high-collared jacket that was so blue it was almost black. Long tails hung to the backs of his knees, making him appear taller. Thick silver cords looped in a scrolling pattern, decorating the lapels, cuffs, collar, and empty buttonholes on either side. The final touch was the sword belted to his waist.

"Holy crap!"

"Well." He blushed, raking hands through his long hair while looking down at himself uncomfortably. "Good afternoon to you, too."

"Sorry, you just didn't look like yourself is all," I stammered as I admired his transformation. I fought to keep the flush out of my cheeks, suddenly aware of how different I also looked. "Afternoon? Is it really that late?"

"Yes, but you earned the rest," he said kindly, stepping toward me. "The servants have outdone themselves. That dress truly suits you."

"Thanks," I replied dumbly as he closed the distance, his eyes drinking me in.

The closer he got, the greater the pull I felt to be in his arms, to reach out and lose myself in the fire I saw in his gaze. But he stopped just out of reach, and my doubts crept back in, eroding the rush of seeing him again.

"I think it's best if we...while we're here..." He fumbled for the words, holding his arms behind him as he spoke. His tone fluctuated from formal to familiar and back again as if unsure of how to address me. His discomfort only added to my own. "We need to be careful about how people perceive us—our relationship. I think it's best if we don't give the wrong impression, to anyone."

My heart dropped to my feet. "Don't you think it's a little late for that? I mean, what about Daggon and Tregr? They already know. Everybody yesterday, don't forget them. I would assume that Ayla does, too."

"That's different. They're friends. I trust them. The people you're about to meet will presume things that will hinder our purpose here. They know only what they've heard. They are not going to understand the world you grew up in, and under no circumstances are you to speak of it. That world is a heavily guarded secret here, known to only a few.

"To have a chance at getting you back to Virginia, we have to honor who they expect you to be: the princess, not the high school girl who loves soccer and painting, or is fond of the knight next door." The corner of his mouth curled into a half smile as he added that last part. Then he grew serious again. "We can't, for your sake, change their perception of you. Not yet. That's why I think it's best for us to keep things...private. Am I clear?"

"Yeah, sure. Crystal. Follow your lead and try not to throw up on the first person I see wearing a crown. What could go wrong?" I asked, my voice light but frustrated.

Something in his face changed after I'd spoken. There was a glimmer, anticipation of something beneath the surface that kept him on edge.

"You are an incredible woman, Adelaide," he said, his voice velvety soft as his posture softened for the first time since entering the room. "They're going to love you."

"That's what I'm afraid of," I whispered sadly. He didn't comment, and that stream between us got a little wider and a little deeper. A shiver of loneliness stole through me, and I folded my arms across my body, rubbing them to get the warmth back.

"So," he started, holding out a hand, "are you ready?"

"I don't know if I'll ever be ready." I sighed, not moving to accept his hand. "But if we must, we must."

"Don't be nervous. You'll do just fine."

"What gives you the idea I'm nervous?"

He smiled as he pried my hands away from my sleeves. He forced them open and placed his hands in mine. I was surprised to feel they were just as sweaty.

"Lucky guess," he grinned crookedly.

I took several calming breaths as he dropped my hands and offered his elbow as an escort.

"Now, let's stop stalling and do this. Okay?"

"Okay," I muttered unenthusiastically. "Let's."

18

Before we left the room, he had insisted on two changes to my outfit. First, he pulled my mother's necklace out of its hiding place, making sure the medallion lay in clear view as it hung past my low-cut neckline. Second, he produced a sleeveless, black shrug that buckled under my arms and had a large deep hood. Walking around like this was sure to attract attention, but I did feel safer observing everything from under the concealing fabric.

My heart pounded as Roah escorted me down a grand corridor lined with gorgeous stone mosaics. In some places, large elaborate tapestries or paintings covered the stonework, their images inspired by the lands and people surrounding this incredible fortress. I wanted to stay and study the paintings, to ask questions about them, but the halls were so quiet I didn't dare speak.

It was still hard to believe I was in a castle, a real castle—Tyler would give anything for an opportunity like this. The majestic structure commanded as much respect as those governing from within. As I moved through the halls, I could almost feel the mantel that the king and queen carried weighing on me. Unexpectedly, the faces of those at the gates of Icel flashed in my mind. *From within walls like these*, I thought, *are made the choices that bring either pain or prosperity to so many lives.*

Word of my arrival must have traveled fast. Everyone we passed stopped what they were doing to stare and bow slightly to us. It was kind of strange. My face was hidden; they weren't supposed to know who I was. I glanced at Roah. Either he didn't notice or didn't want to say anything about it there.

We walked a football field's worth of halls and corridors. After the first few turns, I was hopelessly lost. How did anyone find where they were going without a map?

As we approached the foot of a short set of stairs, we slowed our pace. At the top stood two massive and ornately carved doors. Four armed guards in full ceremonial armor lined the steps leading up to the room. They eyed us impassively. I shrank into the shadows of my hood.

There was no turning back now. I gulped and tightened my grip on Roah's arm.

Just as I thought we were going to collide with the solid wood, the doors swung open.

The room on the other side was long and intimidating, with sets of guards standing beneath massive arched windows. Large candelabras hung from the thick wood beams that supported the ceiling. At least two dozen important-looking people moved around large round tables. The room hummed with discussions and arguments as each group leaned over maps and scrolls of various sizes.

Once again, I saw several ethnicities and centuries mashed together in a collage of fashion and color that ignored convention. Victorian top hats, medieval woven hair nets, and long fingerless gloves were as plentiful as bow ties, high collars, and long coats. I saw the flash of precious metals and noted that while each person was uniquely accessorized, none was without fine jewelry of some kind.

No one appeared the least bit interested in our arrival.

A few steps in, Roah paused, bowing slightly to the figures at the other end. I followed his lead, trying to hide my nervous trembling. When I straightened again, I got a better look at where he had directed

Blood of Moldara 143

our gesture. At the back of the room sat the only square table. It was surrounded by beautifully crafted chairs, two of them much taller and more finely gilded than the others. They were occupied.

"I'm scared," I whispered.

He leaned over, talking just loud enough for me to hear. "We are among allies, I promise. Just remember what we discussed, and you'll do fine."

"I'm trusting you with this. You know that, right?"

He flinched, not meeting my eyes.

"Wait for me here. Speak to no one," he instructed in a low voice. He removed my hand from the crook of his elbow and crossed the room.

I watched him go, feeling like I had been set adrift in an endless ocean. My nerves tossed about from the peaks of optimism to the depths of fear. I held my hands behind my back, massaging one and then the other, grateful for the concealment of my hood.

At the far side of the room, Roah greeted the distinguished figures I assumed were the king and queen. They spoke, but I couldn't hear anything across the din. In truth, I was more than a little awestruck.

The king was no exception to the meshing of fashions. He wore a shirt the color of dark wine, its gold trim enhanced by the golden neck scarf knotted at his throat and tucked into the short collar. The lines of the shirt were impeccably tailored, fitting closely to an impressive physique for someone in his mid-fifties. Over the shirt he wore a wide, leather belt, whose gold buckle and matching sword were just short of being an art piece.

Unlike most of the men I saw, the king's pants were not fitted, nor did he tuck his boots into them. Instead, they looked like a pair of black business slacks. Their hems brushed the ground as he moved, revealing the toe of dark boots with metal soles. The overall look intensified the contrast between his light brown skin and salt and pepper hair.

The queen's outfit was no less elegant, the green of her gown reminding me of new grass in spring. The green silk gathered at her throat disappeared into the perfect ivory lace bodice that started at her chest and hugged the curves of her body to just below her hips. Her tailored, nearly translucent green sleeves flowed beneath the matching ivory lace at her wrists. When she turned to the side, I saw the long skirt's extra fabric was gathered into several layers of green and cream, swirling at the base of the bodice in the back like a bustle on a wedding gown. The whole look complimented her light complexion and strawberry blond hair, giving her a mature yet whimsical appearance.

The other two things that set them apart were their simple, open cut capes and the gold bands I assumed were crowns. Both crowns and capes had been made to match exactly, but it was the simplicity of the capes that drew the eye. Running the length of both lapels and disappearing around the collar were embroidered symbols I assumed conveyed their authority and lineage. Some of them I thought I'd recognized from drawings in my grandpa's journals, but from this distance I couldn't be sure.

The king waved a steward over to consult with Roah, and then an announcement was made. Lunch was ready. Quills and books were set aside as the room cleared out, the steward ushering all but a handful of guards through another large door. I continued standing there, unsure of what was expected of me.

Guards now blocked every door. A shiver moved down my spine as I realized I alone was still standing at the center of the room, the only one besides Roah and royalty. I tried not to look at them, dropping my eyes to the table nearest me instead. Open books, similar to those I'd found in my grandfather's study, spread out over the table. Some were in English, some in that strange trick font Roah had translated for me.

A deep voice boomed from the other side of the room. "But you have returned!"

I startled, looking up. It was the first of their conversation I'd understood. I couldn't tell if the sudden clarity was a result of the cleared room or raised voices.

"I have done what is necessary, my lord. There is still much—" at that moment Roah's voice was not as businesslike as I'd expected for a captain of the guard addressing his king.

"Yes, yes," the King cut him off. "There is still so much to prepare. We can speak of that later." He seemed pleased.

"Yes, my lord."

"We are alone now, as you insisted. So, are you going to introduce the girl or should we call the steward back to do it for you?" he asked, his tone impatient but not unkind. The air of mutual respect in their conversation was palpable, and I got the impression that the king and the captain of the guard were close.

Roah's eyes met mine, his expression steady. He waved me over, but despite my efforts, I found my feet cemented to the floor.

"Well, child, don't keep us waiting," the queen commanded.

With a great deal of effort, I shuffled slowly across the rich carpets, unsure of my place in the room, small and insignificant compared to the displays of those around me. There were guards. There were stewards. There were soldiers, and Roah was their Captain. What was I doing there? Panic bubbled up, and I wanted to run.

As I crossed the room, I kept my eyes fused on Roah. An image resurfaced in my mind; it was of the foreign exchange student I'd thought of on the ride here. I remembered her at school, her head held high as she asked directions in broken English. *I am now a foreign exchange student.*

"Come now, we don't bite," the king directed kindly, gesturing to my hood this time.

I hesitated. I had never before met someone so important. I didn't want my face to betray my terror, so I put on my best poker face and raised my trembling hands. Pulling the hood back, my face emerged out of the shadows and into the sunlight.

Everyone except Roah gasped. I looked to him for assurance. He only nodded, his expression unreadable.

"I can't believe it," the queen said.

"Impossible," the king murmured.

"But she looks just like her." The queen met my eye, and her warmth broke through my fear. I relaxed and forced a little smile.

"Turn your head child. Is that a scar?"

I did as she asked, pulling the collar down to reveal the length of the gnarled skin left from the fire.

They both gasped again, almost troubled by the marked skin. Embarrassed, I repositioned my collar and dropped my hands back to my side.

"Where did you say you found her?" The king turned to Roah, reluctantly taking his eyes off me.

Roah never said a word, but something in his expression gave the king his answer.

"Ah, yes," he responded, nodding knowingly as he glanced at the guards out of the corner of his eye.

"Welcome to Niniever, my dear," the queen began warmly, looking me in the eyes, studying my face as she spoke. "I was grateful to hear you arrived without permanent harm. I hope you have recovered somewhat from your journeys, though I can only imagine what you have endured these past few days. As long as you are with us, we want to make you as comfortable as possible. Please, if there is anything you are in need of, don't hesitate to ask."

"Thank you," I managed, unsure of how to address them. Was I supposed to end with *Your Majesty* or *Your Eminence*? I had no idea.

"I am King Zarian," the man said, gesturing to himself before he introduced the woman next to him with a slight bow of deference, "and this is Queen Tatira. Will you honor us with your name, child?"

I didn't know how to answer. I had been warned not to tell anyone my full name. I flashed an uncertain look at Roah. For the first time since we'd entered the room, his eyes softened. He understood my question and nodded his encouragement.

"My name is Adelaide, but I go by Lotty, sir."

"Adelaide." The king repeated my name with deep reverence, ignoring the nickname. "Are you aware of who your parents were?"

"Yes, sir, I think I am."

"Well, Adelaide," the king broke from his thoughts. "It is quite obvious by your looks that you are indeed the daughter of Norwyck and Mira. If anyone dared dispute that—which I dare say would be futile—the necklace hanging around your neck is all the additional proof needed. It's a miracle you are still in possession of such a significant treasure. No doubt Elion guarded that just as vigilantly as he did you. This is good news. Very good indeed."

Roah had been expressionless through the king's interrogation, remaining oddly still as well. I got the impression they found him unusually tense. Probably something political I wouldn't understand. Did it have something to do with this elusive prince?

"You have just changed the query, my young lady," the king continued. "We have been strategizing for years as to the best way to oust Terrshon. I think you have given us the greatest weapon. No one will be able to dispute your identity. Unfortunately, without your father's ring, it could take years before we can fully take back what was lost. Be reassured though, you have my complete backing in this pursuit. We will have Moldara as our greatest ally once more."

"Thank you." Roah bowed to the king, a hint of something in his eyes. At first, I thought the spark I saw there had to do with the ring, which was securely and secretly tucked away inside my bodice. But no, it was more than that. His eyes softened again as he caught me looking at him. A trace of a grin flashed across his lips. My heart skipped. This was going well.

The queen leaned into her husband, whispering something to him that I couldn't hear. King Zarian's expression changed as the queen finished. The corners of his mouth turned up, revealing a bright smile. His eyes glistened with pride when he spoke.

"You are right, my dear, as always. This calls for a celebration!"

"We have much to raise a glass to," Queen Tatria said. "Adelaide has returned home at last, and our son—"

"NO!"

Roah's yell was so unexpected that even the guards at the doors jumped. Their armor sounded like someone walking through piles of scrap metal and wind chimes. Roah's expression was horrified. He took a knee at their feet, speaking just loud enough for them to hear him. I had to strain to make out what he was saying.

"It's too dangerous. A celebration will forfeit any chance we have of keeping her hidden. If she's discovered, they'll stop at nothing to kidnap her or worse. We have risked too much bringing her this far. Please," he paused, his eyes insistent. "Please, you must see this."

Placing his hand on Roah's shoulder, King Zarian looked into his eyes. He concentrated on reading Roah's expression. A few moments passed before he finally nodded in understanding.

"All right," the king agreed, and Roah visibly relaxed. "I see she has suffered enough. I would hate to be the cause of any more distress. There will be no official celebration just yet, but that doesn't mean we have to forgo such a momentous occasion. Tonight, dinner will be accompanied by music and dancing, as well as fine delicacies. We will make it a masque so she can attend incognito. No one will know that she is here, except for a select few. Will that be enough caution for you?"

I got the distinct impression the king wasn't looking for approval. He was merely informing him of his plans.

Roah nodded once but still wasn't pleased.

I stood there for some time as the conversation continued around me. King Zarian and Queen Tatira discussed how my return would affect the surrounding lands and the people in them, how my life signified a new era. One filled with peace and prosperity, one where their younger son would be leading alongside me.

As I heard this, my eyes instantly shifted to Roah. He had been so poised, so guarded, but his expression had twisted as the conversation changed to my future. Out of concern for me, probably. As I listened to them describe me as the savior of Moldara and them as her allies, I felt all of my choices, the plans I had for my future, gradually being dragged back to the cell in Terrshon's dungeon. I fought down the panic-laced memories of that horrifying place. Once was enough for me.

"Excuse me. I'm not staying."

Everyone turned to look at me; it felt as though all the air had been sucked out of the room. I swallowed hard and continued.

"I appreciate everything you have done for me, but with all due respect, I don't belong here. I have no memory of this place, and a whole life in another world. That is my home now. I just want to go back as soon as possible, so I don't mess anything else up for you here."

I watched their faces, trying to see how they were taking my declaration. I hated to disappoint them, but I couldn't sit there listening to all their impossible plans and not say anything. I glanced at Roah and saw the disappointment before he could hide it. I felt guilty, but I knew it was for the best.

"Now see here, child. Yours is not the only life tied to this issue. You can't just decide something like that on your own," the king said firmly. He looked pointedly at Roah as he spoke.

"Roah, your guard captain, had nothing to do with this decision," I countered with no small amount of irritation. Both the king and queen turned to him with questioning expressions.

For the first time since we had entered the room, he refused to meet their gaze. How dare they look at him like he had somehow failed? I felt protective, irritated at their reactions to my choice. My chin came up as I continued boldly.

"Roah has done more for me than any other living person, save my grandfather, Elion. I owe him my life, but I am not a piece of property here to be used or married or killed for someone else's war. Perhaps if everyone weren't so busy looking for the lost princess, they could be putting an end to Terrshon's barbaric cruelty without a mascot to hide behind!

"And before you say anything, yes, I know about the prince. In addition to every other reason to say no, I am in love with someone else. I'm sorry. I'm sure he is nice, but it's not going to happen—" When I saw the flash of darkness on Roah's face, I stopped speaking. I hadn't meant to say all of that. It had all erupted in a fiery rush. What had I done?

19

"Well," said the queen after a moment of silence. "You don't just look like your mother, dearest Adelaide, you sound like her, too."

The queen's words had been spoken in admiration, but I expected to be clamped in irons and hauled off to the dungeon. Instead, she looked at me with compassion in her eyes.

"It would seem there is much about our plans that must be changed, My King." Queen Tatira placed a hand on the king's sleeve. "It appears that her choice has not been factored into the future that was arranged for her. Our apologies, your highness. We merely thought to fulfill your parents' wishes for you and your inheritance. Of course, you are not a slave to our desires. Though, if yours should change, please let us be the first to know."

She then turned to the king and Roah. "We should speak of this privately. Bring only those you trust. I want contingency plans by sunset. We must know our options."

I swallowed hard. She didn't sound mad, but neither was she as cheerful as before my little announcement. A pleasant resignation filled her face as she waited in silence for the men to agree with her. Both finally nodded, and I let out a pent-up breath.

After a few more whispered exchanges, we were dismissed.

Roah replaced my hood and accompanied me in silence down the cold stone hall. He kept his head held at just the right angle—an angle where I couldn't see his face through his thick curtain of hair, my only way to gauge how he truly felt. My curiosity burned, but the way he carried himself kept me from asking.

He returned me to my room but did not stop at the door. Instead, he guided me out onto the room's expansive balcony. To my surprise, I found that in our absence, dozens of potted plants had been brought out and arranged to create a small private garden.

Butterflies floated between roses, daisies, lavender, jasmine, daylilies, and wisteria. Everywhere I turned, I was met by the most intoxicating perfume. I wanted to lie right in the middle of them and let the sun bake me as I drank in the aroma.

"It's remarkable," I said, breaking the silence that had hung between us.

"I thought you'd like it." The tension remained in his voice, and though he watched me, he would not meet my gaze.

"But where did they all come from?"

"These are from the private garden of the royal family." He pulled back my hood and stepped away briskly. "The prince thought this would be a welcome addition to your room while you waited to dress for dinner."

"I don't know what to say," I fumbled. Knowing the giver, I had to stop myself from pulling the hood back over my head. The whole time my mind taunted, *Your betrothed has sent you an entire garden of flowers! Not a dozen roses, hundreds of them!* "Please thank him for me."

He led me to a small table that had been set up with a picnic. My heart fluttered with sudden panic until I noticed there was only one place setting. I couldn't hide my sigh of relief.

"I saw the table, and for a second, I thought you were going to leave me to have a picnic with this prince!" I laughed at myself nervously. "Oh, my heart nearly leaped out of my chest! Promise you will give me plenty of warning before I face off with that part of this nightmare?"

Blood of Moldara 153

The look on Roah's face killed my smile.

"Roah, I didn't mean—I'm sorry, I—. That was rude. I apologize," I sputtered, guilt at my ungrateful words consuming me. He turned away, leaning against the rail as he watched the streets beyond the courtyard.

"I hadn't realized you were still so set on going home that you'd announce it like that. After seeing the exiled ones at Icel, I thought your feelings about your impact here were shifting." He kept his eyes on the village below as he spoke.

"Of course I'd like to do something to help. Wouldn't anyone? But they were calling for my mother; they need her, not some high school girl from Virginia who keeps putting everyone in danger. I'm just not the answer."

When he finally turned and answered, it was as if from a great distance, the pain in his eyes cut me to my core.

"I know it feels like everyone is planning your life without your consent. You must forgive them. Sometimes people of authority forget their place. You've been an abstract concept for so long that when your presence is a reality, it's hard for them to imagine anything other than their planned outcomes."

I wanted to repair the damage I'd done but didn't know how.

"I have much to attend to if we are to return you to Virginia," he stated stiffly.

"I understand." And I did. He was excusing himself, leaving me alone again.

"Here," he added almost as an afterthought. Striding quickly over to the table, he lifted the silver lid off the tray. The smell of basil, tomatoes, and freshly baked bread made my mouth water. "The prince wanted to make you feel at home, or at least give you a little taste of home, so I had his servants make this for you. I hope it's to your liking."

"Pizza?" I gasped, astonished. It was a perfectly baked, hand-tossed margarita pizza.

"Well, sort of. The cooks had to make a few adjustments," he admitted, "but I think it turned out rather well."

"Thank you, Roah. This is perfect." I took a deep breath, filling my lungs with its aroma.

"Under that," he pointed to an identical silver lid, only smaller, "is dessert."

I reached for it, wanting to see what goodies were concealed there. Roah stopped me.

"No," he said sharply, grabbing my hand. "Not until you've finished your pizza."

I watched him timidly as he stood there, holding my hand. His fingers glided over mine until he seemed lost in the creases of my skin. I flushed with desire as his other hand joined the first, his fingertips studying, memorizing every detail. I saw the longing in his eyes and knew it was in mine, as well. He looked as torn as I felt, although he still refused to meet my eyes.

"Roah," I breathed, afraid to break the spell.

"I have to go," he whispered before I could finish. As I'd feared, his hands released mine, disappearing behind his back as he resumed his formal posture.

"Will I see you tonight, at dinner?" I asked just as quietly, dreading his answer.

"I'm not sure," he admitted hesitantly.

"He's going to be there, isn't he? This prince of yours?"

"Most likely," Roah replied in a cool tone. My heart sank. "He's been trying to get here as quickly as he can to meet you. Last I heard, if all went well, he would be here for dinner, or at the very least, by breakfast tomorrow."

Great, I thought. *Another opportunity to offend people I should thank, and this time I will even have an audience!* I threw myself in the little chair by the table with an angry huff, wishing I could crawl under it and hide.

"Are you at least going to be there?"

"I'm sorry, Lotty, but Daggon is due back any moment with the information I need to begin our preparations. That mission takes priority." I could tell his answer made him uncomfortable. "If I don't get to see you at dinner, I will do my best to check on you before you retire for the evening."

I nodded. He hesitated for another moment before bowing, the way he had once from across the schoolyard. Then he turned and disappeared through the tall wooden doors.

I wanted to run after him, to shake him until he told me what had made him grow more distant. Instead, I sat there looking at the rows of flowers and picked at the pizza.

As I chewed on the crust, the faces of those in the crowd saying my mother's name haunted me again. They saw something in me that I couldn't see myself. Or maybe I could; I was just too scared to admit it. Because the more I immersed myself in this world, the more it took root. The mantle I'd felt on the way to the Chamber Room was there again in my mind, shifting, changing after hearing how my return would, somehow, bring a new era to this land.

I threw the rest of my uneaten crust on the platter, furious I was getting sucked in; that I was letting these people get under my skin and tell me who I was going to be. I was so mad that I'd almost forgotten the dessert Roah had prepared. Anxious for something else to occupy my thoughts, I slowly lifted the shiny lid.

There, sitting on the silver platter, was the pastry I had loved as a kid. I decided that since Roah had given the instructions to the kitchen, my meal was really from him. That way I could enjoy the sweet icing that covered the heart-shaped dessert. I dipped my finger in the gooey frosting and savored its sweetness.

When I went back for more, I noticed a small piece of paper balanced on the far edge of the plate. My name had been written in small elegant script; it was Roah's writing. I opened it slowly and read its two messages written in the trick font he'd taught me.

*D*earest Adelaide,
     The prince you will meet tonight has waited his whole life for this chance with you. He is a good and worthy man, with a heart that is warm and yours for the taking. Please be kind to him.

No matter where your heart takes you, mine is already bound to

yours unconditionally. I am, and always will be, the servant of your happiness.
   – Roah

20

I tucked Roah's note into the bodice of my evening gown next to the ring and my mother's necklace. I didn't need to read it again; I knew his words by heart. And it had taken all of my self-control not to tear it to shreds.

How dare he offer me up to this prince? Had all of his affection been an act, a ruse to get me to trust him, to follow him here?

I had spent the rest of the afternoon pacing and rereading his words. The only thing that gave me the tiniest sliver of hope was how he'd ended the note. *No matter where your heart takes you, mine is already bound to yours unconditionally.*

I had considered tearing away the first half of the note, but in the end, I had not been able to bring myself to destroy a letter from his hand. No one I'd ever cared for—or dated—had come close to writing something so personal for me. I told myself that this was his job, to tell me to give this prince a chance, to be nice, so I tucked it into the front of my dress and waited anxiously.

There was a heavy knock on the door.

"Just a minute," I called, my voice wavering, my palms starting to sweat. It was time, but I wasn't ready yet.

I paused for one last gaze at my reflection.

Hours ago, the same two servants had returned and begun the elaborate task of assembling my ball gown. They'd started with a lightweight black bodice over my silk shift, followed by the petticoats. Inky black ruffles more than two inches long were layered one above the other, halfway up the slip. Then they'd revealed the dress, and I couldn't help a smile.

A deep blue gossamer fabric, nearly transparent when held to the light, had been gathered into row upon row of tight, short ruffles, stacked one above the other, the entire length of the huge skirt. Laid over the black petticoat, the layers of blue became ethereal, fading and deepening the color according to the light.

Next, they'd added a deep blue leather jacket, which covered me from hip to shoulder. It tied in the back like a second bodice and had capped sleeves. The stiff square collar stood straight up like the neck of a vase, revealing the bodice beneath and exposing my throat as if it were an ivory stem. Three large silver clasps held the bottom closed across my abdomen.

Just when I'd thought for sure they were done, they brought in a small trunk full of accessories. Next thing I knew, long black fingerless gloves with silver threads covered my arms from palm to mid-bicep, concealing my scar on my right arm. Generous helpings of silver rings encircled my fingers, with coordinating bracelets on each wrist, over the gloves. A wide pearl and sapphire choker went around my throat and matching chandelier earrings hanging nearly to my shoulder.

My hair had been pulled up into an artful tangle of braids and ringlets. There was a youthful, wild control to the way the two women had woven the different sizes of braids among the curls, pinning them up with tiny diamond-encrusted combs.

To finish off the ensemble, I had been given a stunning mask.

It was made of delicate black leather, overlaid with scrolled silver, sapphires, and pearls. All of it had been delicately worked to give the impression of a magnificent butterfly with open wings. When I placed it on my face, the wing tips began an inch above my hairline and extended down just past my jaw, perfectly framing my eyes and setting off the rose color of my lips. No one would be able to recognize me.

Blood of Moldara 159

The knock sounded again, this time louder. My stomach dropped.

"Coming!" I yelled over my shoulder. Then I turned back to my reflection. "This is completely insane," I hissed, tying on the mask how they'd shown me. I tried to take deep calming breaths, but the corset prevented it. I steeled my nerves as I reached for the door.

When I opened it, three armed men met me, Tregr among them. He bowed when we made eye contact, and the other men did the same. I let out a tiny sigh of relief as Tregr's eyes met mine. At least I still had the walk to the masquerade to prepare my nerves for meeting this prince.

"Good evening, my lady," Tregr began. I stopped him before he could continue.

"Please, not you, too."

He just smiled. "As you wish, my lady." Then he leaned in and whispered only loud enough for me to hear. "In private I can accommodate you, but in public it's not possible." He straightened, giving me a conspiratorial wink.

"Do you like it?" I gestured to the butterfly mask. "They made it to match the one in my stomach. Appropriate don't you think?"

"From what I've seen of these parties, you will blend in perfectly, if that's what you're worried about," he offered, unsure of what was the right thing to say to an agitated girl in a ball gown.

"This is blending in?!" I hissed through gritted teeth. "I have never seen a dress this grand! Or complicated! How is this hiding? How will I not be a beacon?"

"As the prince's guest at a masque, you were dressed to match him," Tregr explained with a casual shrug, "so you won't stand out more than any other couple there."

"I MATCH HIM?" I squealed in a high-pitched whisper, my panic giving way to anger. "A couple? What other surprises aren't you telling me?"

"You need to calm yourself." He looked nervously up and down the halls as he spoke. "There is more, but I can't disclose anything in present company."

"Get in here!" I snapped, stepping back and waving him in. I caught the guards' wary expressions as they looked away from me, and I couldn't help my own glare. Once the door was closed again, I wheeled on Tregr. "Spill it. Now!"

"Lotty," Tregr pleaded, his hands up in surrender as he began. "The first thing you have to know is that Roah saw to every precaution to keep your true identity secret tonight. I am your escort to and from the party, and while you're there, you'll be introduced under an alias."

"I don't know if this is a good idea." I leaned against a high-backed chair, gripping it for strength.

"Then perhaps the other thing I brought with me, the reason I wished to speak to you privately, will help your nerves." He slid his hand into the top of his outer tunic and pulled out a folded piece of parchment. "I've been guarding it until the right time presented itself. It's from your prince. You should've been given it a long time ago. Perhaps this whole mess could have been softened if you knew what awaited you. I believe he would want you to have it now."

I hesitated before taking the sealed paper. The letter looked old and worn, as Elion's had. "Is there no way for me to stall him, to make him wait until I'm ready?" I asked urgently, hoping he could somehow get me out of tonight.

"He's been waiting for this for so long," Tregr admitted gently. "I think, in this case, it will go easier for both of you if you just rip the bandage off as quickly as possible. Get all the secrets out on the table so we can get back to the business of dealing with Terrshon."

My stomach knotted just knowing how close the prince was. Even though I'd been adamantly clear about going home, I had no idea if my words had reached him. I stared blankly at the letter in my hand.

"I'll give you some privacy to read it. I'll be just outside when you're finished." Tregr stepped back through the door and closed it behind him.

I took the mask off as I looked at the letter in my hand. Why did it always come down to paper and pen? Suddenly, I missed the simplicity of texting.

Not wanting to prolong my dread, I broke the wax and started to read.

My Darling Princess,

How I have awaited the day where we would finally meet, and I would be able to make all of your dreams a reality. I, my dear princess, am the key to all that you hold dear. I am the salvation for which you have been praying. I will bring to you all that you desire, and make right what has been wrongfully stolen from you.

I know your life must be filled with despair and discomfort because of the losses you have suffered, and the hardships you've faced, but rest assured that all will soon be righted. I will not rest until all that you have lost has been restored to you.

Fear not, my sweet lady. I have prepared long and hard for any battle that may arise, or any struggle that might face us as we fight for your precious Moldara together. We will not stop until it is ours once more.

As for us, my darling princess, I know I will be able to make you happy. I am sure that we will be able to find comfort and strength in each other's embrace as we rule together, not only over our kingdom but also over our posterity. For these are my greatest desires for us, and I'm sure it is for you, as well.

Until we are able to fulfill these words, Princess Adelaide, I am your most devoted servant

– Prince Zarian

Wow! What a delusional ass! I reread it twice to be sure my eyes hadn't played tricks on me. I felt my blood starting to boil as my eye scanned the paper again. When Roah had described the prince, he'd forgotten to mention one thing: how narcissistic and arrogant he was. This prince was a cocky, hotheaded teenage boy who'd never been told no.

Maybe that's just how the royals were. With no one to burst their egos, anyone might grow to be a man with those same qualities. Roah had said himself that sometimes the royals forgot their place. Well, this guy definitely had.

I crumpled the letter into a tight ball, hurling it angrily across the room.

I pulled off rings and bracelets as I paced, anxious to take some of the sparkle out of my outfit. The letter had confirmed all of my worst fears. I'd escaped one prison only to walk blindly into another. A wild plan formed in my brain, and I rushed to the door. I opened it and motioned for Tregr to enter, closing it quickly behind him.

"I need to see Roah," I demanded in a low voice. "Right now. Take me to him."

"That's not possible."

"What do you mean that's not possible?"

"He's not here," he said.

"What? Where did he go?"

"I can't tell you that."

"Tregr, I don't care what he's said; I need to see him."

"I understand, but it's impossible." Then he quickly added, "He's left the castle."

I groaned in frustration, fearing a subtle trap was already closing around me.

"Fine," I blurted out, exasperated, "but as soon as he's back, you're taking me to him. Understood?"

"Yes, my lady." It surprised me that he addressed me so formally while we were alone. Maybe I had sounded more authoritative than I'd expected. "In the meantime, I am under orders to escort you to the party."

I grabbed my mask and secured it in place, frustrated that I was going to have to deal with Prince Cocky before talking with Roah. "*Under orders*," I repeated, "Seriously?"

Tregr looked pained as he shrugged. "At least your nerves are gone."

"And if I refuse?"

"I would be forced to relay your discourtesy to your hosts, the king and queen, whom I understand you met earlier—"

Blood of Moldara 163

"Fine, never mind," I cut him off not wanting to hear any more. "Let's go."

Satisfied, he extended his arm, opening the door as he did. I took it and followed him down the cool hallway, my head held high. The other men, guards in full uniform just like Tregr, fell in step behind us.

Tregr was right—my nerves were gone, replaced by raw determination. *At least spoiled, entitled princes are good for something,* I thought.

The closer we got to the grand hall, the louder the festivities became. I took the deepest cleansing breaths I could in the tightest corset yet and repeated to myself over and over again, *I am in a real castle, dressed like a real princess and about to attend a real ball.* Thanks to that horrible letter, I was just mad enough to walk through those doors like I owned the place. *If they wanted a princess, they were going to get one!* I set my jaw and straightened my shoulders.

Just before we got to the door, Tregr took my hand, unwinding his arm from mine.

"This is as far as I go."

"You're not coming in?" I asked, my throat suddenly tight when I spoke.

"Don't worry. I'll be right behind you. Since Roah can't be here, he made me promise I wouldn't take my eyes off of you tonight. They," he pointed to the men standing at the doorway, "will announce you. The king and queen are already waiting. Remember, just do your thing." He squeezed my hand with a conspiratorial smile before stepping back.

I stopped as the doors opened, waiting for the ushers to announce me. The enormous hall stretched out in a swirl of colors, music, and mask-covered faces. Once again, I was struck by the mashing together of so many eras, as if nothing ever went out of style but was simply added to the existing motif. Tregr had been right, I wasn't dressed to stand out, but neither was I going to be invisible. Of every variety of dress I noticed, only a few had close to the fullness or length of my dress, and I got the feeling the opulence of my ball gown was a status symbol of some sort.

My conviction wavered. A thousand terrible scenarios raced through my head. *What if I tripped, or said the wrong thing, or insulted my host?* I swallowed hard and touched my mask. I reminded myself I was about to experience the ultimate Ren-fest party, and no one beyond those doors would know I didn't belong. Tyler would've been so jealous and furious with me if I didn't make the most of it.

I would curtsy, smile, be graceful, and act interested. I would be everything a princess should be. Even demanding, if it came to that. It was no different than being in character in a play or at a costume party. A ripple of excitement ran through me as I realized I wanted to do this, to see what would happen if I pretended I was Adelaide, the only daughter of Queen Mira, for a night. Perhaps this prince would listen to her for a change.

As a trumpet sounded, all eyes turned to me.

"An Honored Guest of Prince Zarian, Lady Ashara," a strong voice announced.

I stood there not sure where to go, or even if I could move at all. Everyone's gazes turned on me and low murmurs rippled throughout the room. Slowly, a figure moved through the still frozen crowd, an older man with wise eyes, wearing a simple, modest robe with simple vestments and no mask. When he reached me, he bowed.

"I'm Nachise, a Sage pledged to the service of Niniever. It truly is a pleasure, my lady."

"Thank you, Nachise. That was a beautiful title they gave me," I commented, reminding myself to play the part.

"Yes, it is," he said, an emotion I didn't understand lighting in his eyes. "I recommended it."

"What does it mean?" I asked, hoping his answer would explain his expression.

"Nothing of great importance, for now. I just thought it was appropriate for this occasion. Come, dear." He smiled and lead me through the sea of faces, most of which had returned to their entertainment of choice.

Still, I noticed we walked the length of the room under watchful eyes. Some people glanced from behind fans or under top hats, and others simply stared as they sipped bubbling drinks and nibbled from the full trays of food held by servants circulating around the room. I held my head high as I walked with the Sage, focusing on each step. Now would not be a good time to trip. I followed Nachise up a short flight of stairs to a seat at the head table, a large half circle of carved and polished wood, at which sat the king, queen, and two young men.

My heart skipped a few beats when four sets of eyes found mine.

21

Their faces were all masked. The queen and king's were identical in design, barely hiding their features beneath the jewel-encrusted design, golden vines that wound around their eyes and dripped from their temples. As their costumes also coordinated, it was easy to tell it was them behind the disguises.

Though she was sitting, it was evident that the queen's gown was exquisite. A tall stiff lace collar accentuated her long neck, the design opening just above her bodice. The lace flowed into a gold translucent fabric that cascaded down her arms, covering her purple elbow-length fingerless gloves, which showed off several lavish rings. The deep purple matched that of her simple but shapely bodice. Unlike mine, there were no visible straps or clasp that held it closed. Its only ornaments were the strings of white pearls that hung like a waterfall from the top of her bodice from one side to the other. Yards of purple fabric, with thick gold swirling designs, rippled out from her waist, gathering in several places until it spilled on the ground around her feet.

The king's long jacket, with stiff, angular lapels, was made from the same purple and gold swirling fabric. It covered a white tunic that ruffled at his neck, blossoming along the opening of his dark jacket. There were also ruffles at his wrists, the fabric nearly covering his

Blood of Moldara 167

entire hand. His jacket was held closed by a thick black belt with an intricately designed golden buckle. Several long wide strips of fabric, like coattails, flowed out from under the belt in every direction. They covered most of his tight dark pants, which tucked into his black knee-high leather boots. Polished gold buckles lined the side of the boot.

My anger still fresh, I coolly eyed the masks of the two men who sat with them. They each had short, clean-cut hair, making their masks their most prominent feature. The masks were similar to each other in that both covered them from forehead to jaw, but were open at the chin. Both were designed to look like faces, angular and slightly distorted. Hammered out of metal but made to look like stone, each was polished and finished roughly in different places. Precious stones wound through the deeper crevices of the masks, like veins of diamonds waiting to be cut out of a mountain cave.

The detail was as amazing as it was distracting, making it impossible to guess the features of the men behind them. I couldn't help but notice that one mask was gold, and one was silver. As I looked closer, I realized the one wearing the silver mask had an outfit that perfectly coordinated with mine. I could only guess he was Prince Zarian.

The king stood and the crowd quieted as he addressed them.

"Tonight, we celebrate the return of my son." The silver-masked man, sitting beside the king, stood briefly in acknowledgment.

"His service to our kingdom has kept him from our table for far too long. He returns with a guest who honors our land," the king gestured to me. Following the lead of the son, I waved. "She is here to celebrate with us this night, and we invite her to partake of all the variety that our land has to offer. We are truly fortunate to have them both with us. We invite them to rest from the trials of their journey as we shower them in our gratitude for their continued service."

With the king's announcement, the room erupted. The cheers and applause were deafening. Despite my royal façade, I blushed at the crowd's reaction, hoping there wasn't going to be any more to his speech.

"Now, let the dancing begin." With that, the music restarted in earnest, but it didn't stop the questioning glances in my direction.

"Welcome, my dear," the queen smiled through her mask as she greeted me.

"Thank you," I said, my voice gracious as I could make it. Then I leaned toward her. "I thought this was supposed to be a small dinner."

"This is," she laughed under her breath.

"Oh." I swallowed hard wondering what a large celebration looked like.

Without warning, a server set a large gold platter in front of me. He removed the cover; the aroma of roasted meats and vegetables filled the air. Queen Tatira turned her attention to the food then. Not wanting to interrupt her, I started eating even though I wasn't done asking questions.

It was intimidating, sitting in a room full of people who took every opportunity to steal a glance in my direction. I tried to block them out and kept my focus on my meal. Every time it started to get to me, I looked for Tregr. It never took more than a second to find him standing against a nearby wall, and I was grateful for the few reassuring nods he sent my way.

Though I tried not to, I couldn't help peeking out of the corner of my eye at the young prince sitting at the end of the table. I must have kept my eyes on him for too long because Prince Zarian caught on. I didn't need to see his eyes clearly to know he was looking straight at me. Blood rushed to my cheeks as I quickly turned away.

What was I doing? What if my glances gave the wrong idea? Deciding I couldn't ruin anything more than I had, I opted for conversation.

"If you don't mind my asking, who are all these people?" I asked Queen Tatira as I looked out over the room, trying to keep my eyes off of the men at the other end of the table.

"They are advisers and their families, guardsmen, and other highly important people to either my husband, myself, or our sons."

Laughter erupted from the other side of the table as the brothers shared a joke. I couldn't help but watch as Zarian's older brother relayed an apparently gripping story just out of earshot. There was more laughter and Zarian shook his head as he patted his brother on the shoulder warmly.

"We were lucky to have two sons," the queen said, leaning in, her eyes warm as she spoke. "When they were children I thought they would never learn to get along, but then we lost their sister, who was just two years older than Zarian, to a childhood illness. It brought them closer."

"I'm so sorry," I offered, not sure what to say to such a tragedy. So, there had been three children—the oldest prince, an unnamed sister, and Zarian. I had more questions but didn't feel it the right time or place to pry into something so delicate. I made a mental note to ask Roah about it later.

"Thank you, child," Tatira accepted graciously. "I think you and my daughter would have made wonderful friends. Her brothers took her passing hard, but they have done her memory proud. Laurion, my oldest, became especially protective of his younger brother over the years. Let me introduce you."

My whole body went rigid. This was it.

The queen leaned over, getting the attention of the king and their sons. "This is Prince Laurion, my eldest." She gestured to the taller of the men who had just finished eating. He stood, sliding his gold mask off just enough to reveal his face. The young man, who looked about twenty-five, smiled indulgently at his mother before he spoke.

"My Lady, it's an honor to meet you finally," he gushed as he moved around the table to address me without shouting over the music. It wasn't anything I hadn't expected, but there was something about the way he took my hand and kissed it that made my stomach flip slightly. He was dashing; there was just no other word for it. He flashed a smile that would've had all the girls back at school swooning. "Words fail to express how grateful I am for your safe return to us."

"Among other things, Laurion oversees the relief efforts for the refugees of Moldara," the queen explained proudly. "He's in charge of managing the food, shelter, and workgroups in a way that protects them from Terrshon's cruelty. It's a delicate balance between assisting them, and quietly integrating the members of the younger generation into our population without arousing suspicion. I only wish we could do more."

"Please, Mother," Laurion shushed her as he put an arm around her. "We do much more than the other kingdoms with exiles at their gates, and I am merely keeping proper order and ensuring they are not a burden on our citizens. Someone has to look out for them while they are leaderless."

"That's very generous of you," I said.

"There is nothing generous about it," the king interjected. "It's good training for his future responsibilities." I saw Laurion's smile slip a little before he recovered.

"Please forgive me, my lady, but as it is a night for celebrating, I have some business to tend to. If you'll excuse me, Mother, Father." Then he bowed with a mischievous smile and immediately turned toward a flock of waiting—and I assumed eligible—females. Within moments, I lost him to fluttering fans and gloved hands. *A weaker man would be crushed by that much estrogen,* I thought, reluctantly admitting to myself that I was a little impressed.

"Business," the queen scoffed but her heart wasn't in it. Her smile was too full of love to convey real irritation. "He'll have broken a dozen hearts before the sun rises. Those poor girls. I hope that with his brother's betrothed at hand, he will be inspired to make his choice and finally settle down."

I could only force a smile as I swallowed the lump in my throat.

"And this, as you know, is Prince Zarian." She motioned over to the young man who had just stood, revealing his navy-blue uniform, military in design but from a century I could not place. The button-holes, high-collar lapel, and cuffs were decorated with thick silver cords, spiraling and crossing over one another until they had the look of tendrils of smoke. The overall effect made him look like a recently doused fire that was still smoking. A white silk kerchief tied at his throat, and the buttons on his jacket seemed carved from pearls. Black boots, polished to a high shine, went to his knees, and a black buckler held the ornate silver-handled sword at his hip.

I felt my chest tighten as he bowed slightly, but unlike his brother,

Blood of Moldara   171

he never removed his mask. That didn't bother me. Any curiosity I'd felt about seeing what he looked like was smothered by his obnoxious letter. He moved to join us, and I felt my whole body tense. I stood to meet him, not wanting to be perceived as weak or in need of his assistance.

"It's a pleasure, my lady," he informed me in a low, quiet voice. Though the mouth of the mask was open, it gave his voice a strange echoing quality, as though he were speaking from inside a cave.

"Oh, no. The pleasure is all mine." I hoped my tone wasn't too mocking as I failed to return his bow with a curtsy, but I couldn't be sure.

Just then, the music shifted and started playing something a little slower. I could almost make out the glint in the prince's hidden eyes with the shift.

"We should dance," he declared.

With the king and queen's eyes on me, I knew I couldn't refuse—at least not the first time.

"I agree, best to get the formalities out of the way first," I replied with an eager smile, doing some of my best acting.

Before he could offer his arm, I turned away and marched down the steps to the dance floor. I assumed he followed me since I noticed several eyes following me. When I reached the middle of the floor though, I felt his hand take my elbow. Startled, I paused but refused to turn back to him.

The dancers moved around us as he stepped in front of me. I expected to be lectured on the rules of etiquette and childishly refused to meet his gaze. To my surprise, he silently placed one hand at the small of my back and the other behind his. Confused when he didn't take my hand, I glanced around the room then at him. After grabbing my skirt like the other women had, I followed the direction of his nod and placed my other hand on his right shoulder, vividly aware of the muscles that rippled under my touch. Before I could find the words to excuse my limited skill, we were dancing.

He began slowly, taking small steps until I became familiar with how he led. His steps grew, and we began to float slowly around the floor. I finally heard the lilt of the music; the delicate vibrato of strings and flutes flowed like the current of a river, carrying us and the other dancers around the room. If I had to guess, I would say it was a kind of waltz but easier to follow, the steps like a swaying walk.

He led me through step after step, but he never let me stumble. Instead, he made my missteps part of the dance. He did it so effortlessly that I felt weightless in his arms; as if he were the only thing left tethering me to the ground.

The music changed, increasing in tempo. With the shift in the dance, he drew me closer and reached down for the hand holding the skirt. As if possessed of some unknown instinct, I released the fistful of fabric and opened my palm. He led me through another dance, a patient and decent teacher, twirling and gliding around the room despite my lack of instruction. I tried not to enjoy myself, except it was too easy to lose myself in the flow of the movements and music.

There was something about the way he held me close, the way his body moved in step with mine, that took my breath away. I was grateful for the mask—it hid the flush I could feel on my cheeks. I could hardly string two words together. I had never imagined that a simple dance could have this affect on anyone.

Was this what people meant when they said they had been swept away? Or is this just what it's like to dance with a prince? A distant part of my brain prayed that he could not feel the pounding of my pulse or sense the tremors in my hands. A warm, familiar tension began in my stomach and spread through my whole body, pulling me closer to his confident frame, silencing my usually busy mind.

Time seemed to slow, my awareness of the rest of the room falling away. At that moment, there was only me and the fire that ignited in my palm as his hand tightened over mine. Stunned by my reaction, I started to pull away. He followed, lightly pressing his other hand into the small of my back and confidently pulled me closer.

"We make a good match, don't you think?" he whispered, breaking the spell. His accent was heavy, his voice strange in my ears, parts of it lost in the noise of the party around us.

I felt my whole body tense. The words of his letter, my purpose there, and Roah's face came rushing back into my consciousness. *What was I doing?* I stumbled to a stop, my arms falling away.

"I can't do this," I sputtered, trying to back up.

He caught me by the waist and pulled me out of the path of oncoming couples and into the nearly empty center of the floor. I felt my arms fold across my body as an extra barrier. The things I'd been feeling as I had danced with him called to me like a siren's song, begging me to return to his arms.

"Can't do what?" he asked over the music as the crowd continued around us, unaware. The loud music wasn't helping. Every time he spoke, I had to lean in, forcing me so close I felt his breath on my neck. I tried to ignore the chills it sent down my spine.

"I can't do this," I blurted out. "I don't belong here!"

"I had heard as much," he said, taking my hands and pulling me into our dance position once more. He began to guide me around the floor but this time kept us in the smaller center circle.

"So," I asked, trying to keep my mind off the things I was feeling, "you're okay with that?"

"No," his low voice finally admitted after a long silence. "No, I'm not okay with it. You think something like this happens every day?"

As if to punctuate his words, he pulled me closer and pivoted us around as if it were nothing. For those few steps, I couldn't tell where I ended, and he began. I hadn't even known I could do that, and then there was the heat from his hands radiating through my dress. His steps slowed and he leaned closer still. I felt the electricity between us again, and my breath caught in my throat.

"You don't belong in the Land of the Sages, Adelaide. You belong here, with me." My heart pounded in my chest as he continued passionately, his words becoming tender as his accent caressed each one. "This is your home, your people, and we've all waited so long for this day."

An edge had crept into his voice at those last words. I sensed his anger, and I took the opportunity to step away from his intimate embrace before I continued. I ignored the dancers that flowed around us.

"So is that why you said you were *the key to all I hold dear,* because you've had to wait for me?" I mocked. My anger from earlier returned, putting out the fire his dancing had started in me. "Let me guess, I have a choice just so long as it's the one *Your Highness* chooses for me?"

"That is one way to look at it," he answered, through clenched teeth, his whole body going stiff. "I am uniquely positioned—"

"Tregr gave me your letter," I said, cutting him off. "I found it to be an illuminating insight into the royal mind. Look, I get you've never had anyone say *no* to you before, but I don't like two-faced conceited guys that act like I'm a means to an end. It's just not my thing."

He started to shake his head in protest, but I wasn't ready to relinquish my control of the conversation.

"Don't misunderstand me, I'm very appreciative of everything that's been done for me but getting sucked into your world's drama doesn't make me your prize. The king and queen already know my feelings on this."

I let him chew on that as the song ended. In the silence, I realized that some people had stopped dancing and were staring at us. Without asking, he placed a hand on my lower back and escorted me off of the dance floor. The next song began as we stopped next to a table overflowing with desserts.

"My lady," he began, "your decision saddens me. It affects the kingdom in ways you cannot yet fathom. There is still much you have yet to be told. You clearly are in need of a little more time to consider your options."

"I'm sure you can all come up with a strategy that doesn't involve me."

"This is about so much more," he insisted, "and if I were at liberty to explain it to you—"

"Even if you did, it wouldn't change anything. I'm going back," I said, authority in my tone, "and neither you, nor anyone else, is going to stop me."

He looked around the room, his gaze seeming to linger at the table of the queen and king before simply answering, "Okay."

Now I was confused.

He moved toward me as if to take me in his arms and say more. I immediately stepped back, pushing him away so briskly that he bumped the table behind him. Some of the guests turned to watch. I heard the murmurs of gossip ripple through the crowd and cringed.

"It truly has been an enlightening experience meeting you, Prince Zarian," I announced too loudly, with a forced smile. "I won't monopolize anymore of your time. I'm sure you have so many others waiting for your attention." I turned before he could say anything else and escaped into the crowd.

It was time to find Roah.

I searched the room, looking for Tregr, but before I could locate him, I was scooped up into a much more awkward turn around the floor by an older gentleman who had clearly sampled too much wine.

Three uncomfortable dances later, I finally spotted Tregr. My eyes pleaded with him to rescue me. Thankfully, he understood and cut in before anyone else could steal me away again.

"Take me to Roah," I demanded. "I don't care if he's back yet or not. I'll wait in whatever room you put me until he gets here. I've had enough dancing."

"I'm not sure, but I'll take you to where he'd go first," Tregr said as we exited the room. I was relieved to see that the prince was nowhere in sight.

22

Tregr led me deeper into the castle—up flights of stairs, down corridors, and through arched doorways, until I was sure we were lost. But I was still worked up from having turned down the advances of an actual prince, so I was glad for the walk. Finally, we stood in front of double doors that were guarded by armored statues. One door was slightly open.

Tregr motioned to the open door. "Wait in here. I'll go find Roah and let him know you're expecting him. I trust you'll stay put until one of us comes back for you, and I won't need to find a babysitter to keep you out of trouble."

"Tregr, have I ever done anything that would make you think you need to watch my every move?" As I asked, a flurry of emotions played over his expression. I felt guilty and smiled, quickly adding, "Don't answer that. I'll stay right here. No babysitter needed."

"Good. For a minute there I thought I was going to have to chain you to a chair." He chuckled darkly. He was serious. "I'll be back with Roah soon."

"Thanks, Tregr," I said as I walked through the door.

His footsteps faded as I looked around the room. Not only was it enormous, but it was daunting in so many glorious ways. I took off my

Blood of Moldara 177

mask and wandered over to a writing desk with all sorts of papers and quills on it.

I ran my fingers over the feathers of the quills and the wax used to seal documents. The desk sat against a wall lined with shelves that held books, scrolls, small statues, wooden chests with locks, and many other items that I wasn't sure what their uses were. I looked at every detail, touched everything that begged to be examined, and was awed by every facet.

Tyler would freak out to be in a room like this, I thought. It was possibly the coolest place I'd ever been.

The fireplace on the opposite end had a large shield hanging over it, engraved with a symbol I'd recognized from Grandpa's journals. Two swords stuck out from under its edges. A dark fur rug sat at the feet of several leather chairs close to the glowing flames.

A very large table dominated the center of the room. I was in heaven as I looked over all the objects it held, my inner Ren-geek in ecstasy. There were crossbows in various sizes, daggers, swords with different types of blades, and weapons I had no idea how to use, let alone what to call them—but I loved them all.

It looked like the heavily laden shelves against the walls had spilled several books onto the table as well. Some had been opened to places that talked about survival techniques, history, battle strategies, and something about Sages written in the trick font. That book intrigued me most. I'd heard that word before—Sages—and while I was sure that Ayla had introduced me to one, and my escort at the party had been one, I knew nothing about them.

I set my mask down and leaned over to grab the book. Then, I saw it. I hadn't noticed it under all the clutter, or the small metal talismans that marked it. If I hadn't leaned across the table, I might have missed the entire thing. Lying in front of me was a very large, very detailed map.

I momentarily lost all interest in the book as I looked over the map and read the names: Moldara, Niniever, Bronia, Moorandian, The Flat Lands, Shadiya, Galistan, Valta, and several other names under talismans I couldn't make out. There were more kingdoms than I'd originally thought. A large mountain range ran along the northernmost borders of Bronia, and a great body of water lined the borders of Galistan and Shadiya.

Inside all of these kingdoms were smaller sections. Provinces, Roah had called them. I started to trace the route I'd been on by following the names I recognized. I started with the large city of Moldara, in the kingdom by the same name, and then passed several cities as we traveled to Vanderveld, Elvae, through Icel, and finally to the city of Niniever in the kingdom of Niniever. I was surprised there were no direct routes between any of the cities I'd been through.

As I studied the map, I tried to find the doorway back to Virginia, but nothing was labeled. Then I saw that word again—Sages. I looked closer. In the southernmost portion of the kingdom of Moldara, just before it turned into The Flat Lands, was a small section labeled *The Land of the Sages* and nothing more. *That must be it,* I thought. Everyone here called the place I'd come from "Oldworld" but had said the Sages were the only ones with access.

Realizing this, I started to trace a route between Niniever and that part of the map. It was farther away than I'd first thought. *How long would it take us to travel that far on horseback?* I didn't want to think about it. No wonder Roah had said it wasn't as easy as just jumping on a horse and riding. I guess, with all the travel, I hadn't paid much attention to the distance I'd gone. I also noticed how far back into Moldara we would have to go. Feeling slightly discouraged, I grabbed the book I'd been interested in, walked over to one of the overstuffed leather chairs by the fire, and plopped down.

Staring at the flames, I couldn't help wondering why my life had turned out the way it had. If my returning to Moldara was so important, why hadn't Elion just taken me to one of the farthest kingdoms on that map? It would've been so much easier to grow up here, rather than swallowing revelation after revelation as I had in only a few days. Surely there must have been an easier way. *Why hadn't he taken it? Was I beginning to secretly wish he had?*

As I considered those questions, I couldn't help thumbing through the heavy pages of the book I was still holding, searching for the place

Blood of Moldara 179

where it had been opened to earlier, hoping it held some insight for me. Just as I found it again, footsteps sounded down the hall. Deep voices accompanied them. As they got closer, the conversation became clear.

"When I pledged my support, it wasn't for you to prepare a battalion to take her back," boomed the king's voice. He was clearly upset. "She doesn't belong *there*. She belongs *here*, taking responsibility for her people, fulfilling her duty to my son!"

"She's not ready." I was surprised to hear Roah's voice clearly answering him, defending my choice.

"What do you mean she's not ready? I wasn't ready, but I did my duty, just as you have done yours. The way I see it, destiny has intervened. She is here now, as she should be. We will guide her. What more do either of you need?" the king asked.

"Conviction. Your Highness did not see where she was raised. I have lived there. She has had no preparation, no time to accept her true identity, and you would demand this of her? If we push her, she will break. We can't afford that. We need her, not just alive, but whole and completely committed to our cause. *Her* cause. What are you suggesting, forcing her hand? That would make us no better than the monster we're fighting."

"We are nothing like that man!" the king bellowed. "We honor our oaths and our duty to our people. We do not exploit and terrorize and hold the future of entire nations for ransom!"

"Exactly!"

"Where is this coming from? Is there more you are not telling us, other ways your grand plan has eroded out of your control? Or did that world change you so much you have forgotten your one oath?" the king questioned, a threatening tone lacing his words.

"No, sir, I didn't mean—" Roah's voice turned suddenly repentant, but the king wouldn't let him finish.

"You do not have the luxury or the burden of deciding the fate of an entire bloodline. Need I remind you of all the ways this family's lives are tied to that decision? Would you rob them of their choice to give the princess hers? I don't understand why this is even up for discussion. I remember your grand promises when you took on this challenge. You vowed you would stop at nothing to bring the princess back and restore all that had been lost by this kingdom. Are you telling me that the prince, *my son*, erred in judgment when he committed our forces to this task?"

"Maybe the prince didn't realize how arrogant his promises were, or how foolish he was for underestimating the complications that would arise at every turn. We couldn't know what condition we would find her in, if at all, after all this time. We have corrected for each variable as it has arisen, but this is all still too big a shock to her. I swear to you that I remain confident in our plans. Just give us time."

I guessed the prince wasn't at this impromptu meeting, or he would have defended himself. Or maybe he just let his captain do all the answering for him as he stood there, spoiled and silent.

"So what are you proposing be done now that the gravity of this situation had caught up to both of you? Did you forget where the Land of the Sages is? With all that she has already endured, do you really want to risk all that just to help her hide from her birthright, her duty? Because the next time she meets Terrshon, he might just kill her. Why would you take such an unnecessary risk with all of our futures?"

"I've told you why. She isn't ready."

This was the first I'd heard of any resistance to my decisions. I was still shocked at the amount of pressure he was under to keep me here.

"Then we will guide her," the king said. "No, I have heard your reports of their strange ways and will hear no more of it. I don't know what you saw, but it sounded like the worst kind of prison where she was an inconsequential speck, unimportant. Don't you see? Even her mind was yoked to a false idea of who she was and her purpose in life. Here she can save us all."

The king paused. I was sitting on the edge of my chair, straining to hear Roah's response. Instead, the king continued.

"Or are you so changed from living in the world beyond, that you have lost all sense of your responsibilities and oaths? Do you think you know what has taken the Sages generations to understand?"

"I have changed, but not in the way you claim. Nor am I ashamed of those changes. Every step of this journey has only made me a better person, not someone who would challenge the Sages. But I've also seen what lies beyond, what she has lived with, and we have to let her go back."

"It isn't your place to decide!"

"But it's yours?"

"Yes, it is. Obviously, your judgment has been clouded. I would rather believe that than believe the man we put all our faith and trust in has lost his nerve. Where is the mighty Prince Zarian in all this? That is who I want to speak with. *He* would see the wisdom in my words and honor their counsel. *He* would know his duty and would see reason. *He* is the man that can make the hard decisions."

"With all due respect, he *is* making the hard decision, the right decision. We're not going to take her agency away and keep her here against her wishes. She isn't a pawn to be used against Terrshon. Regardless of her choice, her blood earns her that much from us. Or is that a precedence you're willing to set, that someone of royal birth can be used as a slave?"

"Of course not, you're missing my point," the king answered Roah angrily. "All I am saying is that you need to reconsider your moves. They hold risks that could upset the balance of this world for generations. I can't sit back, in all good conscience, and let it happen. I ask you, if you take her back and she's captured or killed, how are you going to live with that?"

There was a slight hesitation after the king spoke. I held my breath waiting to hear what Roah would say.

"I will concede on that point," he finally admitted. "There is a good possibility things might not go smoothly, and if that were to happen and we lost her, I don't even want to think about the implications."

"Then it's settled. It's time to stop taking reckless chances for childish reasons. She is here and here she will stay, under our protection, of course. I will concede that she needs more time, so we will give her all the time and training she requires to feel comfortable with her responsibilities. We will make her ready to accept her birthright, and her prince, and the kingdom that comes with it. It's what her parents would want us to do for her. I am confident it's what they would have asked of us if they still could."

"It is a worthy plan, my king." I couldn't be hearing this right. *Did he just agree with the king?* "But if I may add another consideration."

My heart eased as Roah continued. "Every day she is here, we risk her whereabouts becoming common knowledge. If word reaches Terrshon, he will stop at nothing to lay his hands on her. With the incident in Icel, the rumors have already begun again. Confirmation of her presence in this court could be enough to start a war. Terrshon has few allies, but they're strong. Valta and Shadiya will undoubtedly side with him. Are you willing to unleash that kind of bloodshed to keep her here?"

The king tried to interrupt Roah, but he cut him off as he continued his argument.

"My men and I know the path blindfolded. If we take her back, the only thing we have to keep watch over is the passage between here and there, not an entire nation. Then we will place all the guards we need on both sides of the falls to keep Terrshon from gaining access to Oldworld. It will be safer and less involved.

"We need to keep the knowledge of her return a secret until she is ready to proclaim herself. Keeping her here risks not only her life but also the possibility of warfare in a land that is ill prepared for it. I saw the people at Icel when Mira's name was murmured. They are hungry for vengeance. We can use that, but not until the time is right. She must go back, not only to preserve her life but also to buy us the time we need to prepare for the battle her unveiling will incur."

Roah finished, and I exhaled. I knew he wouldn't let me down, that he would stop at nothing to get me back home where I belonged.

"I will not concede that. If there is a risk in keeping her here, it is a risk we must take. Going into Moldara is nothing short of a death sentence, and I cannot allow any choice that will endanger her life." My stomach dropped, and I forced down rising panic as I heard the king's words. This couldn't be happening. "This is my final word on the matter. I *will* have your word that she does not leave this castle."

There was a long pause. Then I heard Roah speak in a voice I

Blood of Moldara 183

didn't like. "Yes, Your Majesty, you have my word as a loyal servant of Niniever. I will keep Princess Adelaide safe."

"Good. You will see the wisdom in this soon enough."

I was gasping for air by the time I heard footsteps again. My chest felt like a boulder had dropped on it. My pulse sounded in my ears as it hit me that they were going to keep me here, and worst of all, Roah had agreed to it. *How could this happen?*

Suddenly the door burst open, slamming back on its hinges and closing again with a crash. It was a man in an ornate silver trimmed jacket. His hands obscured his face as they rubbed it in frustration. He stormed over to the large table.

Bam! His fists slammed hard on the thick wood. The sound made me jump.

Leaning as he was, over the table, I couldn't get a clear view of him. I looked closer at what he was wearing because it confused me. I had been so certain the prince hadn't been in the hall for the conversation.

Had he followed me?

I felt trapped. I wanted to run, but I couldn't make my body move.

Still leaning on the table, he shifted his body, reaching for something. As he lifted my mask, the one I had taken off earlier, a familiar voice pierced through me like a knife.

"No," he breathed.

His head shot up, the color draining from his face as our eyes met.

My heart stopped. For a second I wondered if I had finally lost it, gone completely insane. I watched shock and horror consume the face I had trusted most. There was only one explanation for what my eyes were telling me—betrayal.

Why else would Roah be dressed like Prince Zarian?

23

The walls closed in on me, and my chest burned as if all of the air had been sucked out of the room.

Face pale, eyes wide as saucers, he stared at me, my mask still clutched in his hand. For one terrible second, we were both frozen where we stood. Several emotions flashed behind his horrified eyes until he took a step in my direction, one hand stretching out. I recoiled.

He shook his head slowly, his eyes pleading with me, but I couldn't fight the ice that was consuming my heart. I gave into the betrayal, into the panic, and ran. Keeping the table between us, I darted for the door, my shoulder hitting the doorframe on the way out. I barely noticed the pain. The door swung open, and I fled down the cold torch-lit hallway.

"Lotty, No!" The call came from behind me as Roah found his voice. But I didn't stop. I couldn't. It wasn't safe. I needed air. I needed out of this suffocating place.

I ran recklessly through the castle, my footing careless as I fumbled down flights of stairs, around corners, and into unsuspecting people who didn't get out of the way fast enough. Oncoming tears burned in my eyes, but I ignored it. I didn't know where I was headed—I just needed to escape before the walls closed in on me forever.

By the time I stumbled onto a way out, I was nearly hysterical, a storm of emotions dashing me against the rocks of despair. The door opened out to a small, unlit path. Just beyond its stones, I could make out the silhouette of trees in the moonlight. The woods beckoned me, promising comfort and acceptance in their canopy. I ran as fast as my legs would carry me, into the cover and sanctuary of the woods. The tears I'd been holding back were finally loosened, ripping great choking sobs from my throat.

No matter how hard I ran, my dress slowed me. It caught on low branches, leaving a trail of shredded blue fabric as I forced my way deeper into the forest. My shoes cut into my heels and caught in the dirt. I abandoned them. With every step, my stocking feet hit the rough ground, hard. The impact reverberated through me, but I barely felt it.

I still couldn't believe it, but I'd seen it with my own eyes. Roah was Prince Zarian. *How could those two be the same person? How could I ever look at Roah the same way? What else had he lied about?*

I could no more face it than answer the questions blaring in my mind. Rage, panic, and betrayal coursed through me with every beat of my heart. Branches beat at me from every side, shredding my skirts and snagging my hair. Underbrush pulled at my stockings and rocks cut into my feet. Still, I pushed harder into the darkness.

My lungs burned as I sobbed raggedly between gasps of breath. Running and crying in a corset made it almost impossible to get enough air. Removing and tossing aside my jacket wasn't enough. I slowed, clawing at my dress, desperate for more room to breathe, my body shuddering from the exertion. I needed to loosen the seizing around my chest, but the laces were unreachable. Somehow, in all my efforts of escape, my prison had followed me. I was trapped.

Something crashed through the trees behind me. I stopped tugging at my dress and ran, despite the burning in my lungs and the shaking that threatened to consume my entire body. I scrambled through bramble and branches, but the sound continued to gain. With tears blurring my vision, I tripped.

I landed hard on my knees and skinned the palms of my hands. I was hysterical, shaking uncontrollably as the fatigue took me. Devastated to my very core, I pictured Roah—Prince Zarian, I reminded myself—in his masquerade outfit and short hair. Unexpectedly, I retched, dry heaving and gagging through jagged sobs. I struggled back to my feet.

"Lotty, STOP!" Roah's winded cries grew behind me, along with the thrashing and breaking of branches. I forced my unsteady feet back into a feeble jog.

Large hands suddenly seized my shoulders, dragging me to a halt. I attempted to shove him away, but he held my body against his. I tried to break free, and quickly realized it was useless. Fresh panic exploded inside me.

"Lotty," Roah gasped as he held me, "you have to stop! It's just me. I swear," he said between heavy breaths, his voice wild with panic.

"Leave me alone!" I cried between breathless sobs. My body was shaking violently despite my efforts to control it.

"No." Roah held strong.

He wanted to make me listen, to hear his excuse, but the pain was too raw, too biting. I couldn't allow it.

"LET. ME. GO!" I hissed bitterly.

To my surprise, he released me and backed away slowly, with his palms raised. His expression oscillated between anguish and anger.

"You," I spat, backing away from him. "You lied to me!"

"I know," he admitted, leaning over to catch his breath. "But it's not what you think."

When he saw that I had paused in my retreat, he pulled something from his jacket; it was small and shined in the moonlight. He held it out to me, but I wouldn't take it. I wanted nothing from him, but he tossed it to me anyway. It landed in the patch of moss at my feet.

"You'll want to rinse your mouth," he offered. And as much as I wanted to ignore his demand, the acidic residue left on my tongue wouldn't let me.

I grabbed the flask with trembling fingers and unscrewed the top. Expecting something cool and mild, I took a large gulp. Instead, I half choked on the fiery liquid and spat it out. The spiced elixir burned as it slid through my mouth and down my throat but left it feeling better than before. I capped the flask and threw it back at him. It fell to the ground; he didn't reach for it.

"How could you?" I forced out, my voice hoarse from my tears and the drink.

"Lotty, I never meant to hurt you." He took a small step toward me but stopped when he heard the vitriol in my voice.

"This whole time I thought you cared about me, that you—" My body started shaking again as I voiced my fears.

"Lotty, please. It's not safe out here. We have to go back," he pleaded, anger still plain in his voice. But I didn't care anymore.

"I trusted you," I wailed, my voice breaking as my tears returned. I staggered backward, leaning against the nearest tree. My throat burned as I wept. "You were the only one here I could count on, that wouldn't use me, that made me feel safe! How could you do this?"

"I know," he whispered, trying to hold my gaze. He reached out as if to comfort me but stopped when I recoiled. He didn't know, that was the problem. *How could someone like him know what this felt like?* I expected that any second he was going to take advantage of my physical condition, to bind me in his arms and carry me back to his king as the prisoner he'd promised me to be. I silently vowed that that would never happen. I would find the strength to escape. I would claw his eyes out and kick him bloody before I let him take me anywhere.

"I'm so sorry." He choked and my temper flared.

"Stop lying!" I lashed out, my heart fracturing into still smaller pieces. The tears streamed down my face again, my body still trembling as I clutched at my dress and nearly spat each word. "All this time and you were the one I should have been running from! You've been playing me from the day we met! Everything about you, everything you've ever said or promised me was a lie to get me to Moldara, to trap me here!"

His expression was desolate, save for the wild look in his eyes. His shoulders slumped in defeat as his hands raked his now short hair. His obvious distress was disarming.

"You have every right to hate me," he said, his head hung as he spoke, his words growing quiet. I watched as his eyes flashed with bitterness. He was only a few feet away, but it felt like the tiny stream that had separated us had become an ocean. "But I need you to understand, to at least hear why I did what I did, before you—before I lose you completely."

I only glared at him, my chest still heaving from my sprint.

"I truly am sorry," he whispered huskily, his eyes glistening. "You're the last person in the world I wanted to hurt. Please, Lotty, you have to believe that much."

"Believe you? You're joking, right? I don't even know who you are! Do you understand that?" I realized I was shouting, but I didn't care. I looked him dead in the eyes. "You have lied to me at every turn, used what you know about my past to serve your purposes, and manipulated me from one prison into another!"

"I only said and did those things to keep you safe. It was never to hurt you deliberately," his voice half pleading, half enraged as he spoke. "You have every right to hate me. I have broken your trust, but I swear to you I acted out of duty, not malice."

"I heard what you promised the king, your father! It didn't take more than five minutes for you to break the one promise that mattered most—taking me home. What lie were you preparing for me if I hadn't overheard you?"

"I swear to you I have no intentions of enslaving you to this world." The fire flamed in his eyes with every word. "I want you to choose your path for yourself. I would never willingly take that from you."

"But it's too late for that isn't it? You've already sold me out. I heard you!"

"What you heard was a prince who couldn't reject a command without severe punishment." His anger raised his voice to match mine. "I am only willing to give my life up when I see no other way! I never wanted to promise something like that, but what good would I be to you imprisoned or dead? After all I have sacrificed, I wasn't going to allow that."

"What could a prince know about sacrifice?" I scoffed bitterly.

"You're right," he replied, a coldness coming into his voice that gave me chills. "You don't know me. You don't know the absurd lengths I have gone to, so *you* could make your choice, in your time. And yes, of course, I wanted *you* to claim your birthright and all the privileges that go with it! But I wanted you to be sure that you chose it because it was what *you* desired, that you hadn't merely given in to an obligation that had trapped you. I swore to Elion that I would never *willingly* take away your agency, but the king gave me no other choice. I never meant for you to find out like this."

"How did you mean for me to find out? With a letter? Like that piece of work Tregr gave me?"

"NO!" he snapped, raking his once long hair in frustration. I could see him restraining his anger again, but it bled into his words. "It's a relic from a fourteen-year-old boy whose ego needed taming! I grew up. Which is why I was waiting for the right time to tell you, in person."

"And the right time to tell me wasn't when you took me to meet your parents, or when I asked you what the prince was like, or our first date?"

Exasperation exploded on his face.

"Lotty, you want me to believe that if I told you who I was, at any of those times, you would have taken my true identity seriously, or that it wouldn't have changed anything between us?" He accused bitterly, the pressure he had been under finally expressing itself. "Think about it; it's only been two days since I got you to believe that this place was even *real*. I couldn't risk compromising your trust in me any further."

"How do you know what I can and can't handle?"

"You just ran over a mile, into a dark forest you don't know, from your primary safeguard, with only an evening gown to protect you! Do you really need me to answer that?" he shouted, throwing his hands up to emphasize his point.

He was right. I had done that; my lungs still burned faintly with every breath. I merely stared at him, holding onto my tree, unsure of what to say. I had no idea what he read in my expression, but something there made his eyes soften as he leaned in slightly.

"Lotty, you didn't see yourself after you fell in the orchard," he

Blood of Moldara

said gently, swallowing hard before he continued. "I saw you hit your breaking point, and I refused to be another one. But you have to believe me when I say that letter, my behavior tonight, was to protect you."

"Protect me?" I repeated. This was the excuse I'd been waiting for; to prove how badly he had handled this whole thing. But before I could pounce on it, he went on.

"Whether you believe it or not, I am committed to your safety. You saw what your presence means here, what everyone is counting on because they believe you are the only one who can take back Moldara. Can you even imagine what they would do if they had a clue about our true feelings? You want to talk about the injustice of having people decide what your life is supposed to look like?!"

He was truly riled up now. His eyes narrowed as he spoke, and his voice flowed up and down in a range of expression as he paced in front of me. I'd never seen this side of him before. All I could do was watch in astonishment. "Once a union is arranged, those two people are considered off limits to everyone else. And it doesn't stop there. No. Not only are they promised to each other, but they are also considered promised to the people of that kingdom."

A hint of panic laced his voice as he continued. "I pledged to protect and preside over the people of Moldera with all I have to offer, but I have no legitimate power to intervene for those people unless we marry. In your absence, Moldara is a fractured nation at the mercy of anyone with the power to subdue them. And until you are dead or proclaimed, those people are subject to all of Terrshon's whims.

"Your unusual circumstances has given us a window in which we can argue for another solution. But until one is adopted by the royal families of every nation and given the blessing of the Sages, the king and queen will stop at nothing to unite us. Lotty, I was trying to keep that from happening. They had to see you publicly reject me. Can't you see? I was relying on you *not* knowing who I was so that you would be angry enough to make a scene and buy both of us more time to figure this out."

"Can't *you* see what a manipulative, dick-move that is?!"

"I do now!" Roah shouted back, throwing his arms up in exasperation.

Confused, I started to open my mouth. But he held up a hand, cutting me off. I was taken back when his eyes found mine and there was no anger in them.

"When I met you, things changed for me," his said, his voice soft. I could hear the depth of his feelings with every word. "I was selfish. I wanted to know if you could...could love me, for me. Do you know how rare that is in my world? The more time we spent together, the more I found myself falling in love with you. Real love, not the kind of connection made on a scroll with a wax seal. I never expected to feel like this about anyone. So, as much as I wanted to tell you—and there were so many times I almost did—I was afraid," he admitted softly, his eyes gray, vulnerable in the moonlight. "In every other way, I swear that I have been honest with you. You know me. It's just that now you also know where I come from, and why.

"Lotty, from the second I realized I loved you, I questioned our betrothal. Not because I don't want to be with you—the gods know I do—but because this world conspires to have you, in so many ways, for its own purposes. I know the price of being together; what it could cost us both."

His words hung in the air between us. *What it could cost us both,* echoed in my ears, and my heart finally found rock bottom. One truth stood out from his words—he loved me. He was finally bearing his true self, unhindered and raw, and I was running from it. I was running from all the ways this could hurt me, running from what I could not and would not hear.

"What do you mean?" I began timidly, although I hadn't rinsed all of the defiance out of my tone. I wasn't ready to concede my point and admit my feelings, not yet. "You talk as if I only have two choices: to accept my role here or refuse it, but I have to do the job anyway. How is that a choice? How am I not a prize that you and Terrshon are fighting over?"

"Terrshon would kill you to get his way. I would die to give you yours," he answered without hesitation, his eyes passionate in the silver light.

I watched him standing there, his expression as exposed and lost as I felt. I wanted so badly to believe him, but I needed more. Because there was more. I could feel it.

24

"Roah, I need to ask you something, and I need you to be completely honest with me," I said as I finally let go of my tree and took a step toward him.

"I will tell you anything," he said, his eyes and voice full of sincerity.

"How long have you been on this…quest?" I asked, studying his face.

"I started my search for you when I was fourteen, almost six years ago."

"You've been gone for six years?" I marveled. "Wait, that would make you—"

"Twenty years old," he answered, cutting me off.

My jaw dropped. "What else don't I know about you?"

Unbuttoning his jacket, Roah stepped away from me and toward a fallen tree where he took a seat. He rested against the upended roots as if in total submission. Sighing deeply, he slowly removed his gloves, his eyes no longer searching for mine.

"After your parents' death, my life became complicated. I was still bound to you, but no one knew if you were alive or dead," Roah began, the rest of his words gushing from him as if a dam had broken. "That all changed when Elion appeared at our gates. Suddenly I had a purpose, a mission, and even a kingdom that I was once again pledged to serve. I quickly found out that that meant leaving Niniever, my family, and everything I'd known.

"Elion and I traveled through Otherworld. His first lessons were in strategy, combat, and covert evasion. That's also when I left my title of prince behind and took the name my governess had called me as a child. I wouldn't have gotten the kind of training I desired if my title was known. Elion introduced me to Daggon, who quickly became one of the best guards I'd ever known. And Tregr's story, well, that's best saved for another time. Let's just say he has saved my life more than once. I would never want to enter a fight without them both by my side.

"We were three years on the field of battle, as mercenaries under various captains in different provinces. Most of the time, Elion played the role of our steward, tending to wounds and making sure I, most of all, understood the dynamics of conflict between people. Every night Daggon and Tregr stood guard while Elion told me everything he knew about Moldara, Oldworld, and you. My days were blood and sweat; my nights were history lessons and an idealized lost princess. It was an intense education. That was when I wrote that ridiculous letter."

"If you dislike the version of yourself that wrote it, why keep it?" I asked, edging closer but not wanting to interrupt the flow of information.

"At first I was proud of what I was doing," he answered without looking up. "I thought myself quite the hero. You can thank a few of my own near-death experiences on the battlefield for curing me of that delusion."

"You're a prince and your parents allowed you to be in that kind of danger?"

He chuckled darkly. "I'm not sure how much Elion told them. But it wouldn't have mattered if he had. They knew, as I did, that without you or proof of your death, my life was not my own."

"Was it all fighting and danger?" I asked as I took another step toward him. He shook his head.

"The fourth year, Elion got word that Terrshon's men were closing in on our location, and he sent me to a library of the Sages near the border of Moorandian while he drew away Terrshon's men."

Something in Roah's expression darkened, and my blood chilled. "Drew away Terrshon's men? That sounds..."

When he spoke again, his gaze was heavy with sadness. "Elion promised to augment my lessons on Virginia with regular letters. Shortly after I arrived at the sanctuary, the letters ceased."

I counted in my head. It had been over two years since my grandpa was last seen alive. I steeled my heart against the pain that caused as I listened.

"The Sages did their best to finish our education. It was a little over a year before we got official word that Elion had been captured again, but I think Elion had planned for that, too. When I decided to lead Tregr and Daggon past Terrshon's guards and through the caverns, Trell was waiting. These last several months have been a desperate rush to learn the accent and understand how to blend in."

"Your world seems so much more complicated than mine," I offered. "Of course, saying you were all from another country camouflaged everything else. I thought you did a good job."

"Did I?" Roah chuckled bitterly to himself. "Your world showed me exactly how small a person can feel. I struggled with it more than Daggon or Tregr did. I think it was because, in my head, I was still a prince no matter where I was. Horses and crossbows, I knew, but your cars and trucks could not have been more foreign to me. When you'd found out I couldn't drive, I was embarrassed by your reaction. I thought you'd see me as incapable. I counted it a personal victory when you saw me kill the eagle, and when I gave you a ride home the night I found you in the woods."

I couldn't help smiling and flushing in mild embarrassment as those encounters flashed in my mind. I had no idea how hard he'd worked to blend in and seem normal. To me, he had just been the hottest guy at school, who couldn't manage a stick-shift to save his life.

My rage cooled as I pictured home. Thoughts of home brought up memories of every moment that had led to this one. Instead of focusing on my fears this time, I saw his.

A new ache formed around my battered heart. I ached for him, for the pressure he had been under for so many years. I watched him turn his fancy gloves over in his hands, examining them as if he wasn't sure he ever wanted to put them on again. At that moment, an unexpected vision opened in my mind.

I saw a boy who had been bound in his youth to an orphan girl and a broken kingdom. I saw a young man who had made it his personal mission to stand up for a people for whom no one else had been willing to claim responsibility. I saw him entering the Land of the Sages, Oldworld, unafraid and confident. He had dedicated his life to the legacy of my parents and to their daughter, without knowing her.

Only Elion had risked as much for me. Both he and Roah had accepted that other world and my choices without complaint, content to wait patiently for me to be ready. Both had sacrificed and struggled with that choice. Still, they had given up their former lives and identities willingly to protect a secret I didn't know I had. At what price? As I looked at Roah, I realized I would never really know what it had cost him.

The truth exploded in my mind with perfect clarity. He hadn't just been trying to protect me from Terrshon, or a mental breakdown; he had been trying to give me what he'd never had and treasured above all else—a choice. He hadn't failed because he was manipulating me; he had failed because he was just as trapped as I was.

He sat in front of me, broken, just like I was. I couldn't form words, but neither could I stand there silent, knowing how much I'd hurt him.

As I stared into the woods, I thought about the painting of Norwyck and Mira. I longed to speak to them, to run to them, to ask how to move forward when everything had gone so wrong. I could no longer hide from the fact that I was their daughter, any more than I could hide from the price so many had paid for that truth.

"I think you know the story from there," he said, his voice was unsure, haunted.

I felt my body move to sit in front of him. It felt right. I wanted to find the right words for what I was feeling, but I hesitated, unsure. He said nothing.

We sat in silence, and I finally noticed the beauty of our surroundings. The full moon glowed so brightly that hazy shafts of light formed illuminated pools of blue all around us. The sounds of night carried on a gentle breeze and suggested a nearby stream. I shivered.

Roah shrugged off his jacket and draped it over my shoulders. Before he could pull away, I caught his hand in mine, my stomach suddenly full of butterflies. To my relief, his fingers entwined with mine. I rested my free hand on his thigh and he scooted closer.

Emboldened, I pulled his hand over my heart. My pulse raced as I leaned down and kissed his fingers. I heard his small gasp and looked up, afraid I had done something wrong. The fire I found in his eyes felt like a reflection of the one building inside me.

"How do we do this?" I asked, my voice uneven. I knew that, beyond the solitude of these woods, a thousand problems waited to assault us. I also knew there was no one else with whom I wanted to face them.

"Do what?" he asked, his voice cautious.

"Stay together."

I heard his breath catch, and before I could ask the question again, Roah's lips were devouring mine. They moved desperately as his hands clung to me, crushing me against his chest. Fingers moved along my body with every caress of his lips, from my shoulders to my back, up to my neck. Their heat melted me as his fingers glided along my flushed skin.

My lips molded to his, as we both silently pleaded for forgiveness and acceptance. With every caress I tried to communicate my unquenchable need for him to stay with me, to never let me go, to always love me.

I needed him, not only by my side, but I needed him to need me, too. His kisses left no doubt that that was so. His lips moved the length of my jaw and up to my ears. My skin shivered under his heavy breaths. He didn't pull away as he finally spoke.

"I don't know," he sighed, answering my question. His hot breath made my skin tingle with every word. "I don't know, but we'll figure something out."

"Roah," I choked out, afraid to put words to the emotions pulsing through me. "I'm so sorry," I admitted instead, despite the euphoria swirling through me.

He did pull back this time, looking me in the eyes as he spoke.

"What are you talking about? You have nothing to be sorry for."

"I feel like I've wasted your time. Not only do I want to go home, but I'm not who you thought I was. I don't have the training to stay here and rule a broken land. Because of me, you may never have the kingdom you've worked so hard for."

Roah watched me, his expression puzzled. "Just so we're clear, you have done nothing but surprise me since I met you. You escaped several close calls, stood up to royalty without even flinching, and stayed true to yourself under very trying circumstances. You amaze me more than any other person I've known."

He pulled me into his arms. "Don't worry about me not ruling a kingdom. It might have been my goal at one point, but that changed when I fell in love with you. The one thing I've learned is that we can't rush fate. It brought you to Elion and led him to me, despite all odds. Then it brought me to you. We have to trust this path, no matter where it takes us."

"I'm never going to get back, am I?" I said, wishing I had just a little bit of his optimism.

"I promised I would take you home, and I will."

"But what about your vow to the king to never let me leave the castle?" I pulled away. He caught my hands and caressed them as he answered.

"I promised I'd keep you safe. I was very specific with my word choice. That's just what I'm going to do. No matter how I look at it, keeping you here isn't our best option, though the king might say it is. My father and I have different ideas of safety, and I still think you're safer if I take you to Virginia. Since I vowed to keep you *safe*, that's exactly what I intend to do."

"What'll happen when you go against the king?"

"I don't know. But there's still time. We haven't run out of negotiation room yet."

"Roah, I can't let you do something that might cost you your life. How would I ever live with myself if something happened to you?"

"Well," he said, his voice like velvet again, "I'll just have to make sure that doesn't happen."

I reached into the dark and pulled him to me. His arms wrapped around me eagerly, and my corset cut into my side. I gasped.

"What?"

"My dress is being difficult." I chuckled, trying to play off the discomfort. "It's not a big fan of deep breaths or midnight sprints."

"May I loosen it for you?"

"God, yes."

"Here," he said, pushing me back and turning me around. Starting at the bow, he pulled at the long laces. He tugged and jerked but nothing happened.

"Damn strings."

"What?"

"This is ridiculous." He tugged harder.

"Not much experience with corsets?" I guessed.

"How do you even get into these things?"

"You don't want to know."

The tugging stopped and I glanced back to see what he was doing.

He retrieved a dagger from his boot and lifted it to my back. His warm hands traced the length of my corset, searching. My skin flushed with the intimacy of his touch. There was a small tug where he cut away the laces. Gently, he pulled them loose.

The addition of a few more inches of breathing room finally allowed the rest of the tension in my body to ease. I took full, deep breaths for the first time in hours, and a sudden euphoria rose in me. Roah pulled at the laces until his hands reached the top of my now free corset. After tossing it aside, he traced the bare skin above my shift with his fingertips before he turned me around.

When our lips met, he tasted of salt and spice. My fingers

glided over the muscles in his back, and I felt the question in his hands as his fingertips found the edges of my dress. For a second, we were back in the loft, lost in each other's touch, sharing parts of ourselves we were scared to share. But somehow now it felt right.

To answer him, I ran my hands down his chest, stopping at the buckler that held his sword, and started undoing the clasp that would disarm him.

"Are you sure?" he whispered, looking down at me as I dropped his belt on the ground. The sword made a muffled clank.

"I think so." My hands shook slightly. I grabbed onto his shirt to steady them. "I mean, I want this. With you. Can we just have this tonight? Not make it mean more. For now?"

"Okay. You set the pace." His fingers glided, soft as silk, along my cheek. I didn't look at him.

"You're not my first," I confessed, my heart pounding.

When he lifted my chin and his eyes found mine, I forgot how to breathe.

"Should I be concerned?" he wondered, a glint in his eye.

I couldn't hide my smirk. "Nothing's inspired me yet. You?"

"Nothing memorable. Yet."

His hands slid up my arms to my neck, then my jaw, and to my face. His touch was intoxicating as his fingers moved over my skin. I let the sensation consume me, filling me with a portion of his optimism.

He moved closer, and I forgot how to breathe. I forgot that I was in the arms of a real prince, one who had risked his life for mine. I forgot that I didn't belong in this world.

We moved off the fallen tree that had been our bench. Just like when we had danced, we flowed perfectly. Together we settled onto a thick padding of moss that was reclaiming that section of forest. I lay on my back as he leaned over me. Then, his lips found mine. My breath rushed out of me.

"You're crushing me," I managed.

"Sorry." He bolted upright and readjusted.

"Ouch. This isn't working." I pushed him off me. He looked startled. "There's a rock."

"Let's switch."

He rolled me onto his chest, and I settled over him. I leaned in for a kiss, but he rolled me off.

"I found your rock." He sat up, grabbed a stone the size of a golf ball, and threw it. Then, he looked around the clearing. Deciding something, he scooted over to the log and leaned against it. Afterward, he reached out his hand.

"Does this work for you?" I asked as Roah pulled me into his lap.

"Only if it does for you."

"It does." I smiled encouragingly.

His lips found mine and no more words were needed.

We were still passionately entangled in each other's embrace long after the moon had disappeared behind clouds.

"Can we stay like this forever?" I whispered, regretting it the moment the words were voiced because Roah stopped kissing my neck.

"If that's what you'd like, we never have to leave," he answered, pulling his coat over the two of us as we lay back onto the soft moss.

The spell broken, I rested my head against his chest and focused on the soothing sound of his heartbeat.

"I'd like that, very much."

25

The melodies of autumn birds woke me, echoing the singing of my own heart. I listened to their songs as I pressed myself deeper into Roah's embrace, hypnotized by the steady rhythm of his breathing. My eyes fluttered open gradually, adjusting to the early dawn light. A smile grew on my face as he stirred and sighed contentedly. Fingers started tracing light circles on my back.

"I love sleeping with you in my arms." His voice was barely a whisper.

"Me too." I sighed happily. His arms tightened around me, and I relaxed further against his chest.

"I had pictured the accommodations a little more comfortable. I trust you slept better than I did." He groaned as he stretched beneath me.

"That bad?"

"No," he admitted teasingly, sitting us up as he spoke. "I've slept in conditions that make this place look like an extension of the palace. The tree I could have done without." He rubbed his neck.

Then he reached for the small silver flask he'd handed me last night. After swishing and spitting, he handed it to me. I did the same, spitting out the liquid after the fire had completely cleansed my mouth.

"Well, the next time I go running from the castle, I'll be sure to stop at a nice cottage or inn." I handed the flask back, but the look on his face told me he didn't think that was the least bit funny.

"Kidding," I said, trying to ease the tension. "I'm not running anywhere without you, I can promise that."

"It's about time," he proclaimed with a relieved smirk while sliding the silver canteen into his pocket. "There's only so much chasing a guy can endure. I don't know about you, but I could use a break. I'm just glad you stopped when you did, or things could have gotten ugly."

"Uglier than last night?" I returned his smirk with one of my own.

"Lotty, it's not wise to bait someone above your ability," he teased. "The advantage I'd have over you would be utterly unfair, especially in that dress."

"Ha! I'd like to see you try. And what's wrong with my dress?"

"Nothing's wrong with it. It's rather flattering on you. It just allows me to do this."

Without warning, he grabbed my skirt, his hands taking in the first few layers of the tattered silk. Before I could blink, the fabric came up over my head and twisted around my torso as he rolled me back into the grass. In a matter of seconds, he had completely bound me in blue silk. He hovered overhead with a mischievous smirk and a twinkle in his eyes. Pinned to the ground, I was entirely at his mercy.

"Okay, you win," I conceded, after a moment of fierce squirming. "You're way above my skill level, silk master. Can you untie me now?"

"Personally," he began, leaning in so close that my heart froze when he was mere inches away, "I think I like you like this—less likely I'll be clotheslined by a tree."

His lips softly brushed mine, leaving the most desirable sensation in their wake.

"Do you kiss everyone you tie up?" I stared up at him, trying to be serious.

He traced the line of my jaw with his nose. My skin tingled, and I shivered despite the fabric that engulfed me.

Feverishly, his lips crushed mine. His unguarded kiss held nothing back, reminding me of last night. My bonds went slack as he released them to take my head in his hands. I responded to every touch, to every sensation. His lips sent chills through my limbs. I absorbed the surge of pleasure each move of his body sent through me as his mouth tasted mine.

Faint sounds in the distance caught his attention. Roah froze above me mid-kiss.

"What is it?" I whispered against his tight lips.

When the sounds of barking dogs became clear, he sat up and strained to listen. His expression grew serious. "We should head back."

"Is it something to be concerned about?"

"No," he reassured as he finished untying me. "Hunting parties don't come this deep unless they're with a member of the royal family. If I know my family, they're still sleeping off last night, but it's best if we get back anyway, before we're missed."

"As much as I really hate that idea, you're probably right." Thinking about returning opened a Pandora's Box of questions and uncertainty. "So what happens now?"

I'd asked him that same question last night. From his expression, I could see he still didn't have an answer. He graciously helped me to my feet. Then, without warning, he encircled me in his arms, holding me close. I clung to him as a new yearning, deep, and intense, swelled within.

"We take it as it comes," he said softly, "and hope that what waits for us is within our ability to overcome."

"And if it isn't?"

"Lotty, in spite of your prior innocence, you've managed to undo the best-laid plans of princes, kings, and tyrants, just by being you," Roah admitted with an endearing look in his eyes. "I tremble to think of what you will accomplish now that you know the stakes and all the players!"

"You don't know how comforting it is to hear that I'm enough for you, just as I am." I buried my face in his chest. His fingers dug into my back, pressing me closer.

"Never forget that. I know there's still a lot you don't understand about this world, about how your choices affect your people. Remember, you also have knowledge of things that I do not—and some stunning confidence. It just shows up differently than you'd expect."

"You say that like it's a good thing," I grumbled shyly at his compliment.

He pulled away to meet my eye. "It certainly keeps me on my toes and our enemies off balance! That's a trait anyone would value." He bent to pick up his jacket. Shaking the leaves off, he offered it to me. The morning was cool, but I shook my head. He added, "It's getting late. We'd better go."

"I'll be right behind you," I told him as I turned and headed into the woods.

"Lotty, the castle is this way." He pointed in the opposite direction.

"I know," I replied, moving quickly behind some thick bushes.

"What are you doing then?"

"Answering the call of nature. Lady business. Just turn around!" I ordered as I looked for a fallen tree. "And don't listen!"

"On my honor, my lady," he vowed with a grin. His footsteps moved farther away. "Just don't go too far."

As I found an acceptable place to relieve myself, the sound of dogs grew louder. Deep voices of men shouting in the distance now accompanied the barking. I hurried as fast as I could and finished as the commotion intensified. I didn't want anyone to sneak up on me.

Just as I started back, a large dog exploded out of the underbrush, running toward me at full speed. The frenzy of following a scent gave the wolfhound's saggy dark eyes a wild look.

I ran, but the dog was faster. It overtook me, jumping up and knocking me to the ground. I screamed as I went down, calling for Roah. The dog snarled menacingly, barking as he lunged at me. I curled into a fetal position, throwing my arms over my head, waiting for the sickening tear of flesh from its bite. It never came. Shaking, I peeked between my arms and saw it standing over me, its hot breath on my skin, drool dripping from its jowls.

"Lotty!" I heard Roah running in my direction, panic in his voice. His footsteps stopped by my feet.

"Release," Roah commanded in a stern voice.

The heavy mass stepped back, freeing my tightly coiled body.

"Are you okay?" he asked as he knelt over me. "He didn't hurt you, did he?"

"No, I'm okay," I said, still a little stunned. Hearing that, Roah lifted me to my feet, making sure I was steady before releasing his grip. "I take it you know this dog?"

"Yeah, he's one of ours," he said curiously as he peered into the forest around us. Something had shifted in his demeanor, in his stance, even in the tone of his voice. I didn't like it.

"Lotty, can you run?" he asked, urgency lacing his tone.

26

Roah grabbed my hand and took off through the trees, pulling me behind him. The dog led the way as I tried to run as fast as I could, but my nearly bare feet made that difficult.

"I need you to keep up," he yelled over his shoulder, half dragging me behind him.

"That's easy for you to say. You have boots on," I shouted.

He stopped abruptly, and I slammed into his side. He turned and scooped me into his arms. Then he started again, holding me to his chest as he ran.

I clung to his shoulders while we dodged trees and bushes. The dog ran ahead, cutting through the bramble with ease as he led the way back to the castle. Roah was right to carry me; he covered the distance more easily than I could in my stupid dress.

It took some time to move through the trees before they started to thin. In my mad dash last night, I'd traveled farther than I'd realized. When I could make out the silhouette of the castle through the branches, a man appeared, running toward us.

"It's you!" he exclaimed, surprised.

When he got closer, I recognized Hal, one of the men who had ridden back with us from the country manor.

"Of course it's me. Who were you expecting?"

"Are you guys okay? Is she hurt?" he asked, concerned as he looked at me in Roah's arms.

"We're fine," he reassured Hal. "Why the dogs? What's happened?"

"We've been searching all morning."

"What?" Roah's eyes widened, disbelief evident in his voice. "Why?"

"You don't know?"

"Obviously I don't or I wouldn't be asking."

"Sorry, My Prince. I just assumed you did."

The blow of a horn cut their exchange short. It sounded twice, after which the dogs started running in the direction of the castle. Hal froze then, as he had on the road to Icel, with his eyes closed and brow furrowed.

"He is anxious to receive you now," Hal said, opening his eyes.

"*He*, as in my *father*?" Roah asked.

"Yes."

"Perfect," Roah said under his breath. "You didn't include Lotty in your whisper, did you?"

My heart sank as his face became a grim mask.

"No, it will take but a minute."

"Don't," Roah said. "The explanation is best left to me."

"Understood." He nodded, visibly relaxing.

Before we stepped beyond the cover of the forest, Roah set me down.

"Hal, hand me your cloak."

He took it off without hesitation. Roah wrapped it around my shoulders and lifted the hood to conceal my face, completely covering me and hiding my tattered dress from head to bare toe. The hood even disguised my messed-up hair and faded makeup.

Whispering, he said, "Remember, no one can know what happened between us last night. The last they saw you, you rejected the prince. That is our protection, so we must behave accordingly. This guard's cloak will conceal you as we return you to your room. Head high, shoulders back. Stay close. No one will notice you."

"Okay," I agreed, sharing Roah's nervousness. "What's going on?"

"I don't know, but it doesn't look good."

Several more guards in heavy cloaks joined us as we re-entered the castle grounds. Roah didn't say anything more, although the tension rolled off of him like a heavy fog when our guards turned away from the halls that led back to my room. Hal and the other guards said nothing as they escorted us in a tight formation, through the castle, no one slowing until we reached the Chamber Room.

When we got to the oversized wooden doors, they swung open. The room wasn't as full this time. I counted only seven people, the king and queen, Prince Laurion, the Sage Nachise, a tall female Sage with smooth copper skin and arresting glass blue eyes and three other individuals I didn't recognize.

As our group entered, I followed closely behind Roah and Hal. When the king saw us, he immediately stood.

Laurion was the first to break ranks, his face a picture of relief. He rose from his chair as soon as he saw his brother and crossed the room. Everyone remained silent as the two princes embraced.

"I had truly feared the worst this time," Laurion whispered to Roah as his arms encircled his brother. Roah returned the embrace before turning to question their father, who had risen to his feet, a look of barely controlled rage on his face. Though his anger was not directed at me, I fought the urge to shrink back.

"What's going on?" Roah asked the king.

"Maybe you could tell me," King Zarian declared bitterly. "Where did you find him?" he asked Hal.

"The woods, Your Majesty," Hal answered as he went to one knee, bowing his head. "The border of the south forest."

"What were you doing in the woods?" the king demanded of Roah. I noticed that Laurion remained beside his brother and seemed ready to defend him.

"Nothing I couldn't handle."

"I'll be the judge of that!" With the tone the king used, it seemed as if Roah were one command away from being arrested. It suddenly occurred to me that the men at our sides were not an ordinary escort.

"Will someone please tell me what's going on?" Roah demanded. "I heard the horns, I know the protocol. What happened?"

"How do I know you're not a part of it?" the king asked, fuming. "No, I will not divulge any information until I am certain. Explain why all of our evidence points to you."

Roah looked from his father to his brother. "Evidence?"

Turning back with a pointed glare, the king addressed Roah. "Don't think just because you walk in here, acting naïve, that I will be taken in. Your behavior since you've returned has been suspicious, to say the least. And now I discover you've been part of a conspiracy against the very powers that grant you nobility."

As Roah listened to his father, his expression moved from bewilderment to shock. He looked to Nachise and the tall woman beside him, but they looked on impassively. "I am not here to betray you. Aren't my years of sacrifice evidence enough? What more do I need to do to prove that our purposes are aligned?"

"Where have you been these past hours? We searched everywhere. Then you just turn up miraculously in the woods. All of this on the heels of challenging me—"

The queen cut him off, her tone firm. "Let your son explain." She was obviously upset, although I couldn't tell if it was the king's statements or the situation in general that concerned her.

When Roah faced the king again, he'd seemed to have recovered from his initial shock. When he finally spoke, his words dripped with irritation. "My Lord, I promise you, as I did last night, that I am a loyal servant of Niniever. I have done nothing but give my life to its service. I demand to know under what grounds you see fit to question my loyalty."

"Because she is gone!" the queen snapped. The room froze. No one looked directly at her. No one dare move, save one. The king turned toward his queen slowly, as if she were a lit fuse.

I was surprised that the queen didn't think I was standing in the room. Then I remembered I was wearing Hal's cloak, the same cloak as our escort.

She must think I'm just another soldier who had accompanied Roah.

Delicately placing his hand on her back, the king spoke. "My dearest, calm yourself. I am mad enough for the both of us."

"I will not calm myself!" Her voice was cold, her displeasure written on her face. "Laurion found the breach last night when he went to speak with her. Twenty of our men dead at their posts. The circumstance around her disappearance is clear evidence of a conspiracy, a betrayal from *within our ranks*." She turned and locked eyes with Roah and his shoulders tightened.

"If word gets out, it will throw the kingdoms into chaos. Do you understand the position this puts us in?" the queen added, still staring at Roah.

"Your mother is right. You were supposed to have protected her!" The king interjected, his own temper clearly at its boiling point.

The room grew silent. Because his back was to me, I couldn't see Roah's expression, but his shoulders grew rigid. The looks on the king and queen's faces were a mix of disappointment and outrage. After a hefty sigh, the king spoke.

"Laurion and I have been working on theories and contingency plans all night. I know we've had our differences, and I would never consider this lightly, but as much as I hate to say it, all evidence points to you. I'm sorry to have to do this, but you leave me no choice. Guards!"

"Father, wait!" Laurion began, but the two guards from the door joined the armed men who had come in with us. Cloaks opened, and muscled arms pulled polished swords from their sheaths as they surrounded us.

27

"STOP!" I commanded, my voice stronger than I'd expected. I knew what Roah had said about keeping quiet, but the solution to the whole mess seemed too obvious.

I lowered the hood revealing my true, if less than dignified, identity. It was enough. Everyone in the room froze, including Roah. Then he stepped back slightly, turning to catch my eye, but I couldn't look at him. I glared at the king as I advanced on him, his words from the previous night ringing in my ears.

"The prince has done nothing wrong," I practically shouted, defiance pulsing through me. As I continued, I kept my voice firm, assertive. "And if you understood a tenth of what he has suffered to keep me safe, you would bite your tongue off before voicing such vile accusations. I will not stand by and listen to another minute of this arrogant ignorance!"

The king's jaw clamped shut even as others fell open in shock. Nachise and the woman beside him shared a loaded look. I didn't care. I was so livid, I was ready to breathe fire. At that moment, he was every bit my enemy and as guilty as Terrshon. As I continued, I thought I saw a small smile growing on the queen's relieved face.

"Your Majesties, obviously I am safe," I began, not caring how exasperated I sounded, "and once again, your son has proven as good as his word. Is there any other circumstantial evidence you need me to clear up, or can I get *your* word that he is cleared of all charges?"

Roah's expression as I spoke was a mixture of astonishment and concern. I couldn't tell if he was worried about my fate or his own.

"Yes, of course!" Prince Laurion spoke up for the first time. "You have proven his innocence most definitively, my lady."

With the flick of his hand, he signaled the guards, who sheathed their swords and stepped back into formation behind us. Then, in a kind but concerned voice, Laurion added, "No one believes in my brother's innocence more than I, but these kinds of losses cannot be ignored. Could you possibly explain why all of our evidence pointed to his involvement?"

"Clearly you have bad sources," I muttered pointedly as I continued. "I can personally vouch for his whereabouts from the moment he left the king's side until now."

"Oh?" Laurion inquired, his voice suddenly full of curiosity. "So, are you saying that you two were together in the woods, all night, alone?"

I knew what he was asking. My chin jutted up in defiance and mentally kicked myself for not being more careful in providing Roah's alibi. "It was clear to me after last night that I was missing some relevant information, having been gone as long as I have. The woods kept our conversation from being overheard. It was no small amount of information Zarian had to relay, and he was very thorough in his report."

"I'm sure he was. And your obviously distressed appearance?" Laurion pressed, stepping closer. His expression was the picture of innocence and concern, but I thought I saw a hint of pleasure. He knew what he was suggesting, and he knew that I knew. My face flushed.

"I fell."

"Down a mountainside or into the arms of my capable brother?"

"Laurion!" Roah shot his brother an annoyed look and came to stand next to me. "Mother, will you tell me what happened?"

The queen sat, leaning against the high, stiff back, obviously exhausted. She looked like a woman who'd settled one too many sibling disputes.

"We found her room turned upside down and blood in the torn bedclothes. She was gone, and we were positive she had been taken. But when I sent word to you through Tregr, he couldn't find you, either. At first, we thought whoever had kidnapped Adelaide had taken you as well, but then we started to worry. We don't know what Elion taught you. We began to think that perhaps your plans may no longer be in alignment with ours." The queen's expression had stilled, but the remorse shining her eyes as she spoke to Roah was unmistakable.

"Last night you fought so hard to take her back," the king added, "I was convinced that was exactly what you'd done, covering your tracks to keep us off your trail. But that can't be so now, or why would you have brought her back?"

"You should've known I would never spend the lives of our people so freely," Roah simply stated, "and that I keep my oaths."

"I was afraid your time away from us had changed you. I see now that I was wrong," the king admitted. Then he turned, looking at both Roah and me, his expression contrite. "Forgive us, we were wrong to question your loyalty on this matter. It is not an error I intend to make again soon. But the question remains. Who knew enough to act so aggressively against us? Everyone must be questioned. It is clear we have been compromised."

"How is that even possible? She only arrived the night before last," Roah said, his tone full of frustration as he calculated the possibilities.

"Terrshon has finally managed to infiltrate our forces, Father," Laurion offered in disgust, returning to his seat at the table. As he continued, he studied a stack of papers full of names and diagrams. "It's the only answer left that makes sense. But how did his men manage to breach the princess's chambers last night? And why take the time to destroy her room, to give the appearance of a struggle? The twenty guards assigned to her were well seasoned, not easily dispatched. Was he making a point by gutting them within our walls and leaving the bodies in pools of blood?"

I tried to stifle a gasp at how casually he described the carnage, as if he'd just given the morning weather report. It made me sick to know that yet more people had died trying to protect me.

"As she is here, unharmed," Laurion went on, his forehead creasing as he poured over one map after another like a hound following a scent, "we can presume the blood in the room belonged to the men who breached the castle. At least our men left us that evidence of their efforts, a small comfort considering their larger failure. Under closer inspection, our only clues are a vanishing trail of blood and the condition of her room. Clearly, they were here for more than the princess."

I took a deep breath as I forced my hand to stay at my side and not grasp for the chains still tucked into my shift. Roah had explained that people had died searching for my father's ring, but at the time it had been an abstract concept—just a story. Now, I was positive that's what they had been looking for.

"And you have no other leads?" Roah demanded, looking first at his father and then to his older brother. If Roah was trying to hide the urgency in his voice, he was doing a horrible job.

"No. We've questioned all the guards, the servants—everyone found near the room when we discovered it had been ransacked. It seems anyone who could have identified them was killed. We've come up empty-handed on all accounts," the queen added with a heavy sigh. She'd changed out of her gown since the party, but I wondered if she'd slept.

"That doesn't sound possible," Roah said, disbelief lacing his tone.

"It is. Your brother took over the investigation personally when you could not be found," the king confirmed.

"Then they could still be in the castle," Roah concluded as he looked at those surrounding the table. "What are we going to do about that?"

"It's unlikely. I've already sent men to search the castle and grounds, but it's been hours. Before you arrived, I had just called off the dogs. We should localize our manpower, just in case they show up again," Prince Laurion insisted.

"Again?" I asked, my voice strained.

"If they didn't get what they came for the first time, what's keeping them from trying a second time?" Roah's voice was gentle, perhaps in an attempt to not scare me. It didn't work.

"Are we just going to sit by and let that happen?" I demanded. I needed to hear solutions; I was sick of hearing nothing but a list of problems.

A tense silence fell as everyone looked around, each waiting for the others to offer a solution.

"We send her back," a confident female voice said. The tall, striking woman I'd noticed earlier stepped toward the table. At her words, all heads turned in her direction.

"That's out of the question, Devendra," King Zarian's said, his voice more strained than I'd expected. "Sending her back is certain death. We can't allow that."

Devendra said nothing as she stared at the king with those hypnotic blue eyes, waiting. Her cool poise impressed me, her face, framed by tight cherry-chocolate curls, the picture of serenity. As I looked more closely, trying to figure out what her role was here, I noticed her robes complemented Nachise's. Where his were light, hers were dark and very feminine.

"Father," Roah started in a steady voice, trying to mask another emotion I couldn't quite pick up. "Are you questioning the wisdom of a Sage?"

"No, that's not—" the king stuttered, struggling to make his point. "We can't send her back knowing it could kill her."

"Nor can we leave her here for the same reason," Devendra explained, her exquisite voice steady. "It is best for everyone if she returns to Oldworld."

"Husband, she's right," the queen said before the king could dispute the point again. "It is best. The attack has made it clear she's not safe within our borders as we had supposed. Terrshon got too close, and at a great price. He failed this time, but he will not stop. If we continue on this course, then one day he will succeed. We do not want to be known as the province that let the hope of Moldara be extinguished in the hour of its redemption."

The queen had spoken softly, but her words painted a vivid and devastating picture. It was my turn to stare in awe. The king tried not to act stunned, but she might as well have clubbed him.

Roah leaned on the table in front of his father. "What would have been the price of our arrogance if she *had* been in her room when the perpetrators had come? No matter our desire to have her remain here, clearly Terrshon can reach her even inside these walls. Can we, in good conscience, risk even another day with her here? We have to stay vigilant and use all we have in our power to protect her, and right now, that's sending her back."

"The queen and the prince speak great wisdom in this matter," Devendra said to the king. "It would be foolish not to listen."

King Zarian was silent for some time. Then he stood, addressing the room.

"I am not so proud that I cannot hear wisdom when it is presented to me. I will not defy the words of the Sages," he proclaimed, his eyes focused on Roah. When he continued, he released his son's gaze to address the room. "After this attack, it is clear we are not yet prepared for what her return means. That we lack the sufficient ability to keep the princess safe here is beyond intolerable. If the Sages endorse it, then she can wait there, just as well as she would here. She will not return until proper safety measures can be put in place."

I thought my eyes were going to pop out of my head. Was I hearing him correctly?

"Stop looking so shocked, all of you. I am not as burdened by pride as I once was," the king said to both of us before addressing Roah specifically. "We must plan for every contingency. Of course, you will have all my resources and men at your command, all those who are not needed for the general defense of the kingdom and our preparations here. I expect you to use them wisely. She must be protected until she is safely through, and this time I want the passage held against Terrshon until her return. I insist on that. I want you on the road in no less than three days' time."

"Thank you," Roah said sincerely. "You'll have our strategy tonight."

"Fine." The king nodded as he sat. "We will meet here after dinner.

Bring whoever needs be involved in the preparation. I want to oversee it all."

"Very well," Roah agreed. "We have much to do. Please excuse us."

Roah grabbed my elbow as he turned to leave, gesturing for me to raise my hood. We exited the room, and to my relief, the guards did not follow us this time.

28

We walked through the castle, winding up staircases and down long hallways until we reached the room Tregr had taken me to last night. So much had happened since then. Could it have only been last night?

When we entered, Roah shut the door and locked it. Then, he turned, taking my face in his hands, and kissed me desperately. He pulled back while his fingers frantically traced the chains hanging from my neck, following them down my chest.

"Please, tell me it's still there," he said.

Without hesitation, I reached down the front of my dress and pulled at the chain, revealing the ring. Roah grabbed it in relief, releasing it as soon as he'd finished exhaling.

"Lotty, I thought I knew you," he began as he walked over to the fireplace and sagged into one of the overstuffed chairs. His hand clutched what I assumed was a pounding heart. I could relate. My own pulse was still far from normal.

"I'm sorry, Roah. I know you told me not to say anything. I just couldn't—" I tried to apologize, but he stopped me.

"Would you please stop apologizing for doing absolutely nothing wrong?" he pleaded as he held his hand out to me. I crossed the room and sat on his lap. The tumultuous exchange had fueled my need for his grounding touch.

"In your mind, are they or anyone else your superiors?" he asked.

"No, but—"

"Lotty, when are you going to trust your instincts?" he asked. The words hung in the air between us.

"You're confusing instinct with anger," I said in a low voice. "I shouldn't have been so rude. I know I shouldn't have, but something about your father just set me off."

"Are you kidding? You were stunning in the way you handled yourself back there. Truly. I've seen powerful people cower before my parents, and most of the women just swoon after five minutes around Laurion. But not you! You looked them square in the eye and demanded to be seen and heard. Your parents would have been so proud of you this morning."

"Really?" I wondered what they would've said if they'd seen me, or if Elion had.

"Of course! Now we have the Sages' blessing to take you back. Not even the king can go against the wisdom of the Sages without facing severe consequences."

He placed his hand on my cheek as he looked into my eyes, their blue penetrating me to my very core. My heart seized in my chest.

"I love you, Lotty. I love everything about you, especially your temper."

He leaned in and pulled my face close as his lips pressed ever so gently on mine. The connection sent a thrill down my spine, and I savored the sweetness of his touch. When he pulled away, I kept my eyes closed to hold onto the feeling for as long as I could.

"I love you, too," I breathed, afraid of the declaration but needing him to know.

He tensed, and I slowly opened my eyes. When I looked into his eyes, blue liquid fire poured into me. This time, when he kissed me, his kiss burned with desire, and I forgot how to breathe. When we drew apart, I was left dizzy and had to catch my breath.

Blood of Moldara

"Now I just have to figure out how to leave without anyone finding out."

"What?" Maybe I was more disoriented than I thought. "The king has already given you his blessing to take me back. We don't need to sneak out."

"Yes, we do."

"I'm confused."

"There's still a breach in our forces," Roah reminded me. "If they think we're leaving in three days, I am confident they'll be back for you tonight and possibly every night until they find a way through our defenses."

Laurion's description of the soldiers who had been killed in my room flashed in my mind. A tight knot formed in my stomach. More rooms could be filled with corpses because someone was trying to find me here. A knock on the door made me jump, and Roah tightened his arm around my waist.

"I'm not to be disturbed," he commanded.

No answer was given and I relaxed. However, Roah kept eyes on the door, waiting for something.

"What?" I wondered.

He just held up his hand, asking for me to pause.

Then I saw it, a small movement at the bottom of the door. A blur moved toward us, and I tensed, lifting my feet. I nearly squealed when I realized it was a mouse.

Roah relaxed when the little creature stopped at his feet. He leaned down and untied the string around his torso. It had a small tag attached.

"It's Daggon," Roah explained after reading the *D* scribbled in black ink. He scooted me off his lap and stood. "Are you alone?" he asked through the door. A muffled "yes" bled through and Roah opened it.

Daggon slipped into the room quickly, closing the large door and relocking it behind him. As his familiar golden eyes found us, my muscles released a tension I didn't know they'd had.

"I'm glad it's you," Roah sounded relieved.

"I'm glad to find you here and not in the dungeon."

The two men clasped each other by the forearm and pulled in for a quick embrace. It seemed I wasn't the only nervous one.

"I need you to bring my honor guard here—only my honor guard. We have the Sages' blessing to take Lotty home, and I want to leave as soon as possible. I want only those we can trust here to plan our escape."

"Of course," he said, bowing slightly. Then he glanced at me. "What about Lotty?"

"Oh, I'm not leaving Roah's side."

"I agree," Roah said. "It will be easier to keep you hidden if we aren't shuttling you all over the castle."

"Oh, no, I was referring to her dress," Daggon interjected. He turned to me with a boyish grin I hadn't seen on him since Virginia. "No offense, but you look like you were both first-timers, incapable of waiting to undo a few laces, or put down a blanket."

All the eyes in the room turned to look at me, including my own. After a moment, Daggon's low chuckle broke through the remaining bits of my tense exterior and left the three of us in a fit of laughter.

Grabbing his side, Roah finally spoke. "Would you like to change? There's plenty of room in there for you to do so in private."

Roah pointed to a large wooden door to the right of the fireplace. I nodded, getting my giggles under control.

"Make sure to get the women who dressed her before," Roah said as he turned back to Daggon, "and tell the guard to bring plenty of food. We won't be leaving this room for a while."

Daggon wiped a small tear from his eye as he bowed and exited the room, still laughing softly to himself.

A select few of Roah's honor guard joined us soon after, bringing a large meal up from the kitchens. We ate under the watchful eyes of Daggon and three more armed men: Callan, Brokk, and Hoden. Tregr was the last to join us. Roah's shoulders tensed slightly as Tregr entered the room but calmed as soon as he saw my grooming care-takers following him.

Thankfully, there was a bathing chamber in the enormous suite that apparently was Roah's wing of the castle. As soon as I was told a bath was ready for me, I excused myself from the impromptu table. I could hardly wait to slip beneath the hot bubbles.

29

I fell in and out of sleep as I relaxed in the steaming water. Doors opened and closed, voices discussed things in low tones, and the clanking of weapons all sounded beyond the large oak door that separated me from Roah's meeting. None of this alarmed me. The commotion of planning meant one thing—I was finally going home.

A large crash finally brought me fully out of my drifting state.

My water had cooled, and I didn't know if I should call for someone, but the sudden silence unnerved me enough that I didn't want to wait. I got out and reached for a folded towel.

I dried quickly and found a dressing gown. Slipping it on, I wrapped up my damp hair with another towel and made sure the chains holding my mother's pendant and father's ring were tucked into the gown. Everything was still too quiet. Warily, I walked over to the door, being as quiet as possible while I cracked it. I was surprised to see the room completely empty. The weapons that had been on the table were gone. The map and all of its markers—gone. All that had been left were a few books strewn about the table.

I opened the door wider, stepped in, and immediately tripped over something at my feet. I heard a moan as I fell hard into a small puddle, my hands slipping on sticky liquid. When I pulled myself onto my knees, I wiped them on my gown and saw crimson streaks blossom on the white fabric.

I was too shocked to move. Before me a man was sprawled on the floor, eyes closed. Platinum blond hair, soldier's clothes. A corner of my mind filled in the name. Brokk. He'd been assigned to me. The hilt of a weapon stuck out of his chest.

Horrified, I looked around the room for the attacker. We were alone. I touched Brokk's chest to see if he was still breathing. The gentle rise and fall of his chest told me it might not be too late. I pulled the towel out of my hair and pressed it to the gushing wound, trying to keep my shaking hands from disturbing the knife. I remembered a blade could do as much damage coming out as going in if you didn't know what you were doing. My first-aid knowledge ended there.

"HELP!" I yelled, hoping someone would hear and come in time to save him. This couldn't be happening again. "SOMEONE, PLEASE HELP ME!"

Another moan brought my attention to the agonized expression on Brokk's face. I immediately stopped pressing.

"Brokk, I'm sorry. I don't know what to do."

He coughed up blood as he tried to breathe. He was drowning. The blade must have punctured a lung. Brokk tried to say something, but I shushed him. I wanted him to keep his strength until someone came to help, but he insisted that I listen as he forced out his words.

"I know...who...betrayed—" his voice strained as he tried to talk, but he coughed again, cutting his words short.

"Who?" I asked, my voice almost a whisper.

He coughed again. This time he choked so violently he almost couldn't compose himself. When he finally did somewhat, he couldn't hide the pain overpowering him.

"Brokk, stay with me. Tell me who did this to you!" I commanded as I wiped the sweat from his brow. My shaking hands left red streaks across his pale skin. Desperate to comfort him, I pulled his head into my lap, stroking his golden hair as he coughed. I wanted the name of his murderer; I wanted someone to pay for the life that was slipping so painfully out of my fingers. I felt tears burning my eyes, but I couldn't look away.

I screamed again for help, but no one appeared at the door.

I was losing him; he wasn't keeping his eyes focused on me. They seemed to look past me. I tried to get in his line of sight, but he wouldn't meet my eye, as if he couldn't see me. He shuddered one last time before finally going still. I watched helplessly as his eyes relaxed and he slipped away, his head becoming very heavy in my lap as it rolled to the side.

"Brokk!" I cried, shaking his head. I tried to feel for a pulse at his neck—any sign that he was still with me. There was nothing. "Brokk, I'm so sorry," I whispered, wiping tears from my face.

Where was everyone? Why had no one come? Shaking, I got to my feet, determined to find Roah or anyone who could tell me what was going on. Suddenly something across the room moved, and I screamed.

I stopped when I saw it was only Prince Laurion, struggling to pull himself up from behind the table. Blood streamed down his left arm, soaking his shirt and coat. He looked to have taken a solid blow to the head as well, judging from the goose egg forming above his right eye.

"Laurion, you scared me half to death!" I scolded, holding a hand over my pounding heart. "Are you okay?"

Reflexively, I started to move to help him, but something in his eyes stopped me. "Where's Roah?"

"I was hoping you could tell me that," he said angrily, his voice winded.

"He was just here, but I don't know where he is now. What happened?"

His right hand grasped at a wound on his left bicep as he steadied himself on the table. He glared at me in pain as if about to say more, but the echo of boots running down the hall distracted both of us. Out of the corner of my eye, I saw Laurion pull out a dagger to defend us. He stepped closer just as Roah burst through the doors, followed by several of his guards, including Callan and Hoden.

"Lotty!" he cried as he ran to my side.

"Roah!" I was so relieved to see him unharmed. My shaking limbs sagged as Roah reached me. The protective fog of shock lifted from my mind with his touch, and the world rushed in.

"Lotty, where are you hurt?" Taking in my blood-soaked gown, he searched frantically for the source.

"It's not mine," I reassured him in a weak voice as he lowered my limp body to the floor. Kneeling in front of me, he moved his hands over the rest of my still shaking body to be sure. Relief flashed in his eyes before he was serious again, taking my head in his hands.

"Slow deep breaths, Lotty. It's going to be okay. Everything is going to be okay. You are safe."

I nodded as his words registered, trusting his strength. He took the chain around my neck and tucked the ring it bore back under my gown. Then, he turned to his guards. "She's shaken but appears to be unharmed. Watch the door."

I slowly turned my head to where Brokk had fallen but found myself unable to look at him. "Brokk, he's...I tried to help, but he had lost so much blood." The tears came back quietly, and I raised a shaking bloodied hand to wipe them away.

Roah looked over at Brokk's still body and then back to me, anguish filling his face. "Lotty, shh. It's okay. Listen to me. It's not your fault. I shouldn't have left him by himself."

"I'll care for his body," one of the guards said as he moved over to his fallen comrade. Another burly man joined him as they lifted Brokk from the pool of blood and left the room with him.

After they had exited, Roah looked at his brother, nodding at his bleeding arm. "Who did this?"

"I couldn't identify him. His face was obscured, but he wore the seal of the royal guard."

"One of our men?" Disbelief filled Roah's voice as he stood, shocked. I sat on the floor, watching the brothers while I pulled myself back together.

"I saw him with my own eyes," the prince confirmed. "He would have killed me if our father had not been so insistent about my training. I came here looking for you, only to find him attacking the guard at the door. I tried my best to help, but he sliced my arm just before running

Brokk through. He ran off before I could identify him. I apologize, Zarian. I'm not the fighter you are," he acknowledged with uncharacteristic humility.

"There's no need. You did what you could." He turned to his men. "He couldn't have gone far. You six, look for blood. Report back to me at once if you find anything."

The six guards left immediately. Afterward, Roah walked over to his brother and reached for his arm. "Let me have a look. I bet it's nothing the waters can't heal."

"No." Laurion pulled his arm from Roah's hand. "Much has changed in your absence, brother. We began rationing the water a few years ago when Terrshon limited the water to only the royals' portion. I'll not waste what stores remain on something as small as this."

"It's your arm," Roah said, walking back to my side.

"Zarian, your plans for keeping her safe aren't working. Maybe I could help hide her these next few days while you're planning your passage. It's perfect. They would never look for her with me, and I could be sure she isn't seen—take her deep into the castle. Or we could lock her in the dungeon. I know it's not ideal, but I can guarantee they wouldn't be looking there."

"Laurion, I'm not locking her in the dungeon," Roah replied. I exhaled in relief as his words registered in my mind. "Thanks for the offer, but I have made other arrangements."

Laurion's expression grew confused. "You just saw what happened here. Are the lives of your men so cheap? Surely you're not so proud as to refuse help in this?"

"The plan has changed. She won't be leaving my side."

"Oh!" His surprise was tainted with obvious irritation. "Well, that will help you keep her a secret. Zarian, see reason. You can't possibly keep her hidden for three more days without help. Are you waiting until our parents pay for her secret with their lives?"

"Of course not. I'm not going to risk endangering anyone else. We will be out of Terrshon's reach soon enough. Now if you'll excuse me, I have things I need to ready for tonight. Guard, keep watch. I want no one past this point. Understood?"

Blood of Moldara 231

"Yes, My Prince," they said as they placed themselves just outside the door.

Roah didn't wait to hear Laurion's reply before he helped me back to my feet. Once we were safely in the back room, all those bloody images came rushing back. Another person was dead because of me. I hid in Roah's arms as the heartbreak overpowered me.

"I'm relieved you're okay. When I saw the blood, I thought—" His voice caught.

"I'm fine," I said as I nodded perhaps a little too fast. The tremors along my skin subsided. In their place came an icy stillness. Roah cocked his head as he studied me.

"All right, let's get you cleaned up and dressed. This blood may not be yours, but it's still freaking me out. As it is, I'm probably going to have nightmares for a while."

Not wanting to call anyone else up to the room, nor having the time for another bath, Roah showed me a little room off the bathing chambers behind an almost hidden door. Inside was a simple stone room about the size of a walk-in closet. A wooden bench sat in the middle. In the center of the floor, under the bench, was a small metal drain, and hanging above was a small pipe, a device resembling a metal showerhead on the end. One thing I was grateful for in this strange world was the indoor plumbing. I didn't know how they managed that with no electricity, but I really wasn't interested enough to ask.

As my hand fell away from the rubbed metal, I saw Brokk's blood still present in the cracks and lines on my palm. I felt the cold prickle through me as I ran the numbers. Dozens dead in just a few days, because of me.

"It's my fault," I said in a hoarse whisper.

"It's not your fault, Lotty," he said, voice as soft as his touch.

"How can you say that?"

"Because I will not dishonor his sacrifice. It was his to make." The reverence in Roah's words was so unexpected it distracted me from my anguish. "Brokk knew his service could one day take his life. He took a vow to protect those most needed to lead. Brokk did his job out of love for the people of this land. I'm telling you—this was not your fault. I honor his sacrifice and the faith in you that it demonstrated."

"But he didn't know me."

"He knew what you stand for—hope. You are the hope of something better for so many. Don't ever forget that."

But I couldn't be their hope. I had nothing to offer. "Do you think I'm a terrible person for wanting to go home?"

"No, I think you have a big heart that wants to keep people from getting hurt."

We stood in silence for a moment. As I took in his words, I felt the ice around my heart thaw. I could again feel the pain of my grief for Brokk, but I could also feel gratitude for him as well. I hung onto that. After a minute, I nodded. I wasn't going to diminish Brokk's sacrifice with my insecurities. Roah was right. He had fought bravely and he deserved more.

"Thank you," I said.

"For what?" Roah asked, true curiosity in his tone.

"You might not know this, but you truly amaze me. The more I see you in your role as prince, the more I find myself speechless. I always thought there was something different about you, but it took me seeing you here to realize what it was."

He held me tightly, and his words tickled my ear as he spoke. "Thank you," he said, his voice sincere. It seemed he wanted to say more but didn't for some reason. Then he gently pulled away and looked over my bloodied gown. "Still creepy. Let's get you out of that and into something a little less nightmare inducing."

He left me alone to shower, wearing one of those unreadable expressions as he closed the door.

30

As I emerged from the washing area, I pulled at the corners of my new outfit. Roah had laid out a set of simple woman's riding clothes just inside the door. They weren't as comfortable as my preferred jeans and tee shirt, but they were definitely a better fit for riding than the gowns I'd been wearing. The clothes came with a stiff leather vest that fit snuggly over the loose shirt and buckled into straps on the pants. It reminded me of a bulletproof vest but properly tailored for a woman's curves.

I finger-combed my hair and pulled it into a loose braid over one shoulder. Then I double checked that both necklaces were secure—with the one bearing the ring safely hidden—before joining Roah.

A satisfied expression grew on Roah's face as he took in my appearance. "Everything fit then?"

"As well as it can," I answered, accepting the tall boots he handed me. He knelt to help with the laces that ran from ankle to calf. As he did them up, I realized they were made of the same thick stiff leather as my vest.

"You'll need this." To finish off the ensemble, he added a sleeve-less gray cloak that covered me from head to toe. "As soon as you feel ready, they're waiting for us in the annex."

Blood of Moldara 235

I adjusted the cloak's hood over my head, being sure I was completely concealed. I nodded, and he motioned to follow him.

Once outside the room, we were escorted through the castle by at least eight guards. We traveled deeper into the castle than I'd ever gone, to a dimly lit room on one of the lower levels. With our entourage, we nearly filled the room.

"Roah," Daggon called as we walked through the door. "You've been gone for an hour. Is everything okay?" He looked at me and then back to Roah.

"Yes, we're fine," Roah assured him, "but we lost Brokk."

"What? How?" Daggon asked, disbelief filling his expression.

"He was stabbed and killed by the traitor. Laurion was also wounded, but he'll be fine."

"Was your brother able to see who it was?"

"No," Roah said, his tone grave. "He did see that he was wearing the seal of the royal guard."

Daggon didn't say anything as he let that register. Then he leaned close to Roah, talking only loud enough for him to hear. "What if the traitor's in the room?"

"That's why I've changed strategy. If they're trying to get to us from the inside, then we plan for that. I'll tell everyone about the changes at the same time. That way Lotty will know who's involved, what to do, and whom to trust."

Daggon nodded once in acknowledgment. "Very good, Your Grace."

Roah looked around the room. "Where's Tregr?"

"He hasn't returned yet, but we've received a whisper that he's fulfilled his assignment. We expect him anytime."

"Then it begins now." He turned to me and spoke in a low voice. "In a moment, I'm going to ask for an oath from these soldiers. When you hear my words, I want you to remember Brokk. I'm not making this request of innocent bystanders. These are men and women dedicated to an idea greater than any one individual. Those who take this oath are not just doing it for you and me. They are doing it for the family they've lost and for the children whose lives will be decided by this conflict. They are doing it to exact justice on the people who've killed thousands of our own. If you let them see any doubt, you will not just rob them of their hope, you will steal their honor. Can you recognize that?"

I took a deep breath as I realized what he was asking. As much as having more people die for my sake repulsed me, I understood. "Yes," I answered softly, my voice full of reverence.

He grabbed my hand and squeezed it gently. "This is the burden of leadership," he said in a low voice. "I know that every step you take in this world feels like a plunge into the unknown, but I need your help to get you home. I need you to be the brave and confident woman I've come to love. These soldiers deserve the kind of hope that only their princess can give them. Will you do that for me?"

"I don't have to proclaim myself, do I? I'm not ready for that."

"Not exactly."

I took a deep breath, exhaling before I answered. "Then I will trust you in this. Just tell me what to do."

"Good." He smiled as he squeezed my hand again. Then he let go. "Wait for my signal. Be sure to stay hooded until I have their oath."

He walked to the front of the room, and I got a better look at the people he'd gathered together. As I took in their faces, I better understood his need to prep me. I could hardly believe how young they were. The room was half women, and all of them were about my age, dressed in the same clothes Roah had provided me—hair braided, gray cloaks hanging on their shoulders. Unlike me, they wore thick leather bands around their arms and short swords belted to their waists. Bows hung over the shoulders of some. The weapons didn't age them as much as their posture suggested. They could have just as easily been a high school theater troupe as real soldiers.

Their faces were hard, cold masks of indifference. I imagined the pitiful existence that drove a teenager to volunteer for military service at such a young age. I saw calloused hands and lean muscles straining against leather bracers, but no smiles, no ease with their surroundings. I wondered how many of them were orphans. Many shifted from one foot to the other, one hand resting uneasily on the hilt of their swords.

Blood of Moldara 237

Roah raised his hand. "Sons and daughters of Moldara!" he began, authority filling every word. All eyes turned to him and the room fell silent. "You are called here because you are my most skilled and trustworthy warriors, the children of a lost kingdom, sworn to aid its allies until it rises again. You have each served Niniever with unflinching loyalty. Now I am here to request more. It is not a call I make lightly."

The room was so quiet I could've heard a pin drop.

"From this point forward, you must take a life oath. This mission, and the knowledge that accompanies it, cannot be mentioned outside this group under any circumstances. Anyone found breaking this oath will forfeit their life immediately.

"For this reason, I'm extending an out. If you are not ready to give this level of service, for whatever reason, I understand. I give you my blessing. Return to your assigned post now without consequence. But this is your only chance to turn back. Once the oath is taken, you will be required to bear it to your graves or until you are released from it. So, if any of you would like to dismiss yourselves, now is the time." Roah paused as he looked around the room.

None of them moved. No one so much as glanced at the door. Even with that warning, they stood steadfast in their trust that Roah wouldn't make them pledge to something without merit. I was deeply moved.

"This is why I have chosen you," Roah said, obviously touched by the devotion of those he led. "Raise your hand and repeat after me."

They all did as he'd instructed, including Roah. Right and left hands went up, which I found disorganized until I saw what they all had in common. Their palms, every one of them, were scared. Jagged white lines of varying sizes and lengths, some in a zigzag of thick lines, others in spider-web patterns, radiated out from different points on each palm. I imagined them as young teenagers crushing tearshaped pendants in their hands, permanently scarring themselves and pledging their lives to vengeance or death. The scars on their palms were a death sentence if they were caught. It was irrefutable proof of their loyalty to my family. My heart dropped through the floor.

They held up their open palms proudly, a hint of eagerness in their expressions as they repeated after Roah.

"I, Prince Zarian of the House of Niniever, choose willingly to protect with my life what is about to be revealed. Our blood for Creation's Water! Our lives to protect life!" His words were spoken with such power and conviction that it gave me chills.

The soldiers repeated Roah's words, replacing his name with their own. The final words they said as one, their voices echoing off the chamber walls until I could feel the vibration down to my bones. "Our blood for Creation's Water! Our lives to protect life!"

As the sound faded, Roah's eyes found mine. He motioned for me to join him.

My heart pounded, so I focused on Roah, on his eyes. I took deep breaths as I walked to where he stood. If he had the certainty to take a life oath along with those in the room, to protect what he was about to reveal, then at least I could trust that. As I filled the space beside him, he addressed the soldiers again.

"I know some of you are familiar with who stands next to me, but you don't know her true identity. It has been kept from you for her protection." He paused as he lifted his hand and lowered my hood. "I present to you Princess Adelaide, rightful heiress of Moldara."

A quiet reverence silenced the room. The expressions of their faces ranged from utter surprise to disbelief. One by one, they knelt, unable to take their eyes off of me. I was sure most of them hadn't been familiar enough with my mother's face to make the comparison, but obviously they still knew the story of the lost princess.

"I don't believe it," someone whispered, breaking the silence. Low murmurs moved through the room.

"There's too much to explain," Roah began, "and this is not the time, nor the place. But I assure you she is who I say she is. That's why your silence on this matter is crucial. Those who seek to keep the throne threaten her life at this very moment. For the last few years, it has been my mission to keep her safe, and now I'm calling your loyalty due, to join me in that charge."

Heads nodded their consent, and Roah nodded to me. This was the moment he had asked of me. *No pressure, right?* I steadied my nerves as I slowly looked over the faces. They all seemed so young.

"I am Adelaide. I am of Moldara, a home torn as cruelly from you as from me. We've all lost much to Terrshon's violence." I paused, taking another deep breath. Each pair of eyes cut through me to the deepest parts of my soul, and I let them.

"He thinks he has you beaten and on the run." I marveled as a realization came to me. A knowing smile grew on my face as the next words came out. "He thinks I am the greatest living threat to his power, but Terrshon has not truly faced the men and women of Moldara. He tried to orphan an entire kingdom. What is the result? You. Each and every one of you, who no doubt, represent hundreds more just like you."

With Brokk's death fresh in my mind, I continued. "In all my life, I have never met a more indomitable people. I don't know yet where my path will take me, but I do know this—my life is but one flame in an inferno that is waiting for retribution." I let my desires for vengeance coat each word with conviction as I continued.

"*You* are that fire. What you seek to reclaim is greater than one little, lost princess. I know that now. That means this isn't just a mission to put me beyond his reach. It is the first strike against your oppressor. It is the moment he begins to pay for what he took from each of you. When you succeed, you will show the world how weak he truly is." My voice held a tone I'd never heard before. I just knew it felt right. At that moment, I ached for each of them to see in me what I saw in their faces.

"I can't promise you much, but what is in my power to do for you, for Moldara, I will do. I already owe my life to so many. I want you each to know that in this act of defiance, I am humbled by your courage and honored to put my life in your hands."

When I finished, there was only silence. I worried I had been a little too honest, too ordinary. I looked to Roah, seeking assurance. I didn't have his practice for the pregame locker room speeches. I was afraid my words had had the opposite effect.

Then I saw *that* look in his eyes again, the one I was starting to recognize. Astonishment. Pride. And something else. His love for me.

I only hoped I would be able to live up to my own promises.

31

The courtyard outside the stables teemed with brown and gray cloaked figures rushing around in various stages of preparation. Their hoods were secured by buckles at the shoulder like mine; the rest of the cloak was more like a thick-collared cape with armholes. If a cloak caught on a branch, it would separate from the hood, keeping the wearer's face concealed.

Despite those deep hoods, I couldn't help noticing there were more than a few stolen glances in my direction. When I caught them, their excitement and pride shone from the jewel-toned eyes I had come to expect of this world. They were excited—eager even—to ride off into unknown amounts of danger. I wished I shared their enthusiasm.

My leather vest felt tight beneath my gray cloak. My arms and calves were covered by the same thick quilted leather hide as my vest and laced to fit. It was all simple, low-tech body armor. I felt like a warrior peasant, a western pirate, and a medieval forest guide all rolled into one confused mess. This place's inability to stick with one time period only added to my identity issues. It didn't help that thirteen female clones, some just girls, were dressed to match me. I sighed, checking my gear for the tenth time.

The bow Tregr handed me was the one thing that felt familiar in my hands. Tregr caught my expression and showed me how to wear the strung bow while riding, then gave me room to mount my horse. He took each arrow, sharpening their tips between his fingers until he was satisfied with their lethalness. I secured the quiver of arrows to the front of my saddle, within reach if I needed them. I hoped I wouldn't.

I'd told them that I could defend myself if needed. I was a good shot. There was never a question of *if* I would hit my target. It was a question of *could* I. *Could I kill someone if I had to?* The last time I had been faced with that situation, I'd choked. That hesitation had ensured my capture and cost more lives every day. I couldn't let it happen again. I wouldn't.

Roah walked over; anticipation and concern in his eyes as he looked up at me.

"You made riding towards certain death look easy," I said, flashing him half a smile from under my hood.

"And you made driving a truck look as natural as breathing," he teased back before his face became serious again. "Hand me your arm."

I did as he asked, stretching out my left arm. He reached behind him and produced a creamy leather sheath holding a dagger with a sapphire-covered grip.

I gasped. "The dagger." It was the one Roah had returned to me on my birthday, the one my grandfather had mentioned in his letter. "Where did you find it?"

"In the woods by Trell's house," he recalled somberly as he secured it on my forearm. "Thought you might need it here."

"Thank you." I trailed my fingers over the soft leather Roah had crafted into the sheath. I noticed dried blood in the seam and my resolve waned. "Looks like it's already been put to use."

"It's tasted the hearts of every person who attacked us that day. I made sure of it."

"I thought it was supposed to be a symbol of our engagement?"

Roah shrugged, his hand lingering on mine. "That was when other people were choosing your life for you. I think it can be whatever you want it to be now. You ready for what comes next?" he asked, changing

Blood of Moldara 243

the subject before either of us had to comment on the arranged marriage I'd been so dead set against.

"I have to be, don't I?"

"We won't let anything happen to you," he said, giving my hand a reassuring squeeze. "We'd all die to protect you. Remember that, okay?"

"That's what I'm afraid of," I muttered, but the clanging of metal and the tension in the air drowned out my words. My bay gelding shifted beneath me. I pulled on the reigns to be sure he didn't get any ideas.

"Roah," I asked, my voice a little shaky, "I know you haven't been telling me everything because you don't want to scare me. I understand that. But how likely is it that we...that I might need to use this bow? Are we about to get all of these innocent kids killed? You would tell me if this was too dangerous, right?"

His eyes held mine, measuring me as he considered how to answer.

"We ride with the best, but I can't promise you won't need to help them. I hope you'll not be put in a position where you have to take a life to preserve yours, but Lotty, no one here is innocent, or a child anymore." The light bent and illuminated his devastatingly blue eyes as we measured each other in silence.

Roah looked away to glance toward the lowering sun. "I think we're ready now. Remember, keep your hood on and stay close. Tregr, Daggon, or I will always be at your side. Terrshon won't take you again while we live."

He said it so intently I had to look away.

In Roah's absence, Daggon rode up next to me and placed a hand on my horse's neck. He murmured something beneath his breath while he stroked the animal. The horse calmed under Daggon's touch.

"What was that?"

"We aren't the only ones who can feel the tension of this group. He just needed a little reassurance."

"Must be cool, having the ability to talk to animals."

"It's more like inviting them to share my feelings or a specific desire. The words are just for my focus."

"You totally messed with our chickens, didn't you?"

His face slipped into the biggest grin I'd ever seen on him. "And all the horses. You have no idea how many times you walked in on me using my bond. I gave us away at least a dozen times. I thought Roah was going to strangle me."

"Does it work on people, too?" I smiled.

"Not really. I mean, it kind of does on kids for a while, but once they learn to talk, it fades."

"That's so sweet."

"Not when they bite you first. But the rest of the time, yeah, it can be fun."

"When is a skill like that not fun?"

"When you have to ask a creature to do something that will most likely get it killed."

My stomach dropped, and I suddenly regretted my questions. Out of the corner of my eye, I saw Roah turn to his horse and mount up. As if on cue, the remaining soldiers mounted and turned their horses to face him. Daggon left my side, touching each of the horses briefly as he rode around the circle. All nervous prancing ceased. The distant rustling of a city preparing for nightfall was the only sound to accompany Roah's next words.

"It's time." He surveyed the group before him solemnly. "We stop for nothing. We will leave the road and travel through the forest as the scouts send word back, so stay sharp. Remember your oaths. Remember that your first priority is to our Little Sister. If anyone of you fails in this, you fail our world. Am I understood?"

The men and women nodded as Roah urged his dark mount to turn for the gate and the city streets beyond. As I followed him, the group formed around us. When Tregr signaled, servants swung the gates open.

At Roah's shrill whistle, we were off.

We left the security of the castle and the surrounding city as the sun disappeared in the late evening sky. I traced the hilt of my dagger and wondered how long it would be before the king noticed we were gone. Would he be mad that we disregarded his instructions and left without

Blood of Moldara

a word? Would he try to reach through the caverns and accuse Roah of breaking his oath again? If so, could we protect him from that?

Even beyond the city gates, I couldn't shake the hold his father, or any of them, had on our future. Terrshon's words haunted me again: *Your life doesn't belong to you. It never did.*

We stayed in a tight formation, meeting only a few travelers who were so preoccupied with their burdens that they hardly noticed us. I never rode alone; Daggon, Tregr, Roah, and Ayla all took turns riding next to me. It was encouraging to know they were there, though conversations were short and tense. No one in the group wanted to be the one who drew attention.

I'd never traveled long distances by horseback, except to get to Niniever. I'd had the sense then that Roah had been pushing the horses to their limits, and it had still taken a full day. This time he set a different pace, alternating between walking and galloping, depending on the terrain and some internal timer. As much as I wanted to race at full speed back to Virginia, I could see very quickly that the new strategy was less taxing on humans and horses.

It occurred to me that he was careful not to overextend anyone; that way we all had the reserves to make a break for it if necessary. It was one of a million things I noticed as we continued to ride in relative silence. After the sun set, we left the road and traveled for a few more hours before stopping for the night in a small clearing sheltered from the wind by tall pine trees.

Roah dismounted. "This is where we'll make camp. There's a stream to the north, so fill your canteens and water your animals. Travel in twos if you leave the group. I don't want to lose anyone to carelessness, so remember the protocol for reentering camp. Stay within sight of your partner at all times. We will have a watch rotation set up. The watch will be relieved every two hours on the hour. Hal and Chaslynn will start. Remember, we have a long ride tomorrow. It will be an early start, so get some rest."

As soon as my feet hit the ground, Roah's well-oiled machine went to work around me. Some dismounted and untied bedrolls from their saddles; others rode to the stream immediately. One woman came over and took my horse's lead. She gave me a warm but admiring smile before leading my mount away with hers in the direction of the stream.

After Roah dismounted, I was surprised when he didn't look at me. Instead, he handed his horse's lead to one of his men and strode purposefully towards Tregr, who was digging through his dappled gray's saddle-pack. The look I saw on Roah's face wasn't one I wanted to see this early in our travels.

Chills ran through me, and I looked to Ayla, who stood between Enzi and Taft. I threw her a questioning glance. She shrugged. I walked over to help them tend their horses, keeping Roah in my peripherals. When I saw him stop behind Tregr, I signaled Ayla. We both paused to watch curiously as Tregr turned to face Roah.

Without warning, Roah clocked Tregr's face as hard as he could with a clenched fist. I had to cover my mouth to stifle a yelp of surprise. The blow was so intense it sent Tregr to his knees and left Roah shaking his hand for relief. Silence pierced the camp as all eyes turned toward them.

Still on the ground, Tregr reached for his jaw and rubbed it gently. He looked at Roah, his expression one I couldn't read. "That's fair," he said.

Then, Roah stretched out his hand, offering to help Tregr to his feet.

"Don't let it happen again," Roah demanded. As soon as Tregr was standing, Roah turned and walked away.

No one moved as they watched him march through the camp, nor did they dare ask what had brought on the sudden flare-up. I was still so stunned to see this side of him that I didn't know what to say to him if he made his way to my side. I just gawked as he went back to the business of setting tasks and overseeing his troops.

Ayla leaned over to whisper in my ear. "When was the last time you saw Tregr?"

"Just briefly this morning. Before that, I think it was the night of the dance. He had left me in Roah's study…alone," I recalled in bewilderment.

"He left you alone?"

Blood of Moldara

I just nodded wide-eyed, realization dawning.

"Roah must be in an unusually forgiving mood," she offered with a bemused smile as she took in my expression. I just nodded dumbly as we finished rubbing down her mount. When Roah finally turned toward me, Ayla softly excused herself and led her horse in the direction of the stream.

"Hungry?" Roah asked like I hadn't just seen him punch one of his best friends.

"Really?" I tilted my head in Tregr's direction. "No explanation, no confession, just change the subject?"

"He knows what he did and that he deserved worse. It's resolved now."

"For leaving me alone in a guarded castle?"

"For disobeying my orders and putting you in a compromising position."

"But his mistake ended up saving my life."

"Which in turn saved his."

I felt my eyes go wide in shock. Roah simply returned my stare, his expression haunted. Finally, I nodded my understanding. Then I added in my best princess voice, "Well, I'm starving. Who do *I* have to punch to get dinner around here?"

"Let's hope it doesn't come to that." Roah tried to hide his smile as he bowed formally and then held out an arm to escort me. I shook my head and gave him a friendly shove before marching over to the fire the others gathered around. Spiced meat had already come out of packs and was steaming over the dancing flames.

While we waited to be served, Daggon appeared, looking satisfied about something. Then Tregr crossed in front of us, his plate in one hand and a compress covering one darkened cheek in the other.

"What happened to him?" Daggon asked. His hand unconsciously caressed his own cheek.

"You didn't see?" I asked, my tone shocked.

"I was looking for something outside of camp."

"Did you find it?" Roah asked.

"Yes, but what found Tregr's face?"

"I did," Roah admitted.

"You!" Daggon chortled. "Did he lose a bet?"

"More like a princess," Roah clarified.

"Bet he won't make that mistake twice."

I rolled my eyes and shook my head. "So what were you looking for?" I asked, changing the subject.

A large smile spread across Daggon's face as he pointed to the perimeter of the camp. In the flickering firelight, I could barely make out two figures walking on all fours, tails swishing.

"Are those…?" It couldn't be.

"Mountain lions."

"Like real claws, teeth, killer-instinct mountain lions?"

"Yep, but they won't enter camp until after dinner is finished. They just ate."

I gulped. "Well, that's almost reassuring." I leaned into Roah. "What do we need mountain lions for?" I asked in a strained voice.

"Protection. They're the best watchdogs we've found."

"And your bond is strong enough to keep them tame?" I turned to Daggon. "Wouldn't it be hard to tell if they are prepping you for dinner?"

He laughed, hard. "When you entice them with something they want, they play nice."

"And what's that?"

"A good long scratch! You should feel those guys purr when they're happy. It's like a massage chair!"

"They'll watch our backs in exchange for a rub down?"

"It's a lot more involved than that, but I threw in a thorn check and promised them the bodies of any intruders."

"Well, when you put it like that, I feel so much better."

As we ate, I couldn't help glancing at the large cats pacing the perimeter of the camp, their eyes on our group as often as they watched the darkness.

32

I tore my gaze from the mountain lions and found something else to focus on—the way Roah's soldiers interacted with each other. There didn't seem to be a pecking order. Instead, respect and camaraderie ruled the group. Everyone chipped in to do the necessary tasks; no one was too high a rank for a responsibility. Even Roah helped serve food and made sure all had what they needed to be comfortable for the night.

As I watched, I also began to notice a lack of personal boundaries. The tenderness shown through physical contact—an arm around a shoulder, snuggling closely under blankets, and the rubbing of shoulders and feet—was universal and easily expressed for both sexes. None of it seemed to have the normal romantic or awkward undertones I was used to seeing. It was as if everyone was in a relationship with everyone and no one at the same time.

When a sweet young lady, who introduced herself as Hawnah, sat next to me with a kind smile and started removing my boots, the feelings of having my personal space invaded flared. I took a deep breath and had to remind myself that Moldara was a different world with very different traditions. I smiled awkwardly as she proceeded to rub my sore feet. Roah finally rescued me by taking Hawnah's

Blood of Moldara 251

place, a knowing smirk growing on his face as he read the relief on mine.

I saw men braiding the hair of both sexes, women sharpening weapons with their bare hands, and small mixed groups playing cards. And I was pretty sure Tregr was flirting with the guy playing with the fire of a small lantern. It was both confusing and reassuring at the same time.

"Is this about to turn into some kind of weird orgy?" I whispered.

Roah looked around. "On a less important mission, some of them might get that intimate. I know most of them have before."

I must have had quite the look on my face when he turned back.

"It was just as shocking for me to see your world. All those people so isolated, so afraid that every touch, every gesture, every word, was a sexual overture. I've been in prison camps that were less suffocating. It really makes a guy paranoid."

"This doesn't feel like a bit much, though?"

"We don't fear connection here, and there are no institutions that vilify consensual sexual expression. None of us were taught to be ashamed or to hide from the comfort of physical connection. It's not as scary as it looks."

"I can't even imagine what that would be like."

"No reason we can't join them."

"I don't want to be the outsider making it weird."

"Only you can make it weird," he countered, holding out his hand. "Just follow my lead. Let me share this much of my world with you?"

I considered his offer for another moment before nodding and taking his hand. He led me through the soft grass to an open spot in front of the fire. One of the women offered to loosen Roah's armor, and he thanked her, raising his arms. The guy next to me offered the same, and I accepted shyly. He showed me how to remove it to sleep so that it could be put back on in a few seconds. He patted me on the back and smiled when I tried to thank him.

While Roah rubbed out the cramps in another guy's hand and talked about horse grooming styles, I turned to the person who sat next to me—the guy Tregr had been flirting with—and offered a back rub. I felt awkward at first, but no one seemed to notice, so I focused instead on the knot I found between his shoulder blades. After several minutes he insisted we switch, and I was facing Roah again.

He raised his eyebrows in a silent question.

I measured my comfort level and gave him a shy thumbs-up. He stifled a smile, set a hand on my knee and turned back to another conversation. It was surprising how quickly the shared intimacy of such simple acts buoyed my trust in people I'd met only that day. As the last of dinner was cleaned up, people shared laps and more exchanged back rubs as easily as they passed drinks around.

Eventually, the smaller conversations gave way to a group discussion. Around the fire that night, I listened to stories of better times, of family, of love and loss. But most of all, I listened to these great men and women share their experiences of life in Otherworld, the only world they knew existed. So many had suffered from the domination of Terrshon in one way or another. The more I listened, the more I shared in their hatred of him.

When the conversation kept circling back to the journey ahead, people started to retire to their bedrolls. The fire was put out, and Daggon walked to the mountain lions. His soft murmurs were heard across the camp as he pet each cat between the ears. I joined Roah where he had laid out our bedding, wondering how I was ever going to fall asleep knowing those predators were nearby. Without the fire to hamper my night vision, the whole night sky opened up, and I welcomed the glorious distraction. A nearly full moon did little to dampen the brilliant tapestry of black velvet and diamonds that hung above us.

On first glance, it all looked the same as it had back home. I was never much for constellations beyond the Big Dipper, so I couldn't be sure if anything was out of place. The moon was a different story.

"Have you noticed that our moons aren't the same?" I whispered into the dark.

"I did," he answered quietly and found my hand. "The Sages say that it's because ours is younger by as much as a millennium. That's why we don't have all the craters that you do."

"It feels so much brighter without them. Is there other stuff here that's different?"

"Probably. I've heard stories of animals—predator and prey alike—that are almost triple the size of what you're used to."

"Triple the size. Why is that?"

"Domestication and loss of territory. Despite our best efforts, those two things change how each species develops. Every now and then someone turns up at a festival with one or two rare species from uncharted regions to show off, but the Sages always make sure they are returned."

"Wait, does that mean you have animals that we don't?"

"Kind of. I think we have most of the ones you're used to. Some I've never seen. They live in parts of our world I haven't traveled to, but I've been told stories by the Sages. Trell told me once how many creatures have gone extinct in your world. I was horrified."

"Hey, we didn't kill them all. A lot died way before humans had anything to do with it."

"Yes, but you didn't save them, either."

"Ouch."

"No, no, it's just an observation. We have a fraction of the population you do. Sure, the Sages are studying the successes and failures of Oldworld, but there's no guarantee that in a few thousand years we won't make the same mistakes. The more I learn, the more I realize just how young of a world this is. It's full of potential, but potential isn't a guarantee of wisdom. For that we must remain vigilant, learn from our mistakes, and make sure that each generation after us is committed to living in harmony *with* the world, not feeding off of it until it dies."

"How do you do that, smarty pants?"

"Oh, I have absolutely no idea," he confessed, and I couldn't help a relieved giggle. "I just know we have to try—to stay true to the tiny pieces of this world we've vowed to be responsible for."

"That's why you feel responsible for Moldara, isn't it?"

Roah was silent for a minute, and I started to wonder if he'd fallen asleep.

Something rustled behind him, and he went up on one elbow, alert. "It's just the cats." He quickly relaxed, refocusing on my face before continuing. "That's part of the reason. Terrshon is on the verge of tearing this world apart. It's been centuries since the kingdoms were this divided, this afraid of each other. He is a poison that's seeping into everything, a disease I hope we can recover from. Until then, I have sworn on my life to do everything in my power to stop him. For now, that is my contribution to the future generations of this world."

"And how do you do that from Virginia?" The question came out before I'd thought it through. I regretted it immediately. He stopped playing with the loose strands of my hair and lay down again.

"I can't," he finally sighed.

A heavy silence fell over us. I didn't want to think about next week, next month, or next year. Any chance at a future was permanently on hold until we got back to Virginia, and I was my own person again—finally out of a murdering psychopath's reach.

"Time to sleep," Roah finally said. "We have all of the nights after this one to answer your questions. Hang onto that, and the answers you seek will find you." He rolled onto his side, facing away from me. He was still trying to keep up the pretense of a non-relationship between us. After what I'd experienced earlier regarding lack of personal boundaries, it surprised me that he was so cautious.

I don't know how long I lay there, staring through the branches at the stars, trying not to think about the wild predators roaming free in camp. The stories I'd heard around the fire played effortlessly across the movie screen in my mind, their images searing into my memory. Images of families killed, land stolen, dreams ripped out from under them, forced service, endless taxation, greed from those who were supposed to be protecting the vulnerable. My whole body begged my mind to shut up so it could get some much-needed rest, but closing my eyes only made the images more vivid. So I continued to stare at the stars, listening to Ayla's light snoring, which sounded like a cat purring.

A loud screech startled me out of a half sleep. I jolted upright and froze as the fur blanket covering me moved. In the predawn light, I wasn't sure I could trust my eyes. I blinked, and the shadows around me took shape.

A mountain lion had curled up next to me in the night.

I barely breathed as the enormous cat stretched and rolled closer to me. It never moved from its position, but its ears twitched as if it were listening to something. It tensed just as another screech filled the air. This one was directly above us.

The camp stirred but the cat was faster. It leaped straight up in the air, almost fifteen feet, paws reaching, tail swishing like a helicopter propeller. A muffled squawk broke the stillness, followed by an explosion of feathers. The cat landed on the ground next to me, spit the giant bird out of its mouth, and batted the creature like it was a toy. The other cat pounced on the heap of feathers, joining the fun.

A hand gently grabbed mine. I gasped.

"Shh," Roah whispered, eyes fixed on the cats. "Make no sudden moves."

"Why?"

"The bond has weakened."

"How do you know?"

"They weren't supposed to hunt in camp."

Daggon appeared just on the other side of the playing felines. His steps were slow but deliberate, eyes glued to the cats. His usually quiet murmurs were clear one-word commands.

"Friend. Trust. Connection. Calm."

Once Daggon spoke the last word, he was standing right in front of the pacified animals, hands outstretched. He carefully placed one on each forehead and closed his eyes.

This time he was silent, his brow furrowed in concentration. Anyone who woke during the outburst stayed silent and frozen.

Finally, Daggon's eyes opened, and he scratched the cats aggressively.

"Feels good, huh?" he cooed as he worked his way across their shoulder blades. Everyone relaxed noticeably.

"Am I missing something?"

"This is not Daggon's first time dealing with a rogue cougar," Ayla said as she scooted next to me.

"You mean we could have been eaten?"

"No, you'd never eat us," Daggon purred as the cats rubbed up against him. "You're good kitties, aren't you?"

"Their bond never broke?" Roah asked.

"Not even a little," Daggon boasted. "They were protecting us."

I reached for one of the feathers, turning it over in the emerging sunlight. At first I thought it was black, like a crow. But as I looked closer, I recognized its blue-gray color.

"Is it dead?" I demanded, trying to keep my voice steady.

Daggon walked over to the creature and nudged it with his boot. It rolled over and hissed. "Still alive." He started his murmuring thing, but the hissing never stopped. After a few moments, he stepped back. "It's not letting me in. Its mind is broken somehow."

I got up and walked over to Daggon, giving the retriever-sized eagle a wide berth. Roah followed.

"No bonded animal is permitted to be controlled like that," Daggon informed us, his brow still furrowed in concentration.

"It's wearing something." Roah pointed to the leather strap around its neck. He took his sword and with the tip, moved the feathers to get a better look. There, hanging from the leather, was a slice of a geode. I'd seen a similar crystal hanging from the necks of the eagles that had hunted us in Virginia, only this time the rock was purple.

"We have to kill it!" My hand went to the dagger strapped to my arm, but when the creature flexed its claws, I slipped it back in its sheath and turned to Roah. "Give me the sword."

I barely felt the cool metal in my hand as the sword's weight filled it. All I focused on was the light glinting off the purple crystal. I still didn't know how it worked, but somehow Terrshon used it to get information, and I wasn't going to let that happen again. I had to destroy it, and the eagle. Without a second thought, I plunged the blade into the crystal and through the wounded bird's chest.

33

"We need to leave," I said, handing the bloodied sword back to Roah. I walked over to the lifeless bird and pulled the leather strap from its neck. The purple crystal had been cracked in two, but I tossed what was left to Roah, who caught it and crushed it with a nearby rock. The tiny pieces that remained lay scattered on the ground, glinting dully in the early morning light. "This is one of Terrshon's birds. Its necklace is bugged."

"Bugged?" Tregr and Daggon asked in unison.

"It's—he uses it to spy on people. I don't know how it works, but if he's controlling that bird, then someone on the other side of this crystal saw us," I explained, pointing to the crushed shards of purple.

"Trell suspected something like that," Roah said. He turned to Daggon and Tregr. "Your orders were to destroy these on sight in...where we found Lotty. You've still been doing that, right?"

They shook their heads, stunned.

"Are you sure?" Ayla asked, leaning down and sifting through the crystalline pieces. "I've never heard of such a bond."

"It's how he found us in Virginia." I looked at Roah and hoped he would forgive what I was going to confess. "I picked one up the day Conlen almost found us at the old homestead. It was turquoise, but it did the same thing. Terrshon used it to track us. That's how Conlen found me."

Roah's eyes were fixed on me, his expression unreadable.

"He was extremely proud of his little trick rocks," I finished.

"Then he knows we are all here? Together?" Taft asked. He had joined Ayla midway through the conversation.

"We have to assume so," Ayla answered.

"Break camp. Now!" Roah shouted. Breakfast hadn't even been started, and some still sat in their bedrolls, but no one protested. The camp erupted into a flurry of organized chaos.

Ayla's face had lightened a few shades as if she might be sick. She stepped closer to Roah, and our group instinctively closed around her protectively. "If he discovers that I'm leading the force that's taking back the water, we're all dead."

"That's doing what?" I looked to Roah. He gestured for me to wait as he addressed the group.

"We need options. All ideas are on the table."

"We go back," Tregr offered. "Niniever is still an ally, and we can pretend this was a drill."

"And risk assassins killing Lotty and the entire royal family? I won't do it," Roah stated.

"No, we've come this far," Daggon said. "If we push the horses, we can still beat them there. I'll help the scouts make sure the path is clear."

"And if they are already there?" Roah asked. "If they pin us down and we can't fight our way out? Best case, we're killed. Worst case, we're taken prisoner."

"Terrshon would either use our bodies to start a war or hide any trace that we were there," Ayla added. "We will have died for nothing. No, we have to outmaneuver him."

"Is there an option that doesn't get us and everyone we care about killed?" I demanded. "I know you're all doing this mostly for me, but it shouldn't be at any cost."

The group fell silent for a moment.

"There is another way," Taft offered, taking Ayla's hand. "But it will delay your presence at the sanctuary."

Roah's brows came together. "We're listening."

"We split up." Taft perked up when no one immediately objected. "We have connections in the north, specifically the mountain region?"

Ayla nodded and Taft continued.

"We take this decoy strategy a step further. Ayla uses Lotty's name to leave a trail so clear that Terrshon will never doubt it's her. We haven't passed the road north yet, so we make sure his spies see what they think is Lotty's group turn that way. He still fears those regions, and for good reason, but we have people who will hide us."

"Wait, no, this sounds like a bad idea—" I began, but Ayla cut me off.

"We don't proclaim for her, but we help spread the word that their lost princess is alive and looking for allies so that she can take her kingdom back."

"But I'm not doing that."

"Lotty, someone is going to have to do it eventually." Ayla put a comforting hand on my shoulder, but I barely felt it. "Even without you here, you can be the symbol people need to find their courage, to know that they are fighting for the right reasons."

"And you can prove that I'm alive without me here?"

Ayla pinched the bridge of her nose as she considered this new course. "It might work. I know which roads to take and who will spread the rumors. It does delay our other plans, but it is the better option, now knowing we may be found out. Thank you, Taft." She turned to Roah. "If we do this, it will change your mission as well. You and your guards will have to take and hold the waters from Terrshon. I have no idea how long it will be until I can return this far south. Can you manage?"

"We'll do whatever it takes," Roah pledged. "If you lead away the bulk of his attention, it does improve our odds of success."

We all looked at each other, waiting for an objection or another option.

"Okay, it's decided then. I'll inform our people." Tregr gave a slight bow and excused himself.

"Daggon," Roah began.

"I know." He offered his own bow. "I send out some decoys. We'll have to redistribute the horses and make sure Ayla's party is seen on the road north. I'll make sure it's done."

Ayla turned to Taft. "Prepare our things. We will need at least four volunteer decoys, maybe six, if they're willing. We must look like this group for as long as possible."

Taft spun on his heels, leaving a cloud of dust.

Roah and Ayla looked to me, anticipating resistance.

"I don't know, guys. This feels like a really terrible plan," I began. "And I know I'm the one insisting on going back to Virginia, but that was to prevent stuff like this, not make the situation worse. I just can't help but feel we're about to get all of us killed. I don't know if I can live with that."

"Your Highness, I'm positively offended. I didn't make all these contacts, nurture countless spies of my own, and avoid capture for all these years to slip up now." Ayla smirked, a twinkle in her eye. But the spark faded as she continued. "The fact is, whatever comes next has been coming for years. The trick is not to fight the current of events. Instead, you must ride it to where you want to go. That's all we're doing. You're the one Terrshon is chasing, so it's your name we will carry to every corner of our lands. His pursuit of me will prove your existence and send people flocking back to a cause they've been waiting to champion."

"You make it sound so easy."

"Oh no, it's insanely dangerous." A knowing smile spread across her face. "But doing nothing is already costing us everything. It's time to change our tactics, too."

"As much as I hate to say this—I agree," I said. "I know I haven't been here long, but it's clear something has got to change. And if you are that force for change on my behalf, let me help."

"What do you have in mind?"

Making sure no one else was watching as the camp made its final preparations to move, I pulled on the chain that hid my mother's pendant in my bodice. Roah stepped closer, helping to keep the necklace holding my father's ring concealed.

Once the round, wire-wrapped stone was visible, Ayla's eyes went wide, and she shook her head. "No, you just got that piece of your family back. I can't take that away from you again."

"But it's proof, isn't it? I saw the paintings in the castle at Niniever, too. I'm betting that every castle has ones like that. If you can hold up something that everyone knows disappeared with me, then they have to believe you. They have to help you and keep you safe, right?"

Ayla looked to Roah.

"It's her choice."

She hesitated another minute before taking my hands in hers. "With your mother's necklace, these won't be quiet whispers in the dark. My actions will have the full weight of your authority. I will be a ghost—your ghost—haunting Terrshon to keep him guessing and you safe. If you truly want to do this, I swear on my life that this is not the last you will see of your mother's treasure."

"I've never needed a necklace to know who I am. But it has led me to my cousin again. I'm not ready to lose you." I undid the clasp and handed it over to her. "Just promise me you'll leverage it to keep you safe, and you can use it however you want."

She accepted the heirloom reverently, her emerald eyes brimming with determination. "Lotty, I swear to you that I have no intention of dying. I will accept this only so long as you understand that my safety is nothing compared to the opportunity to right the wrongs that have been inflicted upon all of us. I'll always be one of your greatest advocates, but I will place the destruction of Terrshon and the restoration of the people of Moldara above all else."

"It's the most she can promise without betraying her principles," Roah interjected. He placed his hand on my cheek, stroking away the hesitation he saw in my eyes. "I know this is hard to understand. It feels completely contrary to everything you've learned growing up, but your life is more valuable than any of ours." His eyes bore into me, burning to my very core as he spoke. "Even mine. My title as prince holds no significance if it's not coupled with yours. You must believe me when I say we would willingly give our lives to save yours because none of us have the ability or the power to move forward in this if we don't have you."

As I stood there, incapacitated by the fire in his belief, I could see the situation through their eyes. My parents' death had changed everything here, and now that they knew I'd survived, I'd given them hope they'd thought lost forever. They were all part of a struggle I might never fully grasp. But watching how they chose to handle it, I trusted them with my family's legacy.

"I understand and I accept your terms, with one condition of my own. If you find my grandpa—I mean Elion—alive somewhere, you will send him home to me. He knows the way."

Ayla nodded before finally securing the chain around her neck. I watched the stone disappear under her shirt as she excused herself. Roah filled the emptiness with a hug that almost made me feel better about what we were getting ready to do.

The campsite from the previous night disappeared around us as Wapi pushed his hands into the earth. His bond shifted the grass, and a small sinkhole opened up. It started by swallowing the ashes from our fire and continued until the impact of our presence was completely erased. Our mounts were waiting. I got my body armor back on in time for a modest breakfast that barely filled my stomach. Knowing that Terrshon was closing in on us had killed my appetite.

Ayla returned leading her horse and mine.

"Lotty, there is so much I want to tell you, so much I still have to share. But we're on different paths once again." She paused as she took my hands in hers, looking at me with eyes full of an emotion she fought to conceal.

"I know what you mean," I admitted, realizing I felt the same. "Ayla, you have sacrificed so much for me and more I'm sure I don't know about. I don't think I ever got the chance to thank you for all of it."

"And you never have to."

"Yes, I do. I owe you so much more than I can ever repay, but I have one last favor to ask," I insisted, and she nodded. "Promise me this won't be the last time we see each other."

"Only if you swear the same," she said, embracing me. "I'm running out of family, too, cousin. For all my talk of serving Moldara, I fear my heart would break beyond repair if I lost you. We will both find each other again. I can feel it."

I hugged her tightly before she released me. After a slight bow, she turned and walked her horse over to Taft, who had a group waiting.

"Safe journey, friends," she said as she mounted. The rest of her riding party, which consisted of nine heavily armed and skilled men and women, including Taft, Enzi, and Kavish, was mounted and waiting for her. It gave me some reassurance knowing she wouldn't be riding into the unknown without allies.

She looked to Roah before heading off. "Take care of her."

"With my life," he vowed, and I felt my forced smile slip.

As she rode off into the woods in the opposite direction of the road, warm tears trailed down my cheeks. I wiped them with the back of my sleeve. Roah put his arm around my shoulders and pulled me close.

"I keep telling myself that since she and I look nothing alike, this is not as dangerous as we're all making it out to be," I confessed.

"I wish that were true, but with your mother's necklace, the people, and those who rule, will look to her as if she were you. There is no one more qualified for that mission," he said, his voice full of quiet confidence. "Her accomplishments never cease to amaze me. Even with few resources, she can do so much. She will coordinate the support we need. I have no doubt."

"But it's been one danger after another since I arrived. How can you be sure?"

"Her training began long before mine, when she was just a child. She knows how to stay in the shadows, and she has more connections, more allies, and knows more about Terrshon's movements than anyone. She'll keep a low profile or travel where Terrshon's men don't dare go. I wouldn't want to be the one trying to stop her."

"I hope you're right," I said, leaning into his chest.

"Come." He walked me toward my horse and replaced my hood.

"We should be on our way as well. And keep that on. We don't want to be spotted again."

We assumed the same gallop-walk routine we had yesterday, stopping for water and a stretch about every hour or so. I was grateful for the rest; with riding all day yesterday and sleeping on the hard ground, I was only beginning to feel the journey's toll on my body. Mercifully, we stopped for lunch before it hit midday.

The closer we got to Moldara, the quieter our group became. There were soft murmurs from Daggon as he enlisted the horses and other forest animals to conceal our passage, I guessed. Wapi still walked behind us, willing the earth to reclaim its unaltered state, so no one on foot could track us. With his long dark hair flowing in the soft breeze, soft leather pants, and his bare feet, he looked like every picture I'd seen of an American Indian. Only the jewel-tone of his eyes set him apart from those images. It made me wonder why it was the eyes that differed so distinctly when I compared the people of this world and those of mine. It also made me wonder, if I was of Moldara and Otherworld, why my eyes didn't have the same brilliance to them.

34

We stopped in a small clearing a few hundred yards off the main road just as dark was setting in. Once I dismounted, someone took my horse, as they had last night. I looked for a way to make myself useful. Roah was in a deep discussion with Daggon, Tregr, and one of his scouts. A few soldiers were already walking the perimeter. The smell of dinner wafted on the breeze. It seemed I wasn't needed.

I sighed. The feeling of being out of place wasn't unfamiliar to me, but I didn't like being an outsider. Even worse, I was some rare spectacle everyone tried to catch a glimpse of. I missed Ayla and her easy way of making me feel normal. I hoped for the millionth time that she and her party were safe.

Needing some space and a deep stretch, I wandered to the edge of the clearing and started the warm-up routine I did on my runs. I had to keep replacing my hood as I moved, but the inconvenience was worth it as I worked the knots out of my thighs and back.

"Lotty," Roah called as he jogged over to me. He had two bedrolls under his arm and a grin on his face.

"What?" I was relieved to see him in a better mood.

"Come with me."

He waited for me to join his side before we walked in the opposite direction of camp.

"I thought we weren't supposed to separate from the group."

"We aren't. Our people know where we will be. It's a place not many can find."

"But you can?"

"Tregr brought me here to save my life once."

I stopped in my tracks. "You almost died *before* I saw you almost die?"

He spun around, smiling. "What, that little flesh wound? A poison-tipped sword was an unexpected complication; hardly the most life-threatening situation I've been in since Elion brought his crazy plan to Niniever. Of course, I'd pretty much walk any path that leads me to you, no matter how often I must defeat death."

"Great, make *me* your reason to live. No pressure there."

"Don't worry so much. The Spirits aren't ready for me, so I've been told." He stuffed both bedrolls under one arm and grabbed my hand.

"The *spirits* told you?"

"Well, not in a profound conversation or anything. The Sages say only a lucky few actually meet with their ancestors or any spirits and return to tell the story. I'm just guessing."

"What almost killed you before that?"

"The ego of an uneducated prince."

"Now, that I believe. I got a crazy letter from that guy. He needed truckloads of humbling."

"Why your Highness," Roah teased, raising our entwined hands and twirling me under his arm so he could whisper in my ear. "Are you saying you approve of premature maturation through pain and devastating loss? Or do you just like it when I'm begging to have you in my arms?"

"Okay, I'm not a hundred percent sure of that first thing"—I giggled as he kissed my neck and guided me through a narrow overgrown path—"but I do like being wanted, and I have been known to be a softy if begging is involved. Maybe you should try, just so I'm sure."

"I think all this power is going to your head."

"You'd like that, wouldn't you?"

We reached the edge of the clearing and made our way through a narrow, overgrown path. Twenty feet away a mound of grass and moss cut off the trail.

"We'll sleep here." Roah walked to the mound and cleared away a mess of growth and vines. Behind the greenery was a crude wooden door.

The place looked like it was half hobbit house, half wine cellar, with a roof covered in thick moss. Vines and other vegetation had started reclaiming the stone walls, which made the whole place feel like part of the earth. The construction looked ancient but solid.

"My Prince, what a strange castle you have brought me to." I cocked an eyebrow at him. "It seems to be missing like, *everything*."

"Yeah, I wasn't able to keep up on my payments. Turns out crossing worlds to find the woman of your dreams isn't conducive to life planning." He pulled my arm around his waist. "It's not much, but we'll be alone."

"I thought we were keeping up the impression we weren't together."

"We are, but that clearing is used by herders and traveling merchants—which is what our group is going to look like in case anyone is watching. But if either of us is seen among a group that size, so close to Moldara, we make Ayla's job impossible. We can't risk it. Most shelters like this have been forgotten."

"And no one will be sitting out here keeping watch?"

That brilliant smile appeared again. "Nope. Unless a mountain lion counts."

Roah gave the door a good shove before it gave way. Matching his smile, I ducked into the structure.

It was a one-room building with stone walls, a dirty wood floor, and half a roof. There were no windows for light, but with the impromptu skylight, the full moon poured into the space enough to see by. What remained of the ceiling was barely high enough for me to stand upright. Roah had to duck when he crossed the threshold and

Blood of Moldara

nearly hit his head on a support beam when he crossed the room to set up the bedrolls in the corner.

As he stood there half bent to avoid another beam, I stifled a laugh. He looked ridiculously large, as if he were trying to get into a kid's playhouse.

"How did you and Tregr both share this space?" I looked at the bedding spread out on the floor behind him, then back to Roah.

But he didn't answer; he just looked at me. His eyes drank me in, and I bit my lip as anticipation ran up my spine. This was the first time we'd been alone since that night in the woods. He held out his hand, and the thrill of our night together came rushing back.

I threw myself into his arms, our lips crushing so hard I thought I would taste blood. We collapsed on the makeshift bed, and he pulled me into his lap. Our lips moved with each other, and my fingers curled around his collar, brushing the short hair at the nape of his neck.

"I wish you didn't have to cut it so short," I whispered.

"It's just hair. It grows back."

His fingers moved down my bodice and cupped my ass, pulling me closer with a tenderness that told me he knew I was saddle sore. The warmth of his breath on my neck made all my clothes feel too tight. I ached to touch every inch of him, to feel his body with all of mine. The desire to know we were connected, that he was always going to be a part of me, was overwhelming.

I found his armor and fumbled with the fastenings.

"Help me?"

His hands found mine, fingers guiding me until the armor fell away.

"My turn." I sat up, turning to face him.

He rose and pulled out the laces fastening my thick body leather. Once loose, the pieces dropped to the floor, and I took my first deep breath since that morning.

"Better?"

"Not yet," I said as I worked the buttons of his tunic.

He pulled his shirt off in one sweeping motion. Before I could follow his lead, he was kissing my stomach, his hands gathering my shirt as they glided up my sides. I raised my arms and my top went onto our growing pile.

"This is a lot more work than a tank top and jeans." I blushed.

"More time to enjoy the details though," he said as his fingers slowly trailed over my bare chest.

I watched him for a moment. He smiled as he guided me to my back.

He settled over me, pressing his body against mine, his breath hot on my skin. His heartbeat pulsed with mine. My fingers traced the lines of his face, his jaw, his ear, until they curled around his neck. I pulled him to me, my lips searching up his cheek to his ear. My tongue glided gently along the soft lobe and he shivered, his fingers digging into my back. I tasted salt, inhaled his heady scent. His breath caught and he pulled away.

"Wait." I could barely speak but he had to know before I lost all self-control. "We have to be responsible. I've lost track of how many days I've been here. Back home, there's a pill I take. It's for a lot of reasons but—"

He laid a finger over my lips, cutting off my confession.

"I know," he began. "But we're in my world right now. And here, that's something every male drinks each morning in our tea. There's no risk until we stop taking it."

"You're sure? I mean, like, a thousand percent positive?"

"Hasn't failed us in hundreds of years. The Romans should never have let that plant die in your world."

"Stupid Romans."

His blue eyes burned with hunger as he gazed into mine. He stroked my cheeks and then firmly cupped them. Then, he kissed me, the warmth of his lips against mine so sweet that I felt both satisfied and wild with hunger. He moved with confidence as our lips molded together, our lungs breathing the same air. His hands caressed my shoulders, my arm, grazing just above my belly button with his fingertips. My skin rippled under his touch, and waves of pleasure tingled to my toes. He paused, pressing our foreheads together as he took calming breaths.

"We didn't enjoy this as much as we could have the first time," he said, his voice like velvet.

"How so?"

He propped himself up on one elbow and looked me in the eyes.

"I forgot my favorite rule." His eyes played with the rhythm of my heart. "Ladies first."

His smile took my breath away.

He trailed kisses down my stomach past my belly button, until his head disappeared under the blanket. His hands tugged at my pants, but with little success. I loosened my belt and pulled them off. The soft heat of his breath on the inside of my thigh sent a thrill through me, and I swallowed hard, suddenly nervous and more aroused than I'd ever been.

He was confident in his method, and every sensation he created was a new one I didn't know was possible. I relaxed into his touch, enjoying the thrills he coaxed from my body. His movements sent tendrils of pleasure through my hips and down my legs. My hands pressed against his head, my fingers running through his soft hair, encouraging him further. The heat from his touch grew, engulfing my body in a fire I ached to be consumed by. My racing pulse and heaving breaths added to the wild blaze until finally, it rolled through me in waves of ecstasy.

Suddenly, I wanted him. I wanted him more than anything I'd ever wanted in my life. I didn't ask, didn't voice my desires. I just reached down, grabbed his shoulders, pulled him onto me, and kissed him.

His lips were greedy, devouring every inch of me. A current of desire surged between us, filling what our kisses couldn't. It wasn't enough. My fingers played with the waist of his pants, pulling them to loosen—wanting the same thing, Roah kicked off his pants and tossed them onto the pile. I pressed my palms against his chest, feeling the drumming of his heart. He directed my hands down his torso and encouraged me to guide him.

We moved together as one body, one soul. Surges of elation and pleasure coursed through me in ways I hoped would never end. He kissed my neck, my chest, my breasts. Finally, his lips found mine and our breaths united. Pleasure pulsed around us, through us, until it consumed us. Pulling closer, Roah latched onto me and moaned. A rush of euphoria flooded my body, filled my veins, stopped time. He collapsed on me, his full weight stealing my breath. I didn't care. I was still tingling with pleasure.

We lay there, breathing deeply, bodies entwined. Neither of us moved. There was no need. There was no place to be but in each other's embrace as we dozed in a blissful haze. After a while, he started tracing patterns on my stomach. I smiled as wisps of pleasure curled around his touch. My feet found his, my toes gliding along his calf, entangling our legs as I pulled him back to me.

"There's no rule saying we can't enjoy that again," I whispered into the moonlit room.

"I like a woman who knows what she wants." His lips found mine. "And asks for it."

❧

I woke in a haze of pleasure and deep satisfaction. My dreams had been a blur of sensations and euphoria Roah had seduced from my body, feelings I'd only dreamed were possible. But having tasted them, I knew I'd die before being parted from him again. Dawn was still a few hours away, but the sky was already showing signs of the change.

I inched my way closer to Roah, trying not to wake him. Gradually, I pressed my body against his, but he shifted and rolled toward me.

"Can't sleep?" he muttered, his voice blending into the night air as his arm encircled me, fingers gently caressing my skin.

"No," I sighed.

"Here," he said, shifting his body around mine in hopes of making me comfortable. "Maybe this will help."

"Thanks," I muttered softly, allowing myself to relax into him even more. The warmth of his skin and slow rhythm of his breathing finally relaxed my mind and powered down the sensations surging through me. Still, sleep wouldn't come, and I hated where my thoughts were heading.

"Roah," I started, my voice as quiet as the cool wind just outside the door. "What if things don't go well tomorrow? What if this is all a mistake? What if..." I couldn't finish as my fingers clung to him.

He let out a deep breath before answering. "The stories after dinner the other night?"

"You were right," I whispered into the dark. "The more I know, the harder it is to choose a path."

"That's because you're still thinking in terms of right and wrong." He traced patterns on my back as he explained. "Elion used to say that the black and white lines people think of as right and wrong only exist in ledgers and villains. Real life is a series of experiments in a gray area. We have to decide every day who we will be. Some days we do better than others. Even our best efforts and guesses will change in their effectiveness from day to day."

"So how do we know what to do?" I countered, vaguely recalling a similar lecture but unable to remember how it ended. It was comforting to know that as different as our lives were, Roah and I had learned the same philosophies from Elion. My grandfather was somehow with us in spirit, watching over us.

"We stick to the path that honors the best version of ourselves and accept the responsibility and price of that choice."

"No chickening out," I said, understanding his point.

"What else would Elion say to you right now?" he prompted, playing with the unruly strands of my hair.

"That there is always a price. The honorable path is often the one most full of danger. People forget or ignore that the only other option is to sell their soul, their choices, and eventually their lives for a false security, gambling that someone else will shine a light on what they hid and save them from themselves."

"It's a safer option."

"What? Wait in a tower for someone else to fight all my dragons? That's never been safety to me. Or if it is, the cost is too high."

"Lotty, you fear the possible loss of life that may result from this trip. It's understandable; I even expect it, but it's not what I fear. I fear losing myself to someone else's idea of how I should live. Selling my immediate safety for a life of mediocrity, cowering for another's approval, would end up killing me."

"I can't picture you as someone who knows how to cower," I observed quietly.

"Nor I you."

"I promise you, I can be pathetic with the best of them."

"You have deep wells of compassion, empathy, loyalty, and courage within you. I've seen them," he countered. "Do not mistake the excess of those for fear. Do not mistake a price for punishment. See it all for what it is—freedom. It is the knowledge and ability to act decisively and earn the loyalty and devotion of others.

"Whatever happens between here and Virginia, we can both be sure that we chose this road with one purpose—to honor our best selves the best way we know how. Those who die, die doing the same thing. Who are we to take the most important choice of their lives away?"

When he put it that way, I was stumped. I lay silent for a long time, adjusting my overworked mind to his words.

"Did you fall asleep?" he whispered, a hand caressing the curves of my back.

"No, I was just trying to figure out why we have all of our best conversations in the dark, and how do you have so many answers already?"

I felt his body shake as he chuckled beside me.

"Blame Elion," he mused. "I asked him the same questions at least three times a year. His answers were always the same. And I mean word for word, exactly the same. Funny how you don't appreciate some lessons until you pass them on."

"How often do you give yourself that same little speech?" I asked the question as a joke, but I secretly wanted to know.

"Every time I've been afraid I would lose you," he answered wryly, his arm tightening around me.

I couldn't help but smile as I blushed in the darkness.

"Do you think he's still alive somewhere?"

"Elion? That's a mystery I've stopped trying to solve. If he's dead, then there is nothing we can do. If he's alive, then I trust him to find us when the time is right."

"I wish he would come back and teach me all the stuff he taught you. All those years studying under him must have been amazing."

"If he did, would you want to stay?"

I'd felt the question coming before he'd asked it, but it didn't change my answer.

"I don't know. Do you think he'd try to make me?"

"No, that kind of force is Terrshon's way, not your grandfather's."

"Who the hell was supposed to prepare me for all of this?"

"Mable. She didn't know everything, but she knew enough, and she loved Elion. Trell told us that he pleaded with her not to send you away, but she wouldn't listen. She understood just how much danger you were both in if Terrshon's men found you."

"The note on that freaky lamp." The memory of that first clue to this whole mess still blazed brightly in my mind. "I can't believe my grandma waited until she was dying to try to say something! I hope that crazy thing hasn't burned down the barn while we were gone."

"Trell will have taken it to his place to keep it safe and to watch."

"Watch for what? Are you telling me it does other stuff, too?"

"I don't know how the Sages make them, but everyone born into this world has one created for them. They illuminate every sanctuary as a reminder of the people their order serves. No flame can be extinguished until the person they were lit for dies. Then it's usually given to the surviving family to remember them by."

"So, if that lamp goes out, Trell will know that we didn't make it back?"

"Lotty, when we reach the entrance to the caves"—he hesitated, and I tensed—"don't do anything that will get you hurt, even if it's to save one of us. If anything goes wrong, and you get the chance to enter the cavern, you must make a run for it, no matter what. Do you understand?"

"But what if you get hurt? I can't just leave you. I'll be lost without you."

"You can, and you must. The way through the caves is marked. You'll know the signs when you see them. If you go too fast, you will become blindingly ill, but you must go as quickly as you can bear." I could hear him steeling himself against the terror of being separated again, but he was insistent. "I have plenty of soldiers to help if something happens; if we lose you to Terrshon while you have your father's ring, all is lost. Swear to me, swear on your grandfather Elion, that if it comes to it, you will save yourself."

"I swear it," I said, choking on the lie as it came out. I wasn't sure I could do what he was asking, but I knew I could try. "I'll do whatever has to be done."

There was a long pause, and for a minute, I was afraid he was going to ask for more.

"I know you will," he said, his soft, warm lips pressing against the base of my neck.

35

We woke early the next morning and dressed in silence. I was sad to leave our hideaway but anxious to face whatever came next. I sensed the same hopeful tension in Roah as he carried our bedrolls back to camp.

Daggon and Tregr began their pre-dawn reports to Roah while I tied the blankets behind our saddles. Everyone in the group moved about camp quietly as we prepared to leave, as if we could all feel how close we were to danger. The usual banter was muffled and short lived. Thankfully, no one mentioned anything about my and Roah's sleeping arrangements. Even the mountain lions were quick to accept their scraps of meat and disappear into the trees.

Someone passed around cooked oats, fruit, and dried jerky while we broke camp. Roah announced it would be the last hot meal until we reached the sanctuary. Today we would cross into Moldara. Stopping before we made our last camp that night was no longer an option. Anyone who fell behind was responsible for catching up. In the event that things didn't go our way, they would drop back to a rendezvous point.

I noticed an extra round of hugs exchanged by all before we mounted and set off. Within the first few hours, Roah signaled that we'd crossed into Moldara. On cue, our tight formation split in two, until we were strung out along the empty roads. The only clue that all of us traveled together was the uniformity of our cloaks, which we all wore with our hoods up to hide our faces.

As we approached an unfamiliar village—just a tiny collection of huts really—other travelers joined us on the road. Anyone who looked vaguely interested in approaching us got close enough to see our weapons and then decided they had somewhere else to be. Daggon, who'd been my companion since we'd set off, rotated out and was replaced by Roah. I caught a glimpse of other duos making the same adjustments.

Even with all the safeguards and camouflage, there was something about the way people looked at us, as we passed the next village, that put me on edge. Roah didn't like it, either. Their eyes lingered too long and their expressions asked too many questions. Then, a message from one of our scouts was received, a whisper informing us that Terrshon's men had been aggressively patrolling the area. Without hesitation, Roah made the decision to abandon the road completely.

As soon as Roah was sure a whisper had been passed up to the lead scouts, he guided us into a shallow streambed. One by one, as we left the streambed and traveled deeper into the uncut woods, each pair returned to formation. The tension in the group rose.

"Are we going to be okay?" I asked when I was sure no one else could hear us.

"Absolutely. This was always a possible detour. We'll still reach the passage by midday tomorrow."

An hour later, as if to contradict him, a thick fog rolled into the valleys and made visibility beyond the next meadow nearly impossible. Bigger clouds rolled in, and the ride turned dark and cold, putting me even more on edge.

"You don't have anyone in this world that can mess with the weather, do you?" I asked Tregr after he traded places with Roah.

"Not that I know of," he said, one hand fidgeting with a throwing knife as the horses picked their way over rocky soil. "This is Moldara though. The weather around this sanctuary follows no pattern and obeys no season. I'm sure you can guess why."

The gateway.

It felt right that something about that place, where our worlds met, was weird.

The deeper we rode into the fog bank, the more I couldn't stop the goosebumps running up my arms. The mist thickened. Without the sun, it was easy to lose track of time, but even I could tell that our party had slowed considerably.

An eerie hush fell over our group.

The creeping dense cloud muffled the sounds of our passage. When we stopped for the night, our anxiety was almost suffocating. Roah posted guards, and someone took my horse and disappeared into the fog. Few spoke in more than a murmur. We couldn't risk revealing our position or affect the night vision of the watch, so none of us lit fires. Instead, we ate our cold rations in the dark, huddling close for warmth.

Bedrolls were laid out and Hawnah brought us several large river stones. Together, she and Tregr used their bonds to heat the rocks without the use of a fire. Roah showed me how to safely place the hot stone at the foot of my blankets to keep me warm. Tregr and Hawnah repeated this several more times. Once they had heated enough for everyone, Daggon and a red-headed young man named Caid, half carried our two "human heaters" to their bedrolls.

"Are they going to be okay?" I asked Roah as I watched Hawnah collapse on her blanket. Caid stayed with her.

"Yes, but only after a full night's sleep. To be sure, neither will stand watch for the next few nights."

"I didn't think using their bond could do that."

"It doesn't if they stick to the elements they're bonded to. Hawnah can work with the earth, but only the most skilled in her bond can even polish stone, let alone shape or affect it in large quantities. Tregr's skill is with metal, which is typically heated to shape or sharpen it. What they just did together was force their bonds to perform in ways they shouldn't. Tregr found the flecks of iron in the rocks and softened them, which heats them up so he could keep them nearly liquid.

Hawnah was then able to use those softened parts of the rock to shift the entire core. They kept that friction going until the combined heat filled the whole stone, like one of your batteries."

"Wow."

"Yeah, like I said, it requires an extraordinary amount of focus and strength."

"Can they use their bonds too much and hurt themselves?"

"Yes. As I understand it, the first few years of their training are mainly focused on finding and respecting their limits," Roah said.

"How do they know if they're pushing themselves too hard?"

"I've only seen that happen once, with an older man who'd hidden his bond his whole life. No one knew what he could do until a landslide threatened his home and his family. He tried to shift an entire hillside worth of rocks and earth, but suddenly started bleeding out of his ears; then his eyes, nose, and mouth. He died screaming. Despite his efforts, the landslide took his family. The town buried him in the same hillside."

More death. The warmth in my bed was suddenly less appealing.

"Does Terrshon have a bond?"

"No. Not one strong enough to do anything. It's completely forbidden. That much power in one person, a kingdom and a bond, it would make him nearly unstoppable. I can't imagine the chaos."

"But someone has done something to those rocks the eagles wear."

"Even Terrshon has Sages in his court. But what you described is so far beyond what I've been told is possible. I believe you, I do. I just haven't been able to figure out how he is doing it."

"Roah, how old is Terrshon?"

"No one knows for sure, but we estimate his age to be somewhere in his late forties."

"No way, the guy I saw barely looked thirty."

"Another one of the mysteries surrounding him. There are theories, but they are too terrible to consider, let alone be spoken aloud."

I took that as my cue to stop asking questions. His shoulders seemed so tense it hurt to look at him. I offered to rub them, and he quietly accepted; his focus elsewhere. We didn't lie down until the first watch took up its post.

Next to Roah, the darkness was usually a comfort. But that night the mental pictures I had been fighting off all day flashed through my brain. Every death I'd seen since my arrival tormented me. The sight of the whip tearing Oydis's flesh, the sound of her neck snapping under Terrshon's boot, the swords slicing through Nettie's meat and bones, and Brokk drowning in his own blood-filled cries became a looping soundtrack. No war movie had ever prepared me for this reality, and yet my mind took every detail and played it out in true Hollywood fashion.

I shuddered and wrapped my arms more tightly around Roah, willing the images to stop.

My night ended up being more of a series of short naps than deep sleep. In addition to the horror show in my mind, I startled awake at every new sound. To his credit, Roah patiently laid a calming hand on me each time my gasps woke him. Only the cry of a screech owl, hunting just before dawn, was enough to put him on guard. I got my last couple hours of sleep with him tracing patterns on my back as he watched the sky.

The fog lifted slightly the next morning while we mounted up. Being the least seasoned rider, I stifled my groans. Sore muscles or not, I had no desire to linger within reach of Terrshon. Which meant that the faster we rode, the better I felt.

It was almost noon when we entered a small clearing. Roah pulled up his horse and addressed us for the first time since we'd broken camp that morning.

"It's time to split up," he said in a low voice. "The first group to arrive at the entrance will continue through the caves, dispatching any of Terrshon's men they find, and clearing the way for the rest of us. The second group will hold the entrance from this side and protect our retreat. With any luck, our attack will happen so fast there won't be time to mount any serious resistance."

As if on cue, the soldiers each held a scarred palm aloft. The sight still gave me chills. It felt like a promise of violence to come. Without question or hesitation, they split off into their designated groups.

Roah leaned over to me, his eyes determined. "Stay close to Tregr. I'll see you on the other side," he promised.

"You too," I managed, gripping the reins in my clenched fists.

I watched him ride away, and my insides tensed so completely all the warmth went out of me. I felt the ghost of an electric charge running up my limbs as if my body hovered a hair's breadth above a live wire. The thought of never seeing Roah again was almost immobilizing. I was grateful I had a horse to walk for me.

We continued to ride deeper into the surrounding trees, farther away from Roah and the others, until I lost sight of them completely. I knew we would eventually end up in the same place. But when? Like everyone else, I was continually scanning our surroundings. Except unlike the others, I wasn't looking for danger. I was looking for landmarks, anything that might help if I ever needed to return.

As we rode through the woods, I noticed a small clearing up ahead to my left. The fog played with the image, and I almost dismissed it as my imagination. But as we got closer, the mist thinned. Situated in the clearing and extending up the hillside was exactly what I was hoping for—ancient sanctuary grounds.

We encountered the surrounding gardens first. Gravel paths wound between trimmed trees and wildflowers. Simple but elegant benches had been sporadically tucked into the gardens just off the footpaths. Fire-lit torches lined those pathways, illuminating the sitting areas. Wind chimes hung throughout the tamed wilderness, along with one large gong. Etched into its surface was the same broken compass on the ring I was hiding.

As we rode closer, the buildings' details came into focus. This was unlike any holy place I'd ever seen. The structures blended into the hillside as if the earth itself had given birth to them. Cut stone and thick wood beams reached up from the ground in rows of balconies that drew the eyes up. The roofline of the largest building was at least five stories, with high corner peaks and gargoyles keeping watch at each tip.

The exterior looked to have been once painted in happy colors, but the cheeriness had long since faded. A grand set of stone stairs led up to the main building and ended at a set of large wooden doors. The lines looked to have ancient Asian influences, maybe even Tibetan. But the light coming through the stained glass windows that lined the main floor was otherworldly.

The window's images depicted scenes of nature, or the glory and power of creation, not only of human life but also of all living things. The one element all the windows had in common was flowing water. Whether the creation came forth from rain or overflowed from cupped hands, water was a prominent theme throughout all the windows.

Beyond this ornate building was a smaller structure, less used and older, with a strange mixture of Viking and Native American influences. Its facade had been decorated less than the other buildings. Tall skinny openings were windowless, as if the builders had forgotten to install the glass panes when they'd built it. It was less Zen-like than the other buildings but still beautiful. Engraved across the front of the entrance were the words *Sacred Waters of Creation* in large encrypted Sage script.

Coming upon this place was like finding a jewel that had been dropped in the woods and forgotten. But as far as I was concerned, the sanctuary served only one purpose. It would give me the starting point I needed if I were ever to cross into this Otherworld alone.

While we rode past the layered buildings, we were close enough to make out men and women of every age in simple pale clothes with dark-colored tunics, just like I'd seen Soren and the Sages in Niniever's court wearing. Once they saw our caravan, they stopped and watched us pass. A flash of recognition crossed a few of their faces, and one young man reentered a building. When he emerged again, he had a couple more men and women with him, one I recognized.

Soren met my gaze with his wise old eyes, and I relaxed a little. It was too far to call out a greeting, which was fine since I didn't trust my voice. I now counted Soren as a friend, and the warm look on his face was one of pride, of honor. I knew what my face said back to him. *I know where I come from now, just like you said I would.* Soren watched me approach with a knowing smile.

As I was about to end our silent exchange with a passing wave, an older woman rushed out and urgently whispered in Soren's ear. His smile dissolved. He turned to the Sages at his side, speaking quickly and motioning in the same direction we were headed. Several of them disappeared back into the large building while Soren remained watching me, apprehension and worry now plain on his face.

Just as I turned to mention the change to Tregr, I felt a white-hot pain in my left shoulder. An arrow appeared in the neck of my horse. I screamed.

The poor animal fell to its knees with a moan. I flailed but landed on my feet, staggering to the side and grabbing at the top of my injured arm. It burned, and warm blood seeped through the ivory cotton sleeve and between my fingers.

36

Suddenly, I was surrounded by a flurry of circling horses, as if I were at the eye of a storm. Tregr jumped off his mount as the clash of steel sounded nearby. He signaled, and a gray-cloaked woman slipped out of the current of thundering horseflesh. She dismounted, handing me her reins and moving to tend to my wounded animal. Meanwhile, Tregr pulled a cloth out of the pouch slung over his shoulder. He grabbed my arm and wrapped the cloth around the wound, tying it so tightly I cried out again.

"It can't be more than their scouts," Tregr tried to reassure me. "They got off a lucky shot, but there will be more. You have to get back on a horse alone, Lotty. It's the only chance. If you ride with me, they'll know it's you."

I nodded shakily. My arm was on fire, my fingers already tingling from the tight bandage. I moved toward the new horse as if in a trance and felt Tregr's hands suddenly guiding and lifting. I pulled myself into the saddle but stayed low over the horse's neck.

"No matter what happens, stay on your horse and close to me until we're in sight of the waterfall. When you see it, no matter what happens, Lotty, you are to run for the cave opening behind it. Do not stop! That body armor will protect you from a distance, but if any of

Terrshon's soldiers get too close, there are no guarantees. Don't let them get close." He moved to return to his horse, and I grabbed his cloak, my eyes saying what I could not. He put a hand on mine, pulling his cloak out of my grasp as he answered my silent pleas.

"I'll make sure he's safe after I get you through. I swear it."

I nodded, still not able to find my voice.

Tregr mounted, and the circling horses formed around the two of us. Holding the reins tightly, I dug my heels into my new mount and guided the gelding to Tregr's side. I spared one last look back at yet another girl who had taken my place and was relieved to see she wasn't alone. A brown cloak had dismounted at her side, and together they fought off the three attackers who remained. Before I could look for Soren, our horses were running, hard.

Tregr stopped our group at the top of a rise and stood in his stirrups, looking around as his horse danced beneath him. I risked a glance ahead and saw what the fog had been hiding.

Below us stretched a massive gorge. At its head, a towering rock face jutted into the sky. The granite edges came to chiseled points, as if a god had hammered so hard on the world that a behemoth shard had popped out the other side. As I scanned the terrain, I realized the slabs and boulders that littered the valley were a result of the mountain's age. Like wilted petals, the steep slopes were flaking away. Both sides of the ravine grew thick with patches of trees and tall grass. Only the area at the base of the towering granite, around the size of a football field, was clear. And there, where the walls of the ravine met the granite face, I caught my first glimpse of a series of waterfalls that hid the caves.

Chills ran down my spine. I was almost home.

Abrupt movement at the far side of the valley caught my attention. Two riders on horseback—one in brown, and one in gray—were in a full gallop, headed straight for the far cascading falls. Even with the disadvantage of being hundreds of yards away, I knew who rode those horses. Roah and Chaslynn crossed the valley at full speed. *But where were the others? Why had they broken formation?*

That's when I saw at least fifty of Terrshon's men descend the opposite side of the gorge, half their ranks disappearing into the multiple stands of boulders and trees. Roah was a decoy. The rest of his force waited for the enemy on the other side of the trees, setting up a defensive perimeter to cover Roah's flank.

Roah swung around and searched the ridgeline, and his eyes unexpectedly caught mine. Even through the distance, I sensed his urgency, but he turned his horse away from the falls and back towards the fighting that spilled out of the trees and into the valley. Chaslynn let him go without her, and I was just barely able to see her slide to a stop, dismount, and lead her horse through the waterfall and into a hidden cave.

"They're surrounding us," Tregr announced to the group. "Time for the backup plan."

Following Tregr, we began our descent into the gorge. Pairs of riders broke off every few hundred feet. When we hit the tree line, each pairing changed direction, some still heading for the caves, others heading for the fight raging across the gorge. As we descended, I lost sight of all but two other pairs.

After several minutes, we had to slow the horses to a fast walk. The trees were thinning, but the terrain was becoming increasingly challenging to navigate. It took all of my concentration to stay on my horse as we steered around huge bushes and clusters of trees growing around the gigantic slabs of rock that littered the ground.

I urged my horse back to a gallop as soon as I hit a clear patch, still heading for the caves, with Tregr on my heels. With each kick of my horse, the adrenaline pumped faster through my veins, the terror of the fight that had come into view assaulting my ears.

Roah was a hundred yards away when he shot past me on my right, slowing and drawing his weapon as he entered the chaos of horses and swords. The sounds of battle rose behind us. Horses neighed, and men yelled as metal struck against metal. I forced my horse faster, but we hadn't reached the open valley yet. Suddenly, arrows whirled past, striking the ground around us. Some passed so close I could hear them zing by my head.

Another mass of Terrshon's men charged down the sides of the ravine to our left. I called out to Tregr.

"I see them! Keep moving!" He shouted as four of our group finally caught up and surrounded us.

My insides felt like a rope being twisted tighter and tighter until it bunched in on itself and was tightened again. I would have worried about throwing up, but my stomach was stone. My hands tingled and shook as I gripped the reins. I tried not to look too closely at the flashing swords or hear the growing screams of the dying that now came from both sides.

This was it. This was my only chance. I dug my heels into my horse, heading straight for my goal. The last grouping of trees before the valley slowed me again, and my view of the enemy was obstructed. Fear surged through my veins so intensely I was sure my horse could feel it. I was so close I could taste the Virginian air, its sweetness calling to me.

I had to make it.

Caid caught up to my left side. Arrows struck his mount's hindquarters and it screamed, kicking its front legs into the air. The animal didn't fall, yet it couldn't keep up with us either. Caid and Hawnah turned toward the attackers, their swords drawn and crossbows loaded. Tregr tightened the gap between our horses, staying so close our legs touched. Soon the rest of the group disappeared in our wake.

When we finally cleared the last of the trees, I glanced behind us and saw Roah high atop his speeding horse, sword in one hand, crossbow in the other. He had abandoned his group completely and was headed straight for where we had come out of the trees, slashing down anyone in his path.

We were only a hundred yards from the waterfall now. So close, and yet still so much distance to cover. Roah was barely forty yards away from me, fighting to get to my side. His expression was full of blood-curdling fury. As he got closer, he raised his crossbow, aiming it right for us. It was loaded.

"DUCK!" he yelled.

37

Turning away from Roah, I dropped my head until it was pressed against the neck of my horse. As my cheek met its sweaty mane, an arrow zinged overhead. That's when I saw where Roah had been aiming.

Less than ten feet on my left, a man on horseback had appeared out of the trees. Just before he had reached me, Roah's arrow lodged in his chest, causing the man to drop his spear. Tregr suddenly reappeared beside me, a bloody sword in hand. He finished off the attacker Roah's arrow had stopped and engaged the two others that had sprung up behind him.

I turned back to Roah, shock and relief in my eyes, but he was facing the other direction. Another man attacked from the opposite side, and three more closed in on him from behind. I yelled his name, trying to warn him, but the screaming of horses and soldiers was too loud. I looked around for someone to help him and saw that the shallow gorge had become a small battlefield. Blood-soaked bodies lay lifeless on the ground as others continued to fight around them. Even Tregr was busy fending off more assailants, unable to spare an eye for his prince.

We were losing. Outnumbered, and now without the element of

Blood of Moldara

surprise. How many of us were still standing? The carnage, as heart-breaking as it was—terrible and graphic, filled me with guilt more powerful than anything I had ever experienced. I was responsible for this. They were all fighting and dying because of *me*. Fighting with the hope that one day I would change their world. That I would bring about peace and justice. The guilt of my insecurities blasted through me like a cold wind, searing into my heart, and engraving on my bones.

Hopelessness threatened to freeze me where my horse stood until I saw it. White-clad figures, surrounding the battlefield. As if out of a dream, they flowed into the small valley in front of the caves, armed to the teeth. Soren had sent help. The group was heavily armed and outnumbered Terrshon's forces at least two to one.

The Sages cut down Terrshon's mercenaries, one by one, with fluid movements that looked like elegant rage. Their violent dance was terrible and beautiful, and had devastating results. It was obvious Terrshon's soldiers were the least trained of the three groups. Though dressed for the part, they did not move as one force. Instead, each seemed to have their own plan of attack, as if Terrshon had set loose a bunch of madmen on the countryside, and the Sages were dancing among them, restoring order.

As my horse snorted and side-stepped anxiously, I measured the remaining distance to the cave. This was my chance to slip away from the mayhem. Hesitating, I looked back to Roah.

Two of Terrshon's soldiers bore down on him, forcing him between a pair of boulders that would trap his horse. The twisted rope in my gut snapped free. I drew in a deep breath and turned my horse away from the caves. Red-hot fire surged through my veins. I pulled the bow from over my shoulders and drew three arrows from the quiver on the saddle, ignoring the burning running down my left arm. A wild rage filled every part of me until I craved the lives of the two men threatening Roah. I wanted their deaths like I wanted air.

Just as I leveled my arrow, Daggon came up from behind Roah, running straight for his attackers. Catching the nearest one off guard, Daggon knocked him to the ground, stabbing him with his sword as he fell. I took aim at the remaining man and released. A shaft appeared in the man's upper thigh, and he fell to one knee. Roah and Daggon took the killing blow together.

When Roah looked up to see who had wounded his opponent, his expression changed from aggression to disbelief and then horror. For a second, I was angry about his lack of gratitude. Then I realized he wasn't looking at me, he was looking past me. I turned to follow his gaze, adrenaline pumping white hot through my veins as I saw it.

As if in slow motion, a man stepped out from behind a thick tree trunk. He was less than ten feet away, his crossbow loaded and aimed at my heart. He wore the same metal mask as the rest of Terrshon's mercenaries, as well as similar clothing—tight riding pants tucked into leather boots, a leather vest cinched over his tunic, his dark jacket half concealing the weapons at his belt. But it was the look in his eyes that captured my attention. They were cold, calculating, determined. They wanted only one thing, and they weren't going to stop until they had it.

I felt my bow come up instinctively as I heard Roah shout from behind.

"Shoot him!"

In one fluid motion, the two arrows were nocked and aimed.

I felt the string snap and heard a dull thud.

The end of my small bolts blossomed from the man's throat and upper chest as he smiled wickedly at me. Crimson flowed from the wounds, and the man fell, eyes rolling back into his head. I turned back to Roah, expecting to see triumph on his face. Instead, his eyes were wild with horror.

Then, I felt it.

It began as a sharp twinge in my chest. I gasped involuntarily as lightning bolts of pain shot through my whole body. Looking down, I recalled Tregr's warning about my body armor being less effective at close range. The razor-sharp projectile had punched through my leather bodice, slicing my side and cutting deep into my left lung.

Dropping the bow, my hand automatically reached for the wound, but the touch sent more jolts of agony through me. When I placed my hands back on the reins, blood dripped between my fingers.

Blood of Moldara

"NO!" Roah roared from a distance.

I tried to stay calm, to breathe through the pain as I urged my horse forward, but something was terribly wrong. I had to fight to get air with every breath; I couldn't draw enough into my lungs. A heavy weight pressed on my chest, and I couldn't force my lungs to expand.

The only sound I heard was my pulse beating in my ears, bringing awareness to the anguish throbbing through my body. I focused on staying on my horse, but the lack of oxygen and unrelenting pain made it hard to concentrate. It became increasingly difficult to hold myself on the saddle, to keep out the darkness that pulled at the edges of my vision. I slumped over when my horse turned down into a natural trench.

As I was smothered from inside, the world began to spin. I couldn't hold on to the saddle any longer and slipped off the horse. My body slammed into the hard earth, and a fresh wave of agony flared through me. I screamed, and to my bewilderment, it hurt more.

I lay in the clover and brush, fighting for air when, unexpectedly, a pair of hands grabbed me, yanking me off the ground and onto another horse. The pain was so terrible, my breath so short, I couldn't even cry out.

"Lotty, no. Please, no." Cradling me in his arms, Roah held me tightly as he maneuvered his mount. I could only gasp as the edges of my vision darkened. "Stay with me, Lotty! Stay right here!"

I made myself look at him, my eyes full of remorse. He looked down at me, his expression pained, anguished, as he analyzed my condition. I focused on his eyes, feeling life slipping from me. Darkness was rapidly closing in. It comforted me, beckoned me, promising an end to the suffering. I wanted so badly to answer it.

"Don't you leave me," Roah commanded in an urgent voice, reins in one hand, my limp body in the other. "Stay focused on my face, Lotty. Just keep looking at my face."

I wasn't ready to leave him. I didn't want to leave him. I didn't want to go. Not yet. But my eyelids were too heavy; the darkness too enticing. The pressure amplified in my chest with every crush of the horse's hooves, burning away the memory of why I was fighting unconsciousness.

Roah's voice broke through my black abyss as he shook me. "Lotty, hold on! We're almost there. Just a little farther. Please."

Before the darkness completely swallowed me, the reins snapped as the horse made a sudden jerk. Pain surged through me.

Then, everything went black.

38

I was weightless, floating in a dark abyss until a current pulled at my lifeless limbs. Water swirled around me, filling my lungs as I tried to breathe. Hands pulled me, directing my body through the dark water. As I floated, voices echoed faintly. They beckoned me. The voices continued, frantically calling me back. But I couldn't find the surface. I couldn't escape the darkness.

"I'm sorry, Lotty. So sorry," Roah pleaded from a great distance, begging me to respond to him. "I'm going to fix this, I promise, but you have to follow my voice back. Please hear me and come back."

I pushed against the blackness, to reach out to him. I wanted to see him, but my body might as well have been made of cement. Something held me down, and I couldn't escape.

I heard another voice from somewhere far in the distance. This one was frantic. "What have you done? Get her out of there immediately! You tempt forces you cannot begin to understand. No one from her bloodline should ever touch these waters!"

"She's dying!" Roah's voice was louder this time. I tried to open my eyes, to find his face, but the darkness wouldn't release me. "You had your chance to heal her and it wasn't enough. This is the only option we have left!"

"You don't understand." This voice sounded like Soren's, soft and full of pity. Water splashed nearby, and I felt the water around me displaced as someone drew close. "We will hope that her blood has no effect, but we cannot let her die in here. She must be pulled from these waters before the last beat of her heart. One moment longer and we risk everyone's lives."

"Why wouldn't this heal her?"

"There is a limit, my boy. No one is sorrier than I."

"No! This has to work! I won't let her go!"

"Either way, what is done, is done." Soren sighed heavily. "Now that arrow needs to come out if she's to have a chance at healing in here. Hold her firmly. She is probably going to feel this."

Several hands tightened around my body as something ripped through my chest, setting it ablaze.

No all-encompassing darkness came to sweep me away into unconsciousness. One second I was in Roah's arms, in agony, and in the next breath I was standing in the water beside him, all pain gone. Soren and the other Sages had disappeared, and the light was fading. I looked around in confusion, unable to recall when or how I had gotten there. No matter how much I blinked, I couldn't get my bearings.

I stood inside a giant stone chamber. The fountainhead of a natural spring bubbled up from the center of a pool that had been lined with expertly cut stone. Large potted plants surrounded the waters, creating a riot of green in the dim cavern, as if nature were slowly reclaiming what was hers by right. The walls had high, narrow windows with no glass. Instead of a ceiling, I saw an ocean of glimmering stars, as if the whole of the universe was pushing and shoving into this space to look down at me.

"Roah, look up! You have to see this," I said in awe. He didn't answer. "Roah?"

He stood across the pool from me, holding someone in the water. I didn't remember moving away. I pushed through the pool toward him, my anxiety growing with every step. Something was very wrong, but I couldn't put my finger on it.

As I drew close, I stopped, suddenly afraid. Roah was the picture of pain. His eyes were as dark as storm clouds. His brow furrowed, he fought back tears as the muscles in his jaw clenched. He was mumbling something to himself, but I couldn't understand the words. His whole body shook, his muscles trembling while he ignored the blood that dripped from his wounds, coloring the water around him. The pale body he held was as still as death, the face just barely breaking the surface of the spring and causing tiny ripples.

I leaned closer, unable to stop myself from seeing who floated at the water's surface. Somehow I knew it would be me.

It didn't make sense. I couldn't be standing there *and* be in Roah's arms at the same time, but I was. As if to confirm it for me, Roah reached up with one hand and drew away a lock of hair that had drifted across my eyes. His fingers left a smear of blood across my forehead, and he tried to wipe that away too. It was no use. All the water around him had turned bright red.

"Roah?" Again he ignored me. "Roah! We have to go. Something's going horribly wrong here—"

I reached out to take hold of him, to push him to the side of the pool if I had to, but my fingers passed through his shoulder before splashing down in front of me. I reached once more, and my hands passed through his arm, again splashing as they slapped the water.

"ROAH!"

I screamed in a wild panic, but Roah never once looked up or reacted in any way.

WHAT THE HELL WAS GOING ON?!

That's when I saw it.

Out of the cloudy red water, a distinct twist of dark red wound its way along the uneven bottom of the spring and against the gentle current that flowed around me. I followed the strange trail of red to its source, and my mind rebelled. Though the blood from Roah's minor wounds clouded the water, naturally dispersing and diluting like so many drops of ink, my blood seeped and pooled like molasses at Roah's feet. Out of that unnatural glob, the red tendril grew, winding its way toward me.

It went right between my feet. Turning away from Roah, I watched the stream of red grow, snaking its way to a crevice I had not seen before. The crevice became a crack, and then a yawning chasm. From the way the water bubbled and churned on the surface above it, I knew instantly that was where the spring entered the pool.

A little voice in the back of my head told me to run, to get out of the water before my blood reached the source of the spring, but I was paralyzed.

I watched, as if in a trance, as the red tendril reached the chasm. The second the first thick drop disappeared over the edge, the ground shuddered, and a column of water exploded out of the earth. I flinched, finally able to move, only to discover that the current had changed. I got within a few feet of Roah before it sucked my feet out from under me and swept me toward the angry churning pillar of water.

"Help! Roah, please help me! Please, hear me, Roah! ROAH!"

I screamed, fighting against the current. I struggled to reach Roah, but he never looked away from the girl in his arms, both of them remaining untouched by the maelstrom around us.

And then I went over the edge, falling into the dark pit from which the column of water still shot, where it became an endless geyser disappearing into the night sky.

Darkness surrounded me as I plummeted down an invisible chute. All around me the rushing water roared, and I tumbled and rolled in the sucking current until I couldn't tell which way was up. I used everything within to resist, to find the surface again, but in the darkness it was hopeless.

The pressure built up around me until my arms were pinned to my sides. I got in two good kicks with my legs before the water became too thick to move. Panic renewed and I fought harder. I was vaguely aware that my natural instinct to fight for breath was gone. The liquid around my whole body crystallized until I was completely immobilized in the darkness.

Tiny pinpricks of light appeared in the darkness. They sparkled and winked out as often as they lit up. My vision wavered as the water flowed around me; I squinted to make sense of what I was seeing. A

Blood of Moldara

barrage of stars and constellations formed around me, perfectly replicating what I had tried to show Roah in the cavern.

The stars burned brighter still, and I finally understood where I was. It wasn't the night sky as I had originally thought. I was in a cave in the deepest part of the earth. Rock formations, stalactites, and stalagmites stretched out as far as I could see, their surfaces split and cracked like old paint. It was through those cracks that the light illuminated the cavern in which I was suspended.

Their light danced on the water around me until images formed. It was as if the cracks of light were little projectors and the water was my view screen. The images were simple at first. Near me was a great spring. It poured into a wild planet until the world teemed with life. When the land could hold no more, the water overflowed and a second image formed next to the first. I understood that the life force of the water was so abundant it could not stop with one world. Each time it finished one, it began another.

On the original world, a time-lapse video of human history played out over the water. The second world remained wild and empty of humans. An emotion that was not my own rippled through me—longing. The moment I felt it, the people I saw projected onto the water turned as one and looked at me.

Deep longing passed through me again. Ships crossed oceans. The people wore furs, thick woven cloth, and simple draped leather. And while I understood that their journey had taken months to accomplish, the scene reflected in the water took only seconds. Every time the foreign emotion went through me, their heads turned, and they adjusted their direction, always looking toward me.

My fear disappeared, and I stopped struggling against the invisible bonds that held me still. I watched in fascination as the groups abandoned their ships and traveled overland, searching. By that time, I knew what they were searching for. I could feel that force all around me, calling to them, urging them into the foreboding caves hidden among rolling green hills. I felt the ecstasy of the water when the first one of them, their health spent and diseased by the journey, dipped a hand into its healing cold and drank.

The images shifted and the rest of the weary and sick travelers entered the caves where the spring of water originated. One by one, the group moved from the first projected screen, full of familiar history, to the second screen, devoid of people but overflowing with life and vitality. A new world. Otherworld.

My brain briefly registered familiar images on the first screen. Viking voyages. Mongolian hordes. Roman legions marching on cities. But none of the figures could hold my attention. I only had eyes for the several hundred people who had left it all behind.

I watched them build their entire civilization around the spring, where it flowed into their new world. They used the water to heal their sick, water their crops, and wash their clothes. It touched every part of their lives. Gradually the spring began to falter and dry up.

Pain, like the deep ache of an old wound, washed over me, but I knew it was not from the increased tension of my bonds, nor was it entirely my emotion. Whatever force of nature or consciousness the water had was in overwhelming distress as the spring nearly disappeared.

By the time the second and third generations had grown to adulthood, the new world fell in the throes of a violent war. Seven different groups fought for control of the dwindling resource. I wanted to look away from the burning villages and death, but I couldn't.

A man and a woman in their early twenties drew my gaze. They were exceptionally fierce fighters, and though originally on opposing sides, as the number of dead grew, they joined forces. Their years flashed before my eyes in seconds. More fighting followed, and then negotiations. Ultimately fighting broke out again. Their children came of age—most of them no older than I—and they, too, donned primitive armor, picked up swords, and joined the struggle.

The light streaming through the cracks in the rocks flickered, shifting and swirling in a confusion of color until only one image remained. I recognized the place where the spring bubbled up from the crack in the earth. The pool was less than half the depth I expected and completely exposed to the elements. There were no towering walls over the waters, nor with high windows or cut stone

Blood of Moldara

around the edge of the pool. It was still in its natural, unprotected state.

The man and woman appeared, older now but noticeably vibrant, their eyes having taken on the jewel-like quality I had come to associate with the people of Moldara. They embraced each other as they stood in the water, their nightclothes soaked and clinging to them. Tension rippled through the spring as I studied their faces.

She was exquisite for her age, with bronze skin and rich black hair that shimmered in the starlight. Her features were slender and delicate, almost statuesque, and her exotic green eyes were locked on his. His white hair, almost silver against his light skin, shimmered as it fell to his shoulders long and straight, framing his angular and splendidly defined features and making the blue in his eyes look warm and inviting. He pulled her into him, his muscular arms encircling her waist as if he wanted to protect her from something—I just didn't know what.

They spoke to each other, their features twisting with emotion. Though I couldn't hear the words, I didn't need to. Their eyes said it all. Pain. Betrayal. Anguish. Rage. They shared their last moments together in the early morning light. Tears filled my own eyes but again, the emotions were not all mine. Even as I watched, I felt the water begging them to stop.

There was a flash of metal, and before I knew how to react, their arms were around each other, blades plunging through their backs and into their hearts. Horrified, I found myself unable to look away. The hands gripping the knives fell as they slumped away from each other and into the water.

I felt myself scream, but the sound didn't reach my ears.

The image flickered and disappeared, though the feelings did not. Everything the strange couple had felt as they died saturated my body.

A curtain of blood advanced down the same column of water that had brought me there, boiling like approaching thunderclouds. The light bleeding from the rocks dimmed and turned lava red.

I fought against my bonds with renewed urgency. Their blood touched the glowing rocks, and a deep percussion boomed through the water. To my surprise, I was suddenly free. I kicked, swimming for the surface. Seconds later, another boom followed. And another. It was a heartbeat, and it was growing stronger.

The chamber dimmed as more of the bright red blood flowed into the cracks in the rocks. The echoing concussion of the booms changed the current of the water, pushing me back the way I had come. I clawed at the water, struggling to escape the torrent of emotions that were quickly becoming my own.

When my head finally broke the surface, the need to breathe returned. Panting hard, it felt like I had been trying to escape for hours.

The sound of the rhythmic heartbeat evened out. I crawled to the bank of the pool, anxious to escape the water before it sucked me away again, dimly aware that this place was still missing the walls and stones that should have protected it.

Lying there, I heard a woman wailing as if her heart were being ripped in two while she watched, helpless. I sat up. The woman from the vision struggled at the edge of the bubbling red water, bloodstained and scrambling at the edge of the pool, unable to enter. The man, whose arms had held her as she died, was on the opposite bank in the same state. Both hammered at an invisible wall, crying out but unable to hear each other or get close.

Confused, I staggered to my feet. They fell silent and turned toward me in shock.

In a moment, the whole scene changed. The walls returned, their high windows and cut stones once again lining the full, clear pool. The wind whipped my hair across my face, and I looked up. Black clouds rolled above as lightning forked the sky. I blinked and the woman was at my side, brushing away tears I didn't know I had. The bloodstains on her clothes had disappeared, but her face was still a mask of pain.

"Blood of my blood," the woman gasped, embracing me and speaking over the gale force wind. "What have you done?"

"Get away from me!" I choked out, pulling away. The emotions from the water flooded back at her touch. I shook with intensity as I struggled to find words. "I saw you die! You're dead! How can I still see you?"

"There is no time to explain." She glanced at the storm overhead. "What did the water show you?"

"The water?" I repeated, still trying to catch my breath and my runaway emotions. She nodded urgently, her brows rising expectantly, so I continued. "I think it showed me everything. What it can do, how your people got here, the war, your death—"

"It wasn't everything, but it was enough."

"I don't understand."

"Sometimes to end a conflict, one must remove the source. Forgive me. We didn't know the price."

"Why am I here?" I gestured as wildly as the wind swirling around us.

"What we did, it trapped us, bound us to the Waters of Creation until our line is ended or has redeemed our actions, in turn freeing the water. Only one of our blood could have walked between the worlds to learn this."

"Between worlds?" I repeated softly, understanding rushing in. "Am I..." I couldn't finish the thought, couldn't make myself ask the question.

Am I dead?

I didn't have to say it. She understood.

"You cannot remain," she said urgently as lightning struck the pool behind her. "You must go back into the water. You must return to your body. You are now the only one who can save it all."

"Save all of what?" I demanded, raising my voice over the storm.

"The water chose you. Our blood started the curse, yours will end it," she said as her arm went around me and pulled me back toward the water. I felt the same painful reaction to her touch, as if I had become the water in which she had died. "I am Ashara. My husband was...is Markel. Our story is known only to the Sages, and now you. They will know what must be done. To free us is to free the Waters of Creation."

Across the churning pool stood the man she had embraced in death. The wind whipped at his silvery hair, pushing against his bloodless limbs. He watched us in silence.

"I will do what I can, but—" I looked back at her as I voiced the fear screaming in my head. "What will happen to you both if I fail?"

"That which creates can destroy." Her green eyes held mine. The wind blew her hair across her face, and she pulled it away. "Our vengeance on our people, for what they did to us, tied our essence to a natural force and subjected it to our wrath. We didn't know our actions would do this, but I'm not sure that knowing would have changed our actions. The effect has faded after a time, but your blood has awakened the bond. You must find a way to cleanse the water and free us. If you fail, when you die, you and the love that you are bound to will be trapped here."

"Are there others trapped here?"

"Yes."

"Who? How many?"

"All of them," she answered, his face filling with shame for the first time. She looked away. Lightning illuminated the sky again as thunder shook the ground. "Every member of our bloodline who dies comes to this place. We see them emerge from the spring, cursed to wander this in-between place, unable to see or hear us, without knowing why they are prevented from moving on and finding peace. It is the curse we created when we violated the pure and sacred waters of creation.

"You must act before your blood fades from the water. If you fail, we will be trapped forever, consumed, destroyed by the force our blood corrupted. Then, as our punishment, we must watch everything that the water created die."

I blinked, and Ashara was gone. I turned in the churning water and found her watching me from the bank. Her strong eyes willed me to save her, to save everyone, but I had so many questions. Would I be trapped there with everyone else? What did she want from me? How would I accomplish it?

As I watched her, I noticed a change in the plants in the pots around the spring. Their leaves were turning black, crumbling to ash as they wilted and sagged. The wind carried the ash away even as the black rot spread. Ashara's words echoed in my head, along with my own horror. *That which creates can destroy.* What other effects had the corruption of the spring set in motion?

Suddenly, Markel stood in the water next to me, his eyes on fire as he grabbed my shoulders. He spoke over the wind. "If I could take this burden from you, or bear it myself, I would. Time is short. You must go back. Now."

"I'm sorry, I'm just not—"

"Everyone your love touches now will share our fate. You *are* of us," he insisted, one hand coming off a shoulder to cup my face tenderly. The same pain I'd felt at Ashara's touch was in his, but I knew he was trying to convey his strength as well. "You are enough to change this, Adelaide, just you, as you are now."

"How can you know that?"

"Because you can hear us."

I opened my mouth to say more, but he returned his hand to my shoulder and looked back to the bank where Ashara stood, hopeful. I followed his gaze, but she had eyes only for Markel. She gave him the briefest nod, and he shoved me, hard.

I fell back into the swirling tempest, darkness swallowing my consciousness as water closed around me.

39

I gasped for air as pain rushed in. Something held my waist. Then voices, far away.

"She's breathing!" I heard a voice call out.

The crushing pressure on my chest had returned, but not as forcefully as before. My body felt heavy, and my pulse pounded in my ears. Lungs burning, I took another jagged breath. My whole body shuddered. Wet hands pressed gently against my forehead.

"Thank the waters, her lungs are finally showing signs of healing," another voice mumbled from somewhere far away. "Remember, don't let her take the ring off for any reason."

"I know. Lotty, can you hear me?" It was the only voice I wanted to hear.

I tried to answer. I wanted to answer. I wanted Roah to know I was okay, but I couldn't find my way out of the darkness. I was afraid if I opened my mouth, I would start screaming.

"It's finished," a deep voice announced. It was Tregr. "We are hunting down the remainder of Terrshon's men with help from Soren's young Sages. How is she?"

"Better, but still critical."

"Roah, we found one," a new voice added. "He was hiding among the dead on the north side of the ravine. We are holding him for you, whenever you're ready."

"Thanks, Daggon. Both of you, keep a close eye on him. I want answers."

"Our pleasure," Daggon said with a sinister tone.

"Lotty." Warm fingers pressed against my cheek as Roah whispered in my ear, pleading. "Come back to me. Just give me some sign that you haven't left me. Please." I felt a warm, soft kiss on my forehead.

I tried to open my eyes, to break through the fog of agony that threatened each breath. I was so close. I wanted to reassure him that I wasn't going anywhere.

"Roah?" I forced out. The words were barely audible, but he heard me.

"Yes, love. I'm right here," he said, the tension in his voice giving way to relief. I felt the soft brush of his fingertips across my cheek. His body flexed around me, pulling me closer. "Just relax, I've got you. You're safe now."

"It...hurts," I managed through my tight throat. I tried to open my eyes but couldn't. They were just too heavy to lift, and I was too tired to fight them.

"I know. I'm sorry. Try to relax, okay? It will help." His warmth left me as he turned away to speak to someone else. "Help her. She's hurting."

"The Waters of Creation heal, but with wounds this life-threatening they're not a remedy for the pain, I'm afraid," Soren admitted sadly.

"Can't you do something?"

"With a wound that deep, I'm not sure what's safe," he said.

"Please..." The word burned my lungs as I spoke. The pain and pressure in my chest still made it almost impossible to breathe.

"If the pain overwhelms her, we could lose her again," Roah insisted.

Again? I wondered distantly, the images from my time outside my body swirling in a confused mess. I heard myself groan, and the images fled. All I wanted was relief.

"Soren!"

"Okay," he conceded. "Give me a minute to consult the healers and gather ingredients."

"Hurry," I muttered, slurring the only word I could manage.

"Shh," Roah hushed. "Don't talk. Soren will find something to help. It will be all over soon."

I ignored him, forcing my eyes open. I realized why I felt like I was floating. Roah held me so that I lay in a small natural pool lined with expertly cut stone, high walls, and nothing between us and the night sky. I knew instantly where I was. The memories solidified, and adrenaline shot through me, mixing with the pain.

"Roah," I mouthed as my eyes found his face. "Wet. Have to get out!"

I struggled to sit up, to see if Ashara or Markel were watching us from opposite sides of the pool, but Roah held me tighter.

"Lotty, it's okay. It's to help you heal faster. I won't let you drown, but you can't get out. Not yet."

"I saw—" I gasped at the pain, trying to find words for what I had experienced. "They died here...it took me, and I saw—Roah, I have to save it or we'll all be destroyed. It hurts. I have to make it stop, or the rocks will bleed..."

"What did she say?" Soren demanded as he rejoined us.

"Nothing that's making any sense," Roah answered. "I think the pain is becoming too much for her. Tell me you have something."

"I do. It will dull the pain, as well as induce sleep." Soren knelt at the water's edge. He uncorked the top of the tiny bottle, being sure not to spill any. Then he handed it to Roah. "Combined with the water, it should speed her healing."

Roah hesitantly brought the bottle to my lips, slowly pouring the liquid into my mouth. The solution burned my tongue and the back of my throat. Gagging and half choking, my body refused to take in the concoction. My chest flared in agony. Lips on fire, I coughed up the liquid and it dribbled down my chin.

"I know it's terrible, but that will pass," Roah said, the concern in his eyes betraying the calm of his voice. "Just swallow as much as you can. It will stop the pain."

At his promise, I stopped fighting him and the foul liquid. He held the vial up to my lips again. It coated my mouth, then my throat, and finally my stomach, burning like fire. Instantly, my head swirled as the burn spread through my body. Similar to the darts my grandfather would prick me with, wherever the fire touched, my flesh tingled, and my body grew heavier and heavier.

Before I knew it, my eyes were closing again, the blackness pulling at my consciousness. I tried to hold them open for Roah, but I couldn't feel anything anymore. Not my arms. Not my legs. I also couldn't feel any pain, and for that I was relieved. Exhausted, I stopped resisting the fiery fluid pulsing through my veins. It pulled me into that black abyss once more.

40

I wasn't floating anymore. I hadn't been for a while. Oddly, I wasn't wet either. Instead, a soft satin cloud had replaced the water, cradling me as I became aware of my body again.

I took as deep of a breath as I could, fearing the worst. As air filled my lungs, I was astonished to feel no pain. Nothing. The burning had stopped.

Gradually, I flexed my fingers and toes. As the blood flowed faster through my veins, the sensation of being pricked by hundreds of tiny icy needles ran down my arms and legs. I tried to shake the feeling away, but I couldn't get my extremities to move. I groaned at the discomfort, unable to even shiver.

"I think she's waking up," a voice whispered not far from me.

"Are you sure?" a soft female voice asked.

"Look. She's starting to move a little."

"Go get Roah."

A warm hand brushed my cheek, settling on the hollow of my neck. A soft voice counted slowly as fingers pressed harder. A hand settled on my forehead.

Soon after its release, I heard footsteps running in my direction. They stopped at my side.

Blood of Moldara

"Lotty." Roah's voice soothed the ache still in my heart. "Lotty, I'm here."

I tried to answer, but I couldn't get my frozen lips to move.

"Give her a minute, Roah. She's been through quite a lot. Soren gave her rather large doses over the past couple of days. It will take time to wear off."

This time I recognized the voice, but my mind was so lethargic I couldn't remember where I'd heard it before.

"What have I done?" Roah asked in a tone laced with anxiety.

"You did what you saw best, for everyone. She is still alive because of you."

"Yes, but at what cost? Look at her."

As they spoke, I wondered what I looked like. I knew what I felt like. I felt like I was being showered with hundreds of small ice cubes. I was so cold it hurt. I tried once more to stretch my arms and legs and shake off the ice.

"She's moving again," the woman said.

I hadn't realized I was moving until she pointed it out. Lethargically, I could move my fingers and then my arms, but they were still too heavy to lift.

"She's so cold, Brea. Isn't there more we can do to warm her?"

At the sound of Brea's name, a ray of hope blasted through me. Hands pressed firmly on my face again, so warm they burned, melting the ice in my veins.

"Not until she's fully awake. Give it another minute or so," Brea advised him.

As I flexed my arms, I realized why I couldn't lift them. A pile of blankets held them down, heavy, thick ones.

Someone reached under the covers, and fingers stroked the back of my hand, soon intertwining with mine. The fire of Roah's touch shot through me, releasing me further from my icy prison. With all the force I could muster, I tightened my fingers around his.

"That's it, Lotty," he encouraged, his voice optimistic.

It was all I could do to get my mouth to form the words I so badly wanted to say. With the same effort it took to close my hand around his, I was able to get my lips to move.

"Ro...ah." My voice strained as it finally broke free.

"I'm here." Roah's hand formed a vice around mine.

"So...cold." The words slurred and made my mouth feel funny when I spoke.

"I know," he said, slowly rubbing the skin on the back of my arm.

With the heaviness still tugging on my body, it didn't respond to any of my commands. I forced my eyelids open anyway. They fluttered weakly, but when I saw Roah leaning close, it got easier to keep them open.

"There you are," Roah smiled, his face just inches from mine.

I smiled faintly, content despite the lingering chill and stiffness throughout my body. He was with me, and that's all that mattered.

"How do you feel, besides being cold?" Roah asked, worry in his eyes.

"Heavy," my mouth said stiffly.

"I think it's time to move her," Brea suggested. It was the first time I realized she had been watching from over Roah's shoulder. "Soren said to get her blood warmed as soon as she woke up. She's too weak for a bath, but a little body heat from a willing donor while sitting in front of a fire will do just as well. There's one ready in the guest room upstairs. It's not as secure of a room as this one, but I think it will be safe enough tonight," she announced from the doorway.

Roah leaned in, stroking my brow with his free hand. His touch left wakes of fire on my skin. "We won't be going far, and the room will be much warmer. Would you like that?"

Warmer. I wanted to be warmer. I squeezed his hand, not having enough strength to articulate my desires with words.

"Okay then." He smiled. It lit up his face in ways I didn't remember it could.

Roah slowly pulled back the covers and a wave of cold air washed over me. It made my body ache, and I wondered vaguely if I was too cold to shiver. *That's probably not good.*

He scooped me up into his arms. I wasn't surprised when I sagged helplessly against him, my limbs flopping around as if my bones had turned to jelly. I spared a look at my surroundings and realized for the first time where I was—the safe room in Roah's house. Euphoria, as consuming as my pain had been, overwhelmed me.

I was home!

I looked at Roah more closely and saw he wasn't wearing the clothes I had gotten used to seeing him in. Instead, he wore a white button-down shirt with a pair of jeans. I was no longer wearing an outfit from another world either. I was in my very own clothes—a plain long-sleeved t-shirt and the yoga pants I had gotten for my birthday. The only thing reminding me I had been to a totally different reality was my father's ring weighing down my left index finger.

Contentedly, I leaned my head against his chest as he carried me from the room. "We made it," I sighed.

"Yes." Roah kissed me lightly on the top of my head. "You're home."

He carried me up the stairs to the guest bedroom where I'd stayed before, the familiar walls another reassurance that I was indeed home. Roah set me down on the large fur rug in front of the fireplace, and I crumpled into a ball.

I watched while he pulled a stack of pillows closer to the fire and unbuttoned his shirt. Without looking at me, he removed the shirt and placed it neatly on the back of a chair. The firelight revealed a few scars and a muscular frame. It was hard to look away. Roah crossed the room and closed the doors before he picked up the thick blanket lying across the foot of the bed and draped it over his bare shoulders like a cloak.

He knelt next to me. His expression all business, he said, "It's the safest and fastest way to bring up your body temperature, but I know it's intimate. I promise to be the perfect gentleman."

I nodded, and he gently helped me to a sitting position with my back to him. My core temperature dropped another few degrees as he pulled my shirt off my back and over my head without removing it completely, leaving the sleeves over my arms and my front covered. Then he helped me lie on my side, across the stack of pillows facing the fire. I felt him settle in behind me, his warm skin shuddering a little as it touched mine. He brought the blanket around both of us, and I finally began to thaw.

After a few minutes, I realized my earlier guess had been correct. I had been too cold to shiver. Finally tucked in, nestled between the two different fires, I began to tremble, my teeth rattling in my head. Roah reached under the blanket and pulled me closer. Feeling his hand on my stomach, pulling me tight, I was momentarily transported back to that first night on his horse.

Drip by frozen drip, I was thawing, and the shivering subsided. I started to regain the use of my limbs once more, though I was still too weak to move them much. However, I managed to pull the edge of the blanket tightly under my neck, trapping the heat. Time grew irrelevant as we lay contentedly curled in each other's embrace.

"Thank you," I whispered after a while.

"For what?" he wondered, his breath hot against my skin.

"I wouldn't be sitting here if it weren't for you."

"I can't take all the credit," he said somberly. His tone made me wonder what he was thinking, but he changed the subject before I could ask. "How are you feeling? Better?"

"Sort of. I'm warmer, but I still don't think I can stand on my own. It's like I've lost the connection between my brain and my body."

"That's what I was afraid of," he admitted.

"Why?"

"Because of what Soren gave you. The first elixir raised your body temperature so much that you were burning up. To counteract that, he combined two different healing agents: a painkiller, and one that rendered you unconscious to help aid your healing lungs. But he gave you too much. It caused you to go into shock while it lowered your core body temperature."

"In English?"

"Basically, he knocked you out while your body started to freeze from the inside out," he clarified. "Soren had never seen anything like it before. It was pretty scary to watch." His voice was soft as he spoke, his breath tickling my neck.

"But I'm okay," I reassured him, slowly turning back to face him. I saw the concern he was trying to hide. "I'm here."

He closed his eyes and sighed long and heavily. "Barely. Your skin is still too pale, your lips too blue."

"I'm not going anywhere."

"Not for a few days at least."

"What happens in a few days?"

"To start with, you go home," he said, the muscles in his jaw flexing as he said it. "Bill and Karen are most anxious to get back and see how you're doing."

Bill and Karen. I had totally forgotten about them. I turned back to the fire, my emotions conflicted. It seemed like years ago that Bill and Karen had left on their trip and I had been abducted. So much had happened since then. So much had changed that the thought of Virginia seemed foreign, alien almost.

"What has Trell been telling them?" I asked.

"Apparently, you happen to be deathly allergic to mold, which was found in the kitchen when we all went to clean up the house. Your reaction shows up like a severe lung infection," Roah said with a sigh. "So your aunt and uncle called the school to tell them you were out sick while Trell and Brea cared for you. Consequently, you'll be here till next week when Bill and Karen can determine what they want to do with you until they get the mold under control. After that, I'll just be spending more time at your house." He paused as if suddenly unsure. "That is, if you don't mind."

"I don't mind," I admitted softly, still watching the flames as they danced behind the grate. There was so much I wanted to tell him, to ask him. It just didn't feel like the right time. "So what were you and your cousins up to this past week? Just so I know what to say if someone asks."

"Tell them the truth. We were gone. We went home to take care of some family business," he said, a hint of somberness in his tone.

"And was your trip a success?" I speculated, wanting to know what he thought about our experience.

"That's what they say."

"I don't care what they say. What do *you* say?" He didn't answer, and I immediately knew something was bothering him, something that didn't have to do with my healing. "How many did we lose?"

He stiffened. "Twenty-three. That includes the Sages we lost as well."

Twenty-three lives, cut short. I closed my eyes, suddenly sick to my stomach. "Why were the Sages even there? I thought they didn't take sides."

"They came for you, Lotty. They—" He seemed reluctant to expound, hesitating too long.

"Hey," I whispered, stretching out my hand under the blanket. When I found his hand around my waist, I laced my fingers with his, squeezing gently. "I need to know everything, even the stuff you don't think I can handle or understand. No more secrets, remember?"

He squeezed back before continuing. "You're right, you need to know. I had never seen anything like it—Sages engaged in battle. I was raised to believe they train to fight only as part of their self-discipline. They never use it. And yet, without them—" He trailed off, not finishing his thought.

"Then why now?"

"It was you, Lotty." The reverence in his voice brought the images from those desperate moments back with full clarity. "Soren told me the moment one of your bloodline was wounded, that close to that sanctuary, the Sages were bound by oath to come to your aid. They are our first allies now and bound to you. Terrshon will never forgive such an aggression."

One of my bloodline. The words sent a shiver down my spine.

My experience in the spring came rushing back. Had I died? If only for a minute, was that all it took? Ashara's words echoed in my head. *"If you fail, we will be trapped forever, consumed, destroyed by the force our blood corrupted."*

What did the Sages know? I swallowed hard, my throat suddenly dry. It was too much to think about. As I felt the tears threatening, I couldn't stop my mind from scrambling for a distraction, anything to hide from the weight that had settled on my shoulders.

Blood of Moldara 317

"How many others?" I asked.

"How many other what?"

"How many of Terrshon's men did we kill?" My voice became a whisper when the words came. As I included myself in my question, the face of my attacker flashed in my mind. I had killed someone also. My mind was nowhere near processing it.

Knowing he couldn't keep me from the truth, he simply answered, "All of them."

The silence thickened around us. *All of them,* his words repeated in my head.

"How do you do it?" I asked eventually, in awe that he could keep his grief under control the way he did.

"What?"

"Stay so calm about killing people?" I couldn't keep the sadness out of my words.

"Lotty," he answered, his tone pleading for understanding and resigned to my resentment at the same time. "When I ride through villages like Icel and see what Terrshon's tyranny has caused, it fuels my drive to do what's needed regardless of how it might torment me. In time, you will find your own ways of coming to grips with your feelings, as I have.

"Until then, know that those who died did it willingly. You gave them hope of a new future. I accept the burden of making their deaths meaningful by committing my life to their cause. I feel humbled by their sacrifice, not guilty because I could not prevent it. Mourning their loss, as though it were something less than heroic, would dishonor their sacrifice."

"Is that why I'm wearing my father's ring?" I asked. "To honor them?"

"No. The stones in that ring are called Bloodstones," he explained, and my body tensed at the name. "They're mined from the heart of the Waters of Creation and are very rare. Because of where they come from, they can store the healing power that is in the water. That water is the only reason you survived the arrow. The ring is to ensure you recover from the painkillers that nearly took you again."

"Again?"

"There was a moment while I was holding you up in the water—" He hesitated, not sure how to continue. I turned toward him to look into his eyes. They were full of pain, the muscles in his jaw working even while his chin trembled.

"I died. You felt my heart stop," I offered, saving him from having to speak the words. He looked away, nodding. "I know. I saw you holding me in the water. I saw the blood."

That startled him, bringing his gaze back to me. I wanted to tell him more, to explain all that I'd seen—the power of the water, the act that had given the stones their power, and the price my bloodline had paid for it, the curse they had passed to me. But I couldn't find the words.

"I'm glad you decided to stay."

I smiled at him but didn't tell him that I hadn't been given a choice.

He reached for my hand, tracing the edges of the ring as he studied it intently. "Your life continues to be a series of miracles, My Princess."

I looked down at the stone in my father's ring as his fingers trailed lightly over my skin. I remembered the stone being a foggy white color. Now it was clear with tiny red veins across its iridescent surface. It almost looked lit from within.

"After you're fully recovered," Roah continued, "you shouldn't wear it. You should keep it hidden at all times. It's still what secures the throne. There are those who would kill you for the power that ring would grant them. Until you declare yourself, that ring should never be visible to anyone who can't be trusted with your identity."

The words hung in the air as realization set it.

"Just because I got home, doesn't mean it's over, does it?" I was hoping being home would feel more victorious than it did.

"Over?" he asked in a tone that made my stomach flip. "Lotty, we just out-maneuvered Terrshon in his backyard, rescued you from his grasp, killed two regiments of his men while doing it, and cut off his access to the most powerful resource in our land. If my knowledge of battle strategy is correct, then I would call this just the beginning.

Blood of Moldara 319

"Even though we killed all of his men, Terrshon might have an idea of where you are. Ayla's mission will buy us time, but how much, I cannot say. We have to be vigilant in keeping watch. He's smart and will use what he knows about this world against us."

"He'll come back?" I asked, my voice catching in my throat twice.

"Yes. But you won't face him alone ever again, not as long as I draw breath." Roah took in the expression on my face, his eyes fierce and deep. Afraid of what that meant, I forced a half smile and turned back to the crackling fire.

"Hey," he said, brushing my hair back and pulling it behind my shoulder so he could see the side of my face. "We made it. You're safe. As long as we continue to help the Sages hold their ground, Terrshon can't reach us here. That doesn't mean he won't try. It just means he'll have to be smarter, and that preparation will take some forethought. So, in the meantime, we have nothing to worry about except getting you better."

Terrshon only wanted one thing, and he wouldn't stop until he got it. He wouldn't stop until he was forced to, until his power was taken from him.

"What do we do now?" I asked, realizing I was a part of this equation even if I didn't know how to be.

"That all depends on you," Roah answered.

"Me?"

"We're following your lead in this. We did as you asked; you're home. From here we can find support and rally forces, but without your full backing, we can't do anything of impact. If you don't want to be a part of the final battle to reclaim Moldara, then it's all on Ayla's shoulders."

His words were like another wound to my already battered soul. I was not ready to make decisions that big! A part of my brain knew exhaustion had brought my insecurities to the surface, but knowing that didn't make me feel better.

"I feel like I just drank from a fire hydrant, and I don't even know when it slammed me on my back. I need to feel some sense of normalcy. I need time with familiar things. Okay?"

"You don't need my permission. As far as I and everyone under this roof are concerned, you're a displaced queen. It is we who will need your permission to move forward. You don't have to make any decisions now. We will make as much time as we can for you to consider all of your options."

"Roah, what if no matter what I choose, I make everything worse?"

He placed his hand on my cheek, gently turning my face until he could look me in the eyes. "I have to trust in the wisdom that you were brought here for a reason, that the Sages understand the big picture we still can't see. In the meantime, the present is just as important as the future. Let's not forget that."

His eyes locked on mine with a flash of uncertainty, but also with a fire that still made my pulse weak. He leaned closer. I closed my eyes. When our lips came together, the world fell away. All I was aware of was his skin on mine, his need to be with me, the pain of the last few days in the desperate pull of his arms. My soul answered his need with my own. I was lost in his caress until a singular image flashed in my mind.

Roah and I, endlessly imprisoned by the spring, as were Markel and Ashara. Forever trapped but never together, watching the world turn to ash around us. My breath caught, and my body tensed in his arms. *What if, because of those intimate nights in the woods, I was already so connected to Roah that I had condemned him to share my fate?* As I searched the memory, I realized that Markel and Ashara had said as much.

Everyone your love touches now will share our fate. Did he mean just Roah, or did this curse also apply to Elion, Mable, Bill, Karen, Tyler and anyone else that had a place in my heart? Where did it end? Was I dooming everyone I'd ever cared about? The full implication of Markel's words exploded in my mind.

I pulled back, my heart pounding so hard my hands shook. Confusion washed over his face when I shifted in his arms to settle back in front of him, trying to hide the fear I knew was in my eyes. When the moment passed, his quiet voice broke the silence.

"You're right. You should rest. Soren won't be pleased with me if

Blood of Moldara

you don't recover like you should," he said, fumbling with his words in the firelight. There was something in his voice I didn't like, a slight distance I hadn't expected, especially after everything we'd been through. "Get some rest. There'll be plenty of time to talk later." He kissed my neck softly.

"Okay," I agreed, not sure what to say if anything at all. I had hurt him when I pulled away, but I didn't have words for the nightmare my subconscious mind had conjured. *How did I reassure him when I couldn't calm myself?* Suddenly aware of his arms supporting me, I wanted nothing more than to relax into his warmth and drift away from the weight of it all.

I stared into the swirling flames of the fireplace, and he finally tightened his arms around me. Curling my still weak body into his, I decided to trust his words—to trust that we would have time to talk later, time to process everything that had happened so that I would know what move, if any, I should make. To trust that somehow, I would find out what had happened when I'd died, what it all meant, and what was required of me. I was still drowning in questions, but there was at least one life raft to which I could cling; I knew what was at stake now, and I was going to find a way to save Moldara, to save everyone I cared about, if it was the last thing I ever did.

EPILOGUE

Terrshon moved purposefully through the great hall. He had long ago converted the useless space into an elaborate map room. More than a dozen waist-high stone pillars were scattered across the diagram of his known world. Each marked the location of his emissaries—the eagles that were his eyes.

A servant entered through a side door carrying the evening meal. The bent old man didn't look up to acknowledge his king, but Terrshon saw his shoulders tighten in fear. It had once amused Terrshon to find new ways to torment Ninlore. Long ago, Terrshon had learned how to break a mind and control the damage done to the body. Ninlore was Terrshon's first subject, but he was far from perfect. It had taken many more victims to perfect his craft, to choose the marks that became permanent and devoted a person to his service completely. Ninlore's ticks and obsessiveness was Terrshon's reminder that it was possible to break a person more than was useful.

Blood of Moldara

That day he had no patience for the old man. He waved Ninlore away.

The king circled a pillar, eyeing the round stones that sat in the glass dish. Each had been cut into several thin slices, the flat sides polished and set facing down. The patterns within the geode were only half of the stones' beauty. The rest was in their twins. He picked up the stone that had been resting at the far edge of the bowl and held it in both hands. His face strained, and a picture formed on the surface of the stone.

The stone had many facets, though each showed the same image, as if the picture had been forced through a kaleidoscope. After another moment of concentration, the single image of a familiar house came into focus. Terrshon had been told it was the home of Adelaide's adoptive aunt and uncle. The image wasn't clear, but it was obvious no one was there. His confidence that she was still in Moldara was affirmed.

He set the stone down and picked up another. In this one, he saw the outside of a dilapidated barn. Several figures moved about the structure. Terrshon recognized his men's fighting gear, as well as the style of clothing in which Adelaide had arrived. They appeared to be instructing and outfitting the new arrivals. It was confirmation that one of the three squads he had sent had breached Trell's defenses.

The next three stones were dark, signaling that their twins had been destroyed. It was also likely that the eagles that had born the gemstones were lost. Terrshon tossed the stones across the room with a flick of his wrist, distantly aware of them shattering against the floor.

Impatiently, Terrshon crossed the room.

He stopped at the pedestal on the border of Niniever. After reviewing two stones that revealed nothing, the third bore fruit. An image of Prince Laurion feeding scraps of raw meat to one of his eagles materialized. When Laurion saw the change come over the bird, its eyes altering and its posture become threatening, he pulled out a scrap of paper and held it up in front of the stone at the bird's neck. Terrshon leaned in eagerly.

I have seen the ring. It is time to discuss terms.

As he took in the news, a delighted grin twisted Terrshon's face. He released his control of the stone, and through it, the bird, just as the door to the room swung open.

"Commander Waygar is here for you, My Lord," the guard at the door announced.

A burly man wearing a heavily soiled captain's uniform was thrust into the room. He was immediately restrained by two more guards, who forced the man to his knees before taking up posts by the door. He looked around uncomfortably. His usually masked face was exposed, his garish scars made more fearsome by the flickering torchlight.

"You're late."

"My King, I—"

"And you are alone? I told you to bring the girl directly to me this time, Waygar," Terrshon crooned in a singsong voice as he returned the stone to the bowl in front of him.

"I didn't have enough men to—" Waygar struggled in the quiet of the chamber, aware that all eyes were on him. He held his chin high as he continued in a steadier voice, "I have returned to request reinforcements."

"Explain your incompetence before my patience expires, Captain," Terrshon threatened as he wandered distractedly from pedestal to pedestal.

"It was a trap," Waygar began, the words tumbling over one another in a rush. "All the reports said that we outnumbered them. Your men knew to only kill brown cloaks since we could not be sure which gray cloak was the girl. But as soon as they realized our strategy, the women refused to be taken alive. We had them surrounded, but we never had a chance.

"It was like something out of our nightmares, as if the fog itself gave birth to an army of wraiths. They moved soundlessly among us, cutting down men like it was all part of some terrible dance. I am ashamed to say that the courage of your men failed, Sire. I heard men screaming and crying, begging for the redemption of their souls before they, too, were put to the sword. By all the powers of creation, I swear to you, I never have in my life seen such a horrific sight."

Blood of Moldara

"My armies are not made of cowards, Captain," Terrshon objected coolly as he arranged the stones in yet another bowl.

"But neither were they prepared to stand against the Sages, My King," Waygar confessed in a hushed tone.

Terrshon suddenly burst into laughter, and the temperature in the room seemed to fall several degrees. The guards shifted uncomfortably, and Waygar broke out in a cold sweat. When the king's amusement was spent, he spoke as if to a child.

"You expect me to believe that the Sages took lives on the field of battle?"

"On my life, I swear I saw it with my own eyes, My King."

"Let's say I believe you." Terrshon's mirth gave way to calculated curiosity as he finally turned his full attention to Waygar. "Was their wrath directed at both sides of the conflict?"

"At first I thought that to be the case, but then I saw that where they went, only our men fell."

"Where is the girl now?" the king demanded, an anticipatory smile hinting at the violence to come. His eyes bore into Waygar until the man felt the answer explode out of him.

"I don't know. There are reports in the north—"

"Reports?!"

Waygar's face twitched nervously, causing the unsightly scars to pull at the skin on his cheek. When Waygar regained his composure, he amended his answer, the words emerging as if they'd been strangled out of him.

"That is to say, I know of five possible places our spies have reported seeing her since the battle. I had one account of Prince Zarian himself carrying a girl from the battlefield. I've had others of her being wounded. At least three of the girls we killed could have been her, but none had the necklace. Since then we've had reports from our informants that she's been spotted everywhere. Hiding out among the Sages, traveling the road heading to the northern mountain territories—"

"But you are sure Prince Zarian was with them?"

"Yes," Waygar offered quietly.

"You're trying to convince me that Prince Zarian, the boy who ran from his title, becoming no better than a peasant himself, has somehow conscripted the Sages?" Terrshon mused, as if in a trance. His mind was an electrical storm of thought, one hypothesis after another striking and being discarded. If only he knew the secret that pathetic prince had leveraged to bend the Sages to his will.

Control of the Sages was the control of information. Two Sages sat at the council of every court in the land. They oversaw all education, managed and regulated the tradesman, and were the voice of the common people, but Terrshon had learned long ago that they kept all the best secrets for themselves. Terrshon had only ever fantasized about that kind of power.

"I would not believe it myself if I had not been there," Waygar offered. "Which is why I brought proof—another witness."

At Waygar's signal, the guard at the door stepped to open it. A young man, still in fighting gear splattered with blood, was dragged in by his collar. The guards dropped his trembling body beside the captain. Obviously wounded, the man's face had drained of all color. His gaze darted around the room in a desperate search for an exit.

"This sniveling whelp is all I was able to salvage from the battle. Trey claims to have seen Prince Zarian fighting alongside the Sages," Waygar said in disgust.

Terrshon gestured impatiently, and a guard pointed a spear at the wounded man's heart as he lay on the floor.

Trey whimpered, babbling as he shrunk away from the blade. "I am a true believer! We owe the Powers of Creation our lives, all of us! The Sages are the holy keepers of the Waters of Creation, the fountain that brings life to our world, to all worlds. But they have turned against us, My King! They fell upon us like reapers to a harvest. To be slain by a Sage is to have one's soul extinguished forever!"

Terrshon shook his head, his face pinched in growing irritation, as if a headache was coming on. "Why is this one talking now?"

"They wore no armor." Trey's quivering voice went on, his panic rising with each word until he was hysterical. "They carried no sigil. They offered no quarter. I lost my horse. The men around me fell. The ancestors forgive me! I tried to fight. I knew it was wrong, but still I tried. I thought I was about to die, too. Then I saw the prince. He was wounded and covered with other men's blood, but I am sure it was he, Your Grace. He rode past us with a body in his arms. That's when I ran—"

Trey's last words were cut off as a stone spike erupted through his chest. Waygar struggled to keep the shock from his face as he looked to the guards for reassurance. They didn't meet his eyes, but their knuckles where white as Terrshon laughed, his words full of fascination as he released his grip on one of the stone pillars. The spike in Trey's chest retracted and fell back into the floor.

"You know, I wasn't entirely sure that would shut him up."

"This is but a sampling of the effect the Sages had on the weaker minds in our ranks. And there is more." Waygar rose uncertainly to his feet. No one moved to stop him, so he went on. "The Sages have taken control of the water. Their doors have been closed to all travelers, and they now prohibit passage within a mile of the Sanctuary. Every day, more soldiers arrive to help them defend it. So far, no one knows where they come from. Perhaps Zarian offered their help in exchange for the Sages cooperation. I cannot say for sure. I only know they control the water and the cavern entrance, My Lord."

Terrshon leaned against a pedestal, turning his attention to the guards at the door. "Bring Poyus in," Terrshon ordered. One of them immediately straightened and left the room.

The guard returned with a muscular man in his late twenties wearing a uniform. He had a shiny bald head, numerous piercings in both ears, and several weapons at his belt. Unlike the others who served Terrshon, his face was smooth and unmarked except for a long thick scar that started on his forehead, cut between his eyes, and angled across the top of his nose. Poyus stopped next to Waygar and went to one knee, his head bowed.

"Poyus." Terrshon measured the man who had joined them, his voice low and menacing. "I assume you have heard of the fate of the two regiments sent to retrieve our lost princess?"

"I have, My King," Poyus answered with hunger in his voice.

"Can you describe for me the qualities of a captain of my army?" Terrshon crooned, the excitement back in his voice.

"A man who would die before he fails you," Poyus hissed fervently.

"And is that man in this room with me?" Terrshon questioned petulantly.

Poyus's head came up, a sneer distorting his scarred face, his eyes narrowing like a wild animal closing in on its prey. The bald man sprung from his place on his knees. Before Waygar realized what was happening, in one smooth motion, Poyus pulled out his captain's sword and stepped behind him.

He kicked Waygar back to his knees, and the aging man hit the stone floor hard. Waygar's cry for mercy was interrupted by the blade that burst from his chest. He looked down, his mouth open in a silent scream as he grabbed at the weapon. Just as quickly, Poyus withdrew the sword, slicing the old man's fingers to the bone. Blood gushed out of the hole in Waygar's armor. He coughed red and slumped to the floor.

Poyus stood behind the fallen captain, his chest heaving, holding the sword ready in case his actions were challenged. Terrshon kept his face a mask of indifference, but he was thoroughly pleased. Poyus had performed better than anticipated. He would serve well as long as he passed one more test.

"Surrender your weapon to your king, soldier!" Terrshon commanded.

Poyus straightened up from his crouch and lowered the sword. Terrshon pushed off the pedestal and approached. Poyus held the sword out to him, handle first.

"On your knees," Terrshon hissed as he accepted the still dripping blade. Poyus locked eyes with him but obeyed.

Terrshon stood over Poyus, the tip of the blade resting in the notch above the man's sternum. The room was deathly quiet as Poyus pulled out a dagger from his belt and cut open his shirt. The cloth fell away exposing a scarred, muscular chest.

Without flinching, Poyus slid his fingers along the flat of the sword, the blood still dripping from his kill, and brought the now crimson fingers to his chest, drawing a crude circle over his heart. Never once did he look away from Terrshon's measuring gaze.

Terrshon moved the tip of the sword to the circle and began carving. In four simple strokes, it was done—an upside down triangle with a notch in the top bar, the blood of the previous captain mingling with the new one.

Terrshon stepped back. "It would seem you are my new captain, Poyus."

"I am yours to the final death, Your Majesty," Poyus promised as he rose and accepted the sword that Terrshon handed back to him.

"Never forget that," Terrshon commanded, the tone of congratulations giving way to impatience. "Your first assignment will be to reorganize my forces. You will search for men unwilling to engage in a battle with the Sages. Persuade the ones you can. Kill the rest. Make an example of their cowardice. Make sure people see it. I need strong, capable warriors for the conquests that await us."

"With pleasure." Poyus grinned, the scar across his face giving him a twisted expression.

"Your second task is to ascertain the actual location of our lost princess and bring her to me. Be more ruthless than your predecessor, succeed where he failed, and I will reward you beyond your wildest dreams. Fail me, and there won't be enough left of your body to feed the worms."

Poyus bowed and excused himself. As the guards dragged the bodies out of the room, Terrshon began to pace.

Adelaide was alive. He could feel it. His men would find her again, and this time he wouldn't wait. She would be his queen, and he would make her suffer for causing him such trouble.

The thought of calling her his queen was akin to calling his horse royalty simply because it was ridden by him. He had never wanted a queen, but he would have to keep her alive until he had a male heir. After that, he imagined it would depend on his mood. He would, of course, be the one to raise the child, to guide him in all of the skills that had made his father great. Just then, an idea so poetic formed in his mind that he wondered why it had not occurred to him before. The first person he would teach his son to break would be his own mother.

The thought thrilled him to his core. He would raise the grandchild of Mira and teach him how to destroy that vile woman's hope for the future. It was the perfect antidote to the most destructive queen Moldara had ever known. His only regret was that he could not reach back through time and compel Mira to watch her own grandson destroy everything she'd worked for, to crush the child on whom she'd pinned all her hopes. Terrshon's heart pounded as the fantasy unfolded in his mind.

He spun on his heel and returned to the far side of the map, to the area that marked the land of the Sages. Terrshon picked up one last stone. The image that formed on the rock was that of a young man. He sat outside at a table under a large tree, surrounded by books and other things with which Terrshon wasn't familiar. He didn't recognize the boy, or the surroundings, so he willed the picture to focus on the paper on which he was scribbling. At the top of it, Terrshon read a name: Tyler Anderson. He remembered that name. Adelaide's adopted cousin. Elion had articulated it only a few times, but it was enough.

"So you're the young man Elion tried to hide from me," Terrshon said, gloating. "I think it's time I gave your life purpose."

ACKNOWLEDGMENTS

Writing this story has taught me more about myself than I ever thought possible. I am a better person because of Lotty, Roah, and Moldara. I sit and ponder possibilities more now than I did before I created Otherworld and, because of that, my world—Oldworld—holds more beauty and magic than it had before. I am forever changed because of Moldara and thrilled it is now out for everyone else to discover. But that wouldn't be the case if it weren't for a few very creative, dedicated, and talented people who helped me bring this story to you.

J. Norwood! My Winchester, Wonder Woman, and soul sister! Your Developmental Editing skills continue to challenge me, and I love you for it! I am so thrilled for the collaboration we did on this story! You make me a better writer and a better storyteller. I love how badass you are and only hope someday I can write a death scene as well as you do! I love you sista!

Tony, My Love! I have no words to express how much your love and support means to me. Thank you for encouraging me to continue to follow my passion. You still make me blush!

My kiddos! Your love and encouragement keep me going! Especially when you get excited about what adventures Lotty and Roah find themselves on and beg for spoilers of what happens next. I love you all to the moon and back!

My Family! Especially those who've read this story. Thank you for indulging me when I'd start talking Moldara. I love you all.

Carrie and Aunt Jill! Your endless support and asking for more is what helps me press through on those bad days. Hugs!

Myth Machine! Again, thank you for believing in me and Moldara and loving it as much as I do!

Leslie Lutz! My Copy Editor. Thank you for making this manuscript shine! Your Jedi skills are amazing!

Cora Younie, A.E. Blackwell, Jill Land! Thank you for sharing your proofreading skills and adding your enthusiasm to this story.

AND MY DEEPEST THANKS TO YOU,

MY READERS

*For loving Lotty and Roah
as much as I do,
and getting swept away
in their adventures
with all of us!*

Coming Soon...

BRIANNE
EARHART
& J. NORWOOD

CURSE OF
MOLDARA

CURSE OF MOLDARA

I HAVE A LITTLE SISTER
AND HER BLOOD IS NOT MINE
I GUARD AND WATCH OVER HER
AND OUR LIVES ARE ON THE LINE
WE WILL ALWAYS PLAY IN SECRET
TO KEEP HER FROM THE LIARS
SO ONE DAY SHE CAN SAVE US
FROM THE TORMENT OF THE FIRES

Lotty and Roah have returned from Moldara but the price of doing so has not yet revealed itself. New allies are looking to them for leadership, old friends are coming back, and their enemies are multiplying faster than any of them know. In his pursuit of Lotty, Terrshon's men now hunt for a new prize, Tyler. But Tyler's world is about to change in ways only Elion has foreseen. Meanwhile, Trell and Brea are rushing to train and care for the wounded that fought for their lost princess. But using the Waters of Creation suddenly has a heavy price. Roah is struggling to balance his oaths to Moldara and his desire to stay beside the woman he's fallen madly in love with. And it's up to Lotty to learn all that she can about what happened to her in the Waters, before they all lose everyone they've ever loved.

Can't wait for the next chapter in this epic story?
Sign up to get the latest updates,
join the rest of Moldara's fans,
discover the newest fan merchandise
straight from the book,
get extra goodies from the author,
and so much more at:

Join all your fellow fans in celebrating your old favorites and be a part of discovering new obsessions and new books. Myth Machine is here to bring more of the fandoms you love into your daily life.
Don't see your latest obsession?
What are you waiting for?
Create a fandom of your own.
Make it your masterpiece
and share it with the world!

ABOUT THE AUTHOR

Author – Brianne Earhart

Brianne Earhart spent most of her childhood dreaming up stories. She would pretend there were knights and fairies living in the woods behind her house, her animals could talk to her, magic was a superpower, and that her imaginary friend really did have a house in that fallen tree across the horse trails. Struggling with learning disabilities throughout her schooling, she was very insecure because reading was a challenge. Her imagination and creative expression were her safe place and creating stories through works of art, her liberation. After years of self-education, she had enough confidence to trade her paintbrush for words and create The Moldara Series.

Brianne Earhart loves being outdoors, creating art, all things yoga, and dark chocolate. She lives with her husband, Tony, and their 5 kids by a lake in Northern Idaho.

ABOUT THE CO-AUTHOR

Co-Author – J. Norwood

Jennie has been taking apart stories, to see what makes them connect with people, for over 20 years. Her extensive background in live theater productions and new startups finally came together at her first writing conference, where she saw the industry disconnect between authors and their fans. Myth Machine is the next evolution of a publishing concept that's she's been developing for the past 4 years. As a development editor in her own right, Jennie bridges that elusive gap between art and business, leading the Myth Machine team through every stage of growth. Connecting fans to more of what they love, bringing that community together with fresh stories in the digital realm as well as our daily life, is what she lives for.

Blood of Moldara - Copyright © 2017 Brianne Earhart & J. Norwood

Curse of Moldara - Copyright © 2018 Brianne Earhart & J. Norwood

All rights reserved. Published in the United States of America. No part of this book may be used or reproduced in any manner whatsoever without written permission except in the case of brief quotations embodied in critical articles and reviews. For information, address Myth Machine at info@mythmachine.com

This is a work of fiction. names, characters, businesses, places, events and incidents are either the products of the author's imagination or used in a fictitious manner. Any resemblance to actual persons, living or dead, or actual events is purely coincidental.

Cover Illustrations Copyright © 2017 by Myth Machine, LLC

Cover design by © Alfie

Book design and production by Myth Machine, LLC

Development Editor J. Norwood

Editing by Leslie Lutz of Eliot Bay Editing

Author Brianne Earhart photograph by Robin Johnson

Author J. Norwood photograph by Evan Lurker

BLOOD OF MOLDARA

THE TOUCH OF FIRE, EVER SHARPENS OUR BLADES,
THE TOUCH OF SPIRIT, EVER TAMES OUR BEASTS,
THE TOUCH OF EARTH, EVER SHAPES OUR ART,
THE TOUCH OF AIR, EVER SPEAKS OUR TRUTHS,
THE TOUCH OF WATER, EVER HEALS OUR WAYS.
MAY IT RETURN TO US SOMEDAY

Lotty has been torn away from the only home she's ever known and swept up into a world that was supposed to be just a bedtime story. But now the monsters of her childhood are real, the fate of an entire country hangs in the balance, and everyone she meets wants to use her. With her parent's killer closing in, Lotty must decide who to trust and find a strength she lost when her grandpa disappeared so many years ago. When Roah tries to protect her from a fate he can't escape he will set in motion a curse that alters the future of Moldara forever.

MYTH MACHINE

Join the Fandom Now

Made in the USA
San Bernardino, CA
03 July 2018